Wise Follies

Grace Wynne-Jones

Published by Accent Press 2007

ISBN 1905170637/9781905170630

Printed and bound in the UK

Cover design by Joëlle Brindley

The publisher acknowledges the financial support of the Welsh
Books Council

Extract from *Reference Back* by Philip Larkin reproduced by kind
permission of Faber and Faber.

Extract from *Come To The Edge* by Christopher Logue reproduced
by kind permission of Faber and Faber.

Extracts from *The Road Less Travelled* by M. Scott Peck M.D. have
been reproduced by kind permission of Random House U.K..
Copyright © 1978 M. Scott Peck, M.D.

Acknowledgements

A big bouquet of thanks is due to my wonderful agent, Lisa Eveleigh of the Lisa Eveleigh Literary Agency for all her insight, support and encouragement. Bundles of thanks are also due to Hazel Cushion and everyone at the wonderful Accent Press for all their enthusiasm, savvy and publishing prowess. I am also very grateful to Joëlle Brindley for the wonderful jacket artwork. A big 'Thank You' to Puddy and also to friends and family who have been so supportive and encouraging and to Clare Ledingham. And of course I must mention the main character of Wise Follies, 'Alice' herself and our mutual 'friends', who gave such help and guidance in their own way, and who taught me a great deal.

'The heart has its reasons that reason knows not of.' Blaise Pascal

Chapter 1

MY NAME IS ALICE Evans. I'm thirty-eight, single, and very keen on art and gardening. I'm also growing increasingly fond of my cat and watch far more television than I used to. I've been celibate for over a year and occasionally find small spiky hairs on my chin. I don't think these two things are necessarily connected. I think my not having sex has more to do with my being rather disillusioned with men in general. Get me on the subject of men on a chin-hair day and I can sound as knowledgeably resigned as any political pundit. This is because I've been waiting to meet my Mr Wonderful for years now, but he still hasn't swooped me off on his white charger. In fact, I think by this stage he's probably married or become bisexual or a Buddhist.

In my more realistic romantic moments I remind myself that men are not the answer anyway. They are just another question...and a very puzzling one at that. There's even a book called *Men are from Mars, Women are from Venus*. Certainly many of my romantic entanglements have a fairly inter-galactic feel about them. I wish I could summon Captain Jean-Luc Picard from Star Trek to help me sort them out.

'Love yourself' – that's what the self-help books scream at me. And I've been trying to, I really have. But the sex isn't great and when I give myself a hug my arms only reach my shoulders. I know so many lovely women, I dearly wish I could become a lesbian. The thing is, I'm just not that way inclined.

As you may have guessed, I didn't expect to be single at this stage in my life. Neither did my housemate Mira. We were under the impression that our Mr Wonderful would just inevitably turn up, as he usually seems to in films. As time passed and the biological clock started ticking, we attempted to speed up the screening process. In an effort to be businesslike we even drew up a long list of men we would not countenance:

'No men who go on and on about themselves on the first date and don't even get your name right.'

'Indeed.'

'No men who wear sunglasses in midwinter without good reason.'

'Agreed.'

'Or fanatical golfers.'

'Certainly not.'

'Or men with mobile phones perpetually stuck to their ears.'

'Absolutely.'

'Or limp hand-shakers. Or men who say they'll call and then don't.'

'Or the really really difficult ones.'

'Ah yes – Alice's specialist subject.'

'Not any more.'

I suppose you could say we'd got rather picky. We realized this when we saw the list had grown to cover almost everyone, and therefore couldn't be right.

I think one of the reasons I'm still alone is that for ages and ages I only went out with the 'specialist subject' Mira referred to: difficult men. They seemed to draw me to them like magnets. If there was a difficult man in the room I'd find him. Obsessive meditators, alcoholics, workaholics, arrested developers, brilliant nerdy types with unfashionable sweaters – I sensed their misty sadness and frayed longings before we even spoke. I looked into their big bewildered eyes and saw my own. They were different. Broken in some way. They wouldn't drag me blithely to their bonny beaming mothers and announce, 'Here's Alice. You'll love her. She's just like us.' There was no 'Us' they could refer to. Unless, of course, they were married. I think what I hoped was that we could be mixed up together and this would be somehow comforting. The thing is, it wasn't. We got our love ingredients all jumbled up. It was like trying to make chocolate sponge pudding with tomato sauce.

I think I've got past my 'difficult men' phase now. What I want these days is a more adjusted man who'll stay around. Preferably someone who's as sexy as Daniel Day-Lewis and almost as wise as the Dalai Lama. A man who's warm and kind and funny and sees straight into my soul. The thing is by the time you're in your late thirties many of the desirable men you meet are someone else's and it's a right pain in the ass. You glance at their left hand and – ah, yes – there's another glint of gold. Of course, some stinkers don't tell you they're unavailable until you're hooked, but the more responsible ones do – over and over again – by being rather liberal with their 'we's'. Their blatant plurality is almost offensive. I think they do it to remind themselves of their 'we-ness' as much as you. And even if they don't say the 'we' word themselves someone else eventually does for them. 'Yes – he's a lovely person and his wife/live-in partner/girlfriend is lovely too.' They say it so quickly that you feel like they're part of 'Neighbourhood Watch' and you've been caught skulking. It really pisses me off. It's just the kind of thing that has greatly increased my enthusiasm for painting and gardening.

I love gardening. It's so sane and straightforward. Once you've read one book about it you'll have grasped the basics. It's a predictable pleasure. There's no 'we-ness' about it. After months of tender care your geranium will not, for example, announce that it has another owner or 'isn't ready for this kind of commitment'. If it needs more space, you simply replant it. The nutrients it requires are well documented and not subject to random alteration. You can indulge your broodiness for, say, camellias, way past menopause. Plants also bring you close to nature and remind you of the transience of things in the nicest way. Sometimes, standing in my garden on a moonlit night, I feel such comfort in my smallness. In the part I play in the grand scheme of things. Only as crucial as a wave is to the ocean. Part of something so huge that, for a moment or two of deep bliss, I even forget my dreams. At such moments finding Mr Wonderful does not matter one whit, but as soon as I go inside it does again. 'Transcendence is a hard thing to hang on to,' as my friend Annie says.

I'm sitting with Annie now at my distressed-pine kitchen table. She is one year older than me and has a smile that's as sweet as Winona Ryder's. She has honey-blonde hair that frames her pretty, thoughtful face and has no shortage of male admirers. She is a puzzling exception to the 'we-ness' syndrome. It doesn't seem to affect her at all. Sometimes I suspect she's found an 'available men' EU stockpile and is keeping it all to herself.

'These are nice mugs, Alice,' Annie is commenting as I plug in the kettle. 'Are they new?'

'Yes, I got them free with my supermarket saver points,' I reply, reaching into a cupboard for the Bewley's Earl Grey tea bags.

'You should have waited until you'd got five thousand points and applied for a Toy Boy,' Annie chuckles, and I smile. It is one of her older jokes. Another is that I should practise being more adventurous by attempting to sneak nine items through the 'Eight Items Only' check-out.

'Maybe you should find yourself a Toy Boy, Alice,' Annie adds cheerfully. 'They haven't developed any nasty habits and are great in bed.' She almost purrs as she says this and I know she's remembering Serge, a French exchange student who could do incredible things with grapeseed oil.

'It's all very well for you to talk,' I reply resignedly. 'You're not as insecure as I am. You don't mind when your young men get sense and find someone their own age, but I would.'

'I had to beg Serge to go back to the Sorbonne,' Annie protests. 'I persuaded him it was in his best interests, but he still cried and cried.'

'Yes, but he was French,' I reply as I look out the window at the May afternoon. I glance at the delphiniums, which seem a bit subdued, and then my gaze drifts to an upstairs window of the house that overlooks the garden. A handsome young man seems to be dancing on his own. He's wearing a tight black T-shirt and denims. My interest is, of course, purely aesthetic. I went to life-drawing classes some years ago and know a good set of biceps when I see one. The young man is jumping around as if he's in a disco. He's holding what looks like a can of aftershave, pretending it's a microphone. The song 'Shiny Happy People' is drifting bouncily through his open window. He's obviously attempting to be R.E.M. The whole band. He must be that new chap. The one who's just moved in. I saw a furniture truck outside his house the other day. A pretty

5

woman was struggling to wedge a huge framed poster of the Manhattan skyline through his front door. Oh dear – he's sensed that I'm watching him. He's glancing out the window at me. I turn away quickly and start to make the tea.

'What were you looking at just then?' Annie enquires. 'You seemed deeply engrossed.'

'Oh, I – I was just studying the delphiniums,' I mutter. 'I think they could do with a bit of that well-rotted organic manure I bought the other day.' I don't tell Annie about my new neighbour because I just know she'd insist that I ask him over for lunch or something. Immediately. Any suggestion that he might be far too young for me would be treated with an airy dismissal. She has no shame about that kind of thing.

'Did you know that Mira is taking up windsurfing?' Annie asks as I start to pour out the tea.

'Yes, she did mention something about it,' I sigh. The enthusiasms of Mira, my housemate, no longer surprise me.

'I love to hear of people taking up new interests.' Annie's voice is slightly muffled by a chocolate-covered Polo biscuit.

'Well, Mira is certainly developing lots of new interests lately,' I reply, in as non-judgemental a manner as I can manage. 'In fact, at this precise moment she's at a motorcycle maintenance class.'

'But she doesn't have a motorbike.'

'I know. It's part of her training.'

'What training?'

'Her training to become an eccentric spinster. She's getting very dedicated about it. She's given up on romance completely. She says if she had a choice between a man and a Mars bar, the Mars bar would win out every time.'

'Oh dear, what am I going to do about the pair of you?' Annie clucks maternally. 'You haven't been out with anyone for ages, Alice. Don't you miss the sex?'

I look at her forlornly. 'I'm deluged with sex, Annie, didn't I tell you? Sex, sex and more sex. It's driving me up the wall.'

'Gosh!' Annie leans forward excitedly. 'Have you been having orgies without telling me?'

'Of course not,' I groan thinking of the glossy woman's magazine I work for. 'Sarah keeps asking me to write about sex lately. You'd swear it had just been designed by Terence Conran.'

'Oh, I see.' Annie sits back in her chair and fiddles with a teaspoon. She was clearly hoping for a more exciting answer.

'Sometimes I wish I worked for the kind of magazine my mother used to read,' I continue dejectedly. 'You know, the ones full of knitting patterns and cake decorations and tips on stencilling…even if the women in the short stories were a bit like the Canadian Mounties.'

'How so?'

'They always got their man.'

'Just tell Sarah you need a change. I'm sure she'll understand,' Annie says briskly. Annie knows Sarah, the magazine's features editor. She was one of our pals at college.

'Sarah's not as malleable as she used to be,' I reply. 'Sex sells, you see, Annie. People want it.'

'You don't seem to be too enthusiastic about it.'

'I think I would be enthusiastic about it again,' I sigh '…if I met the right person.'

'Oh, you will, Alice.' Annie regards me tenderly. 'Of course you will.'

'I can't believe the last time I slept with someone was fourteen months ago,' I continue morosely. 'I was with Eamon – you know, that fellow I went out with for a while. We were in his house and he had the Ryder Cup on in the background. Ian Woosnam had a birdie.'

'What's a "birdie"?' Annie frowns.

'I dunno. He had one anyway. People cheered.'

Annie has begun to study me rather concernedly. I know by the way she's pausing that she's about to say something blunt. 'Alice, you're going to have to start being more proactive,' she announces.

'What do you mean?'

'More proactive about men. You're going to have to get out there and find one. There must be far less of this lounging around evening after evening watching *Emmerdale* and saying "Fancy a cuppa?" to Mira. It's getting far too cosy.'

'Oh, really,' I reply, trying to really emphasize the irony. 'And this from the woman who watches every soap opera on the schedules. Even the ones on cable.'

'Yes,' Annie agrees patiently. 'But the difference is I sometimes go out afterwards. I'm sociable. I haven't developed hermit tendencies like you have.'

I listen resignedly. Annie has always been more daring than me. When we were at university I was the one who bought an Afghan coat and burnt joss sticks and said I was going to India, but she was the one who went there.

'What about joining a dating agency?' Annie urges. She's really getting into her stride now. 'You could choose your dates yourself. They supply photos and personal details. Or you could put a personal ad in a newspaper. Lots of people do that these days. There's no stigma to it.'

I grimace and start to pull at a loose button on my cardigan. As Annie starts to tell me about an 'acquaintance' of hers who met a 'very nice' chiropodist through the personal columns of the *Buy & Sell* magazine, I begin to wonder why she and I are still close friends since we're obviously so different. I think it's mainly because we share the same background. We grew up in the same village and have known each other since we were kids. We know the naughty pleasure of testing half-dried cow-pats with our sandals, pressing on them until they released their thick green ooze. We know what it's like to scamper through fields of long tickling grass and sweet meadow smells. Of finding plump cream mushrooms on a dewy morning and rushing home with them to see if they were the ones that could be fried. Of testing our gumboots in that mucky place where the cows drank from the river. Of being free in a way few city children know and so unsophisticated that we regarded the Eurovision Song Contest as a crucial cultural event. We used to be so similar but somewhere along the line Annie became braver than me, more savvy and less prone to disenchantment. I don't know how this happened but it did.

'Alice! Alice! Come back from Wonderland, will you?' Annie is waving her hand in front of my face.

I stare at her, somewhat startled. I have a tendency to drift off in mid-conversation.

'You haven't been listening to me at all, have you?' she demands.

I regard her bashfully. 'I'm sorry.'

'I was telling you about a singles dance that's being held at the Island Hotel this weekend. Look – there's a big ad about it in the paper.'

'Oh, is there?' I mumble cautiously, wondering how to sidetrack her. I glance at my watch. 'Gosh, is that the time!' I exclaim. 'I really should be getting on with some work. I'm rather late with an article about masturbation.'

Annie doesn't say anything. She's looking rather exasperated.

'There's this place in New York where you can get orgasm lessons,' I continue cheerfully. 'They sit in a big room with vibrators. Eric McGrath would be fascinated.'

'Who?'

'You know, the boy I sat beside in primary school. He was the first person who told me where "men put their thing". I thought he was making it up because I wouldn't let him borrow my Monkees ruler.'

Annie's exasperation lifts and she chuckles. 'Eric McGrath...goodness, I'd almost forgotten about him. He kissed me behind the bicycle shed once. It was awful.'

'Oh, yes, that's right! You told me. Your braces got stuck together and you were sure it would lead to pregnancy.'

We're both spluttering with mirth now like two gleefully naughty little girls. All the differences between us have gone, if only for a moment.

As Annie leaves I wonder if she's right. Maybe I do need to become more proactive about men again. Go out more. Be less fastidious. The Gold Blend man is most unlikely to run out of coffee in my vicinity. Romance isn't going to come to me out of the blue – that's become painfully clear. Just as I'm thinking this the phone rings. I approach it wearily. Someone's probably phoning Mira. Her friends tend to leave rather complicated messages. I reach resignedly for a notepad as I pick up the receiver. But the call is not for Mira.

It's from a man. And it's for me.

Chapter 2

THE PHONE CALL WAS from Eamon. The last man I had sex with. He was ringing to invite me out to dinner. I must say I was extremely surprised. Eamon hasn't contacted me in ages. Even though it means missing a particularly interesting episode of *Coronation Street*, I've accepted his invitation. In fact, I'm sitting with him now in a swish French restaurant. Céline Dion is singing about everlasting love in the background.

Eamon looks older than his thirty-nine years and is quite handsome in a restrained, well-ordered kind of way. He takes regular exercise and is generally moderate in his views and lifestyle. He is very practical and methodical enough to save coupons from the back of food packets and get cut-price dinner-sets. His longings don't seem to lunge at him, like mine do at me, and he doesn't talk much. Not usually anyway. We are very different.

He is currently surveying the wine list and I'm wondering whether to order the lobster or play safe with the Chicken Kiev. The lamb sounds pretty good too but I can't bring myself to consider it. Lambs to me mean fluffy white creatures gambolling through spring meadows. It may sound sentimental, but that's just the way I am. I'm frowning at the menu. I wish there wasn't such a large selection. I wish someone would just march up and say, 'Here, take this,' and get it over with. Procrastination has been a bit of a problem for me for some time now.

As you may have gathered, I am not in love with Eamon. If I was I'd be gazing into his dark brown eyes and not fretting about whether to ask the waiter if the chicken is organic. I'd be scanning his solemn, perfectly symmetrical features tenderly. I would have asked him what he is thinking at least five times instead of wishing I hadn't read my weekly horoscope in *The Sunday Times*. Apparently the sun is changing signs and Neptune, 'the planet of deception', is in a challenging aspect to the 'unsettling' Uranus. There is also talk about intensified feelings being triggered by a Full Moon. I should have stayed with the gardening column.

'What are you having?' I ask Eamon. He has picked up his own menu and has looked at it for about ten seconds.

'The lobster,' he announces, with exemplary lack of equivocation. I bathe in his decisiveness for a brief moment. Whatever one may say about men, they can be very soothing.

'Yeah, I think I'll have the lobster too,' I reply, closing the menu firmly before I'm tempted to scour it again. The starter was easy. We opted for salads.

'I'm so glad you could come,' Eamon is saying as he unfolds his thick linen napkin.

'Well, thanks for inviting me,' I smile chirpily. 'I haven't eaten in such a swanky place for quite a while.'

Eamon seems unusually pleased at this revelation. 'So you haven't – mmmm – been going out much then?' he asks, smiling.

'No, I haven't,' I concur. 'Ah, here come our watercress salads. My! Don't they look pretty!' My exclamation is entirely sincere. It's so nice to feel pampered. No one has stuffed a tomato for me for a very long time. Eamon looks at me happily. I know he finds women rather complicated so my simple delight in my salad must be rather reassuring.

As I tuck in, he refills my glass of wine and I glance at him gratefully. He's wearing a very fetching taupe-coloured Armani jacket and looks highly presentable. I really liked the skilful way he ordered the wine and the diligent manner in which he enquired whether I was warm enough and if he should ask the waiter to return my rose-coloured wool shawl. His attentiveness is comforting. He seems so masterful and grown-up sitting there. We fit in perfectly with the other couples in the restaurant – his casual but perfectly groomed appearance somehow compensating for the fact that my Laura Ashley floral-patterned cotton dress is inadequately ironed. There are four yellow freesias in a vase on our table, which is covered with a crisp linen tablecloth. I touch them tenderly. The luxuriance of the setting seems almost sensual. I suddenly realize that I've been missing this kind of thing – when we used to date, Eamon frequently wined and dined me at nice places. We tended to eat in virtual silence so I entertained myself by earwigging on conversations nearby, which were often fascinatingly indiscreet.

However, this evening Eamon is far more talkative than usual. He tells me that he has had his kitchen redesigned and that his cousin has given him a book called *Talking to Ducks – Rediscovering Joy and Meaning in Your Life*. He says the name of this book carefully, as though it is some sort of secret code. Getting to know Eamon requires being alert to these sorts of signals, because he rarely speaks of his own emotions directly.

I restrain myself from asking him about the 'duck' bit. I have talked to ducks myself occasionally and they haven't answered back. 'That book sounds interesting,

Eamon,' I say encouragingly. 'I could certainly do with a bit more "joy and meaning" myself.'

'Yes, you can borrow it if you like,' he smiles affectionately. 'I knew it would appeal to you. I'm afraid I haven't got beyond the first chapter. I haven't much time for reading these days.'

I look down at my napkin and wonder if Eamon ever will find the time to address his more murky personal issues. The fact that he mentioned such a book at all must, however, be in some way significant. 'Are you doing a bit of mid-life reappraisal?' I ask gently. 'It's all the rage these days.'

'I suppose I am in my own small way,' he agrees, most surprisingly. Then he says, 'Ah, here comes the lobster,' and I know he's decided to swerve off the subject as deftly as Jensen Button in an Alfa Romeo. Eamon prefers cars to feelings. He likes the way you can just open the bonnet and sort things out there and then, so his evasion does not surprise me. On the rare occasions that Eamon has been open with me, he has done it in his own good time. Any attempts I've ever made to get him to 'open up' have resulted in emotional withdrawal.

Sometimes it seems like a little game of his. A 'now you see me, now you don't' kind of thing. It's a kind of defence I suppose. Though he appears strong, silent and sophisticated, deep down Eamon is very sensitive and doesn't really want people to know it. I sensed this side of him the first moment we met at a friend's barbecue two years ago. Frankly, I think it's what drew me to him in the first place, so of course it was rather exasperating to find he had walled this side of himself off quite so neatly. Bits of it slip out sometimes in conversation, and when they do he almost seems relieved. But, just as quickly, he tucks them back into their box and it's as if

15

they were never there at all. Because of this our conversations tend to be rather bland – as though we're skirting around something. It can get very lonely and is one of the reasons we drifted apart.

Though we are still skirting around things in this swish French restaurant, I do sense that Eamon is trying to be more open. I sense he is working up to something, however laboriously, and I wonder what it is. I order chocolate mousse for dessert and he has profiteroles. As we drink our post-prandial liqueurs I restrain myself from playing with the melted wax on a tall vermilion candlestick and listen. He's telling me more and more about his house and things he's had done to it. He is looking at me fondly as he speaks, as though these details somehow involve me. Then, after a generous glass of chartreuse he suddenly announces, 'But the place is far too large for just one person, Alice. It's just a house, not a home. I need someone to share it with me.'

'You could advertise in the "Flat Sharing" section of *The Irish Times*. That's how I found Mira,' I reply.

He looks at me with such obvious disappointment that my tentative decoding is confirmed. When he said 'someone' he meant me, though he doesn't seem able to acknowledge this. Instead he starts to talk about a Van Morrison CD I gave him for his birthday and how he often plays it in his car. He says that the Fair Isle sweater we chose together is now one of his favourites and that even though he's tried to follow my chocolate sponge pudding recipe, his puddings never taste as good as the ones I make myself. He says he doesn't have much time for cooking anyway. He buys most of his meals pre-prepared at Marks and Spencer. When he starts to tell me, rather nostalgically, that he came across my 'occasional' toothbrush in his bathroom recently, I decide it is time to broach the matter he is obviously avoiding.

'Eamon – are you suggesting that we get back together?' I ask.

'Yes! Yes, I am!' he grins delightedly. 'I'd like you to move...to move...' He fumbles with his napkin. He just can't seem to spit it out.

'Move in with you?'

'Yes! In fact, something a bit more than that.'

'A bit more? In what way exactly?'

He doesn't reply. Instead, he reaches across the table and takes my left hand in his. He presses it tenderly and looks rather pointedly at my marriage finger.

'Is this – is this something to do with marriage?' I enquire cautiously. I'm beginning to feel like a contestant on Name That Tune.

'Oh, yes, Alice. It is. Absolutely.' He looks at me with great relief. I stare at him, gobsmacked. Even when we were dating Eamon had seemed a confirmed bachelor, though now he has decided not to be his decisiveness should not really surprise me. Eamon approaches life the way he ordered lobster from the menu. He scans his alternatives and swiftly reaches a decision. I often wish I was more like him.

After his pronouncement, neither of us speaks for at least half a minute. It feels like half an hour. 'Why didn't you say you felt like this before?' I eventually ask, taking a gulp from my glass of Grand Marnier. 'You haven't contacted me in ages. You seemed to have forgotten all about me.'

'Oh, no, I hadn't, Alice,' he replies earnestly. 'I thought about you a lot – it's just – it's just that I've been away on assignments. I've been incredibly busy.'

I get that forlorn feeling you get when someone says they're going to transfer your phone call and clearly doesn't know how to. The 'bleep' just doesn't sound right, and neither does Eamon's explanation. Being 'incredibly busy' wouldn't have stopped me from contacting him, if I'd wanted to.

'Eamon' – I begin the sentence cautiously, but with as much firmness as I can muster. 'Eamon, I think you should know I'm not at all sure we're suited.'

Eamon does not seem surprised at this remark. 'I've been thinking a lot about commitment lately,' he says slowly. 'My younger brother got married last month and it just didn't seem right.'

'What do you mean?'

'I'm the older one,' he frowns. 'It should have been me.'

'I don't think they keep scorecards about that kind of thing.'

'I went to the wedding alone,' he continues dolefully. 'My sister kept saying, "Where's Alice? Why didn't you bring Alice?" And I thought, "Yes, why didn't I? Why isn't Alice here?"' He says it somewhat reproachfully. I shift uncomfortably in my seat.

'Life has got rather bland without someone to share it with – but it was never bland with you.' His tone has changed to fond nostalgia. 'I've been remembering all the good times we had together and wondering why I let us drift apart. We could both wait forever to meet our ideal person, but what is "suited" Alice?' He looks at the wine bottle as though it might speak. 'We're comfortable together. We have similar interests. I find you attractive. Sexy too.'

I watch this lob land in my court with a rogue bounce. It's hard to respond to compliments with an overhead smash, and yet I want to be truthful. 'Look, Eamon,' I sigh. 'You're a handsome, intelligent man and, yes, it is true we are quite comfortable together. Sometimes. That pine shelving you put up has been invaluable. And I think all those subtitled movies we saw together did improve my French. But we don't have that many similar interests, do we?'

'We're both alone, Alice.' Eamon looks deep into my eyes. 'We're both nearly forty and, maybe, want a family. That, added to the rest, adds up to quite a lot.'

I wish he hadn't said that word. Forty. It wasn't fair. Sometimes I feel as though I've got romance mixed up with tennis. I really don't want to be 'forty–love' – that is, loveless, like some score at Wimbledon. As Eamon speaks I can almost hear the old biological tick tock, and other tick tocks too. He seems to be treating his proposal like some sort of business agreement. The romantic side of me is, frankly, rather offended.

I just know my Mr Wonderful, if he exists, would have found a better way to broach this subject. He would have looked deep into my eyes like Tom Hanks stared at Meg Ryan in *Sleepless in Seattle*. But maybe watching too many Hollywood films has skewed my judgement. Maybe Eamon is right to treat marriage in this methodical manner. There's no 'whoosh' about his proposal. No sudden dislocation. It's nothing like the rabbit holes I have so frequently wandered into. It seems practical. Sensible. So why am I gripping the edge of my seat so fiercely that my fingers have begun to ache?

Eamon leans towards me earnestly. 'Look, I'm going to Peru tomorrow.'

'Peru?' I repeat, somewhat startled.

'Yes, I'll be away for five months. I know I should have mentioned it earlier but it does give you time, Alice.

19

Time to decide what your answer will be. I sense you need that.'

'Yes, I do,' I agree with considerable relief. 'Leave it with me,' I add, as though he's put a memo on my desk. 'I'll let you know what my answer is when you get back.'

Eamon studies me carefully. He's a consulting engineer. He knows about construction. About the weights that things can take. Is he surveying me to see if I could bear him? There is always a heaviness about him. But would I just add to it? And what would he add to me?

After the meal, Eamon drives me home in his new Audi. As we cruise along the dual carriageway I press the buttons of the car radio, trying to find something brazen and unsentimental. 'And now we have Laren Brassière's new CD, "Little Fishes",' an Australian disc jockey says with practised brightness. As a loud wailing sound invades the car I lunge towards the control panel and surf on to Barbra Streisand who is singing 'I Am a Woman in Love'. I wince and am about to press the buttons again when Eamon says, 'Leave that on. It's nice'. He glances at me tenderly, conspiratorially, as though I am 'A Woman in Love' myself. But I'm not, that's just the point. I'm not.

And I wonder if I ever will be.

Chapter 3

I HADN'T MEANT TO tell Annie about my meal with Eamon. The thing is, I let it slip that I got home rather late last night, now she wants to know the reason.

'Yes, what did you get up to last night?' Mira adds unhelpfully. She's just appeared in the kitchen and has plonked her very wet wetsuit beside me on the floor.

'Look, could you put that thing in the bathroom?' I demand irritably. 'Just because you've taken up windsurfing doesn't mean we have to have bits of the Irish Sea dripping all over the lino.'

Mira pours herself a mug of freshly ground coffee and makes a face at me. 'She dashed out of the cottage wearing her Laura Ashley dress,' she murmurs sotto voce to Annie before she picks up her wetsuit and, with mug in hand, pads barefooted out of the room. She knows she'll be able to prise the details from me later.

'Was it a date?' Annie is leaning towards me excitedly.

'Yes,' I mumble.

'Oh, Alice, you've met someone. How wonderful!' Annie almost spills her tea at the news. 'Who is he? Come on...give me the juicy details.'

'Oh, all right,' I sigh, 'if you must know it was Brad Pitt. You know how he's been pestering me lately.' I look at her, hoping she will laugh. Far-fetched claims that Hollywood actors have been competing for my company are among our older jokes. 'We went by Learjet to Nice,' I continue. 'I had asparagus for starters.'

Annie eyes me stonily. 'Who is he?' she repeats.

I look wistfully at the cat who is stretched out and purring on a cushion. I have a good reason for not wanting to tell Annie about Eamon. She believes that he and I are completely incompatible. I think it's something to do with a dinner party I gave when we were going out together. Annie didn't like the way he just sat there and didn't help me with the food, or the crockery, or the conversation. I told her he was shy, but she wasn't impressed by this excuse. She also didn't like the way he'd disappear for days on end to play golf but 'didn't have time' to go away on holidays with me. I complained to her about all this myself, in great detail, so I suppose I have contributed to her bias. The thing is she doesn't know the 'other' Eamon. The one who sat with me in that restaurant. The one who is masterful and attentive and sporadically sensitive. The one who watches me closely while I'm daydreaming and then gives me a little smile.

Annie herself is watching me – watching me with the resolve of a woman who bakes her own brown bread on a routine basis. I take a deep breath. It's obvious that I'm going to have to tell her about Eamon's proposal. And so I do.

'Of course, you said "no",' Annie chuckles, as soon as I've spilled the beans.

'No, I didn't actually,' I mumble, making a trellis with my fingers. 'He's in Peru for five months. I said I'd give him my answer when he gets back.'

'You're not actually taking this suggestion of his seriously, are you?' Annie is looking horrified. I really didn't think she'd react quite so dramatically.

'Well, it does seem worth mulling over a little,' I reply mildly. 'I mean, it's not every day someone asks you to be their wife.'

'Your answer must be "No".' Annie says it most urgently. 'You don't love him. You know you don't.'

'Yes,' I agree resignedly, 'but he is quite practical. I mean, he put up that pine shelving very well. He's very obliging, Annie. And he's not at all difficult.'

'Oh, Alice.' Annie reaches out and pats my hand. 'You poor sweetie. I didn't realize you were feeling this – this romantically demoralized.'

'It's not just that.' I pick up a biscuit and start to munch it. The crumbs trail down a corner of my mouth but I'm too preoccupied to wipe them away. 'I'm trying to be sensible, Annie. If I want to have a baby I'll have to get round to it soon. And I'm tired of these pipe dreams of meeting Mr Wonderful. Fantasies about him cheer me up on rainy evenings, but they don't hug me when I get into bed. I can't whisper to them, spoon up with them. They don't give me cuddles – and I need cuddles.' I stare at her bleakly. 'I'm lonely, like Eamon. I don't think either of us realized just how lonely we are until now.'

Annie rubs my back comfortingly.

'No man has shown a romantic interest in me for ages,' I continue. 'Eamon may not be Mr Wonderful but he wants me. I'd almost forgotten what being wanted feels like.'

'Oh, Alice, what has happened to your self-esteem?' Annie asks. 'You're pretty and interesting and kind and…and a very talented painter,' she adds loyally, knowing this will please me. 'If you're determined to marry then there are some very pleasant men I could introduce you to. Men who are far more suitable.'

I regard her with tender exasperation. 'You've already organized quite enough dinner parties on my behalf, Annie. And, anyway, the men you introduce me to are already half in love with you. It is a tribute to your sweet and unassuming nature that you don't realize this, but it's a fact.'

'Of course they aren't in love with me!' Annie says this with great vehemence. She looks just like she did at primary school when the teacher wouldn't believe Alan O'Callaghan had given her a Chinese burn. 'And what about Ernie?' she adds, glancing at her watch worriedly and reaching for her handbag. 'Ernie took your telephone number. He liked you.'

'Yes, and he also borrowed my hand-painted silk scarf and didn't give it back.'

'What!'

I hesitate. 'Look, I hadn't meant to tell you this but...but Ernie is a transvestite.'

'I don't believe it!' Annie exclaims.

'Yes, he is. He admitted it to me after a number of Guinnesses in O'Donnell's pub. He wanted to dress up as a woman on our next date, and I'm afraid I said I'd find it too embarrassing.'

Annie is staring at me, dumbfounded. She is clearly distressed that her matchmaking went so awry.

'But he was very nice,' I add, now desperately trying to console her. 'And' – I smile at her wryly – 'he gave me some really good tips about exfoliation.'

'Oh, Alice, I'm sorry.' Annie grimaces at me apologetically. 'I'm beginning to understand why you've developed hermit tendencies.' She gives me a hug and starts to head purposefully out of the room. 'Sorry to dash,' she adds, 'but I've got to collect Josh from playschool.'

'How is Josh?' I ask, as I open the front door for her. Annie is a single mother and Josh, her five-year-old son, is one of my favourite people.

'He's decided he wants to be Wayne Rooney,' she smiles, then she pauses and adds anxiously, 'Alice, I know you've had some sobering romantic experiences, but I do hope you'll start going out a bit more. I – I really do think you need to explore your options. Especially…now.' She says the 'now' bit very firmly and I know she's referring to Eamon's proposal.

'Yes, you're probably right,' I find myself mumbling, I don't like seeing her this fretful.

After Annie has left I find myself wishing that she and most of my other female friends didn't have such strong opinions about romance. For example, Sarah, the features editor, claims that finding Mr Wonderful is a bit like tracking down some extremely rare and fleet-footed mammal and Mira makes flat, disturbing pronouncements like, 'Love often finds you when you've stopped looking for it.' The minute you do this, apparently, you are as in demand as Sellotape at Christmas. What she doesn't mention, however, is that not looking for love probably has to find you too. Find you after years of spent illusion. Find you when you've turned into a sturdy soul who rings up radio gardening programmes and talks excitedly about brassicas. The minute you start doing this, apparently, Mr Wonderful tracks you down with the unlikely determination of the man in the Milk Tray ads. He swoops you off while you're still mulling over whether to relocate your rhododendrons.

I head grimly towards my laptop computer and the subject of solo sexual stimulation. As I do so I glance at the photo of my mother, smiling wistfully out at me from her silver frame. I wish she was still alive. I wish I could ask her about Eamon and about so many other things. Because I know she heard whispers in other rooms.

Whispers from another life that she might have lived, and now I often hear them too. Sometimes I think I mislaid a part of me a long time ago, and I just can't seem to find it. Without it everything seems different, yet I'm not sure what it is. And maybe that's why I so often find myself dreaming of the carefree childhood days Annie and I so seldom speak of. The days when the loudest whispers came from the wind as it blew through the tall trees by the river. The time when I loved Aaron and Aaron loved me, though we would have giggled if anyone had said it. I somehow need these memories, and yet if I could run away from them I think I might. For they are the 'long perspectives' Philip Larkin wrote about in his poem 'Reference Back'. The long perspectives 'Open at each instant of our lives' that:

...show us what we have as it once was,
Blindingly undiminished, just as though
By acting differently we could have kept it so.

Chapter 4

I THINK ANNIE IS right. I do need to get out and meet more people. I doubt if I could manage that 'singles dance' she spoke of. Maybe joining an evening class would be a good tentative step towards sociability. An adult education brochure from the local college came through the door last night. I think I'll opt for figurative painting. I've a nice photo of my childhood home in my album and I'd like to try to capture it in oils.

I rather wish I hadn't started to browse through that album actually. It's made me very nostalgic. Even more so than usual. I didn't know I'd kept quite so many photos of Aaron. He's smiling out at me from every second page. As I look at his big wide smile memories come flooding back to me, startlingly undiminished. It's almost as if I'm back in the small country village I grew up in. It's as if he might tap gleefully on the window any moment.

Aaron was my first best friend. He lived near me in a big house. He had long legs and a mop of browny blond hair and was very keen on ants. He kept some in a special container. You could see what they were up to through the perspex glass. He also had one of those strange things between his legs I learned was called a 'willy'. I'd seen a bigger one on my father when he was having a bath, and on that man who didn't manage to keep the towel wrapped around him on the beach in Ballybunion. But, apart from his willy, Aaron and I were very much alike. He was a bit more daring than me, and he had a catapult. But we could finish each other's sentences. And frequently didn't need to speak at all.

Most afternoons, on the way home from school, Aaron and I used to go into the shop run by two spinster sisters – the Delaneys – and buy some pink marshmallow mice with proper tails. The Delaney sisters handed them to us with thin, careful hands. They always had the radio on and one bar lit on the electric fire. They were in their fifties and had Never Married.

Never Married. Those words had a strange ring to them when I was a girl. A bit like Never Washed, only marginally less surprising. I studied the Delaney sisters as though they were a kind of finch in one of Aaron's bird books. What on earth made a woman 'never marry' and therefore be 'alone', even if she lived with her sister?

'We just never met the right man,' Ethel said when I asked.

This was not in fact entirely true. Agnes, her sister, had met the 'right man'. I'd heard Mum talking about it. The thing was he lived in England and if Agnes went to join him who would help Ethel run the shop and look after their elderly mother? So she'd stayed in the village and this man was never mentioned, to us anyway. But when Agnes was behind the till she always had the radio on more loudly.

Primary school always had a smell of old apples to it. A sandy-coloured man called Mr O'Donovan gave us 'special' French lessons late on Thursday afternoons. You had to pay for them so only about half the class stayed on.

Mr O'Donovan used tapes and a lot of them were about a certain Monsieur Thibaud, only sometimes the tape went funny and he was called M on S i eeeeur TH I I b a uud. I liked when that happened. Mr O'Donovan used to get annoyed and started to fiddle with his machine while the rest of us got a break from Monsieur Thibaud, who seemed to lead an incredibly boring life. He told us all about himself in French. He got into his car and he got out of it. He went into a shop and reached into his pocket for his purse. He counted things very carefully, saying every number. He said 'hello' in many different ways and repeated his name and where he came from over and over again, as if we hadn't heard him the first time. He went on and on.

Mrs Forrest, the Sunday School teacher, did too. The best way not to let her get to you was to pretend she was a television. She was supposed to be talking about Jesus, but she went on a lot about herself. For instance, the Feeding of the Five Thousand might remind her of a picnic she'd organized when there hadn't been enough bread rolls. If it wasn't for the felt pictures I don't know how we would have put up with her.

The felt pictures were great. You could move say, Jesus, around, but the felt background remained the same. You could put donkeys on roofs and sheep in boats. You could move entire mountains.

Aaron's Dad was very keen on taking photographs. Mine wasn't. I had to pester him about it. 'Take one now – pleeeease,' I'd plead at family gatherings. 'Look – Berty has a rose stuck in his collar. That would be a good one.'

Berty was my Aunt Phoeb's Yorkshire terrier and she fussed over him far more than she fussed over her husband, Sean. Berty had piles of toys and doggy chocolate and stuff like that. He was rather neurotic. Aunt Phoeb had to be adored by someone and she'd groomed Berty for this task. When she was absent he was desolate. When she returned he was ecstatic. In the long bits in between he watched her and waited.

Uncle Sean didn't mind all this because he was a fanatical golfer. 'I'm going to play golf,' he'd say, as if the words themselves would clear a smooth, respectful space around him. Sean seemed more married to golf than to my aunt. She was not one of those wives who watch their husbands trot off on some ostensibly pointless pursuit with an indulgent smile. His preoccupation with small white balls eventually made her lose respect for him. She used to tell my mother he was 'running away' and 'shirking his commitments'. In fact she became so angry with him about it one began to feel a certain reluctant sympathy for his absence. Though people spoke of marriage as the 'icing on the cake', my childhood observations led me to believe it was sometimes more like marzipan.

I wonder if marriage to Eamon would make me revise this opinion.

I'm looking at the adult education brochure again as I munch my breakfast. I decide that I'd better ring the college today before all the painting classes are booked up. Then, as I make myself a cup of coffee, I notice that the stray cat who has adopted Mira and myself is padding around the garden hungrily. He isn't hungry actually. I know this because when I tried to feed him he just looked up at me in a bewildered manner. Mira must have given him breakfast before she left. I don't know what he's waiting for – love perhaps. The thing is, any time I try to stroke him, he just runs away. I open the back door and address him sternly. 'Look, I'm tired of this charade,' I say. 'You'll just have to conquer your fear of intimacy or you won't get any more Whiskas.' This of course is a lie, and he knows it. Cats are rather like men in that way.

The handsome young man who's just moved in – whose house overlooks the garden – is playing 'The House of the Rising Sun' on his guitar. He must be sitting outside. I can hear him quite clearly. He pauses at every chord change. All his chords sound much the same – a sort of loose twang. He's singing very earnestly, lending great emotion to every word, but he's off key half the time. He moves quickly on to Donovan and then Paul Simon. He doesn't seem to be looking for a song to play so much as one that will play him. That will spring from the instrument with its own volition. I hope he doesn't make a habit of serenading his neighbours in this manner. I'd have to buy earplugs. The cat, however, seems fascinated by the noise. He jumps on to the wall to have a look.

'Hello, puddy. Come to give me a bit of encouragement, have you?' I hear the man saying in what sounds like a slightly American accent. The cat doesn't run away. He usually does when strangers talk to him. Maybe he's getting tamer after all.

I glance in the hallway mirror before I leave. Dear God, I've got another small spiky hair on my chin. I know this can happen when one gets older, but why? Where on earth do they come from? I glance at my watch. Oh dear, I'm late. Time does funny things in the morning. It seems to speed up when I'm at home and slow down as soon as I reach the office.

'Blustery day,' says Mrs Peabody, my elderly neighbour, who's picking up a carton of milk from her doorstep as I blast out my front door.

'Yes, but quite bright,' I answer, smiling from the teeth out. I can't do a proper smile yet. It takes me a long time to wake up properly. I sometimes wonder if I've ever managed it completely.

'It's quite mild, but there may be showers later,' says Mrs Peabody, who is an avid listener to weather forecasts.

'Indeed, there is some patchy cloud,' I agree. 'Well, I'd better dash if I'm going to get my bus.'

As soon as I get on the bus I put on my Discman earphones. It's a good way of not getting into conversation. When passing acquaintances on the street one can observe the rituals of friendliness and distance. When they plonk themselves beside you on a bus you have to summon up a plausible personality, and I haven't been feeling plausible for ages now – especially not this early in the morning.

Sometimes I find myself staring at men on buses. Men who, perhaps, have a toddler on their knees who they are being nice to. I watch them burying their faces sweetly into their child's hair and wonder if I could have spotted their potential, say, ten years ago. Back when they were probably as footloose as I still am. Could I have spotted this tenderness under, say, four pints of Guinness and a World Cup T-shirt? Someone obviously did. Someone who knew that tenderness was what she needed.

I take out my Discman and turn on my meditation CD. According to it I am on a beach and feeling enormously calm. An American voice is telling me that I am someplace between Naples and Fort Myers. I like that he presumes my acquaintance with these Florida locations. That he thinks that maybe I jump into a jeep and speed off to them at weekends with a stash of Budweiser cans in my trailer. The thing is, I don't seem to have studied the map too carefully this morning because I don't end up on a beach. I visit my imaginary villa in Provence instead.

32

It's a wonderful villa. It has green wooden shutters and the front door is framed by bougainvillea. I wear silver rings with big interesting stones when I'm there. I go for long sunny walks in loose cheesecloth dresses and picnic in lavender-covered fields. I collect baguettes from boulangeries and watch lizards sunbathing. There's a small town nearby and it's full of friendly people. I sit with them at sidewalk cafés. Whole afternoons slip by without my noticing. I also paint wonderful landscapes which sometimes end up in Paris. I keep hens and don't care when I find hairs on my chin. I am extremely happy. And though I am nearing my stop – I can tell this without even looking out the window – I linger at my villa for a small stolen moment longer. I need these patches of reverie and meditation – I need them badly. For not only am I in transition between locations, I am in transition between myself. Commuting from the leafy centre of my deepest longings to the stern suburb of necessity.

As soon as I sit down at my desk Gerry pops his head over the open plan partition that separates us. 'Is it the fourth or the fifth?' he asks.

'The fifth,' I reply. I have only become so sure of dates since Gerry has started asking me them. In some way he has shifted the responsibility.

'Do anything exciting this weekend?' asks Cindi, stopping by my desk. She always asks me about my weekends with great eagerness. It's as if, after years of fairly prosaic replies, she believes I'm suddenly going to announce that Colin Farrell popped by for supper on Saturday. Or that I briefly joined the Folies Bergère and only just made the dawn flight back.

'I had quite a dirty weekend actually.'

'Wow! Really!' Cindi leans forward excitedly.

'Sorry, Cindi – I was just referring to the state of my cottage.'

Cindi has a bubbly, pretty face. She is, as usual, perfectly groomed. Every morning she gets up early so she can wash her shiny blonde hair and twirl it into shape. My hair, on the other hand, is as unruly and untamed as ever. I get it cut at a posh place every so often and then forget about it, until even I can't avoid noticing that I'm beginning to resemble a Pyrenean sheepdog.

I want a Pyrenean sheepdog. I want...

'Can I borrow your stapler for a moment?' Humphrey has grabbed it before I even have time to answer. Humphrey is tall and solemn and has a pony tail. He works in Design and lopes along the corridors in a preoccupied manner. He has numerous staplers of his own, but he does something to them. When he presses them they click like they're supposed to, only the staple seems to fold in on itself instead of going through the paper. 'Have a nice weekend?' he asks, as he's about to sprint away.

'Yes,' I reply, because any other answer would flummox him.

'Do anything exciting yourself?' I ask Cindi, who is clearly waiting to be asked. As I say this I plug in the new kettle I got to ensure a regular supply of Earl Grey tea without having to face the mysteries of the office kitchen. People who use it have to bring in milk on a rota and Lesley, the receptionist, gets very shirty if there's any spilt sugar on the sideboard.

'I met Jason on Friday,' she replies. 'I've decided that he's far too intellectual for me. He confiscated my Jilly Cooper and gave me a book by Gabreel G-Garnia Marq-Marq... Oh, you know who I mean. He's Colombian.

Has a moustache. Jason's turning out to be just like Leonard – you know that guy who went ballistic when I said that Bizet was a type of bathroom appliance favoured by the French.'

I smile sympathetically and start to brew my badly needed cuppa. Cindi watches. 'Like one yourself?' I ask, as I have been asking her every Monday for some years. She's quite young – in her mid-twenties – and seems to need someone to spill the beans to. The beans vary enormously and frequently include long descriptions of the vagaries of the No. 20 bus route.

'Oh, thanks, I'd love a cuppa,' Cindi smiles. 'I'll just go and get my mug.' Then she races off down the corridor in navy Capri pants that show off her slim toned legs. Cindi has a pretty floral mug, and she keeps it very well. She washes it each time she uses it, whereas I just give mine a quick run under the tap in the Ladies at the end of the working day. I don't even have a nice mug. I use one I found in the office ages ago. It's a kind of muddy brown.

I take a deep, desperate swig of my first fix of tea.

Bergamot – that's what they put in Earl Grey tea. I sometimes burn Bergamot oil in my aromatherapy burner. It's good for lots of things including depression, agitation, despondency and mood swings. I'd drink it neat if that were allowed.

As soon as Cindi has had her tea and headed back to her office, or 'orifice' as she prefers to call it, Natalie walks by. Natalie has developed a nice little niche for herself in 'celebrity interviews'. She likes to think of herself as being very 'down to earth' and frequently speaks of famous people in a manner which implies that she is in no way impressed by them. Something I sense she believes is impressive in itself. There are so many famous people she isn't impressed by that I dare not surmise what she makes of me. I'm rather frightened of Natalie actually. We used to have lunch together sometimes. I managed to retreat from them by saying that I was 'very busy' and was going to have lunch at my desk. My desk has become a kind of unofficial shelter. Little by little I've been stealthily appropriating office partitions and I now have four of them surrounding me. There's only a small entry gap, but sadly this doesn't seem to deter people. I've got prints of pictures by Matisse, Rembrandt, David Hockney and Chagall on the 'walls'. I also have plants, a needlepoint cushion on my seat and an art deco lamp I found at an auction.

I do need a place to hide in. I used to be very open with people when I first joined the magazine. When they asked me how I was I went into too much personal detail. It was in no way soothing. Though they gobbled it up and passed it on and discussed it, they really didn't tell me that much about themselves.

I don't blab nearly so much now. For example, I've discovered that when colleagues ask me about 'my holiday' I can give them small, neutral details without feeling under any obligation to mention my torrid affair with a tennis coach. Or that his 'forearm' instruction was frequently extracurricular. The place where I should speak more is probably at the editorial meetings. We have them fairly regularly. The production schedule dictates that we deal with seasonal features in advance. Our discussions of spring and summer, autumn and winter, have little to do with the conventional calendar. For example, people are frequently in their winter woollies when we are busy discussing safe tanning. No wonder Gerry keeps asking me what date it is.

36

The younger contributors tend to be very perky at these meetings. Suggesting all sorts of topics, and angles and interviews and 'hot' issues for 'today's woman' while I listen rather warily and doodle. They sound so enthusiastic – as if they don't realize nearly all of these things have been written about before. Many times. I said this to Sarah once.

'Of course most of the best stories have been covered already,' she smiled. 'It's making them seem fresh, new, finding interesting angles, updating them, that's the challenge.'

I bet if I spoke up more at those meetings I wouldn't be asked to write so much about sex.

I pick up the phone and start to dial. 'The number you have dialled has been changed – please place the digit two before the number and start again,' a resigned voice tells me. Every single number in my phone book seems to have been altered. And the new phones themselves have so many features that they require a small manual. This building is awash with 'time-saving' new technology. Just trying to keep up with it takes ages.

My phone starts ringing. It's Sarah. I know this before she speaks because I hear the clang of her earring. 'When will you have that "Sex Alone" article ready, Alice? I'd like to see it before I finalize the artwork,' she asks brightly.

'I – mmmm – I'm just tidying it up a bit,' I mumble. 'I – I should have it for you this evening.'

'Well, keep it nice and light. We don't want any references to Monet or anything like that.'

'Of course.' Sarah knows that art is my real passion.

As I put the phone down I realize it must be coffee-break time in ad sales. I know this because they've turned on the radio. Anita Baker's 'Sweet Love' from her album

37

'Rapture' is wafting out at me. That song is obviously about some very Wonderful Man. Old, familiar longings are swirling round me in great gusts. Suddenly I am miles away from this office. I am no longer the person who has just circled 'Frazier' carefully on *The Irish Times* television page with a blue biro. I am the girl who put donkeys on roofs and sheep in boats in felt pictures.

I want to break out. I want to get honky and funky. I want to feel like a jazz tune floating out of a New York brownstone. I – I want to go out and buy a Snickers bar.

And I do.

Chapter 5

I CAN'T BELIEVE IT...I've met a Wonderful Man! And just when I'd given up on them too. It happened last week. And in the most unlikely circumstances. I feel as though I'm David Attenborough. I feel I should be crouching in some jungle with a camera crew, talking in hushed tones. 'We'd better be quiet, this species can wander off rather easily,' I'd tell them. 'Notice the distinctive markings. He may be the only one who is not in captivity. His name is James Mitchel.'

The hour before I met James Mitchel, I was typing frantically at my kitchen table. 'Rub some fruit yogurt on his chest,' I wrote, 'and then, very gently lick it off, letting your tongue linger sensuously round his nipples while...'

I paused. I pause a lot while writing articles for the magazine. Sarah wanted me to enumerate all the sensuous things women can do with items that benefit from cold storage. 'Sex Comes in from the Cold' – that's what she's called the article. I was in a bit of a quandary about whether to include mayonnaise.

'Mira, would you lick mayonnaise off a man's inner thigh area?' I called out.

'No,' she replied. 'Have you fed the cat?'

'Yes. He doesn't seem to like that bargain brand we bought. He's getting very fussy.' Then I looked at my watch and exclaimed, 'Gosh, I'd better hurry or I'll miss my evening class.'

I'd wanted to do 'painting' but when I rang up the college the class was booked up so I'd decided to opt for 'pottery' instead. I'd heard the teacher was called James

Mitchel and I was sure he'd turn out to be past middle-age and ordinary. I was sure he'd be wearing those sort of broad clumpy sandals and one of those synthetic shirts. I suspected he might even smell a bit, but as long as he was kind and encouraging I wouldn't mind. Sometimes you have to delve a bit to find a person's beauty. But, when I entered room 5B of St Benedict's High School I realized James Mitchel's beauty was entirely obvious.

He was standing before a group of gobsmacked ladies and four vaguely interested men. He was saying, 'Hello. It's good to see you all. Before we start let's get to know each other a little. As you may know, my name is James. James Mitchel. Now, you tell me yours.' And then he looked at me because I was standing nearest to him.

'My name is Alice – Alice Evans,' I told him in an abrupt, almost curt manner. I was already, somehow, on the defence.

'Thank you, Alice,' he said, and as he did so his eyes looked straight into mine in a very piercing way. He gave me a little smile and then turned to the others. I studied him carefully as he talked to them. I studied his lovely high cheekbones, his mischievous, but kind, smile. His skin was tanned and smooth, with just enough lines to give his face character. He looked around my age. He was wearing an American football jacket in a jaunty, trans-Atlantic way. He was the kind of man who'd stand out at an airport. If he was a plant he'd be some kind of orchid.

Once James knew our names he told us about basic pottery techniques and then we went to our wheels. I stared at mine warily, as though it was something I'd suddenly been called upon to reinvent.

'We'll just play around a bit tonight so you can get used to using clay,' he told us. 'Don't take it too seriously. Just have fun.'

I went to the large slab of clay and grimly cut some off with the wire cord put there for that purpose. Then I went to a table and belted the clay around a bit like you're supposed to. In fact I made it thud against the table with considerable force. James saw me doing this and gave me a little, knowing smile. 'It's just friendliness,' I told myself. 'Teachers are supposed to be friendly. I must remember that. I'm here to learn about pottery. This class is supposed to be serenely sociable. A place where my longings do not lunge at me and men don't matter. A little clearing. A cosy spot in which to learn how to be incremental – how to take small steps towards less volatile satisfactions. Oh, why does he have to keep looking at me like that!'

I became determined not to be tantalized by James Mitchel's outer beauty. I decided he probably wasn't even a nice person. 'He's probably awfully vain,' I told myself. 'Those sunstreaks in his hair were probably done by some fancy salon. And that small tear on the right knee of his jeans is most likely intentional. Goodness – he's wearing those broad clumpy sandals I don't like. Well, that does it!' I felt the antagonism mounting. I convinced myself that he almost certainly had a girlfriend or wife stashed away somewhere. He was too handsome not to have been grabbed.

The next time I felt him watching me I turned around, determined to give him a hostile glare, but there was something about his strange, almost compassionate expression, that made me quickly turn back to my wheel.

Clay is not easy to centre on a wheel – not if you're trying too hard. You have to sort of feel it into place.

41

Guide it. Otherwise it bumps disconcertingly against your hands as it turns and won't shape properly. James saw me struggling. He came over.

'Don't force it, Alice.' That's what he'd said. 'Be firm and gentle. Relax.'

I'd wished he wasn't standing so close. He smelt so nice, and it wasn't just shower gel. It was him. What he'd just said was so right. Not just about pottery, but about life too. Who was I kidding? I didn't dislike James Mitchel. James Mitchel was gorgeous.

'And just let your elbow rest there and that will steady your hand so you can guide the clay while the other hand draws it upwards,' James Mitchel said, his blond fringe flopping boyishly over his lovely face. Upwards and upwards the clay was moving.

James Mitchel stood beside me, watching the clay growing erect between my hands. His proximity was like a heat haze. The priapic connotations of what I was doing were beginning to make me terribly flustered.

'Go on, Alice,' James urged. 'You're almost there.' Small beads of perspiration were gathering on my forehead. I closed my eyes briefly, trying to summon up some sort of calm. As I did so I felt the clay acquiesce. I stuck a finger, slurp, into its centre…and something like a vase began to form.

'Well done.' James touched my shoulder briefly but, it seemed to me, with considerable feeling. Then he moved on to someone else. I paused for a moment, an almost post-coital glow surrounding me. 'Get a grip of yourself, Alice,' I told myself sternly, but I still felt tingly. I hadn't felt like that in ages. I looked around, wondering if anyone else had Noticed. They hadn't. They were as intent on forming misshapen mugs and ashtrays and bowls as ever.

Though James Mitchel had moved away, my radar was now on the alert. I was aware of every glance he made towards me, ostensibly watching my progress. But surely those glances had more to them? 'Oh, come on, Alice. Don't be so silly,' I told myself. 'He's a man for goodness sake, and you know what they're like.'

But did I? Did I really? They couldn't all be the same. That's what the Delaney sisters who had Never Married said about, say, peaches. 'Don't press them, dearie – they're all the same.' But it wasn't true. It was just convenient. James Mitchel was on some journey too. I could sense it. But his mists, unlike mine, had cleared. It was obvious. I saw it the instant I looked into his eyes. A sweet, unsought-for recognition…the most seductive thing of all. I turned back to my vase with an almost religious intensity. I already knew that I'd lick mayonnaise off James Mitchel's inner thigh area if he wanted. Even coleslaw, if that's what he'd prefer.

By the time the class finished I did have some sort of vase made. I had to discard a number of others, but the one before me was the best. It was not the kind you'd buy in a shop. It was not the kind you'd boast about. It was rather squat and heavy actually. It didn't have conviction. James saw me staring at it. He came over. 'Don't worry, Alice,' he said, as if reading my thoughts. 'By the end of term you'll have made all sorts of nice things. It just takes practice. It just takes time.'

'Yes,' I agreed humbly. James Mitchel was so right. Things do take time. I forget that sometimes. I get impatient. He wasn't impatient. Maybe he'd been sent to teach me all sorts of important things.

'You should glaze this.' James was studying my vase. 'I like it. It's a nice shape. And it's the first thing you've made here. It's important.'

'Is it?' I stared at him gratefully. I have a tendency to dismiss my own efforts too easily. To not give myself enough credit.

'Of course it's important,' he smiled, and then he walked off to talk to someone else and I knew I'd have to learn to share him. He's just that sort of person.

As I walked home I told myself sternly that I mustn't get infatuated with James Mitchel. I hardly knew him. And it was plainly part of a recognizable pattern. Indulging in complete cynicism for a while and then, suddenly, converting dramatically back to a kind of Mills & Boon idealism. 'Poor, dear Eamon out there in Peru,' I found myself thinking. 'What an innocent you are about me.'

Even so, as soon as I reached the cottage I went to my laptop computer most eagerly. The 'Sex Comes in from the Cold' article had to be ready the next day and thoughts of James Mitchel had made me much more enthusiastic about it.

'Get some chocolate chip ice-cream and feed it to him slowly on a silver spoon,' I wrote. 'Then kiss him gently, sharing its delicious sweetness. Let what you're feeling roll over your tastebuds. Pretend that you are tasting ice-cream and him for the first time. Don't hurry. Linger in the moment and enjoy it. These things take time...'

Chapter 6

SOME THINGS SEEM TO take a very long time. Especially this concert. We've only been here half an hour, but it seems like four. 'Be who you really wanna be,' a singer called Laren Brassière is screeching at us. 'You're not some sideshow monkey, dancin' on some lead. Find your tune. Your very own. Only it, and not some streetcar slowin', not some man, can really take you hoooome.'

I really want to be at home right now. This concert is dreadful. Even the bits of moistened tissue paper I stuck in my ears have only slightly muffled the noise. Mira dragged me here. She says I've become obsessed with James Mitchel and need distraction.

I still only see him once a week – at pottery class. I must see more of him. I must. I make love to him every night, but he doesn't know it yet. Very occasionally I wander around the roads near his house, hoping that we'll meet. I've started numerous letters to him. They go: 'Dear James, I hope you don't mind me writing to you out of the blue like this...' and then they stop.

Mira says I'm behaving as if he's 'the last good man'. She says I've got the whole thing completely out of proportion and if passion has this effect on me I should marry Eamon. She says Eamon's proposal has sent me into a panic about something, and I'd better find out what it is. I wish she hadn't dragged me to this stupid concert. I don't see how it can possibly help.

Ever since Mira decided to become an eccentric spinster she's had a very low boredom threshold. A deep need for diversion. She's been seeking out the oddest people she can find, and Laren Brassière is certainly different. For example, all she's wearing is a see-through négligée with only a bra and pants underneath. In a boudoir setting this ensemble might look 'come hither' but here, on Laren, it clearly says 'fuck off'. Tall and slim with long black hair that does not appear freshly washed, she seems in her late thirties. Though her lips have a surly confidence, her eyes are huge and almost girlish as they peer out at us.

'Bugger it anyway, and I'm missing Gardeners' Questions too,' I think, as the jangled, mangled music continues. Snatches of it sound like the garbled noises that emerged during French class when the Monsieur Thibaud tape went funny.

'Plastic!' Laren is now screeching into the microphone, occasionally curling her body slightly as if riding out some psychic twinge. 'Plastic! Plastic! Plastic!' From what I can make out from the lyrics, which break over us like shards of glass, the song is about people. I feel as though I'm listening to nails being scraped across a blackboard. I look at Mira, hoping that's what she's feeling too, but she just sits there entranced.

Laren is prancing around the stage now. It's impossible to ignore her. Everybody is watching her intently. Even the ones dragged here to lend support to battered wives – that's the cause the proceeds of this concert are going to. Tattoo-less women – women who might as easily be watching Neil Diamond. But there is something about their faces that makes it clear they aren't. They are looking at Laren Brassière as if for clues. Shocked in some way, but not as much as they'd expected. For though Laren Brassière is both rude and lewd – some of her gyrations are really quite outrageous – there is more to her than that. Even I can see that now. It's in her eyes. There's something almost innocent and

46

bewildered about them. And yet she's obviously not a woman anyone could batter easily. Like James Mitchel, she has conviction.

Laren ends her encore with what looks like a microphone blow job, and then slinks sullenly off-stage. 'Wonderful,' says Mira dreamily, and with a strange glint in her eyes. 'I must meet her.'

'What?'

'Laren. I must meet her. She's so – she's so...'

'Weird?'

'Yes,' Mira agrees blissfully. 'Come on. Let's go to the bar next door. She's probably there. They all go there after shows.'

I sigh. There's quite a good film on Channel 4.

Mira is right. Laren is in the bar. She's slouching over the counter having a pint with her band. She's surrounded by a small group of cautious female fans, many of whom are way past adolescence. They are trying to look as cool as Laren herself. Every so often they throw gimlet-eyed glances in her direction. I glance carefully at her too, though not as carefully as Mira. For it is clear that Laren Brassière is a deeply eccentric woman who does not need spinsterhood as her excuse. As I stand near her I notice that she frequently laughs long and loud in mid-conversation and for no apparent reason. What's more, the bra under her see-through nightie isn't even clean.

'Let's go,' I say urgently to Mira, suddenly deeply fearful. She doesn't seem to hear me. Her eyes are shining. The last time I saw them shining like that she was with Frank, the married man she had a passionate affair with. The man I don't think she's got over, even though she insists she has.

'Let's go,' I say again. For I suddenly know that Mira feels herself close to the 'tune' Laren sang about earlier, and I'm not at all sure it's one I'd like hearing.

'Mellow out, Alice,' Mira says, suddenly slipping into California-speak.

'So, are you going to talk to her then?' I demand. 'You said you wanted to.'

'I dunno,' Mira replies, a little shyly. 'Maybe later.'

I scrutinize Laren once more...trying to identify her strange attraction. Maybe it's because she has somehow sidestepped the proprieties most of us have been saddled with for years. Seen in a certain light, that could be a cause of gratitude. This emotion has certainly spilt over on to Mira. She's talking with a cluster of fellow fans. They're agreeing that the evening was 'different'. They're discussing the aggressive sound-system and Laren's clothes. Then they move on to other topics, because that's what adults do. They're drinking rather freely and, as they talk, small expletives and scowls occur. Slight grimaces twitch upon their lips and when their laughter comes – about men and marriage maybe – it is way too loud.

I have a sudden yearning to get into conversation with Laren myself. I want to ask her how she came to be like she is – and if it's preventable. The thing is Laren looks like she wants a conversation as much as I need to know more about smiling. She's scowling. Scowling into her drink and lighting up cigarettes offered to her by her equally weary drummer. She absent-mindedly scratches her elbow every so often. Someone I knew used to scratch their elbow like that – who was it? Now that I'm closer to Laren she seems strangely familiar. Have I seen her somewhere before? Glimpsed her on a poster in Virgin Megastore perhaps? From snatches of conversation I gather she and her band are waiting for their equipment to be loaded into their van. They are not waiting around because they want to. I should have known that. Then a skinny fellow wearing a sleeveless T-shirt and tattoo comes over to them, says something, and they drain their glasses.

'Fuck the terrapins – I'm not putting up with them.' That's what Laren says to a man with long blond hair as she rises from her bar stool. I've heard that voice before. I know I have. It's nothing like the nasal whine she sings with. As she turns to grab her packet of Gauloises from the counter I look at her. Really look. Burrowing beneath the layers of lurid make-up and spiky, dyed black hair. Like a grainy picture – obscured by its own white spaces – another face flickers for a second in front of me. And then it's gone and, as the sharp, streetwise features of Laren Brassière condense, I feel even more bewildered. I am now sure I know Laren from somewhere, but I simply can't place her.

The bar is closing. 'Look, I'll drive home,' I tell Mira. 'I've drunk far less than you.'

'OK,' Mira agrees swiftly. She sways a bit as she hands me the keys and keeps exclaiming 'Oops!' and giggling as we push our way through the crowds. As soon as she gets into the car she slumps inebriatedly into the passenger seat. Then, as I turn the ignition key, she starts to doze.

As I drive Mira's car along the dual carriageway I am still puzzling about Laren. Where on earth did we meet before? Do we go to the same hairdresser? No – no it's more than that. She's someone from the past, I know she is. The face I glimpsed through all that make-up seemed a grown-up version of the one I knew. Could she be someone from school? Could she be... Laren MacDermott?

The thought seems so preposterous that I'm tempted to stop the car in a lay-by. Maybe I drank more this evening than I'd thought. Of course Laren Brassière couldn't be Laren MacDermott, my meek, mild-mannered friend from school. The girl who cried every time Eric McGrath made the back of her bra ping open by pulling at it through her sweater. It's just that she speaks like her, and they both scratch their elbows and have the same face and first name.

By the time I've parked outside the cottage I have pretty much accepted that Laren MacDermott is now Laren Brassière. I am still finding it very hard, however, to find any explanation for her mysterious metamorphosis. As I walk up the pathway and Mira lurches after me, I recall that Laren never spoke about becoming a singer. The last time we met she was about to do a beautician's course in Edinburgh. We were in Bewley's Cafe on Grafton Street and shared a plate of chips. She did send me a postcard from Scotland. She didn't write much on it. It was just a quick scribble to say she'd found a flat. She didn't give me the address so I wrote to her care of her parents. She never replied. I was a bit disappointed, I suppose, but not that surprised. People do tend to drift apart after school.

As soon as we get into the cottage I fill a large glass with water and insist that Mira drinks it. She got through a considerable number of vodkas this evening. 'You don't want a hangover, do you?' I fuss protectively.

'Laren was wonderful, wasn't she?' says Mira, cradling her glass of water reverentially.

'She certainly was unusual,' I reply tactfully. I've decided not to tell Mira that Laren and I are acquainted.

She'd almost certainly want me to invite her round to dinner. She'd probably arrive in a bodystocking or something.

'I wish I'd spoken to her,' Mira continues wistfully.

'Well, I'm very glad I didn't,' I think, remembering that I'd wanted to ask Laren how she became what she is. If I had she might have asked the same thing of me – and I really don't know what I would have told her.

I feel frightened suddenly. 'Life is a narrow bridge,' Aaron told me that once. It was a quote he'd heard somewhere. 'Life is a narrow bridge and the important thing is not to be afraid.' But I am. I wish I wasn't. And even more so now that Mira has started to laugh beside me.

Loudly, and for no apparent reason.

Chapter 7

LAREN MACDERMOTT, THAT IS Laren Brassière, is the reason why I like neon tetras. They are small tropical fish with streaks of blue that flash iridescently, especially in certain kinds of light. She had an aquarium full of them in her bedroom. Laren was a 'day girl' at secondary school, but I was a 'boarder'. I wasn't allowed to leave the school grounds until fifth form, and when I did it was often to go to her house. I stared and stared at her small fish. In some way they seemed to represent hope and how it can flash at you suddenly, iridescently, at the most unexpected moments.

I loved Laren's home. It seemed to me the home of someone who should be carefree and happy, even though she wasn't. She thought her bum was too big, her nose too long and her hair too lanky. She didn't even like her teeth, which were perfect, and was very keen on Leonard Cohen's more lugubrious songs. When I visited her mum used to give us mugs of tea and biscuits. It made me feel like I was back on civvy street. Ever since I'd been thrust into boarding school at twelve I'd felt as though I was in the army – a reluctant soldier sent to some perplexing front. I felt a certain identification with the joke that went 'her parents couldn't afford to send her to boarding school so they locked her in the attic for a while.' I would have far preferred to be in the attic actually. At least it would have been 'home'. While Laren dreamed of meeting a 'Wonderful Man' – initially I simply dreamed of freedom.

Laren's 'Wonderful Man' back then was Leonard Whiting, who starred with Olivia Hussey in *Romeo and*

Juliet. She even persuaded me to skip 'games' one afternoon and go to the cinema with her to see it. But, somehow, the headmaster found out about this misdemeanour and I was gated. Laren's mum, on the other hand, was just glad she was taking an interest in Shakespeare. I cried and cried at the unfairness of it. And afterwards I stared harder at the neon tetras than ever. Luxuriating in the way they darted with such carefree competence, in their big, beautifully maintained aquarium – completely unaware, it appeared, of their restrictions. And as I did so, Laren's dreams of meeting some 'Wonderful Man' began to grow on me. It seemed some way beyond my own high walls. At weekends I sometimes stayed with her and she took me to films. Films where some man saw some woman at an airport and their eyes met and that was It. And then some schmaltzy music swelled the cinema and I was so moved I couldn't even chew my Milky Mint.

Laren said she was going to marry young and have loads and loads of children. As a teenager I didn't mention marriage myself, but I did want to be in love. And paint. And travel. And wear skirts as infrequently as possible. I had no idea of the kind of life I might be leading when I was thirty-eight, but I'm sure I didn't suspect for one minute that I would grow so very keen on horticulture. In fact I only bought my cottage in Monkstown, County Dublin, five years ago because it had a garden at the front and at the back.

Each of them is now brimful with seasonal blossoms. Tonight, as I walk back up the pathway after work, I pause in royal fashion before various plants and have a brief chat with the new scented geranium, saying that I hope she's settled in. Then I hear my elderly neighbour

Mrs Peabody calling 'Cooee, Alice' and go over to her. She's standing at the wicker fence.

'Sorry to ask, dear, but would you do me a small favour?' she says. 'Could you pop round to the corner shop and get me a loaf of bread? My knees are a bit stiff today.'

'Of course I will,' I reply. As I say this the man who's moved in round the corner saunters by breezily and calls out, 'Hello, Mrs Peabody,' in a cheerful manner. Goodness, they know each other already. And he's even stopping for a chat. He's standing at Mrs Peabody's small iron gate. As Mrs Peabody says, 'Come here for a moment, Liam, I'd like to introduce you to my neighbour,' he opens the gate and walks up the pathway. I study him with detached interest. It's hard to tell what age he is but maybe he's a bit older than I'd thought. Around thirty perhaps, though he could easily pass as twenty-five. His broad, calm face looks mature, almost philosophical, but there is definitely a youthful twinkle about his deep brown eyes. He is tall and dark-featured. In fact he looks a bit Jewish. I've always admired those sorts of looks but since I've met James Mitchel other men's handsomeness does not seem to affect me. That's just the way it is with love, I suppose.

'Alice, this is Liam,' Mrs Peabody tells me. 'He's just moved in to a house on Half Moon Lane.'

I'm about to say I know this, but then think better of it. It's best not to admit to voyeurism to new neighbours. 'So, how are you settling in, Liam?' I ask politely, trying to look him straight in the eye.

'Well, I still have piles of boxes lying around the place, but I'm getting around to them gradually,' he replies, equally politely. 'It's a lovely area. And I like being close to the sea.'

I was right, he does sound slightly American. Maybe he spent a few months in New York once and brought the accent back as a souvenir. I pick up accents quickly myself. Only the other day I was interviewing someone from Manchester. After an hour I was beginning to sound like one of the Rovers Return regulars on *Coronation Street*.

'So, how's the gardening going, Liam?' Mrs Peabody asks, a trifle slyly it seems to me.

'I've mowed the lawn but that's about the extent of it,' he replies, his calm face clouding suddenly. I recognize that bewildered, half-apologetic expression. It's one of my own. 'Gardening's completely new to me,' he continues, switching to a brave smile that's almost as dazzling as Richard Branson's. 'The last place we lived in was an apartment. The only bit of greenery in it was a rather rampant cheese plant.'

'Ah yes, there it is,' I think. 'He said the "we" word.'

Mrs Peabody doesn't seem to notice Liam's 'we'. Instead she turns to me and says, 'Liam and I met the other day when I was doing a bit of pruning. He asked me what the soil type is round here.'

'It's alkaline', I reply automatically.

'Yes, I told him that.' Mrs Peabody looks at me approvingly. 'Alice is a most accomplished gardener,' she announces. 'I'm sure she'd be glad to advise you about your garden, Liam.' She turns to me and adds pointedly, 'Wouldn't you, dear?'

'Mmmm,' I nod, somewhat unenthusiastically. Liam seems a nice enough young man, but I have no particular wish to become acquainted with his garden. I have quite enough to do in my own.

Liam is looking at me carefully. 'Some gardening advice would be most welcome,' he says, 'but I don't want you to feel under any obligation…mmmm…' He has clearly forgotten my name.

'Alice,' I prompt.

'I can get some books about it,' he continues. 'I believe the basics are fairly straightforward, though by this stage I think my clematis may require counselling.'

As he says this Mrs Peabody's telephone rings. 'Excuse me for a moment,' she smiles, and starts to walk away stiffly.

I wish her telephone hadn't rung just then. I don't want to be left alone with Liam. What on earth am I going to say to him? I doubt if we have much in common. Though I may admire his appearance aesthetically, he doesn't seem my type at all. I wish he'd just go home to his girlfriend. When he said 'we' he must have been referring to that pretty woman I saw wedging a picture through his front door the other day. I glance longingly at my own front door and fidget around a bit. I jingle my keys and even stifle a yawn. It's been a long day and I want to watch *Eastenders*. But Liam is not getting the message. In fact he is now leaning languorously against Mrs Peabody's fence. I am beginning to rather dislike him.

'My house overlooks your cottage, doesn't it?' he says suddenly.

'Yes, our gardens do adjoin,' I agree a trifle primly, letting my gaze drift to Mrs Peabody's roses.

Liam smiles. What is he smiling at? 'So that must be your cat who sits on my wall sometimes,' he observes.

'Yes, probably.' I say it rather wearily. I'm simply going to have to make my excuses and go. I glance at my watch. 'Goodness − is that the time?' I exclaim. 'It's been nice meeting you, Liam, but I'd better be off. I have to go to the shop for Mrs Peabody. She wants me to get some bread.'

'I was just going to the shop myself,' Liam replies. 'I'll get the bread for her when I'm there.'

'Oh. Thanks.' His offer has made me feel flustered. What excuse can I now give for my getaway? 'Well, I'd better go anyway,' I begin. 'Because I have...I have...'

'You have things to do?'

'Yes. Yes, I have things to do,' I agree quickly.

'Bye then, Alice' he says, as he turns to go. 'It's been nice meeting you.'

'Yes, missing you already,' I mutter sardonically to myself as I head eagerly for home. I'm just about to scurry into the cottage when I hear Mrs Peabody calling out 'Cooee, Alice!' again. I sigh and go over to her. 'Liam's getting your bread,' I inform her. 'He was going to the shop anyway.'

'Oh, what a nice young man he is,' she clucks approvingly. 'Since you're here, Alice, could you pop into my cottage for a moment? I'm sorry to impose, but I'm a bit worried about Cyril. I'd like you to have a look at him for me.' Mrs Peabody doesn't see things clearly up close these days. She obviously thinks she may have missed something.

As I go into her small cluttered sitting-room I see that Cyril is standing on his wooden perch, and is staring ahead stonily. Cyril is Mrs Peabody's budgerigar. He got out of his cage the other day, and he hasn't been the same since. Now he doesn't like being in the cage, or out of it, apparently. He's moping. He's moping for the Australian outback, it seems to me. A brief flight around suburbia has not soothed him. I know just how he feels.

'Hello, Cyril,' I say. 'How are you?'

He doesn't reply of course. The only word Cyril knows is 'bollocks' and he only uses it on a good day. Mrs Peabody says he picked it up from her handyman. She keeps wanting Cyril to say 'Who's a pretty boy then?' but he won't.

'I think he looks a bit more chirpy than last week,' I tell her. 'He's just taken a little bit of seed.'

Cyril has taken a bit of seed but he doesn't look chirpy. In fact he looks deeply disillusioned. There is no need to tell Mrs Peabody this.

'Oh, really!' Mrs Peabody beams with pleasure. 'Maybe it's the Russ Conway. I've been playing him Russ Conway. That usually cheers him up.'

'Well, I'd better be off then,' I say, giving Cyril a sympathetic look.

As I open the front door of my cottage I hope, as usual, that something wonderful has arrived in the post. A letter, perhaps, from James Mitchel saying he 'cannot keep his love a secret any longer'. What greets me on the hall mat this evening is, in fact, a hand-addressed letter in a blue envelope for Mira and a forwarded catalogue for thermal underwear addressed to myself.

An aunt of mine called Hilda was concerned about the skimpy cotton dresses I wore about ten years ago. She lectured me about thermal underwear with the zeal of a Jehovah's Witness. She also put me on the Damart mailing list. I should really write and tell them that I have become a many-layered person in my life and in my clothing, though I'd strip off real fast for James Mitchel. I really would.

As far as I can tell James Mitchel doesn't have a girlfriend. Mildred, who's the class snooper, hasn't discovered one anyway. Even though she's seventy she fancies him a bit herself. Who wouldn't. Especially in those tight black Lee jeans that show off his nice firm bum. He has long toned legs too, and broad shoulders, and strong arms. His hair is genuinely sunstreaked from sailing. 'Boats may be safe in harbour, but that's not what they were made for,' he said the other day and as I listened I knew – I just knew – he could teach me to be less afraid. That he could whoosh me up in the mistral of his wonderful calm enthusiasm. That he could send me scudding.

The descriptions of James's outdoor pursuits are so bracing. I almost lean on the words as he says them, as if into a strong sea breeze. They are such a refreshing change from my own introspective tendencies. But I think what's clinched it is the massage.

James Mitchel knows how to do massage. He has been trained. He has the certificate. How blissful it would be to lie naked with him. To have his big broad hands knead me all over. How beautiful it would be to stare deep – deep into his eyes. He can probably make love for ages. We'd be surrounded by lit candles and muslin. We'd probably have to leave little snacks lying around to sustain us – like those tantric sex devotees. Sex with James Mitchel would be a meeting of souls as well as bodies. It would be spiritual. Transcendental. Uplifting things like that become more important as you get older, and of course they help you not to care about your bum wobbling a bit. It would be completely unlike sex with someone younger – say, Liam. Not that I'd want to have sex with Liam. I really wouldn't. I have no interest in him, and he'd never ask me to have sex with him anyway, so I'm just using him as an example.

With Liam, for example, I'd be terribly self-conscious. I'd just know he'd be noticing my cellulite – even though there's not that much of it. And the fact that my bum's a bit too big and I have a hair on my chin, and my breasts aren't as pert as they used to be. I just know he'd be comparing me to women his own age and wishing he was with one of them. It would be very demoralizing and I'd have to insist on low lighting. I wish James Mitchel had moved in round the corner instead of Liam. That way we'd be sure to get to know each other better. I'd keep popping by in low-cleavage dresses until he had to ravish me.

I've bought some low-cleavage T-shirts to wear to pottery class. I put 'Golden Wonder' on my face, Fidgi perfume into my shoes and tie bright scarves around my hair. I'm not sure James notices, but I have my dreams to console me. For he has moved into my imaginary villa in Provence already. He massages me nightly and I do the same for him. When we buy baguettes in the local village old people smile at us knowingly. We might even start a family soon...

If only we could get off the subject of ceramics.

Chapter 8

MY LOW-CLEAVAGE T-SHIRTS have obviously had some effect because James Mitchel chose me the other evening. He chose me when he needed someone to demonstrate the 'coil technique'. Basically this involves rolling clay into long strips and coiling it round on itself. It's a technique that's particularly common in Africa, apparently.

'Alice – could you bring your bowl over here?' James asked me. I naturally complied with his wishes. He and I stood at a table in front of the whole class. 'Alice has rolled her clay out very uniformly,' he said, while I blushed with pleasure. 'See how she's built it up – rounding it out so that it makes a pleasing curve.' I looked down at the table and tried to look bashful. I tried to hide the fact that I was absurdly pleased. Mildred was regarding me rather enviously. Her own bowl was pretty good, but I didn't care. My feelings for James Mitchel seemed to have made me a bit ruthless. When he picked my bowl up and showed the class how I had smoothed the insides carefully, I wanted to kiss him.

He was standing very close to me. More close than seemed entirely necessary. I began to wonder if he was using this demonstration as an excuse. An excuse to be near me. At one point his arm reached across mine and our warm, naked skin touched. I could even feel his little hairs. He didn't pull his arm away from mine immediately. It lingered for a moment...almost longingly. Of course this could have happened because he was distracted – Mildred had just asked him a question – but I think there was more to it than that. I suppose that's why I stayed behind and offered to help him clean up after class.

It's really not fair the way people leave the pottery wheels. They don't clean them properly after they've used them. They sponge them out all right, but they don't bother to get at the stuff that's wedged into the corners. The stuff that dries in and becomes even harder to extract. They leave globs of clay all over the place and don't even rinse their sponges properly. They become all squishy and mucky and you have to run them under a tap for ages to get them clean. They leave the utensils around too. They're supposed to go into a big wooden drawer, but some of them are left on the tables. They're also supposed to put the clay objects they've given up on into a bucket which has some water in it, only sometimes they try to stick it back on to the unused clay in the big clear plastic bag. I began to feel rather angry on James's behalf as I scurried around the studio, trying to make things shipshape. But I was very glad to have an excuse to be alone with him too. Sharing these somewhat domestic tasks with him had an intimate feel to it. It was as if we were a couple suddenly – a couple clearing up after the kids had gone to bed.

The fact that we didn't speak much seemed to make the situation even more loaded. The clay, as it squelched between my fingers, seemed deeply sensual – and the silent rhythm of our movements felt quite carnal too. The way James wiped the tables seemed so masterful. So full of hidden meaning. It was almost like one of the more restrained scenes in that film *The Piano*. The early ones where the daughter was scampering off somewhere and Holly Hunter and Harvey Keitel were alone in his mountain shack. I wished there was a musical instrument in the room and I could play it with sudden brilliance.

James hadn't spoken for ages. The sexual tension in the room was so thick I almost had to push my way through it as I scrubbed and wiped and rinsed. I wondered whether he was wrestling with his conscience. Trying to subdue his emotions. After all, teachers aren't really supposed to become involved with their pupils. But this was different. I wanted to tell him that. This was way beyond ceramics. This was a man–woman thing. I suspected that he was realizing this. Every so often he looked up and gave me a small, grateful smile. If he did speak, it seemed to me that he might say something wonderful. It would come out as a sort of husky groan, a deep rasp of longing. 'Put that J-cloth down and come here, Alice.' I furtively slipped a Silvermint into my mouth.

James was perspiring a bit. I could smell it. It was a lovely smell. Clean and male and lusty. I wanted to snuffle into his armpits like a truffle pig. There are many smells to James Mitchel, and all of them are blissful. I could enthuse about them the way a wine expert might enthuse about her favourite muscatel. 'A hint of sandalwood wafting through the sweet flowers in a summer meadow, a hint of sea and pine leaves – and something else so wonderful I cannot name it...' that kind of thing. I wished it was dark outside and that the lights would go out for some reason. That way we'd have to grope around and probably bump into each other and it would Happen. James would take me in his arms and press me so close to him that we almost melted together. He'd press his mouth against mine, urgently, hungrily, for a long, deep, delicious kiss, our pheromones dancing.

Thinking all this made me rather self-conscious. I was determined to appear businesslike – even searching in the cupboards to see if there was any Ajax. I scrubbed those plastic table-tops until they shone. I scrutinized them carefully. They were clean, there was no getting round it. Any moment now, James and I would have to leave, leave with our passion completely unaddressed. How very poignant it was. I sighed deeply as I gave my J-cloth its final rinse.

And then James said something. 'Come here, Alice, I want you...' As I stared at him, he seemed to hesitate. 'For a moment,' he added quickly, but I barely heard him. I wanted to run, arms out, grab him. I didn't. I approached him slowly, cautiously, like David Attenborough might a mountain gorilla. I didn't want to frighten him away.

'What do you want me for, James?' I asked tremulously. Then I gave him a very encouraging smile. I looked at his earlobes and thought how I'd love to nibble them. I was very glad I'd had that peppermint in my pocket.

He seemed so tall as he stood there before me.

'Alice, I was wondering if you'd like to...?' He was looking straight into my eyes.

I fluttered my eyelashes in as coquettish a manner as I could manage. 'I'm sure I would, James,' I thought, almost quivering with nervous excitement. 'Go on. Please, just ask.'

'I was wondering if you'd like to look at the new glazes I mixed the other day. One of them might be suitable for your coil bowl.' He was pointing enthusiastically to some large plastic containers full of viscous coloured liquids. As he peered at them with a deeply preoccupied expression it became clear that romantic lunges were very far from his mind. He had that rolled-up sleeves, 'isn't this interesting?' expression that one often sees on children's television.

I gazed at the glazes too. Numbly. Uninterestedly. The humiliation of it. I'd almost thrown myself into his arms and there he was mulling over pottery all the time. He was clearly trying to be kind to me, but not in the way that I'd wanted. 'I fired some samples of these glazes,' he continued, as he picked up some small ceramic squares from the table. They were all different colours.

'I – I like the sandstone,' I mumbled, trying to force a little smile. 'The – the sandstone is very nice.'

'Excellent choice,' James beamed. 'Well, Alice, thanks so much for your help. Don't wait – I'm sure you're keen to get home. I'll lock up.'

'Good-night then, James.' I looked at him longingly.

'Yes, good-night, Alice,' he replied, producing a large bunch of keys from his jeans pocket.

As I walked home I wondered how I could have misread James's signals quite so drastically. It hadn't been like *The Piano* at all – more like *Blue Peter*. It was so very humiliating. And disappointing. That Silvermint had been entirely unnecessary. The self-deception of the evening made me squirm.

But at least James had been friendly. He had used me to demonstrate the coil technique. He smiled at me so gratefully. Yes – yes – that was something. Surely one day – one day very soon perhaps – James might take me in his arms.

This is the fifth time I have asked James about 'raku' – a type of Japanese lead-glazed coarse-grained pottery. He sounds slightly exasperated as he goes over the details again. I have to find a way of talking to him somehow. Asking him if I could open a window only took five seconds. And admiring his sherbet-coloured shirt was equally brief. 'James, ravish me – here – now, or during coffee break,' I want to tell him. Instead the conversation somehow slips on to slipware and then porcelain until Mildred, who's been trying to make a jug for the past four weeks, asks for his assistance.

This is the final night of term and I'm getting desperate. Even though I ask James questions I already know the answers for, I can't seem to broach the one I am most doubtful about. I can't seem to ascertain whether the tender interest he takes in my ceramic endeavours extends to any romantic interest in myself. I'm being far too meek. I stare up at him as though he is a mountain. I search for emotional footholds from my base camp. In fact, I'm just about to gingerly attempt a slight ascent of my beloved and tell him I like his aftershave when he says he has something to tell us.

'I am infatuated with Alice Evans. I simply must share this with you.' How wonderful those words sound, only James Mitchel isn't saying them. He's standing near the door and is solemnly informing us that he is moving to West Cork. He's opening a pottery studio there.

I'm gobsmacked. I just stand there trying to keep my expression calm, while emotions go off inside me like popcorn. Then I start to smile idiotically, as though absurdly pleased.

'West Cork is such a lovely place,' I sort of squawk.

'Yes, it is. So picturesque,' people agree as they head calmly, unbrokenly, back to their clay. Someone says they have brought in chocolate digestive biscuits for the tea break as a special treat. They've all just accepted it, like it's no big deal. But I can't accept it as I pretend to study my newly glazed vase with an expression so rigid with sadness, so expressionless, it makes my cheeks ache.

By eight-thirty I've worked myself up to it. 'James,' I say, softly, tremulously, as he passes. 'James, I'd like to buy you a drink after class. You've been such a good teacher.'

'Oh, Alice.' James gives me his gorgeous smile. 'That is really very kind of you, but I've arranged to meet someone later.'

'Oh.' I try not to look too disappointed. 'Oh, well, maybe another time then.'

'Yes.' James looks at me most kindly. 'Yes, maybe another time.'

'Why don't you suggest another time?' I think. 'Oh, James, please do.'

But he doesn't. Instead he says, 'These are very nice,' as he gives my pottery an end-of-term inspection.

I stare at the pottery too. Eventually I manage to speak. 'It's kind of you to say that, James,' I mumble dejectedly. 'But Mildred's jug is far nicer. Look, my ashtray's got hardly any sides to it, the mugs don't have proper handles. The dish is too heavy. And the vase doesn't look like a vase at all. It's a kind of humiliated bowl.' And as I say this I realize I sound a bit like Laren used to when she enumerated her perceived deficiencies.

'But what about your coil bowl?' James asks.

'Yes. Yes, I suppose that's OK,' I mumble.

James smiles. 'You set yourself rather high standards, don't you, Alice? Perfectionism and happiness don't sit too comfortably together. Be easier on yourself. These things take time.'

I look up at him adoringly. These are precisely the kinds of words I need to hear. James Mitchel is perfect for me. He can't go now. He can't. I look deep into his beautiful eyes hoping to see some loneliness. Some longing. I don't.

But as he moves away he touches my shoulder. Gently but, it seems to me, with a definite poignancy.

I had a very strange dream last night. I dreamt that Eamon and James Mitchel got married. I was at the wedding. Eamon's dress was a big billowy satin job with a long train and lace veil. James was wearing a morning suit and a wide smile.

'You can't marry Eamon,' I told him. 'I love you. You must marry me.' He just laughed. A long and hollow laugh.

'What about your proposal?' I then hissed at Eamon, who was fiddling around with a bow.

'You spent too long prevaricating about it,' he replied sharply. 'And anyway, James knows how to do massage.'

'I could learn massage.' The organ music had now started and I was running up the aisle after them both. 'I could. I really could. Let's make it a threesome. A ménage à trois.'

They ignored me. I slunk into a pew and sat down rebelliously. And when the vicar appeared he looked remarkably like Laren Brassière.

I've been having a number of strange dreams lately, since James announced his departure. Occasionally I am a Los Angeles-based 'romance guru'. From the vantage of my high podium I urge women to only date men who give them organic vegetables as love tokens. 'On the first date he should give you a parsnip,' I tell them authoritatively. 'On the second, broccoli, and on the third, lettuce. The fourth date is the big one. If he brings a cauliflower I would strongly advise marriage.'

Sometimes I dream that I am resitting an important exam – one I know I've already taken. 'Look, I did this years ago. I don't even know the current curriculum,' I tell the stern scrutineer.

'Go to your desk, Miss Evans,' I am told, which I do, most despondently.

I am despondent these days. 'James Mitchel would have had that drink with me if he really cared,' I think. 'It was all so one-sided. I've been such a fool.' When I get home from work I slop around the house in ancient clothes and haven't even bothered to mow the lawn. I've been eating far too many take-aways and have let the washing-up pile high in the kitchen. I have known for some days that I should wash my hair. It's as though something shiny has gone, leaving just a slight, shimmery marking in its wake. In fact if James Mitchel wasn't a Wonderful Man, he could almost be a snail.

Added to all this angst is guilt, because pining for some man I hardly know is, of course, dreadfully politically incorrect. I'm supposed to know that if you put Mr Wonderful on a pedestal even he will probably expect you to give it a good rub over with Ajax. And anyway, these days us women are supposed to be 'the men we wanted to marry'. I'm simply going to have to work on my 'male side', along with my 'female side', my 'higher self' and of course my 'inner child'. If I do marry Eamon he'll be gaining a whole community.

Now it's Tuesday evening and I'm listening to the radio. A man is talking about some monkeys who put their hands into a grid containing peanuts and then got trapped. 'And the strange thing is they weren't really trapped at all,' the man is explaining. 'Because if they'd stopped clenching the peanuts in their hands they could have pulled free.' As he says this my doorbell rings.

It's Matt, an old friend from university. 'I haven't seen you in ages, Alice. Where have you been hiding?' he exclaims.

'Oh, I've just been sort of– mmmm – busy,' I answer.

'I met Mira the other day,' Matt says as he follows me into the sitting-room, which is looking dreadfully unkempt. 'She told me that you've "received a proposal of marriage".' He smiles delightedly at the formality of this sentence. 'She wouldn't go into the details. She said you'd tell me yourself…if you wanted to.' He looks at me hopefully.

'Would you like a cup of tea?' I reply.

'Yes. That would be lovely.' Matt picks up a stack of old Sunday papers from the sofa and sits down.

I go into the kitchen and plug in the kettle. 'Still not taking sugar?' I call out.

'Yes, I have my Hermesetas with me,' Matt answers smugly. 'But I wouldn't mind some biscuits if you have any. I only had a salad for lunch.'

I reach into the cupboard and extract some chocolate digestives. Matt is slightly chubby and has been trying to lose weight for some time now. This seems to mainly involve not taking sugar in his tea and does not prevent him, for example, getting through an entire tube of Pringles crisps in one sitting. As I place four biscuits on a plate and make the tea Matt peers in at me.

'Need some help?' he asks.

'Yes, you can carry the milk and the mugs.'

'This is an unusual shape,' he comments, picking up a mug I made at pottery class. 'Where did you get it?'

'It's an Alice Evans original design,' I sigh. 'Don't worry, I'll use it. You can have a proper one.'

'You made this mug yourself? Well, you clever little thing.'

'Yeah, but the handle's not on right. It's all skewy.'

'Well, I find its skewiness rather pleasing,' Matt says solemnly. 'In fact I insist on using it myself.'

I look at Matt gratefully. One of the lovely things about him is that he tends to find flaws endearing. This may be because for years he thought he was skewy himself. His schoolmates used to call him a 'Spaniel' because of his blond curls and docile nature. They couldn't understand why he hated rugby and spent hours reading about the Renaissance when they were reading Biggles.

He couldn't understand it himself for years. In fact, he began to believe he was a complete aberration until he discovered there were other people like him. Boys who looked at other boys with fascinated shame and yearning. It was called being 'gay' apparently, even though it didn't seem that jolly initially.

He's come to terms with it now though. He's had some very nice boyfriends but, like me, he hasn't met his Mr Wonderful. Sometimes I wonder if we should both just forget about romance and move in together. We're very comfortable in each other's company.

I can tell by the way Matt is drumming his fingers on the arm of the sofa that he's just itching to find out who proposed to me. He'll be patient about it, though. He won't press me for details until he feels I'm ready to broach the matter. Matt notices things. I'm sure he has noticed that I am looking a bit miserable, but he hasn't mentioned it. He's not the kind of person who feels impelled to point that kind of thing out.

'So, Alice, when did you take up pottery?' he's asking.

'Oh, I did some evening classes,' I reply dully. 'I'm not that good at it really. I wanted to do painting but it was booked up.'

'You must do a painting for me one of these days,' he replies. 'I'd buy it from you.'

'Would you?' I sit up in my seat more brightly.

'Yes, of course I would.'

'What sort of painting would you like?'

'I'll leave it up to you,' Matt replies.

'Oh, OK,' I mumble, already beginning to feel a bit doubtful. I'm not as confident about my painting as I would like to be.

'So you got that framed. I'm so glad.' Matt is looking at a seascape I did some time ago. It's hanging by the French windows. The way Matt has steered us on to the subject of painting is a measure of how well he knows me. He seems to have an uncanny sense about what will cheer me up. He stands up and goes over to look at the painting more closely. 'I love the colours,' he enthuses. 'If you could do something like that for me I'd be right chuffed.'

Matt occasionally uses north of England expressions because he studied architecture in Manchester. Before that he did a degree in English at Trinity, which is where we met each other. I think what first drew us together was our earnestness. We felt rather intimidated by the big books we pored over in the library. We spent too much time in that library actually, scribbling and reading and trying to understand. We underlined too many sentences. It all became too important. Eventually we realized this and, as we learned the art of fecklessness, we felt as euphoric as Mole in *The Wind in the Willows* when he deserted his spring cleaning.

We used to talk for ages in the college canteen, holding on to our mugs of coffee as the cleaners tended to grab them. The lugubrious observations of certain foreign intellectuals seemed to cheer us. We rolled their names around sensuously on our tongues. We were sure we'd end up somewhere foreign, since we already felt expatriates. We thought this made us special, until we found out it was as common as muck. We joined societies. In 'Improvisational Drama' we spent whole evenings pretending to be trees. 'When you leave here you will be on a higher level of confusion.' That's what various lecturers told us. It sounded like a joke at the time.

I really could do with more clarity now. I wonder how I should go about finding it. 'Matt, do you still go to those meditation meetings?' I ask as he returns to the sofa and reaches for the last chocolate digestive.

'I do when I have time. I find it quite helpful and I particularly like the cat.'

'The cat?' I repeat, wondering if this is a branch of feline meditation I haven't heard of. I certainly find looking at my own semi-stray cat very soothing, especially when he's sprawled out in a blissful manner on his cushion.

'The owner of the house we meet in has a Burmese cat,' Matt explains. 'He miaows very loudly when we chant. Even when he's put out of the room we hear him downstairs. He seems to have an affinity with Sanskrit.'

'I wonder if I would too,' I murmur dreamily.

'I'm sure you would,' Matt smiles, then he adds gently, 'Look, Our Kid, I'm going to have to go soon. Are you ever going to tell me about this marriage proposal of yours?'

I stare into his kind blue eyes. It really isn't fair of me to keep him in suspense like this. I pick up my mug of tea and sigh. 'Oh, all right, if you insist,' I say. And then I tell him about Eamon and James Mitchel.

'What do you think I should do, Matt?' I ask, after I've given him the details. 'Should I marry Eamon? Go on, be honest. Tell me what you think.'

'I'd love to give you advice, dearie,' Matt frowns. 'But I just don't know what to say.'

'Yes, you do,' I pester. 'I'm sure you have an opinion.'

'Maybe I do.' He looks at me inscrutably. 'But my opinion isn't important – you'll have to work this out for yourself.'

I pull sulkily at my pearl pendant.

'You can notice what you want, Alice,' Matt continues.

'What do you mean?' I enquire wearily. He's obviously slipping into philosophical mode. He does that sometimes.

'You can be your own witness. You can watch and see what you need. Allow the answers to come to you. Don't force them, just relax.'

'Oh, Matt, you sound just like James Mitchel,' I wail miserably. 'Why did I meet him? I wish I hadn't now.'

After Matt has gone I realize something. I realize that I'm growing rather tired of comfort eating. And watching distraught American people talk about their complicated lives on cable TV. My Mitsubishi colour portable may be very nice, but it's not very satisfactory as a Significant Other. I must galvanize myself somehow. And I must stop going to work with greasy hair. Any moment now Oprah Winfrey may jump through the television and give me a stern talking-to. She's such a very proactive person.

I rise stiffly and shuffle into the garden. As I do so I try to recall some uplifting phrases.

'It's not what life does to you – it's what you do with what life does to you.'

Yes, yes, Alice. Come on. Come on.

'Go with the flow.'

'Love and approve of yourself.'

'Feel the fear and do it anyway.'

'Women fly when men aren't looking.'

'Monsieur Thibaud is a nit.' No, no, that last one's not right.

I take out the mower and mow the lawn a bit, pacing lethargically up and down as though trying to console a blubbering child in a buggy. I scatter a thin mulch of grass clippings on to the herbaceous border. I watch the cat chasing a bumble bee as it flies away. The hanging baskets look dry – again. I go inside to get the watering can.

Later that night I feel marginally more contented as I snuggle under my duvet. I have washed my hair, shaved my legs, removed the hair from my chin and thoroughly scrubbed my face with peach kernel cleansing cream. I also reek from a mixture of the fruit-smelling potions people keep giving me lately. They come in small baskets that are now dotted around the place and adding to the cottage's clutter.

I really should unclutter the cottage a little. I read a Feng Shui article the other day and it said one should rid oneself of unnecessary items. It also instructed me to keep the loo seat down and to put crystals in certain places. I even had to relocate my bed because it was, apparently, facing the wrong way. As I did all this I thought of my parents. Though their own lives were rather complicated I don't think they ever worried about whether the loo seat was in the right position. In fact, should I go and check on it now? No. I've done quite enough fretting lately. I must try to relax.

I reach for my Walkman which contains a meditation tape about finding my 'higher self. 'I've almost forgotten the exact shape of James Mitchel's nose!' I think happily. 'Soon he will just be a stranger.'

'There is a wise, deep, knowing part of you,' an American voice is saying. 'Take deep, deep breaths. Release. Release. You are in a wood. You are walking along a small mossy pathway. Then the pathway broadens and you are in a clearing. A clearing full of light. Stand there for a moment. Feel the calm. The serenity.'

I try to. I really do. But, as usual, I drift off to my imaginary villa in Provence. And James Mitchel is still there...

'You're not supposed to be here, James,' I tell him sternly. 'This is just squatting. You're a most unsatisfactory Wonderful Man. I'm not even sure I like you any more.'

James does not listen. He's ripping off my T-shirt. He's exploring my crevices, my conduits, with his hands and with his tongue. He's massaging my hills, my mounds, my valleys. His hair is tousled as he trails its golden tendrils deliciously along my skin. 'Ma chérie,' he says, for we are now bilingual. Then he plunges deep within me. It's blissful. But I do rather wish something.

I do rather wish that when he came he wouldn't always shout 'raku!'

Chapter 9

EVERY TIME I MENTION James Mitchel now Mira starts humming The Wombles theme tune. She says she does it to alert me to the extent of my obsession and that it's meant kindly. She says she's heard quite enough about strange glances and enigmatic looks and lingering shoulder pats, and I have too.

I suppose I like talking about these things because they bring James into my days, even though he has left my vicinity. I keep hoping that if I say them enough they'll become more tangible, more convincing – but they haven't convinced Mira. She thinks I'm using James Mitchel to distract myself from some dull ache in my soul. She says women often use men to distract themselves from thornier issues. She also says I might find flying lessons therapeutic.

Apparently a divorced friend of hers took up flying recently and finds it so exhilarating she no longer besieges her ex with late-night phone calls. I imagined myself careening round the skies with bug-eyed terror and decided I would opt for something a little more sedate. Horse riding perhaps, or sailing. I told Mira this and she gave me the phone number of a woman called Josephine who's an avid sailor. I phoned her and that is why I am now clinging grimly to my seat in a yacht on the Irish Sea.

There's a huge wind blowing and the yacht is keeling over to one side in a very dramatic manner. There is also no land in sight. Heaven knows what's going to become of us. I'm terrified. I desperately want to go home. The women I'm with – Sandie, Laura and Josephine – seem to be relatively calm. They're busy ducking, winching, steering and pulling. The thought of shipwreck doesn't seem to bother them, or going overboard, or ending up on a desert island without Sue Lawley. Every so often I scream when the boat lurches more dramatically than usual and a big wad of water smacks against my yellow oilskins. No one hears me. I'm drenched and my copy of *The Accidental Tourist* by Anne Tyler is decidedly soggy too.

The enormity of my misapprehension regarding this sea trip is evidenced by the fact that I actually brought a novel and a small sketchpad with me in case I got bored. The afternoon had started off so calmly. There was just a slight breeze. When this breeze grew a bit stronger it seemed bracing, but now that it's a gale I've started to talk to God.

I've obviously come on this boat by mistake. I try to scream this realization to the rest of the crew, only the statement tends to turn into 'Aaaargh…' as the yacht gives another dreadful heave and plunges into an enormous wave.

'Oh, God, please, please help me,' I start to moan as Josephine scrambles along the deck towards me. She's leaning over me. She's shouting something. Maybe she wants me to man the radio or send up a flare. It's either that or launching the life raft. I try to smile up at her bravely.

'Alice!'

'Yes!' I screech.

'Alice, would you…?'

'What?' I roar. The wind is blowing her words away from me. It's like talking to someone on a dodgy mobile phone.

Her face is almost touching mine now. The wind is whipping up a tassel on the hood of her jacket. 'Alice,' she says earnestly. 'Alice, would you like a bar of chocolate?'

I stare at her.

'Fruit and nut or just plain?' she adds, delving deep into her pocket.

'Plain,' I reply, grabbing the bar from her as the boat tips over even further. Then, as she turns to scramble back across the deck she says, 'Great day for sailing,' as though she expects me to agree with her.

'Oh, well, at least I have some chocolate now,' I think, trying to reassure myself. I feel the bar in my pocket. It has eight slabs on it. If we do get stranded somewhere I could eat, say, two slabs a day. I check the fastener on my safety harness for the twentieth time and attempt to hum one of Elgar's Enigma Variations. I simply have to try to calm myself somehow. I scan the horizon. Goodness! Is that land! Yes, it's Dun Laoghaire harbour, and we're heading towards it. I almost sob with relief.

Sandie, Laura and Josephine are now discussing what a brilliant afternoon it was over pints of Guinness. We're in a yacht club and I'm having a pint of Guinness myself but I'm not saying much. I'm quietly euphoric just to be back on dry land. There wasn't a gale today, apparently. Just a very strong wind. Next weekend they may sail over to Fishguard.

'Would you like to join us, Alice?' Josephine enquires with a mischievous twinkle.

'No, thanks,' I reply rather firmly. They all smile at me and I smile back bashfully. 'Oh dear, my terror must have been so obvious,' I think guiltily and yet – and yet my smile has broadened and, as the others start to laugh,

I do too. Maybe it's just relief, or all that fresh air, or the Guinness, but it feels wonderful. It's like we're high on something. 'I was frightened,' I think. 'I was frightened, and it doesn't matter. And I still have a bar of chocolate in my pocket…'

I take the bar out. I break it carefully into four slabs. 'Goodness, Alice, we ate ours ages ago,' Laura exclaims, as I offer her a piece. We're all munching now and chatting and giggling. Part of me is watching, tenderly. I want to savour this. I need these moments of sweet silliness. I need them badly. For it seems to me suddenly that there are many ways to pull anchor. And maybe this is one of them.

Chapter 10

MY AFTERNOON'S SAILING HAS provided me with some excellent anecdotes. I've embroidered them up a bit and have been dining out on them for days. I've even added in some nautical terms like aft and fore. In fact just the other day I was explaining the meaning of 'port' and 'starboard' to Mira, when she smiled at me warmly and said, 'You know something, Alice, you haven't mentioned James Mitchel for a whole week.' I felt like a star member of AA – and I don't mean the Automobile Association.

I often wish there were AA type meetings for the frequently bewildered. If there were I bet I'd go on a regular basis. We could meet in a hotel room somewhere and air our 'issues' in a sympathetic atmosphere. We'd know that we all have small, scared, cowering creatures inside us, and once we start to bully them, we do it to other people too. In fact I bet if people were more open and sympathetic with each other in general more marriages would work. They wouldn't have to provide such compensation…we wouldn't come to them with such a big bag of dreams.

I must have been lugging a huge trunk of dreams along with me when I met James Mitchel. I really didn't realize I still had quite so many of them. I thought I'd managed to trim them down like travel books advise one to do with luggage. You're supposed to put all the things you want to pack on a bed and then only take half of them, only I still tend to end up with two suitcases. And the funny thing is there is always one item I end up wearing more than all the others. One skirt or blouse, or dress or sweater that ends up being indispensable. It doesn't seem special when I pack it, but unpacked it immediately announces its appropriateness. It's one of life's many mysteries. And my infatuation with James Mitchel is another.

I must try to stop pining for him. I really don't want to become like Cyril, Mrs Peabody's budgerigar. He's so busy missing the Australian outback that he's hardly noticed the tasty sprig of millet I left in his cage the other day. Maybe James Mitchel is my Australian outback and Eamon is my sprig of millet – something quite tasty that I'm stubbornly overlooking. After all, very few of my married friends have ended up with the man of their dreams. They went for men who understood their dreams rather than embodied them all. Though they might once have longed for someone as passionate as Heathcliff they're rather relieved that they didn't get him. Kindness, tenderness, a sense of humour – that's what proved most seductive in the end. They seem so sensible as they sit at my distressed pine table telling me about their new chintz suite or little Jamie's viola lessons. If they've recently dined out at a restaurant they tell me the entire menu. Having kids seems to make them deeply appreciative of any personal pleasures they manage to grab. A friend called Bridget once spent twenty minutes telling me about a recent bath.

She'd just had a baby girl and had taken to having showers. This was because she was breast-feeding and little Chloe always started to bawl just as she herself was reaching for the Badedas. But one amazingly serene evening this didn't happen and four weeks later Bridget described her bath to me as though it had been a four-week cruise on the Caribbean.

'I lit a candle,' she told me, her face glowing at the memory. 'I poured in the Badedas and watched it foaming under the tap. I turned on my Garth Brooks tape and stepped into the water. Honestly, Alice, as I lay there I felt a kind of weightlessness I have never felt before. I wonder...' she looked at me dolefully. 'I wonder if I'll ever have a bath again.'

'Of course you will,' I reassured her. I'd talked to enough new mothers to realize such statements are prompted by sheer weariness. Motherhood tends to be far harder work than they'd realized. In fact I've heard so much about it I really don't know why I'd like a baby of my own. It must be genetic programming.

'Stay single, Alice,' that's what Bridget told me the last time I met her, which was some time ago. We were out on one of her 'I have a life of my own' evenings, which don't happen very often. Her husband had been working late a lot and she was in a feisty mood. 'They've done studies about it you know – single women are often happier than the married ones,' she continued. 'Men get more out of marriage than women. That's what many of those studies conclude.'

'Yes, I know, I've read them,' I replied, wondering how any study could measure such a variable thing as human contentment. Bridget seemed to be envying my freedom, while I was cooing besottedly over photographs of her daughter. Faraway hills tend to seem greener. I wish they didn't. It can be rather confusing.

I discovered something rather confusing about Eamon last week. A friend of his told me that earlier this year he 'disappeared'. He was gone for some days, apparently. It was most unlike him. He hadn't phoned work or anything. He missed appointments and left his phone off the hook. When people went to his house they found

'Riverdance' playing over and over on the stereo system. They were extremely worried.

When he did eventually turn up he looked weary and unshaven. He hadn't washed and had mud on his shoes. He said that he'd been 'camping' and had forgotten to tell people. 'Look, there's a tent on the back seat,' he said. And indeed there was. He completely refused to talk about it further.

'When exactly did this happen?' I asked. Somehow I was not surprised by the answer. Eamon had 'disappeared' around the time of his proposal to me. One week before it in fact.

'I suppose he needed to get away to really think things through,' the friend said. 'He'd often said he was lonely – dissatisfied.'

'Really!' I replied, considerably surprised. I didn't think Eamon said things like that to other people. He finds it hard to be open, even with me.

Funnily enough, I've begun to find the idea of Eamon's 'missing days' strangely appealing. They hint at a kind of extremity I didn't know he was capable of feeling. His steady, rather plodding behaviour has given no hint of this covert wildness. I like a bit of mystery in a man. But I'd like a little less of it in Mira.

Mira and I met four years ago when I advertised for a housemate. The minute that half-eaten muffin fell out of her coat pocket I knew I'd like her, but I never suspected she'd become quite this puzzling. For example, she keeps going into hairdressers and getting her hair cut, even though it doesn't need it. It's so short now she'll have to leave it for a while, unless she wants to resemble Sinead O'Connor in the earlier part of her career. She's bought Laren Brassière's tape and plays it every evening and she's also begun to suspect there's something valuable in her stamp collection. She stopped collecting stamps when she was ten. She's taken the album to various experts and says they just flick through it. 'They can't possibly value five hundred stamps in a minute,' she complains.

I've been trying to be non-judgemental but I do rather wish Mira would drop this eccentric spinster thing and take up something more conventional. If she went deeply New Age, for example, I wouldn't mind at all. I'd like to have more crystals and jasmine oil and aurasoma bottles around the place. We could say things like, 'Have you cleansed your aura lately?' and buy an even more bewildering array of herbal teas. Just as I'm thinking this I hear Mira open the front door.

'Hi there,' she says, giving me a tired smile. She's wearing a blue beret, a multi-coloured silk Indian scarf, dungarees and a big woolly cardigan she knitted herself. She's heading for her bedroom and I know the first thing she'll do there is put on the huge furry slippers her brother gave her. She's grown extremely fond of them lately, in fact she sometimes wears them to the corner shop. When I say this looks a bit odd she answers, 'Oh, I do hope so.' 'It's hard to feel purposeful while wearing these slippers,' she once told me and that, of course, is why she's so fond of them. I need a pair of slippers like that. I really do. I used to have slippers as a girl. When I put them on I felt different. I felt my slippers feeling. I didn't even have to buy them. My parents bought them for me. Sometimes they were pink and furry and sometimes they were plainer. But they were always gentle. An acknowledgement that life needs soft places...times of retreat.

My runners are now my slippers. Another sop to the fake athleticism I and many of my friends seem to share.

They're comfortable, but they've too much purpose. They're not slightly silly. I miss my soft, silly shoes.

When Mira reappears she curls up on the old and very creased leather armchair in the sitting-room. 'Like a cup of tea?' I ask.

'Yes, please,' she says gratefully. She has put on her earnest round-rimmed spectacles and is looking at her mail. She's opened the blue envelope and is looking at its contents. Her hand is trembling slightly.

'Who's it from?' I ask.

She hesitates before replying, 'It's from Frank.'

Frank is one of the reasons Mira says she wants to be an eccentric spinster. They were involved for a year. It was love with a capital L and the London Symphony Orchestra in the background. Frank was wonderful in all sorts of ways. The thing was, his wife and daughter thought he was wonderful too.

'I would never, ever leave them. I couldn't – they trust me,' he used to tell her. 'But I want you.'

'I want you too,' Mira agreed sadly. But as time passed she found there were lots of things about him she would gladly ditch. The long, lonely weekends, for instance. The needy but clipped phone calls and the furtive meetings in obscure locations. The passion of it all was blissful, but the secrecy was oppressive. She began to think him selfish.

'It's not like that,' he'd protest, almost in tears.

'Yes, I know,' she'd agree. 'It's not like that. But it is like that too.'

They parted eventually. Mira put her foot down – she was wearing Nikes. 'It's just too complicated,' she'd said.

So now he's gone, but every so often he sends her a letter to remind her that she is not forgotten. She keeps them carefully in a small, hand-carved rosewood box. She thinks they will meet again, in another life – she believes in reincarnation. She went to someone once who told her that she and Frank had been together before – about a hundred years ago. She was his concubine. She's also been a Chinese peasant, an Indian soldier, a Spanish nun and a member of the Court of Versailles, apparently...and that's just for starters. You wouldn't think it to look at her.

As I bring Mira her tea I notice something. I notice this time she hasn't placed Frank's letter in the rosewood box. She's torn it into a clump of tiny pieces. She's slumped in her chair and is staring at it. I study her worriedly. I can see by the deep silence on her face that she doesn't want me to speak. I sigh and return to the kitchen. I usually cook the dinner if I'm home first. I peer into the fridge. According to the stickers a number of items in there will be inedible a minute past midnight. I take them out and try to cobble together some sort of meal.

'Grub's up, Mira,' I call out. There is no answer. 'Food's ready!' I yell. Still no reply. I go to the sitting-room. 'Mira, dinner's ready, didn't you hear me?'

She looks up at me apathetically. 'Actually I'm not very hungry,' she announces. 'Maybe I'll have a toasted sandwich later.'

I frown and look at Frank's torn-up letter, which is still lying on the coffee table. 'Oh, come on, Mira,' I coax. 'Just have a small helping. It's Marks and Spencer lasagne and there's some salad too. It looks very tasty.'

'Oh, all right,' she mumbles, rising wearily from her armchair. She follows me into the kitchen and we commence our meal in complete silence. Mira does go silent occasionally. In fact sometimes she's almost as evasive as Eamon.

I wish she'd tell me what was in Frank's letter. It must be something to do with the letter. She's looking so sad and she's hardly touched her dinner. Wine. That's it. I'll get some wine.

'Mira, would you like some wine?' I ask. 'We've got that open bottle from the other evening. We might as well polish it off.'

'OK,' she replies glumly. When I bring the bottle to the table she grabs it and fills her tumbler right up to the rim. She gulps it down and I wait for it to make her more loquacious only it doesn't. In fact if anything she seems to have retreated even further. She's definitely brooding about something. Dear God, I hope she doesn't become like Cyril too.

'Mira,' I say gingerly, 'are you all right?'

'What do you mean?' she frowns.

'It's just – it's just I saw you'd torn up Frank's letter.'

A pained expression flits across her face and then changes into an ironic smile. 'Yes, I thought I'd follow your artistic leanings and make a little collage.' She takes another gulp of wine and stares at the table. I decide not to probe the matter further. The subject of Frank is obviously about to be swept under the carpet again. In fact, I think Mira's been sweeping quite a lot of things under the carpet recently. I wish our underlay could talk because she clearly isn't going to.

As soon as we finish our meal she starts to whip the plates from the table and almost throws them into the washing-up bowl. They clash together dramatically while she grabs the Lemon Quix and aims. She's making this small domestic task seem like something out of a Quentin

Tarantino movie. I decide to leave her to it and exit the room swiftly.

When Mira reappears about ten minutes later she seems a good deal calmer. We watch *The Simpsons* together and then I get a sudden urge to go for a walk. I get antsy sometimes, restive. There are moments when I could leave this cottage with just my passport. There are moments when I could dash to the airport and get on a plane without even asking where it's going. It's the wild wanton part of me. The Snickers buyer. 'Mira, let's go for a walk,' I say. 'It's quite a sunny evening.'

'Where do you want to go?' she asks.

'I dunno. Where do you want to go to?'

'I hadn't thought of going anywhere,' she sighs. 'I was going to fill in my membership form for the South Seas Club.'

'What?'

'The South Seas Club. It's for people who are interested in the South Seas.'

'I didn't know you were interested in the South Seas.'

'Well, I am, now. The women wear grass skirts.'

'Sorry?'

'The women members wear grass skirts at meetings. It sounds fun.'

'Well, yes, it certainly sounds…' I leave the sentence unfinished and look at her ruefully.

For sometimes it seems to me that Mira may be taking her eccentric spinster thing just a bit too far.

Chapter 11

MY WALK TAKES ME past my new neighbour Liam's house. I hear raised voices as I walk by and can't resist glancing quickly at the front window. Liam is seated and a pretty woman is glowering at him…the same woman I saw helping him move in some weeks ago. She must be his girlfriend. She's standing by the mantelpiece, her arms gesturing wildly in a Latin manner. 'How could you!' she's shouting. 'How could you lie to me like that when all the time you were with…with her!' Her face crumples in anguish and she throws herself despairingly on to an armchair. I feel like rushing in and belting Liam with my handbag, but I don't. Domestic squabbles are best left private, unless they get out of hand. That little bollocks Liam has obviously been unfaithful. I quicken my step and mutter 'Men!' to myself. 'Life would be so much simpler if we were hermaphrodite, like snails.'

For some reason this observation reminds me of James Mitchel, but then a lot of things do. The *Home and Away* theme tune, my pottery mugs, American football jackets, blond hair brushed a certain way, almost anything really. I see the local Methodist church in the distance and start to scurry towards it as though I'm dashing for a bus. The argument I overheard when passing Liam's house has discomforted me. The woman had seemed so anguished. 'Maybe there's an evening service on,' I think. 'I could do with some distraction.'

The pebbles in the church's long driveway crunch in a comfortingly familiar manner as I walk towards the heavy wooden door. They evoke memories I thought I'd forgotten. Sunday mornings from long ago. In fact, as I enter the stone porch I almost expect to bump into Mrs Pemberly carrying her big hymnal.

One of the high points of church for me as a girl was when Mrs Pemberly played the organ. She was only allowed to do it once a month because she was ancient and a bit strange. She'd start off real slow so we had to drawl, then she'd speed up suddenly so we had to gabble. Sometimes she came to a complete halt for about five seconds and we had to try to carry on without her accompaniment. When she rejoined us it was never in the right place but at the right tempo, for a while anyway. It was wonderful. I giggled and giggled while the adults frowned and clenched their hymnals and struggled to sound spiritual. Sometimes I looked up at Jesus in the big window above the altar and saw that he was smiling gently. Probably at the Five Thousand, because they were with him in the window. But perhaps just a bit for Mrs Pemberly too.

After the service Mrs Pemberly would beam smugly at us as though she was Artur Rubinstein and no one disabused her. We'd nod and greet her politely and then leave. There seemed a tacit agreement that we would not rob Mrs Pemberly of one of her last illusions. I think I learnt more about Christian forbearance through Mrs Pemberly than through any sermon.

There is obviously not going to be a sermon in this church tonight. As I enter the large solemn building I see that it's empty. In fact I'm surprised that it's open at all. 'Oh well, maybe I'll just have a little sit down anyway,' I think, wishing the wooden pews looked a bit more cosy. At least it has the familiar smell I remember from my childhood. Aunt Phoeb said it was old bat droppings, but I think there's more to it than that. The smell of stillness, maybe – combined with a bit of old cologne, and sweat, and hope. I don't know who plays the organ here. In fact I haven't been to this church in ages, which is not to say I'm not interested in spiritual matters. I am.

I've read quite a lot about God and I've learnt people have an incredible number of opinions about him, or indeed her. Or it. Or them. Or us. Or nothing at all. I've prayed and meditated. I've danced in a circle holding hands and singing 'The Earth Is Our Mother'. I like the way the Buddha smiles. I believe in the power of unconditional love, only I don't seem to be much good at it. I've been told we all have Guardian Angels, and want to believe it. In fact I do sometimes believe quite a lot of this stuff – it's just that there's so much of it around. Believing there is someone up there watching over us is not always easy. But then, as Annie says, believing that there is nothing there at all is, in a sense, equally amazing.

Maybe I wandered into this church because I feel like talking to somebody. Spilling the beans. After all, Mira is in such an uncommunicative mood this evening that I might as well try Jesus. I haven't done this for ages and ages – not since my late teens. I sigh and look up at the high-domed ceiling.

'Jesus, I hope you don't mind but I need someone to talk to,' I mumble, somewhat embarrassedly, then I look around furtively. Good, there's no one in the church to overhear. 'I've been feeling a bit miserable for some time now and I'm not sure what's causing it,' I continue. 'James Mitchel cheered me up for a while, but now he's gone.' As I say this, I sigh deeply and decide to kneel.

'Why do I get these longings, Jesus?' I ask, no longer trying to conceal my desperation. 'Why do I sometimes grieve for things I cannot name and so often feel afraid? What am I here for? I'd really, really like to know.'

Jesus remains silent. It's like speaking to a therapist but at least he doesn't charge eighty euros an hour. I begin to doubt if he's there at all, but I keep talking. It must be all that wine I drank at dinner.

'I don't understand death, Jesus,' I continue. 'I don't understand birth either, and life and even my DVD player can be most bewildering. What are we supposed to be doing here? I know there's a lot of goodness in the world, but have you looked at the news lately? Where does hatred and suffering and bigotry come from? Where's all this love that you went on about?' I stare up at the ceiling feistily, then I begin to feel a little guilty about my tirade. The art of cross-examination does not necessarily involve examining crossly. And anyway it is up to us to decide to love each other. No one can force us to do it. I decide to soften my tone.

'Of course there is quite a lot of love around really, if you look for it,' I say, trying to be more even-handed. 'Love is an interesting word, isn't it, Jesus? It seems to me there should be at least twenty words for it because there are so many different types. My father used to say romantic love only lasts four years and I think he may have been right.'

Jesus does not comment. It's like talking to Eamon when he's watching golf on television. I begin to feel a little impatient. 'Look, Jesus,' I say in a businesslike manner. 'I'm sure you're very busy but I'd just like to ask you one further question. Is it necessary to love the man you marry? Eamon says it isn't. He says liking someone is more important. He says like can lead to love, but it doesn't often happen the other way around. I've given men piles of love, Jesus, and sometimes they've just sprinted off with it. But I don't think Eamon would sprint off with it. He only runs if he's chased.'

I finger my pearl pendant. 'People go on a lot about falling in love, Jesus, but in my experience it often feels like landing – landing on something a bit lumpy. I've got all this love sloshing around inside me, Jesus. Love that I don't know what to do with. I've been waiting for ages for someone wonderful, like James Mitchel. It's like a bus or something. You know how it is. The longer you wait for one the more reluctant you are to leave the stop. But if I was going to meet him – this wonderful man who'll love me – surely he would have turned up by now.'

Silence. What on earth am I doing in this church? Why on earth have I been blabbing on like this? I seem to be getting just as eccentric as Mira. I rise from my kneeling mat and sit on the wooden pew and as I do so I suddenly feel desperately alone.

They hit me sometimes, these waves of grief. For some moments they're almost unbearable, until they go away.

Because I'm not used to being as alone as I am now. I used to belong to something once. I was part of a family. There were people who had to take me in if I needed it. Put up with me. I still can't quite believe that they are not around. As the damp sods landed on their graves I knew things would never be quite the same and I just wasn't ready for it. People rarely are.

My parents died, with a small interval between leavetakings, when I was in my early thirties. My grandparents and Aunt Phoeb have gone too, though Uncle Sean is still an avid golfer. I often wish I had brothers and sisters, but I don't. And I don't want to think about all this here in this empty church. It's just too sad and anyway I'm getting used to it. It doesn't bother me so much now. I have my friends and my garden and my painting. And a job too – lots of people don't have that. I can go to a therapist if necessary. Jesus doesn't have to listen to me. Yes, I was silly to come into this church. I don't know what I was expecting, but it's obviously not here.

I feel a sob rising in my stomach. No, I mustn't cry. It is entirely unnecessary. I must get a grip on myself and toughen up. Be less sensitive. I must become more like the kind of woman who could marry Eamon and be happy. I know I can do it if I try. It will mean giving up some dreams, but I think it's about time I did that anyway. I lower my head humbly. Yes, Jesus was quite right not to indulge my middle-class whingeing. If he exists at all I'm sure he has more important things to do.

I pick up my jacket and leave the pew. I walk down the aisle slowly, looking around me, trying to at least appreciate the architecture. So many people have put work into this place. I look at the carved cornices, the stone plaques, the huge windows. They seem just another testament to human longing. Part of our huge wish for meaning. Almost endearing in their innocent faith. I sigh deeply and am about to pull the heavy wooden door open when my gaze is drawn back. The last rays of the summer's evening are shimmering through the clear glass above the altar and I look up at them, surprised. For though it is nearly sunset, the light seems to be intensifying. Filling the high domed building with a deep and dappled peace. I get a distant sense of an infinitely gentle presence. A witness. And just for a moment it seems to me that I am not alone in this building after all. That something has heard my sadness and did not find it too meagre or ordinary or unimportant. That it is seeking to offer me some consolation in its own mysterious way.

I stand there for a moment, comforted but uncomprehending. Is this just another dream, or something real and true? Am I as steeped in illusion as Mrs Pemberly at her organ?

I dearly wish I knew, as I step outside into the dusk.

Chapter 12

LIAM AND ELSIE – I'VE discovered that's his girlfriend's name – are giggling in their garden. 'Put that thing down!' Elsie is spluttering.

'No way, José,' Liam replies and then I hear the sound of running and water splashing and squeals of indignation and delight. He's obviously chasing her with a hosepipe.

'I'm soaked,' Elsie is protesting. 'Stop it, you brute, or I'll throw out your Fats Waller tapes.'

'You wouldn't dare.'

'Oh, yes, I would.'

I hear scuffling sounds and shrieks of laughter. They've obviously patched up the argument I overheard the other day. 'Got you!' Elsie shouts triumphantly. And then they both start giggling again. Suddenly a jet of water shoots up over the boundary wall and lands, splat, on the front of my T-shirt.

'Oh, for God's sake!' I exclaim. Elsie and Liam are silent for a moment, startled.

'Is that you, Alice?' Liam calls out. 'Sorry if we splashed you. We didn't mean to. Honest.'

I don't reply. Liam and Elsie are now talking in hushed tones. The hosepipe chase has obviously ceased. I hear them walking away and their back door closing. They must have gone into the house.

I start to remove some slugs from the geraniums. The small ones seem to be the most greedy, and they're hard to find. As I do this I wish I hadn't overheard Liam and Elsie. I don't like these private glimpses into other people's lives. Sometimes I feel like Alice in that children's book, peering through a keyhole. I see or hear people laughing and playing in the distance and I so long to join them, but I just can't open the door. And the silly thing is I think I must have locked that door myself. I don't know why or when I did it, but it's happened and now everything seems different.

I pick up a snail that is munching on a nasturtium and think of James Mitchel. Maybe I was hoping that James Mitchel would bash down that door and find me. Find me the way Aaron did when we played hide and seek. Aaron always managed to seek me out, even in the most unlikely places. I don't think anyone will ever search so hard for me again. Search to see the truth of me. Who I really am. I put on so many disguises these days only a keen eye could see through them. Sometimes they even fool me.

Eamon does not know any of this and I will never tell him. He is in such deep disguise himself that he wouldn't really understand. If I ever speak to him of James Mitchel it will be as an anecdote. I'll describe what happened in a way that would make him laugh. You know you're getting older when you bear your scars as funny stories. You try to laugh and laugh at the things that once made you cry. You even dress up the details for dinner parties, digging into your store of broken dreams, finding the comic detail that will twist them into absurdity. And yet every time I do this I know something very precious is getting lost. That it is watching, anguished, as it sees itself misrepresented. I suppose one of the things I fear is that one day it may turn away and not watch at all. That it will leave me, and only the laughter will remain. Many of my dreams are already beginning to seem silly, but what is there to replace them? And how did they start anyway, where did they come from? I dearly wish I knew. Maybe that is why I sometimes dip into the past for clues, try to see the clear beginnings. And yet more often it feels like I am walking through a wood of memories, completely lost.

I run my hand over the wet part of my T-shirt. I must go inside and change. I'm getting far too introspective lately. Eamon wouldn't approve of it at all. He doesn't believe the unexamined life is not a fully lived one. He seeks distraction like Mira. Maybe they're both right. In fact if I do marry Eamon it is just possible that I'll take up golf. Eamon says trying to get small balls into tiny holes in the distance is very therapeutic. And then of course there'd be the gin and tonics later in the clubhouse with men in brightly coloured jumpers. I wonder what the women wear. Slacks, I suppose, not jeans.

I used to be so dismissive of golf, but I'm not so much anymore. I used to see it as a kind of emotional bunker, but maybe we all do feel stuck in some bunker in a way. We get out our sand wedges and try to soar on to the green. The grit flies, but the ball often doesn't move that far. Maybe there is a certain wisdom in accepting the situation. Trying to make the best of it.

I leave my container of slugs and snails by the door for relocation to the park later. Then I go inside. I see that Mira is busy in the sitting-room. She's making a 'grass skirt' for her South Seas Club meeting. She is using green crepe paper and seems very contented. In fact she's smiling.

'Why are you smiling, Mira?' I ask.

She looks up at me cheerfully. 'I was just remembering how Frank used to sniff.'

'Did he? I didn't know that.'

'Oh, yes, when he got excited about something, he'd sniff most persistently.' She's started to giggle. 'There was no need for it. It was just a habit. It sounded so funny.' She's started to laugh. I try to join her. She's turning Frank into an anecdote. Soon he'll be a story she tells at dinner parties. Not her lost love at all.

After I've chortled with Mira about Frank's sniff for the appropriate length of time I go into my room and change my T-shirt. Since I seem to be in a rather Cyril mood this evening I decide to distract myself by doing something practical. It's high time I got rid of some of the clutter that's been accumulating under my bed and I might as well do it now.

I thought it was all files of old newspaper clippings I'd kept as background research for articles, but it turns out that it isn't. Because among the first things that I find is a picture of Aaron and myself eating sticks of candy floss. I recognize the location immediately. It was taken when we were on holiday with my parents in a small seaside village. The time we stayed in the 'B&B with the bouncing bedsprings'.

I tear it up and put it in the bin along with a review of a book called *Nasty Men: How to Stop Being Hurt by Them Without Stooping to Their Level*. There is no way I want to be reminded of that seaside holiday, even though it spawned numerous family anecdotes in later years. There came a point at which my mother was even able to laugh about meeting Gilbert, her first love, as we walked along the strand. 'Do you remember, Alice, you thought he was wearing a dress?' she'd say and my father would look at her warmly and we'd all have a little giggle. But I don't want to think about all that now. I toss out a feature called 'Are Men Necessary?' and another about sperm banks. I pause briefly to look at an article about why an English dictionary dropped the term 'New Man' from their listings. They decided there weren't any. I could have told them that.

By the end of the evening the clutter under my bed has filled up one large black rubbish bag. I look at it smugly. Throwing out things you don't need can be so satisfying. Of course next week I'll probably find that I need one of those clippings, but you can't hold on to everything. You have to make space for things. Maybe you have to make space for new dreams as well.

It's time for bed. I wash and undress quickly, then I curl under the duvet cosily. The cat is lying at my feet and I feel rather privileged. This is a new thing for him. He's definitely getting tamer. He doesn't jump off the bed when I move, like he used to. His deep contented purring is very restful. I wonder if he will ever let us pet him. It would be so nice. I close my eyes, intent on drifting off to a deep and dreamless sleep, but I start to doze instead. And as I do so the picture I tore up, the picture of Aaron and myself eating candy floss, starts to float in front of me, stubbornly intact. It's awakening memories I wanted to forget. I turn over, trying to shake them off, but they will not go away. Half asleep, I am drifting back in time, even though I do not want to. I can see Gilbert and the way my mother looked at him. I can feel the seaspray as Aaron and I scampered on the sand. I can see Posy and Tarquin looking deep into each other's eyes. In fact the memory of that seaside holiday is now so startlingly clear that I can almost hear the bouncing bedsprings.

They were 'at it like rabbits' – the couple who ran the B&B in the coastal village we'd all gone to for a 'bit of peace'. Aaron had come with us. I was eight at the time and I shared a bunk with him in a small room. The couple in the next room, Mr and Mrs Allen, the B&B's owners, fascinated us. They bounced up and down on their bed far more than Aaron and I had ever done. And they speeded up real fast before they stopped. Mrs Allen made great big yelps in the middle and Mr Allen grunted. 'They're having sex,' Aaron said.

'What's that?' I asked.

'I'm not sure, but I know it's noisy,' Aaron replied. It became clear that my parents had also heard the sounds of passion from the flinty look Mum gave Mrs Allen when she asked her how she liked her egg.

Mr and Mrs Allen seemed to like each other a lot. Sometimes, when Mrs Allen was going upstairs with a pile of clean washing, I'd see Mr Allen giving her bottom a quick pinch and she'd squeal with indignation and delight. When I told my father about it he said that kind of thing happened when you were newly married. Romantic love only tended to last about four years, he said. You had to find a new kind of love after that, if you could, but it didn't tend to be 'so giggly or obvious'.

'What is romantic love?' I asked him. 'That,' he'd said, pointing to the cover of a slim novel my mother was reading. It was called *Moonlight* and the cover featured a man and woman who looked like they wanted to eat each other. He was handsome and she was beautiful. Their skin was tanned and they were staring deep into each other's eyes. There were foreign-looking flowers in the foreground.

Mum only read that kind of book on holiday. I turned it over and read the big bright words on the back: 'When Posy first met Tarquin Galbraith, the dashing millionaire oil tycoon, she disliked him immediately. With his thrusting arrogance and glinting dark eyes he...' Then my mother appeared and said, 'Give me that, Alice,' rather brusquely, so I never found out why Posy had obviously come to find Tarquin Galbraith less repellent.

We had some sunny days on that holiday, but there were some damp grey drizzly ones too. The kind that can make one traipse off to places and then, having traipsed there, sit down and stare out of cafe windows for rather too long. Aaron and I would, frankly, have been far less fidgety if we had been allowed to stay in the B&B's cheery sitting-room and watch TV, but my parents did not approve of that kind of aimlessness on holidays, so we had to go along with their adult type of aimlessness instead. It was on one of these days that we met Gilbert, my mother's first love.

It happened after Dad had poured himself four cups of tea from the Seaview Restaurant's capacious cream teapot. When he tried to extract a fifth just a dark brown stewed dribble emerged. Aaron and I had long since finished our fizzy orange drinks and had started to campaign for candy floss. 'Oh, all right,' Dad had sighed, lifting his mac wearily off the back of a bentwood chair.

My mother, who had been reading 'Stress. Ten tips to help you relax' in her women's magazine, also rose and then we spent some minutes hunting for a bag of pot-pourri she'd bought and which eventually turned up in Dad's pocket.

'Why didn't you tell me you'd taken it?' she'd demanded. 'Why didn't you?' And, as we trudged along the seafront her words seemed to follow us and generalize, until I began to wonder if our neighbour was remembering to feed my tortoise. Then Aaron shouted that he thought he'd seen a humpback whale, and we didn't wait to hear someone say that this was most unlikely, but scampered over to where the sand was wet. And standing there with him it suddenly didn't matter that the day was wet and damp and drizzly and that though we stared for ages we didn't see a 'cetaceous mammal', as it was called in one of Aaron's big books. The wind was fresh and was blowing all that didn't matter from us. It was full of lovely sea smells and helping to turn the waves into white horses with flying manes.

I wrote 'Alice' and he wrote 'Aaron' in the wet sand with a stick. We found a huge rock pool and stared in at the anemones and crabs and shrimps and fish. We'd almost forgotten we weren't on our own when my parents called us.

'Did you see the whale then?' my father smiled. We didn't answer. I looked at my mother. Her face seemed frozen. She was staring at a man who was walking towards us. Then she turned around and started to scurry off in the opposite direction.

'Frances,' Dad called after her. 'Frances, the B&B's this way.' She didn't seem to hear him. She darted into a concrete shelter, which I knew from my explorations contained a long wooden bench.

'Did I say anything?' Dad addressed me perplexedly. 'What on earth made her rush off like that?' And then, looking up at the man who had now almost reached us, he knew.

'Hello – er – Gilbert,' he said.

'Hello – er – Benny,' the man replied.

The interesting thing about Gilbert was that he seemed to be wearing a brown dress. I could just see the hem of it peeping out from under his big grey mac. He had a long serious face, windswept dark hair, big eyebrows and eyes as brown as my father's fifth cup of tea. They grew even darker, yet somehow more shiny, when they looked past us and saw my mother, who was now emerging from her concrete shelter and approaching us with an expression I suspected she'd been practising. Even though I was only eight I knew that, sometimes, one needed to go away and prepare a face for certain situations, such as being called upon to explain why one had scrawled 'Monsieur Thibaud is a nit' on the underside of one's desk. But I couldn't work out what it was about Gilbert that had made this necessary.

'Hello, Gilbert,' Mum had said, holding out her hand in a jolly fashion. 'How strange bumping into you here. Are you on holiday?'

And the conversation went on like this for some ruthlessly cheerful moments until Mum said, 'Well, Benny, we'd better be off, if we're going to – you know...'

'Yes, indeed,' my father agreed forcefully.

'Bye then,' Gilbert said.

'Yes, bye then,' Mum replied. And we set off at such a brisk pace away from him it began to feel like a getaway.

'Why are we rushing?' I asked.

'Be quiet, Alice,' Dad replied. And when I looked at Mum I saw her eyes were shiny, but not in the way Gilbert's had been. My mother wanted to cry. She looked so sad. So full of yearning. Once she looked back quickly, wistfully, at Gilbert as he walked away in the opposite direction. 'She doesn't want him to go,' I thought. 'She wants to be with him. With him instead of us.' I reached out and held her hand tightly.

My parents let us get on the dodgems on the way home, and the roundabout, and the pretend train, and the big swings. The candy floss was a doddle too. Gilbert had come in very handy, somehow. They gave us the coins as we asked, hardly even counting them. They laughed and waved as they watched us. It didn't fool me.

'Who is Gilbert?' I asked, as we walked back to the B&B with the bouncing bedsprings. 'Why does he wear a frock?'

'He's a monk,' Dad answered tersely.

'Is that why you talked to him?'

Dad sighed. 'We talked to him because he was once your mother's boyfriend.' Mum looked at him sharply.

'Was he a monk when he was Mum's boyfriend?'

'No. That happened later. He found he had a "vocation". That's why he and your mother parted.'

'Were Mum and Gilbert in love?'

My mother and father glanced at each other warily. 'Let's all just stand here quietly for a moment,' Dad announced suddenly. 'Let's see if we can hear the mermaids singing.'

'OK,' I agreed, while Aaron giggled. We knew what mermaids were. We'd seen them in books. Mum was fidgeting a bit and when Dad tried to put his arm around her she pulled away. I knew this mermaid thing was a ploy to stop me talking about Gilbert but I still listened earnestly.

Yes. Yes. I could hear something. A small sweet song with no words amongst the waves. 'I heard them. I heard the mermaids singing!' I almost said, until I looked around and saw Aaron had wandered off and was looking for flat stones to skim across the water. My mother was consulting her watch. And my father was picking up an ice-cream wrapper.

Some years later I discovered my mother and Gilbert had once visited that very same seaside village together. Perhaps that is why she had wanted to go back there. And maybe that's why Gilbert had also found himself walking along the seashore on that drizzly afternoon and Mum, Dad and I had seen him instead of Aaron's whale.

Mum left her novel, Moonlight, half-read that holiday. I even snuck it into my bunk one evening and was reading about sultry looks and passionate embraces and Tarquin's hard manly thighs when my mother came in and confiscated it.

'You're too young for books like that,' she told me.

'No, I'm not,' I replied. 'It's interesting.'

'Women like me read silly books like that to cheer them up,' she replied sternly. 'They're not meant for girls your age.'

'Why do women need to be cheered up?' I asked.

'Because – because some things aren't quite what we thought they'd be.' She smiled gently. 'Look, you two scamps settle down now. I don't want any chattering. It's been a long day.'

As she turned off the light and left the room I thought, 'It hasn't been a long day. Not really. Maybe she just felt it was because she didn't listen for the mermaids or even look for Aaron's whale. "Some things aren't quite what we thought they'd be." That's what she said women felt.' I clenched my teddy fearfully. 'She doesn't even believe in Posy and Tarquin really,' I thought. 'Is that what happens when you get old and marry?'

I saw *Moonlight* peeping out from the rubbish basket on the day we left. I decided to nip back and retrieve it when my parents were loading up the car, but when I went back into their bedroom it was gone. 'Mrs Allen must have taken it,' I decided. 'She wouldn't find it silly.'

'How long have you been married, Mrs Allen?' I asked her later, as she stood on the porch to wave us all goodbye.

'Don't be so nosy, Alice,' Mum chided, though I knew she and Dad had mused over this question themselves and decided Mr and Mrs Allen must have married recently. Their love was still so very giggly and obvious that it must be new.

'Mr Allen and I have been married for ten years, dear,' Mrs Allen answered cheerfully and my parents grew very still for a moment and stared at each other. They were obviously completely mystified, but I was smiling. I was smiling for Posy and Tarquin and myself...and Aaron. But I'm not smiling now, as I remember all this, curled up under my duvet. Salty tears are coursing down my cheeks like tiny waves. I'm crying. I'm crying for Posy and Tarquin and myself...and Aaron.

Yes, though he has gone, I am crying for Aaron too.

Chapter 13

MIRA SAYS WE'VE GOT to find a name for the cat. 'He's obviously decided we're his owners,' she said at dinner. 'He's not a stray anymore. What about calling him Fred?'

'Oh no!' I protested. 'That's far too ordinary.'

'Well, that's what he is. He's an ordinary cat.'

'No, he isn't!' I exclaimed. 'He's special.'

'Really. In what way, exactly?' She smiled at me.

'He's intelligent, and very sensitive to moods,' I explained earnestly. 'He's sympathetic and can be very understanding. Look at him now, he's listening. He doesn't want to be called Fred. I know it.'

'Well, what name do you suggest?'

I took a deep breath. 'Tarquin,' I announced. 'I think Tarquin would suit him.'

'No, it wouldn't,' Mira frowned.

'It's got a nice ring to it.'

'It's fecking stupid.'

'No, it isn't. Tarquin Galbraith, the dashing Texan oil millionaire...'

'What?' She frowned at me.

'He was a character in a romantic novel my mother wouldn't let me read.'

'Well, she has my sympathy on that one,' Mira smiled. 'You've quite enough romantic notions as it is.'

'Oh, come on – let's call him Tarquin. Just for fun.' She didn't reply and I knew she was relenting.

Tarquin is being rather naughty actually. He's frightening Cyril. I know this because as I pop by to have a chat with Mrs Peabody I notice him staring at Cyril hungrily through the sitting-room window. Mrs Peabody can't see him because of her poor eyesight, but Cyril obviously has. He's looking nervous and glum. Maybe he knows budgerigar is Aboriginal for 'good eating'. He hasn't said 'bollocks' for ages.

'Perhaps you should move Cyril upstairs, Mrs Peabody,' I say. 'He might like a different view.'

As I return to the cottage Tarquin follows me. He's definitely become more friendly lately. He stares at me even more frequently. Sometimes he even cavorts flirtatiously at my feet, looking up coyly. He miaows if I'm late home. He brushes his tail against my legs when I please him. If I lean gingerly towards him he sometimes reciprocates, letting his pink nose briefly touch my own. Yes, he definitely is special, but he must stop frightening Cyril.

'Posy wouldn't approve of you scaring a poor little budgerigar,' I tell him, recalling *Moonlight* and its steamy jacket.

Suddenly I am remembering the cover of that book very clearly, only now Tarquin Galbraith seems to have turned into James Mitchel and Posy is myself. We are staring into each other's eyes as if we want to eat each other. Dear God, I still haven't forgotten about James Mitchel. What on earth am I going to do?

I head grimly for my word processor. Sarah has asked me to write a feature on sex out of doors. 'Sex Where They May See You' – that's what she wants to call it. I sit down wearily. I really must get out of the habit of bringing these articles home but there tend to be a lot of interruptions in the office. The phone rings imperiously almost every five minutes and people tend to pause and chat as they pass my many partitions. Then of course there's Cindi, who seems intent on keeping me up to date

110

with office politics. Apparently Natalie, the one with the nice niche in celebrity interviews, has her eye on Sarah's job, and Cindi herself would like Natalie's if this vacancy occurs – which is most unlikely. There's also a rumour going round that I myself am interested in poaching the 'Male Matters' column from a woman called Edna, which is completely untrue. I think it started at an editorial meeting when I actually spoke up and mentioned an up-and-coming landscape gardener because I hoped Sarah might ask me to interview him.

'Sounds a possibility for our "Male Matters" section,' Sarah replied. 'It's been getting a bit stale lately. Could you look into it, Edna?'

Edna glowered at me and I think that's how the rumour began. The edited version of this interchange seems to involve me implying that the column has got 'a bit stale lately' even though, of course, it was Sarah who said it. That's how ridiculous the office can get at times. We're all supposed to have a hidden agenda and I don't, which people find very hard to believe. Conspiracy theories are so much more entertaining. Every time I see Edna now I have to say how riveting her last column was and this is mollifying her very gradually. I dearly wish Sarah would try to mollify me and stop asking me to write about sex.

I stare glumly at the screen of my computer. The 'Sex Where They May See You' article is needed by tomorrow. 'Bring a light blanket with you as pine needles and dry grass can be quite prickly,' I type. 'Try to find a secluded spot where there won't be interruptions and you can feel at ease. Men sometimes like the idea that they may be spotted, but women tend not to. This, of course, is not a hard and fast rule. Some women find the idea that they may be seen a turn-on too...'

Hard and fast...that pretty well describes the way Eamon did it. Did it in that field and on that beach and by that hedge and under that pine tree. He pestered me. Pestered me until I relented. He has a thing about 'sex close to nature'. It's his only unusual feature, and one I could do without. It can be very uncomfortable and chilly. Ireland just doesn't have the climate for that sort of thing. And it's too small. Even at midnight in the wilds you might bump into someone you know. But Eamon loves the subterfuge. When he saw figures way in the distance he'd speed up, obviously excited. 'It's all right. They can't see us,' he'd pant. 'We're rabbits, that's what we are. Little creatures in the wild.'

Now that I think about it, maybe a bit of outdoor bonking was what Eamon got up to when he 'disappeared' earlier this year. It would certainly account for his weariness and the mud on his clothes and the tent in his car. Eamon often brings a tent along on such occasions in case it rains. He even plans passion methodically, though it would be unlike him to go away without telling anyone...unless...unless he was desperately in love.

I bite the top of my biro so hard that it splinters. Could it be that Eamon is wildly, madly, hopelessly in love with someone else and wants to marry me just because he cannot have her? People do that kind of thing sometimes. I've read about it. No, of course not. I sit back in my chair and smile at the very suspicion. He's not that kind of person. If he thought his feelings for someone were getting that intense; he'd play squash. He is a well-ordered, sensible man and likes things to be neat. His feelings for me are neat, I'm sure they are. They're not all jumbled up with memories and longings and wistful glances at the past. I used to resent his linearity but now I

112

almost admire it. Maybe if we do marry I can learn to be more like him.

This thought is supposed to calm me, but somehow it doesn't. In fact, as I type out the article I find myself feeling increasingly angry. I'm remembering how Eamon coaxed and cajoled me into doing something that went completely against my wishes. He only seemed to be concerned about his own pleasure as he peeled off my undergarments eagerly in some corner of a field. Suddenly, unaccountably, I am almost hating him. If he was in this room now I'd be tempted to give him a good kick. How dare he. How dare he reduce the act of love to something so lonely. So bleak. He didn't even care if the blanket underneath me got damp. He was completely wrapped up in his own urgency. As I lay beneath him, bewildered tears sometimes misted my eyes. He didn't seem to notice them. 'You are so lovely, Alice,' he'd moan, but he wasn't saying it to me. There was some other Alice there in that field, lying on that blanket with him. He didn't see the real one with tears in her eyes who was staring at the stars.

I read through the article, which I have almost finished. Then I type: 'I must make one thing clear, however, and it is this: if you don't feel like having sex outdoors don't do it. There is a lot more to life than sex – such as self-respect. Don't be pestered into it. Men can be very selfish sometimes. If keeping your relationship going means having pine needles up your bum each week, then you may be better off without it. Remember, there are quite a number of interesting evening classes available if you find yourself alone and bored.'

'What's all this about?' Sarah is waving my article fractiously.

113

'Since you've obviously just read it, I don't see why I need to tell you,' I answer with uncharacteristic feistiness.

Sarah moves around in her seat agitatedly. 'There's no oomph to it and the last paragraph is completely inappropriate.'

'Why?'

'It just doesn't fit in.'

'Why?'

'Because the article is supposed to be light-hearted and fun – not a lecture on self-assertion. We've done self-assertion. We've done it piles of times. You're quite right to state that women shouldn't be coerced into this kind of thing but, frankly, that could have been said in a sentence.'

I sit down on a Habitat cane chair and glare at her.

'What I've written is true. I have the grass stains to prove it.'

Thankfully the phone rings before my mutiny mounts further and Sarah answers it. Someone is trying to argue with her about a design issue, but she's not having it. Whoever it is should know that it's usually pointless arguing with her. Sarah can sound plausible on almost any subject. That is her talent. You wouldn't guess she has this steely side to her at first. She comes across as a career romantic. Her office always has fresh flowers in it, and she tends to wear soft, feminine clothes. She has a delicate silk-lined basket of lavender pot-pourri by her phone and a photograph of her husband and small daughter in a silver photo frame.

As soon as she gets off the phone I decide to sidetrack her away from the vexed subject of my article. 'Sorry I couldn't make your Friends of Georgian Dublin soirée the other night, Sarah. How did it go?'

'Oh, fine. You really should have come. I could have introduced you to Nathaniel.'

'Who's Nathaniel?'

'Haven't I told you about him?' Sarah's face lights up. 'He's a wonderful interior designer. He's going to marblize the sitting-room next. Aquamarine. To evoke the Aegean.'

'How nice.'

'That silly woman Leonora kept referring to him as my "Toyboy". "Do have a peanut, Leonora," I said, proffering a bisque reproduction of one of four téton Sèvres bowls – they're supposedly modelled from one of Marie Antoinette's breasts. She recognized it immediately from *The World of Interiors*. That shut her up, I can tell you.'

'I'm sure it did.'

Sarah tends to move her arms around in a Gallic manner. As she does so, waves of Giorgio drift towards me. Sarah wears a lot of expensive perfume. She buys it with leisurely discernment at airports because, unlike me, she doesn't get into a dither about whether the plane will ever get to where it's going. She doesn't find herself thinking about Eternity – and I don't mean the aftershave.

Another thing Sarah does is she makes disconcerting pronouncements such as: 'What you have to remember about men, Alice, is that they are basically like dogs'. Because of this I simply mustn't tell her about Eamon's proposal, or James Mitchel. She's bound to tell me to put them both on leads.

'Anyway' – I can see from Sarah's brisk expression that she's going to tug us briskly back to business – 'when you've lightened up that 'sex out of doors' piece I want you to look into the whole area of supermarket

115

singles evenings. I'd suggest that you linger around the oriental food section.'

'Meet strange men?'

'Yes. Even more strange than usual.' Sarah gives me a conspiratorial little smirk. 'What was the name of that boyfriend of yours who thought if a woman changed her hairstyle she was about to leave?'

'Al.' I release the information grimly.

'Ah yes, of course,' Sarah smiles. 'That short bob really suited you.'

As I leave Sarah's office I wonder, yet again, if I should go back to 'mainstream' reporting. The thing is I'm not at all sure I have the temperament for it. I worked for a local paper some years ago and was definitely not the Bob Woodward of the suburbs. I seemed to mainly cover local spats about minor planning permission issues, dreary council meetings, cat shows and resident association uproars about, say, dog poo on the pavement. Rotting seaweed also proved to be an explosive issue for coastline dwellers, and heavy traffic on small roads and noisy neighbours were also hardy perennials. I felt a deep sympathy for the people involved in these dilemmas. I tried to understand all the various permutations – in fact, I probably tried to understand them too much. I'd talk to people for ages and then I'd ring them back to make sure I was quoting them correctly. I wanted to be fair to everyone and rang up 'experts' to confirm I had drawn the correct conclusions. I gathered a long list of people who were prepared to be quoted on various subjects. Who were good at sounding plausible.

'Tell it to me in a sentence.' That's what the News Editor used to bark at me. And of course I found I could. Eventually. I began to discern the extraneous. The unnecessary. I stopped gathering too many quotes because there just wasn't time for it. Half an hour, that's all I had for some stories. I began to feel a small exhilaration at all I wasn't saying. What I'd learned to leave out. And yet what I hadn't space for was, in a sense, what interested me most. Which is why I eventually decided to freelance in 'features'.

But I still sat with more hardened hacks in their preferred hostelries. I imbibed small measures of cynicism, along with full pints of lager, and revelled in their conviction. I listened to them talking about politicians and all the things they wished they could print. What should be done and why about crucial national issues, which sometimes gleefully included how a reporter called Anto could be persuaded to part with his corduroy jacket. A jacket he had worn daily for at least ten years.

And then slowly, almost imperceptibly at first, I drifted away from them. For journalists are, in general, deeply curious. They have to be. And I was no longer quite sure of the 'angle' I might offer them on my own life. And then Sarah offered me this job on the magazine and I grabbed it. I'd grown tired of the insecurity of freelancing. The sheer hard slog and whimsicality of it. I also needed a decent salary if I wanted to buy my cottage. Joining the magazine made perfect sense. Or at least it used to. Now I really want to leave. In fact, if I'm absolutely truthful, this is one of the reasons why I'm considering Eamon's proposal.

Eamon gets a good salary so if I married him I could leave the magazine. We wouldn't need the extra income. Yes, there are many very solid, practical reasons why I should marry him. Looking back, I'm quite amazed at how het up I got the other day about our 'sex outdoors'. Of course Eamon can be a bit unreasonable occasionally.

Everyone is sometimes. I'd just have to take a firmer stand with him about certain things. Be more assertive. I'm sure he'd understand. He's a good, kind man though, funnily enough, I sometimes think he and Mira would be more suited. She wouldn't mind his long silences because she has them herself. She'd like his practical, no-nonsense approach to relationships because Frank has really put her off the more high-flown stuff. Yes, in many ways they are extremely compatible...though I'm not sure what he'd make of her membership of the South Seas Club. They're planning to hold a meeting in my cottage tomorrow.

I bet Posy and Tarquin Galbraith never had to put up with this kind of thing.

Chapter 14

IT'S NOT JUST A meeting, it's a 'bi-monthly beach party' and the South Seas Club are currently holding it in my sitting-room. There are seven women – including Mira – and four men. They are swaying gently to exotic music and weaving strange patterns in the air with their arms. The women are wearing bikini tops and 'grass skirts' made from crêpe paper. The men are wearing shorts and multi-coloured shirts. All are barefooted and none have been to the place their club is named after. Evelyn Waugh was right, you sometimes have to modify the truth to make it plausible. I bet if I told Sarah about this beach party she'd think I was making it up. I look at the huge poster by Gauguin that Mira has Blu-Tacked to the wall and have a sudden desperate longing to go to the garden centre. Maybe I can sneak out and get a nice big terracotta pot for my hydrangeas.

As I furtively exit the cottage I wonder if I should write an article about the South Seas Club for the local newspaper. Odd people tend to make good copy and I seem to be meeting quite a number of them lately. I'm so preoccupied with these musings that I don't notice Annie approaching.

'Hi, Alice! Are you off somewhere?' she calls out. She's with Josh. 'I was just popping by for a cuppa. I haven't seen you in ages.'

'I'm sorry, Annie – I can't offer you a cuppa chez moi this afternoon,' I reply.

Why?'

'Well, to get into the cottage you'd need a visa.'

'What?' She squints at me.

I explain, adding, 'Come on. Let's go to California instead.' She studies me guardedly.

'California,' I repeat, 'you know, the new café. Haven't you been there yet? It's just down the road.'

As we talk, Josh fidgets. 'Smell my hair,' he demands suddenly. He's obviously feeling a bit left out.

'Oh, my poor sweet pea. Did you feel ignored?' I bend to sniff his honey-coloured curls. 'Mmmm – lovely. Timotei?'

'Silvikrin,' Annie smiles.

I hold out my hand and Josh takes it. I like pretending he's my son. I like taking him into the corner shop when Annie's off somewhere and buying him bright toys and sweeties. I love it when he runs to me, arms out, for a hug. He's taken to asking quite a lot about the 'Birds and the Bees' lately, and Annie has not fobbed him off with any tales of storks. Because of this he thinks penises are great. A kind of novelty item. He frequently refers to them.

'Mum, why don't you have a penis?' he asks loudly as we sit down on one of the California Café's comfy cane chairs. Annie looks like she's about to go into a detailed answer, so I say briskly, 'Who wants a chocolate chip cookie?'

'I do!' Josh shoots his hand up eagerly. He's just started school.

I go to the counter and order two cookies, a brownie, two cappuccinos and a fizzy lemonade. As I wait for them I look around. It really is a very nice café. The kind of place you could sit in quite happily reading a book. There's a smell of cinnamon about it. And fresh baking. The mugs are nice and big and in a beautiful shade of golden yellow. The décor is also bright yet cosy, and there's a large teddy bear wearing a straw hat by the till.

Some pictures on the walls are for sale. I gaze at them dreamily, wondering if some of my own paintings might be displayed. Then I see Liam. He's sitting by the window. I look away quickly. 'Oh, blast it, he would be here,' I think. 'Maybe he and Elsie have had another row.'

'Hello, Alice.' Oh dear, he's talking to me. He's seen me.

'Hello, Liam.' I give him one of Sarah's tight philosophical smiles though a Laren Brassière scowl would have been more sincere. I don't know why, but for some reason I seem to have developed a dislike of my new neighbour. Even the fact that he has leather patches on his rather worn tweed jacket suddenly seems deeply irritating and he really should get his hair cut. His fringe is far too long. What on earth does Elsie see in him? He's not even faithful. I feel him looking at me again and I glare back at him, no longer hiding my distaste.

'Who is that man who said hello to you, Alice?' Annie asks as I return to the table with a heavily laden tray. 'He seems really nice.'

'He's a new neighbour of mine and I don't think he is nice, actually,' I mumble.

'Ask him to join us. Go on. I like the look of him.'

'No.'

'Does Alice have a penis, Mummy?' Josh interjects.

'No, dear,' Annie replies patiently. 'Only boys and men do.'

'So he has a penis!' Josh is pointing at Liam, who's obviously heard Josh's exclamation and is trying not to smile. I have a sudden desperate need to talk about my amaryllis plant.

'My amaryllis did really well this spring,' I announce. 'It had four beautiful blossoms.'

121

'How nice,' says Annie. 'Have you told Eamon you're not going to marry him yet?'

'No...would you like a cutting from my begonia? I could make up a nice hanging basket for you. It would look great on your patio.'

'Thank you, Alice, but I think I'll pass on that one. I sometimes forget to water that geranium you gave me as it is.'

'I know. I have to give it a good soak every time I visit. I think you should know, Annie' – I take a comforting sip from my big bright mug of cappuccino – 'that I can't help being slightly suspicious of people who forget to water their plants. Don't you hear their plaintive little squeaks?' I smile as I say this, but I am not entirely joking.

'I do water it, Alice,' Annie protests mildly. 'Just not quite as often as I should.'

'I've got some spare nasturtiums I could give you. They're fairly easy to keep and they self-seed. You can even eat the flowers – add them to a salad or something. They make a wonderful garnish.'

'Oh, Alice.' Annie regards me with tender exasperation. 'Do stop casting nasturtiums at me. Just tell me here and now that you're not going to marry Eamon. It's been worrying me.'

I am aware that Liam is listening to our conversation. He is camouflaging this fact by gazing too studiously at his book which happens to be *Howard's End* by E. M. Forster, who is one of my favourite authors. I frown at him and lean towards Annie, almost whispering. 'Look,' I say pleadingly, 'let's not talk about all that men stuff now.'

'I know what it is, you're just broody at the moment, Alice,' Annie replies airily. She's one of those disconcerting people who never believe other people overhear. 'There's piles of sperm around if you really want it. You don't have to have Eamon's.'

'Sperm! Sperm! Sperm! Sperm!' Josh repeats happily, as usual picking up the one word I would have preferred him to ignore. Then, as I squidge up my last bit of brownie and munch it, he starts to make loud swishy noises with the straw he's using for his fizzy drink.

I glance at my watch. 'Look, I have to go,' I say. 'I promised Mrs Peabody I'd buy Cyril a cuttlefish bone and I simply have to get to the garden centre before it closes.'

'Give that neighbour of yours a nice smile before you leave,' Annie is leaning towards me conspiratorially.

'Please keep your voice down, Annie. He can hear you.'

'Of course he can't. He's just your type, I can tell. He's even reading E. M. Forster.'

'He's far too young for me,' I hiss.

'No, he isn't.'

'Yes, he is. I've tried the younger men thing and it's never worked.' Neither has the older or same age men thing, of course, but I don't mention this. I lean towards Annie irritatedly and whisper, 'Anyway, he has a girlfriend.'

'You could still be friends,' Annie replies stubbornly. 'Some of the best relationships start off that way.'

'Yes, that's what Eamon says,' I comment slyly. I rise from my chair and reach for my handbag. 'You're most unfair about Eamon, Annie,' I add reproachfully. 'He's a very nice man and I'm getting tired of the way you go on about him. It's just not fair.'

Annie just sighs and looks forlornly at the table.

'Bye then,' I say, then I add, 'Goodness, where's Josh?'

Josh has snuck away from the table, as he often does in cafés. I notice that he is now standing beside Liam. They're chatting away in a very friendly manner. I decide to exit the café swiftly and as I do so I overhear Josh asking Liam something.

He's asking whether fizzy lemonade and chocolate chip cookies ever fall in love.

Chapter 15

EAMON HAS SENT ME a postcard. It features a llama who looks a bit pissed off. 'Dear Alice,' he's written in his tidy hand:

'Thank you so much for your letter. I was very pleased to hear that you may take up golf. Maybe we could even do a bit of golfing on our honeymoon – if you say 'yes' to my proposal, that is. There are some wonderful golf courses in the Algarve. By the way, I've bought you a nice sweater made from llama wool – hence this choice of card. It's hand-knitted and in a very simple, but pleasing design. Looking forward to seeing you again. Love, Eamon.'

I read through the postcard again at least four times. I'm trying to read between the lines, as I so often do in our conversations. I must admit I was expecting him to send me a letter. Oh well, he's probably very busy. I'm not sure I like his suggestion of a golfing honeymoon, but perhaps it's sensible. I know a lot of people spend their honeymoon mooning over each other, but I don't think we'd be that kind of couple. Still, the Algarve sounds nice. I could get a tan and bring my sketchpad with me. We'd probably dine out in wonderful restaurants. Eamon has highly developed culinary tastes. In fact, he's already done a draft menu for the wedding reception, if we have one...

Our wedding – dear God – what a very strange thought.

I always thought that if I got married Dad would be there to 'give me away'. That he'd be standing beside me smiling protectively, as he so often did through the years.

'The kind of man you need to find, Alice, is one who will appreciate you,' he often said. This was nice because it implied I had virtues that required recognition.

When I reached thirty my father never implied that I should grab the first half-decent man who would have me. An option some of my female relatives only half-jokingly suggested. 'Marry marriage, Alice,' Uncle Sean would sometimes add. 'People change but the institution itself can be quite desirable.' He always smiled knowingly when he said this while Aunt Phoeb looked like she'd like to take a good swing at him with a sand iron. Even my mother, who had once been extremely finicky about men on my behalf, reached the point when race, creed, colour and even love didn't seem to matter that much. 'Company, Alice,' she'd say. 'Company. There's a lot to be said for it.' I suppose you could say they worried about me, and their worries became my own.

Over and over again marriage was offered to me as a solution, though the problem it might solve was never clearly stated. 'Marriage is about compromise, Alice,' Aunt Phoeb often said and Mum looked at her in warm agreement. For by then my single state seemed to be regarded as just plain stubbornness. They were growing old. It really wasn't fair of me to keep them waiting.

Dad didn't take part in these conversations, but he talked when I needed him to. All through my childhood he had been encouraging. For example, he tended to say 'very good' about samples of artwork I showed him – even drawings that I myself was not entirely satisfied with. Because of this I began to suspect that he was without discernment. A harsh judgement which I saw later was unfair, because he believed people need encouragement. Even now when I paint huge, unlikely landscapes, I draw some comfort from the knowledge that Dad, at least, would have liked them. He was on my side long before I was. Long before I even knew I had a side to be on. If he was here now what advice would he give me about Eamon? I so wish I knew.

Talking of advice, Mrs Peabody's handyman, Willy, has told her that she should find a mate for Cyril. 'He's lonely,' he told her authoritatively the other day. 'Budgerigars are gregarious creatures.'

Mrs Peabody has become determined to find a partner for Cyril, and has asked me to help her. In fact, I am now in a pet shop with her and am scrutinizing Cyril's potential Significant Others conscientiously while she fidgets eagerly by my side.

'What are they like? Oh, I do so wish I could see them better,' she keeps saying. 'Old age is such a bugger.'

Mrs Peabody is not known for her expletives. I register a mild surprise and continue my inspection. 'I think Cyril would like a cheery mate, don't you, Mrs Peabody? A bird who'd take him out of himself.'

'Maybe.'

'What about her?' I look in at a yellow and green beauty who is darting us coy glances. Mrs Peabody squints into the cage.

'She is definitely a she, isn't she?' she asks the assistant.

'Yes, she is.'

'Does she talk?'

'Not yet, but I'm sure she will, given time,' he replies. 'She's got an affectionate temperament. Good breeder too I'd bet.'

'What do you think of her, Alice?' Mrs Peabody is peering at me earnestly.

'Well, Mrs Peabody,' I reply, 'she's definitely the most alluring budgie here.'

'We'll take her,' Mrs Peabody announces. As she snaps open her purse I begin to mooch around the shop. I do not go over to the tropical fish, though I feel drawn in their direction. Instead I look at the huge array of doggie gifts, and this reminds me of Berty the Yorkshire terrier and his sad adoration of Aunt Phoeb. How the mystery of the cupboard to the left of the back door enthralled him. For it was there that all the love gifts for him were stored. He often stared at this, his secular shrine, most thoughtfully. Sometimes he even barked at it, hoping perhaps that it would dispense its goodies direct and he could thus dispense with Aunt Phoeb's perplexing intervention. Berty looked at that cupboard the way we humans often look for God.

'Feck the terrapins.' This announcement comes from a gruff female voice behind me and somehow does not sound unfamiliar. 'I've told you to get rid of them. I'll flush them down the boghole. I really will.'

I turn slowly. Warily. A man with blond hair and a tattoo is leaning over a large tank and Laren MacDermott, that is Laren Brassière, is scowling furiously beside him.

'One more terrapin and I'm leaving.' Laren's voice has turned into a growl. 'I really will leave you this time, Malcolm. I mean it.'

'You always say that, honey,' Malcolm drawls. 'Now shut the feck up.'

'You shut the feck up yourself, dickhead!'

Mrs Peabody is staring, gobsmacked, in the direction of this interchange. 'Don't listen to them,' she's telling Cyril's prospective mate. 'I don't want you picking up rude words.'

As the assistant transfers Cyril's partner into the small cage we've brought with us I dart wary, excited glances at my old schoolmate. She's grown quiet, thoughts of departure evidently themselves now gone. She looks rather resigned and bored as Malcolm lifts the small creature he's selected and its legs thrash the air desperately. Then they both suddenly turn towards the counter and I find myself facing them.

'Hello, Alice!' Laren beams. She looks astonished but genuinely pleased to see me.

'Hello, Laren,' I smile back. What on earth am I going to say to her?

'How strange that we should meet each other here, in a pet shop,' she announces, as though the location somehow pleases her.

'Indeed,' I agree politely.

'Remember how you used to love my aquarium?'

'Yes, absolutely,' I reply. I don't know why I added 'absolutely'. It's a word that's frequently used in the office lately. It implies such complete agreement that people change the subject, which is probably what one wanted.

'So, Alice, what are you doing now?' Laren asks.

'I'm a journalist.'

'That sounds interesting.'

'Yes, I suppose it does,' I reply.

'I'm a singer.'

'Yes. So I've heard.' I look at her guardedly and wonder if I should tell her I've been to one of her concerts. No. It would be best not to mention it. She might wonder why I hadn't spoken to her afterwards.

'I've often thought of you, Alice,' Laren smiles at me most warmly. 'We haven't seen each other in so long. When was the last time we met up?'

'In Bewley's on Grafton Street,' I reply. 'You were about to go to Edinburgh.'

'Ah yes, of course,' she says. 'We shared a plate of chips.

The blond man, Malcolm, seems to be growing rather restive as he listens to our conversation. Laren notices this and sighs. She looks at the struggling terrapin and then at him.

'This is Malcolm, my husband,' she says wearily. Malcolm holds out his free hand and I shake it.

Silence. The terrapin squirms. I stare at it. In normal circumstances it would seem an obvious subject of conversation. I remember the budgie. 'I – that is my neighbour and I – have just bought a budgerigar.'

'Really.' Laren looks at me, somewhat bemused.

Malcolm is talking to the assistant now and Mrs Peabody is waiting for me by the doorway. Laren and I don't seem to have anything further to say to each other. I wonder how I can acknowledge this without appearing rude. 'Just coming,' I call out to Mrs Peabody, adding, 'Well, it's been lovely meeting you again, Laren.'

Laren is not listening. She has started to scribble something on to a scrap of paper. She thrusts the grubby note, which I see bears her address and phone number, into my hand. 'Give me a call, Alice, soon,' she says. 'Let's have a proper chat.'

'Yes. Yes, I will,' I reply, though what this 'proper chat' might entail is a complete mystery. There is no doubt that some people can recede from you. Locating the intimacy Laren and I once shared would now require binoculars. As Laren and Malcolm leave I stare at the grubby note fearfully. And Mrs Peabody's new budgie chooses this moment to squawk her first word.

Which sadly sounds remarkably like 'feck'.

Chapter 16

I'VE BEEN WONDERING IF I should phone Laren, but I don't think I will. I think having a 'proper chat' with her would be most uncomfortable. I wouldn't want to talk about Eamon and his proposal either. I wouldn't want to tell her that I am feeling most bewildered, though I probably would. She was far more bewildered than me when we were at school together. She used to look up to me in a way, but I don't think she would any more. She's the one who's found her answers now, however odd they may seem. There is a possibility that she might gloat a bit about this, and I really couldn't bear that. I'd prefer her to keep her illusions about me so I've conveniently 'lost' her telephone number.

But I haven't lost James Mitchel's.

Yes, I have obtained James Mitchel's telephone number. I rather wish I hadn't, but I have. It happened when I was in a drapery store hunting for some net curtains for the kitchen window. I was doing this because sometimes, when I gaze out into the garden, I notice Liam, my new neighbour, looking at me from an upstairs room. Our eyes meet for a moment and then we both look away quickly. It's most unsettling. Net curtains are definitely called for. In fact, I was just buying them when I bumped into Mildred, the pottery class snooper.

'Hello, Alice!' she said. 'Been doing any pottery lately?'

'No, I haven't actually,' I replied.

'It's such a pity James had to move to West Cork like that, isn't it?' Mildred eyed me meaningfully.

'Yes, I suppose it is,' I agreed. 'Has he opened his studio there yet?'

'I don't know, dear,' she replied. 'But the young man he's sharing his cottage with – Sean, I think he's called – is going to be holding a yoga weekend soon.'

'What?' I frowned at her.

'Mo, the man who runs the craft shop, told me about it just now. He and James know each other quite well. Sean will be giving the yoga instruction and James will be doing the vegetarian catering. Apparently he's an excellent cook.'

'Oh, is he?' I replied dully. I was trying not to be impressed.

'Have you done any yoga, Alice?'

'Yes, I have attended some classes.'

'You might enjoy that yoga weekend then. It would be nice to get away to West Cork for a break, wouldn't it? And it's quite reasonable.' Mildred delved into her bag and produced a leaflet. 'I told Mo I'd pass these round,' she said. 'They give all the details.' She handed the leaflet to me. James Mitchel's home address and telephone number were in big bold letters at the top.

'No, I don't think I'll bother with it,' I said, handing the leaflet briskly back to her.

'Oh, keep it anyway,' she said, popping it into my bag. She's a very persistent kind of person.

I look at that leaflet sometimes. It both disquiets and comforts me. I have wondered at great length whether I should go on the yoga weekend, but I've decided not to. It's high time I gave up on James Mitchel. He's far too wonderful for me. It's becoming plain that I'll probably settle for Eamon, my Mr Mediocre. A bird in the hand is worth two in the bush, they say, and frankly I've spent quite enough time hunting for James in the shrubbery.

Even so, not phoning him has made me feel a little sad and I've decided to seek distraction like Mira. I've been doing some freelance articles for the local newspaper. They especially liked the one I wrote about the South Seas Club and have asked me to do other assignments. It's great. I've done freelance features for local newspapers before but I'd forgotten how cheering they can be. A reminder that behind the muted tones of the suburban savannah, some people are daubing their lives purposefully with great colourful dashes. On occasion one even meets someone who is authentically eccentric.

I tend to do my reports for the newspaper at weekends, but today I took a day off 'in lieu' from the magazine and interviewed some rather intriguing people. One of them was a woman who saved frogs. Earlier this year four hundred of them reached adulthood in her back garden. Now most of them have hopped off elsewhere for a while before returning to her pond to breed. But she still has four American bullfrogs as year-round residents, plus the fifty newts.

'I just love frogs,' she told me, as if I might somehow have remained ignorant of this fact. She lives alone and looked very happy. A good deal happier than many married women I know. She must have had many, many handsome amphibians in her life, and she'd obviously never had the temerity to kiss them. 'Princes may be fine for other people,' she commented when I alluded to this fact. 'But frogs are just fine for me.' I don't know why but there was something in the tilt of her head when she said this that reminded me of Princess Diana.

After the frog lady I interviewed a man who was very keen on Esperanto. And then I went to talk to the owners of a cat called Floribunda Flossie – a local Siamese who had won the Best Siamese Kitten prize at the Siamese and All Breeds Cat Club's recent show. Floribunda was curled up in her basket with a hot-water bottle, thermal blanket and a catnip mouse.

The pièce de résistance of the day was meeting a man who's in charge of a university botanical garden. As I wandered around the huge glasshouse which, amongst other things, boasted bananas, mangoes, sugar cane and lemon trees, I wondered whether Mira might be allowed to hold one of her beach parties there. I was enthusiastically learning about the conservation of rare plant species when I guiltily remembered that Sarah was expecting me to have my 'Supermarket Singles' article ready the next day and I had done absolutely no research for it. So I reluctantly had to finish my blissful botanical discussion and race off to my local shopping centre, which is where I am now.

It is, thankfully, Thursday – the evening of the week when complete strangers are encouraged to approach each other, perhaps under the guise of a shared interest in tortellini. I am glad I have an assignment as I pick up my shopping basket because I often get a bit lonely in supermarkets. In fact, if I marry Eamon I think one of the things I'd savour would be shared strolls through the aisles. I'd love to have someone to discuss the merits of various brands with. Someone to buy special titbits for, to linger with by the delicatessen. Eamon would want to buy good wine and I'd listen in as he talked to the assistant about Zinfandels and Cabernets and Sauvignons. I'd enjoy his knowledge, though I'm not sure I'd be so keen on drinking his chosen vintages with his friends later on. I don't seem to have much in common with them. They're mostly men and they talk a lot about cars, business, politics and sport. They love their wives and children, if they have them, but they don't seem to crop up in conversations that often. When they do one sometimes gets disquieting glimpses into their domestic arrangements. As I head towards the supermarket's toiletries section, I recall a rather sobering conversation with a man called Doug. It occurred when I and some of Eamon's friends were having drinks together in a pub. 'Goodness, I must get home,' Doug had announced suddenly. 'I said I'd let Judy out this evening.'

Normally I would let a remark like that slide by as a colloquialism, but I'd just covered a feminist conference and was in a feisty mood. 'What do you mean "let Judy out", Doug?' I asked. 'You sound like you're referring to the cat.'

Eamon glowered at me and I glowered back while Doug smiled tolerantly. 'I said I'd look after the kids,' he explained. 'She wants to go off to a film with some friends.'

'Ah, that's nice,' I said, giving him a muted smile. At least he was prepared to babysit.

'Have a quick pint before you leave,' a man called Alan suggested. Eamon's friends seem to say that kind of thing a lot.

Doug glanced at his watch. 'Make it half a pint,' he replied. 'I'll have half a pint and then I'll go.'

'I think you should go now, Doug,' I commented. 'The film will probably be starting around eight. You're going to be late if you don't hurry.' By this stage Alan had left the table to order Doug's drink and the others were shifting uncomfortably in their seats. They seemed to be trying to ignore what I'd said. It was as though I'd farted.

Eamon leaned towards me. 'Look, Alice,' he said somewhat embarrassedly. 'I'm sure Doug has every intention of being home on time. Calm down, will you? Just let him have his drink in peace.'

Alan brought the drink to the table and Doug stared at it. I did too. 'What film is Judy going to see?' I enquired.

'Mmmm – gosh, I'm not sure.' He lifted the glass to his lips. It left a creamy moustache as he pondered. 'I think it's something to do with eternal sunshine.'

'Really!' said Eamon. 'Sounds interesting. Is it something to do with global warming?'

'It must be *Eternal Sunshine of the Spotless Mind*,' I said. 'Yes. That's a good choice. That will cheer her up.'

Doug looked at me strangely. He did not linger over his half pint. He drank it quickly. He reached into his pocket for his car keys and jingled them. 'See you then,' he called out. Then he was gone.

Will Eamon become the kind of husband who'll say, 'Gosh, I'd better get home, I've got to let Alice out?' and if he did could I bear it? That's what I'm thinking as I approach a neat row of perfumed body sprays. I pick up a container of Impulse and look at it. The ads for it often feature a man running after a woman with flowers in his hands. Though she's a stranger, he sniffed her as she passed and couldn't let her get away. They laugh gaily. They may even be falling in love. I frown and put the can back on to its shelf and as I do so Charles Aznavour starts to sing on the supermarket sound system about 'Feelinks'. I sigh and look around. This aisle is almost empty. Maybe I should try the oriental section as Sarah suggested. I head off towards it and as I do so a man with a very large baguette sticking out of his basket smiles at me rather warmly. I walk past him briskly and reach the corner of the next aisle, where a man in a navy blue jumper is explaining the merits of freshly ground coffee to his small, precocious daughter. She has pigtails and is doing ballet steps as she listens. 'Mummy says we mustn't forget the Sharwood's Plum Sauce,' she informs him and he nods gratefully. They are obviously quite a team. They belong to each other. I get a sudden wave of yearning as I walk away from them. Suddenly I wish I could just leave this supermarket and go home.

No, I must speak to some people. Get some quotes. But how can I tell the ordinary shoppers from the ones who are here for romantic purposes? Just as I'm thinking this I see Liam. He's looking rather closely at a packet of basmati rice. I'm rather surprised Elsie isn't with him, but then again maybe he's come to this supermarket singles evening in search of fresh romantic liaisons. I wouldn't put it beyond him. After all, I did overhear Elsie accusing him of being unfaithful. I must get away from him fast.

I head towards the Italian section. I try to talk to a man who is stuffing his trolley with home-made pasta; only it turns out he actually comes from Italy and doesn't speak much English. I try to explain that I am a journalist on an assignment but it's not getting through to him. He's saying, 'Oh, signorina, yes, yes. We go for dreenk. I like that.'

'No. No,' I say. 'No go for dreenk with you. I am journaleeste.'

'Jornaleestah. Ah. So. We go restaurant maybe? Spaghetti bolognese?' He's saying it very eagerly. I sigh with frustration and look around, hoping a fluent Italian speaker may be in the vicinity but instead I see Liam again. He looks at me quickly and turns away as though trying not to laugh. 'Oh no, he probably thinks I've been propositioning this poor man,' I think glumly. 'And I suppose I did in a way, but only for a quote.'

I start to make wild gestures with my hands implying that I have to go, only the man seems to be interpreting them as great romantic excitement. 'Yes, yes, we go now,' he's saying and starts to steer me towards the check-out. 'Me Enrico. You share my trolley. Like so.' He takes the one item in my shopping basket, a tin of Whiskas, and relocates it. I grab it back.

'Aw – signorina!' Enrico looks at me most reproach-fully.

'Enrico, sorry. No go restaurant with you. Misunderstanding.' I point to my watch and add 'busy' then I call out 'ciao' as I scurry away – straight into Liam.

'Hello, Alice,' he says. 'Doing a bit of shopping?'

'No, I'm on assignment,' I reply with as much dignity as I can muster. 'I'm a journalist and I'm doing research for an article.'

'What kind of article?' Liam studies me with his calm brown eyes.

'An article about supermarket singles evenings,' I reply trying not to get flustered. The music on the super-market's sound system has changed to Michael Bolton singing 'Soul Provider'. I love that song but I wish they weren't playing it right now. It's lending a sort of emotional significance to our meeting that is entirely inappropriate.

'Ah, yes, I saw a notice up about that when I came in here,' Liam comments, almost too casually it seems to me.

'They have one here every Thursday,' I reply. 'Super-market singles evenings are becoming quite popular actually. Especially abroad.'

'I suppose there's something to be said for them,' Liam replies solemnly. 'Though when a woman approached me just now and started talking about courgettes I was a bit baffled. I've got so used to calling them zucchini.'

'Ah, yes, that's the American word for them, isn't it?' I look at him curiously. I'd like to ask him more about his background – his accent definitely has a trans-Atlantic twang to it – but I decide not to. I don't want us to become too familiar, and anyway I've got to get on with my research.

'So, Liam, I suppose I'd better let you do your shopping,' I say politely.

'OK, ciao then, Alice,' he replies, with just the hint of a smile.

I race away from him towards the bakery section. The supermarket is about to close in ten minutes and I still haven't got any quotes for my article. I talk to a sleekly groomed middle-aged woman who turns out to be married and not love hunting at all.

'One man is quite enough for me,' she sighs wearily as the assistant hands her a gooseberry tart. A younger girl who's buying some doughnuts just giggles when I ask her if she's come here to meet a boyfriend and, as the man with the very large baguette in his basket starts to approach me again, I decide to leave.

I'll just have to make that article up, I think, as I trudge homewards gloomily. Though perhaps I can use Liam's comment about zucchini and the 'One man's enough for me' quote. And of course the tussle with Enrico over the Whiskas. That would add some comic relief.

As soon as I reach the cottage I turn on my laptop computer.

'If you want a man with passion, then try pasta,' I type. 'Bring out the Latin in him by humming something operatic and wearing vibrant colours – though if he turns out to be legitimately Italian you may need a phrase book. If you want someone a bit more exotic then linger around the oriental foods wearing patchouli oil and a saffron-coloured scarf. Only engage in conversation with men who cook basmati rice from scratch rather than using the boil in the bag method. Pet foods are good if you want someone a bit cosy and kind, especially if they buy the more upmarket brands and titbits. In the plant section I would watch out for a man who bothers to buy Baby Bio. Any man who is kind to his plants must be a cut above the rest. Steer clear of men carrying very large baguettes in a suggestive manner.'

I continue with these authoritative gross generalisations, interspersed with quotes and anecdotes and bits of description for 'colour', until I have reached two thousand words.

'Wonderful,' says Sarah happily, as she reads my article the next day. 'It's got loads of oomph.'

'I'm so glad you like it,' I smile, then I look at her pleadingly. 'Sarah could you give me a break from articles about sex and men and love hunting for a bit? I really do need a change.'

'Funnily enough I was just going to talk to you about that,' Sarah replies. 'I want you to write about being an extra on a film for a day. Here,' she hands me a letter, 'this gives all the details.'

'Oh, Sarah!' I feel like kissing her. 'Thank you so much!'

'Yes, it should be interesting,' she replies calmly. 'Now to get back to this supermarket singles evening article – I'm afraid I don't quite understand the concluding sentence.'

'Why?'

'Well, Alice', she looks at me wryly, 'I don't see why women who are shopping for love really need to know this particular bit of information.'

'What bit?' I lean forwards nervously. I'd written the article in such a tizz I hardly remember what it said.

'The bit that says' – Sarah starts to titter. 'The bit that says "Jam-jars are totally unsuitable for frogspawn".'

'I think that must have strayed in from another article,' I mutter.

'Well, I'm glad you're taking an interest in ecology,' Sarah smiles at me kindly. 'After all, frogs are so much easier to find than princes.'

'Yes, absolutely,' I agree sadly, remembering James Mitchel.

Chapter 17

I'VE DONE IT. I wish I hadn't now. It was stupid. Impetuous. I wish Mira was here so I could talk to her about it, but she's on a canal with her cousin. They've hired a barge. She asked me to join them but I said I wanted to get on with my painting. I'd hardly done any painting since Eamon's proposal and I'd begun to miss it. But I should have gone on that barge with them. I really should.

This evening began in a balanced, productive manner. I was almost serene as I made myself a nice, nourishing dinner, straightened the books on the bookshelf, watched *Coronation Street* and loaded the washing machine. Then I went to my canvas and got on with a painting I've already got a name for. It's called 'The Dolphin Smiles'.

I'm fond of dolphins, but then nearly everyone is so it's not something to brag about. I suppose one of the reasons people like them so much is because they smile – all the time. The dolphin in my painting isn't smiling. My dolphin has a choice in the matter, so I suppose you could call the title ironic. But, though my dolphin's mouth is a straight line, his eyes are shining with happiness. He's happy because he doesn't have to smile. I know exactly how he feels. It has long been a cause of sadness for me that certain emotions are thought suitable for indiscriminate display, while others live more furtive, shadowy lives. It seems to me that people's smiles are often like the dolphin's, and I long for a world where we can wear our many faces without shame.

I was deeply engrossed in my painting – elated even. The house seemed quiet without Mira so I turned on the radio. I'd meant to find something chatty and restful on Radio 4, but 'Have I Told You Lately That I Love You?' by Van Morrison wafted out at me from some pop station instead. I loaded my brush with indigo and added it to the horizon I was painting. Tarquin brushed against my legs, miaowing up at me. It was almost his dinner time.

'Yes, OK. In a moment,' I told him. His miaows increased in frequency and his gaze grew disapproving. He now not only insists on premium brands, he has also developed strong preferences as to the ingredients. He set off purposefully in the direction of the kitchen, turning round halfway, commanding me to follow.

'You really are becoming a very bossy cat,' I told him. 'Patience. Patience, dear. Some things take time.' I couldn't help recalling that James Mitchel had said much the same to me at my first pottery class. As I trudged into the kitchen and opened a tin of Whiskas I began to feel rather unsettled. Patience is one thing, but months of procrastination are quite another. Suddenly, unaccountably, I knew that if I didn't phone James then, there, at that very moment, I never would. And I had to.

I scurried to get the leaflet, not daring to analyze the impulse further. I even worked out a plan of action as I tremulously picked up the receiver – the yoga weekend was long over, so I couldn't use that as an excuse for phoning him. If things got sticky, that is, if he couldn't remember who I was, I was going to ask him to recommend a new pottery teacher. And if things got friendly I was going to ask him to dinner next time he came to Dublin. I was going to say I'd like him to bring some pottery samples from his new studio because I might be able to get a photo and small write-up about them in the magazine.

I dialled quickly with damp fingers. I felt itchy and antsy and strangely determined. I jumped slightly at the ringing tone and then listened to it carefully, as if counting footsteps. Any moment now…I almost clattered down the receiver. But I didn't. I took deep breaths like an opera singer preparing for a small, perplexing aria.

And then I heard James Mitchel's voice telling me he wasn't there.

I had to force myself to leave a message on the answering machine. I just said who I was and left my number. As soon as I'd done this I realized I shouldn't have. Because this way James Mitchel could phone me at any time – perhaps catch me at a moment when I am in no state to follow through on my brazenness.

It is now an hour later and I am appalled by the improbability of my action. I wanted a peaceful, painterly weekend, and now I jump with terror every time the phone rings.

I decide to distract myself with a favourite CD. I thought I had Nanci Griffith on the stereo system, but Mira must have slipped on Laren Brassière for a quick blast before she left. As I turn the thing on, hoping for some soothing ballads, Laren's voice comes out at me. More softly than usual. Almost tender.

'Why did we do it?' she is singing. 'Why did we stare so, so hard at the little fishes in my room? What were we searching for? I hope that we will find it soon.' I turn up the volume and almost press my ear against the loudspeaker. Laren's voice is nearly a whisper. But not for long because she suddenly starts to screech 'Oh yeah, yeah, yeah! Oh yeah!' so loudly that it momentarily makes my ear go numb.

'Dear God!' I think. 'Are those lyrics about me? About us? They must be.' And then the phone rings and I leap into the air.

The call turns out to be for Mira. A man is phoning to say he has her loom. 'Her loom?' I repeat.

'Yes, her loom,' he agrees. 'She can collect it on Tuesday.'

As I hang up I wonder how on earth my life has come to be this perplexing. I dearly wish I had a loom myself to help weave all its strange strands together.

The first day of James's not phoning has a certain intensity. The ways I imagine him responding to my message vary wildly. At one moment he is saying to himself: 'Alice Evans. Who on earth is Alice Evans? The name does ring a slight bell.' At others his face is radiant with joy – but slightly troubled too. At such moments I imbue him with my own fears and hopes regarding intimacy. 'Dear, darling Alice Evans,' he's thinking. 'Dare I phone her? Dare I tell her how I really feel? After all, I do live in West Cork and long-distance relationships can be so complicated.'

Ambivalence is, I suppose, what I'm mainly feeling. Ambivalence about men in general. If James Mitchel does phone I suddenly fear I may exclaim, 'How dare you! How dare you pester me like this when I'm seriously considering a proposal of marriage!' – though I would, of course, just be addressing my own longings.

By Sunday evening I'm a little less leery of the phone, though as I study it I realize that, in a subtle way, it seems to have already acquired some of the characteristics of James Mitchel himself. For instance, there's something almost smug about its silences now – as if it knows something that I don't. Whether he called while I was out buying a Chinese take-away. Whether he's the kind of man who tries to phone once and then gives up, or waits for a while and then dials again and again until he gets an answer. For a wild moment I wonder if I should plunge it ruthlessly into a bowl of cold water.

As Sunday evening dawns, hope has been replaced by a dull resignation. I am reminded of the country song that goes, 'If nobody calls, it's me.' Listening to James's silences while I try to paint is, frankly, boring. I finally reach a point when, if he does call, I'd be tempted to say, 'I've lost interest in you now. Please go away.'

I'm enormously relieved when Mira returns, tanned from her weekend on the waterways. After I've made her a mug of tea I tell her, somewhat shamefacedly, what I've done.

She's surprisingly non-judgemental. 'At least it's something real,' she comments. She says women like me do things like that sometimes and I shouldn't feel too bashful about it. She says she'll field phone calls for me so at least I'll know who they are from.

Now a week has passed and Mira and I are blissfully listening to good old Colin Derling going on about organic manure on Gardeners' Questions. We rather like the idea of maturing into the kind of women who contact Gardeners' Questions with simple dilemmas. Mira keeps telling me I should make my life more simple. 'Simplify. Simplify.' That's what she says, though she often doesn't seem to follow this advice herself.

'How do you simplify things, Mira?' I ask her anxiously. 'It sounds like a rather complicated thing to do.'

'You have to remember what you've learned. What you know,' she says. 'We all know what we need – deep down.'

I try to smile gratefully at this insight, even though I don't feel like smiling at all. I don't feel like smiling because I don't think I know what I need deep down any more. I think my needs have got so mixed up with my wants and fears and hopes that they're all jumping round inside me in a panic, like stray cats stuck somewhere far too small. They're demanding all kinds of fish heads to distract them: love. Painting. Celibacy. Television. Emigration. Marriage. Snickers Bars. Oh, well, at least James Mitchel kept them entertained for a short while.

But how I long for a serene, sensible, uncomplicated life. I really do.

Chapter 18

I ALMOST LOST MY moustache a moment ago. It happened when we all had to cower after the shots rang out. It was most interesting.

I tried to cower with great feeling. I tried to reel in shock and then I covered my mouth – I gave a little screech and widened my eyes in terror too. I was trying to stand out in a small way, but I don't think they noticed. There are just too many of us and there's an awful lot of smoke. They're blowing the smoke at us from some kind of machine. It doesn't smell too bad – in fact there's a tiny whiff of juniper aromatherapy oil about it.

So this is what being an extra on a film is like. I must say it's a wonderful change from writing about sex, though I rather wish I didn't have to be a peasant. I'd hoped I'd be one of the women who are wearing those nice long dresses with lace collars. The thing is, I arrived a bit late and they had enough women by then. So they put me in this scratchy ancient tweed suit with muck all over the knees. They put a bit of muck on my hands and face too. Not real muck – but it looks like it. Then they stuck my hair under a big tattered old hat and gave me a stick. The moustache came later. A young, driven-looking woman raced up to me and shoved it on.

There seems to be an awful lot of waiting around with filming – so I suppose in some ways it's not that unlike real life. We wait around for something interesting to happen and don't quite understand the pauses. We get rather bored and start grumbling about wanting cups of tea and things like that. Little posses are sent off to find a tea urn, which is eventually located. As we drink our tea we wonder what there'll be for lunch and ask if anyone has seen the film's big stars, Mel Nichols and Julia Robbins. I saw Mel Nichols just now actually. He'd found a quiet corner and was saying his lines into his polystyrene cup. He was picking at it a bit too – the way one can with cups like that. I liked seeing him picking at his cup. It was a special moment.

I think we're supposed to cower again soon. The cowering we did earlier was just a rehearsal apparently. 'Life is not a rehearsal' – Sarah's got that on a bit of sticky yellow paper by her desk. I'm so glad she sent me on this assignment. It's almost made me forget that James Mitchel hasn't returned my phone call, and probably never will. Even Eamon's proposal seems like a distant dilemma. Maybe if I can cower with enough conviction a Hollywood producer will spot me and whisk me off to Beverly Hills.

I must try to get some quotes from Clara, the woman who seems to be in charge of us extras. She's so busy; I haven't seen her stand still all morning. She's rushing around this set like a blue-arsed fly with a walkie-talkie. She's taking care of small but crucial details, such as making sure we aren't holding coke cans during filming.

We're to take off spectacles and brooches and earrings and cover any glinting buttons too. The camera picks up these things, apparently.

Today's filming is being done in a small country village. They're using real buildings only they've altered the exteriors to make them look the right period. They've done a brilliant job. You really would think you'd stepped back in time. The film is set in Ireland during the early part of this century. It's a love story, but there are skirmishes in it too. In fact, I'm waiting to take part in one of the skirmishes right now. It happens when a man is addressing an outdoor meeting about Irish freedom. Shots ring out and the crowd – that's me and about four hundred others – cower for a moment but don't run away. I myself would have run away. I would have scuttled into the local bar before you could say 'Steven Spielberg' – but this moustache seems to have changed my character enormously. Maybe I should keep it.

The film's love story starts straight after this outdoor meeting. One of the men in the crowd goes into the local hotel and meets a mysterious and very beautiful woman who's taking refuge in an alcove off the reception area. They fall in love immediately – which, of course, is how it should be done. But after this happens the handsome man discovers that the woman's father is a high-ranking officer in the British Army. This is a right pain in the arse because the handsome man is devoted to the Irish cause. Love does win out in the end, apparently, but not before they have caused themselves, and piles of other people, a considerable amount of heartache. Frankly, I wonder if they wouldn't have been better off saying 'so long' when things got so complicated – but, of course, there wouldn't be a film then, would there? I have a tendency to back away from difficult situations, but maybe you have to face them if you want your life to have some glory.

Goodness – is that Elsie over there? Liam's girlfriend. She's got a lovely velvet dress on and loads of make-up. Her hair looks as if it's been styled too. Maybe she's one of the extras they're using in a close-up. They have to look just right. She's with a man in a smart brown suit. She's eating an ice-cream, and he's sharing it. He's taking long suggestive licks from her cornetto. They seem to know each other very well. Goodness, he's nibbling her ear! He's brushing a stray hair from her face, and now they're kissing! Perhaps it's a rehearsal. No. I doubt it very much. It seems entirely authentic. Poor Liam. She's cheating on him. But then, of course, he cheated on her too. They obviously deserve each other.

The director is shouting into his megaphone again. He says he wants us to look scared when the shots ring out. We weren't looking frightened enough before apparently. I'm sure I was. I'm good at being frightened. I'm not that great at uncertainty, and there's a lot of it about.

What on earth can be holding things up? The director told us we were to look frightened and then he went off somewhere. People are starting to slouch around again and are looking for somewhere to sit. I simply must have a pee. I can't wait any longer. I'll dash into that pub and be back in a second.

Oh darn – there's a queue. Still, they can't have started filming yet. The crew all looked very engrossed in obscure matters a moment ago and Mel Nichols wasn't even on the set. I better check my moustache is on right. Little details like this do matter. The camera could just turn in my direction. Some people must get singled out – even in a crowd.

But as I sit down on the toilet seat I hear a loud English voice shout 'Action' and I know my moustache and I are not going to be part of this Hollywood epic. I've missed it. Missed the final 'take'. The one they must be using because now, as I pull up my scratchy tweed pants I hear the director shouting through his megaphone: 'Perfect. Thank you, ladies and gentlemen.'

I can't believe it. It's just not fair. I cowered more convincingly than any of the others. If only they'd waited for a moment I would have been back in time. But life doesn't wait for you, does it? That's what I've been learning lately. If you straggle too much you miss things.

I've missed piles of things. It's quite possible that I'm even going to miss love – the thing I want most of all. Because life isn't like romantic movies. If I was Julia Robbins I probably wouldn't even see Mel Nichols when he walks into the hotel where they're supposed to meet. I'd probably be buttering a scone or something.

I push my way through the crowd in the pub, my eyes misting. Once I get outside I stand, blinking in the sudden sunlight, wondering what to do. I suppose I should go home. I'm good at that. But I have to hand this scratchy suit and other stuff back to wardrobe first. I'm so disappointed. My big day on a big film is all over and I'm not even in the thing. I'll just have to face the fact that I'm not a Hollywood kind of person. I live a small life, and must adjust my dreams accordingly. There is a certain comfort in resignation, not just about this but other things too. Some of them swim in front of me now, almost taunting me for my stupidity: James Mitchel will never ever phone me. Beautiful letters do not arrive in my post. There is no Wonderful Man out there waiting to meet me. I will spend most of my honeymoon learning how to play golf.

I feel like throwing myself, wailing, to the ground, but I know I must practise stoicism. Most people 'live lives of quiet desperation' – that's what Thoreau said. It's true. I see Clara. She's studying some notes on her clipboard. She looks very busy. Too busy to be interrupted by the likes of me. I can ring her for those quotes if necessary. I walk humbly by her, my resignation less scratchy now. Less painful. I'll go home and give the herbaceous border a good weeding. Yes, that would be a sensible thing to do.

Then, just as I've almost reached wardrobe, I hear Clara calling, 'You. You there. Come here for a 'moment.' I turn around and see she's pointing at me. I go back to her. What on earth can she want?

'You missed the last scene, didn't you?' she says, looking at me sternly. 'I saw you coming out of the pub. What were you doing in there?'

'I went to the ladies.'

'Couldn't you have waited?'

'Not really. I must have drunk about five cups of tea.'

'Well, go easy on the tea for goodness sake,' Clara smiles tolerantly. 'We can't have you running off like that the next time.'

'What?'

'We could use you in some of the next scenes since you weren't in the last one.'

I feel a sudden jolt as life does one of its abrupt gear-changes. 'What did you say?' I peer at Clara as though at a very confusing script.

'We can use you in some other scenes, but you'll have to hurry.'

'Hurry. Hurry where?' This sudden transition from resignation to elation requires a kind of emotional athleticism I am not in training for. I couldn't bear to be caught straggling again.

'Where do I have to go? Where do they need me?' I'm scouring the set for the director and crew.

'In the hotel. But you'll have to smarten up first. I'll bring you to wardrobe.' Clara strides off and I scurry after her. In fact, at one point I'm in front of her, and she has to tell me to slow down.

Though I'm excited, I'm surprised to find my feelings about this sudden turn of events are not entirely clear cut. My recent resignation had felt rather seductive in its certainty. Though it was sad, it did seem to offer some kind of lacklustre liberation. A severing of dreams. And now hope was back on the line again like an inconsistent lover – offering no certainties, just its sweetness. And no excuses as to why it took so long to return my many, many urgent calls. But, as I change into one of the long dresses with lace collars I so longed for earlier, I forget these variegated ruminations. The colour of the day is suddenly bright and beckoning, making hesitation not only stupid…but impossible.

There are only ten extras in this bit and we're pretending to have afternoon tea. It's so much nicer than being a peasant. I've got some make-up on and my hair has been put up in a bun. I can't believe it! I'm part of the big scene in the hotel where Mel and Julia meet!

After the usual waiting around we get some instructions. 'We need a reaction shot,' says the director, then he explains that this involves us extras looking towards a window as the shots ring out outside. We're to look shocked, even though the shots don't really ring out because, of course, that happened earlier. We just have to pretend they do. I'm so excited. As he shouts 'Action!' I give a little gasp and widen my eyes. I clatter my teacup down on the table and put my hand to my face.

'What's your name?' the director asks when we've done some rehearsals.

'Alice Evans,' I tell him eagerly. It's happened! He's singled me out. Maybe I'm going to have to stand up and shout 'Help!' or something. I'd be good at that.

'Alice,' he smiles at me patiently. 'You can leave the teacup on the table. And clutch your bag instead of putting your hand to your face. It won't look natural if it's overdone.'

'But I wasn't overdoing it!' I want to protest. Like all the best actresses I have given my 'character' some thought. I have to get right into things – it's my nature.

So I know, for example, that my 'character' is nervy and well-bred and called Jessica. She lives in a big house nearby and has a husband who's away a lot. She paints watercolours of local plants and plays the pianoforte. She isn't used to this kind of thing.

'OK,' I tell the director humbly, trying to keep a mutinous look from my face.

Once the 'reaction' scene is 'in the can' as we film people say, we're used as background when Mel Nichols comes in. We don't ogle at him, of course. We just chat away quietly and pick at our sandwiches. I hope to God that big sound boom over there doesn't pick up the conversation I'm having with the woman opposite me. Though she's wearing a bonnet she insists on talking about her recent trip to France via the Eurotunnel.

We're background again as Mel and Julia Robbins emerge from their first meeting in the alcove. And then, as Mel leaves the hotel and Julia stares fondly after him, four of us afternoon tea ladies are told to rise in a leisurely manner from our seats, collect our belongings, and exit the hotel too.

The first time we do this hotel exit scene I'm gripping my handbag tightly, grimly determined to look relaxed. But after we've done it over and over again it begins to feel rather ludicrous. In fact, in the final take 'Jessica' seems to have lightened up considerably and is giggling. The director doesn't seem to mind.

And that's it. This bit of filming is over. It must be because the crew is moving to another part of the set. I'm wondering if I could sneak into another scene when a woman, who looks a bit like Maggie Smith, suggests we female extras head off for a drink together. Most of us agree to this immediately, probably because we do desperately need some way of slipping back gently into ordinary life.

There's a pub with a lovely view just down the road apparently. After we've changed and I've left 'Jessica' behind with wardrobe, we walk there. Some of the women are veteran extras. They talk about being prostitutes and nuns and rabble and prim Victorian housewives.

'He stayed in his trailer with his script and dog eating wine gums,' one says of a rising star she has worked with. 'Between takes he watched cable TV.' I listen, fascinated. These are the details one Needs To Know.

Once we get to the pub someone says that there's a river nearby which is great for a summer dip. We're rather hot and sticky so, with much laughter and giggling, we decide to at least give it a look. We're feeling rather wild and worldly – like a brat pack. If Brad Pitt turned up right now, we'd probably just say 'Hi'.

We've been up since the wee small hours and now it's a very warm and golden late afternoon. The kind of afternoon that seems to belong to memory, even while it's happening. When we reach the river, having trekked across some fields, we see that it is fat and smooth, lazy and bright. It looks rather like the river Aaron and I used to play in when we were children. It meanders through the green meadows and is shaded here and there by trees. Cows look up curiously at us as we walk by them, looking for the special spot one of us knows.

We're there. It's beautiful. The river is wider here, almost a little lake. There's some yellow sand at the edge. It looks like a tiny beach. There is the sound of bees and birds and the occasional glint of a dragonfly. The plop of a fish rising. I decide I'll have a sedate little paddle. Then someone takes off their clothes leaving on their bra and pants, and the rest of us do too.

Everything seems so still, even in the midst of all this movement – of people splashing and shouting 'Oh, my God – it's cold.' Yes, it is cold. Very cold. I decide to go back to the comfort of the grassy bank, but instead find myself splashing forwards, letting the river lift me. Then I shout and squeal and dig my toes deep into the sand. I sound as feckless and carefree as Elsie and Liam did when they were chasing each other with that garden hose. I am part of this playfulness. I am not just listening to it from the other side of a wall.

When we emerge from the river we take off our sopping undies. As we dry ourselves with our clothes we chatter about uncomplicated things. We name our favourite actors and actresses, though we can hardly name each other. It doesn't matter. At times like this I know very few things do. We may never meet each other again. But we won't forget this late afternoon, almost evening now. It bubbled up from somewhere inside us. It took us to this river. And now it's time to leave. To move back towards the village and the pub. As we walk we wonder if anyone saw us in our undies, even though we were shaded by some trees. Somehow we don't mind if they did. We don't mind at all. Especially Mel Nichols.

Now I'm sitting outside the pub on a wooden bench. I have a glass of wine in my hand and am staring gratefully at the distant hills. All this afternoon I've been 'living in the moment' as my self-help books suggest. I've been part of a team. It felt so nice.

People sometimes compare working on a film to being part of a large family, and now I see why. There's an intimacy about it. Though the practicalities of filming are vast and complicated, at least for a little while a lot of people are dreaming the same dream. Playing make-believe. Dressing up. The lady from wardrobe even allowed me to keep my moustache. I have it in my pocket.

Sitting here with a glass of wine in my hand, I can understand why actors get hooked on being other people. There's a liberation to it. A letting go. We have so many different sides to us. Even when I'm sitting dourly at my desk there must be a part of me that's waiting to squeal and shout playfully. That's waiting to dig her toes deep into the sand and then plunge forwards – letting the river lift her. I think this is the part of me that doesn't want to marry Eamon. She has been telling me this most urgently. She has been whispering it for some time.

'Wait for love, Alice,' she says to me.

'That's what I've been doing,' I reply rather impatiently. 'I've waited and waited, and now I'm getting tired of it.'

'Ah, but what kind of love have you been waiting for, Alice?' she persists. 'Is it the one you need?'

'Oh, please don't bring up semantics,' I scold. 'Life's quite complicated enough as it is.'

But life doesn't seem so complicated now as I sit outside this pub. I'm not longing to be somewhere else, as I so often am. I am not wishing anything was different. The warmth of the day is still within me. I don't seem to have just left 'Jessica' back at wardrobe, I seem to have left the 'Alice' I've been living with lately too. She'll probably return with all her conundrums when I get home, but this Alice doesn't care. This Alice is much more simple.

And what's more she hasn't any knickers on.

Chapter 19

I REALLY ENJOYED WRITING that article about being an extra. It was such fun. We've got some lovely photographs to go with it. The film publicity people have sent them on.

I'm so looking forward to seeing the film when it's finished. I'll bring a posse of friends to the cinema and I'll sit on the edge of my seat waiting for the hotel scene. 'That's me!' I'll whisper, and they'll scour the screen dutifully. I hope they show the bit where I clutched my bag when the shots rang out. I winced and gasped a bit too. It was done with considerable feeling.

'Did you get Mel Nichols's autograph for me?' Annie is now asking eagerly. We're sitting in my garden. It's a sunny Sunday afternoon.

'No, I'm afraid I didn't,' I sigh, realizing that Annie would have got his autograph if she'd been on that film set. She would have marched right up to him. She's so much more daring than I am. 'He was very busy,' I explain. 'But I did get quite close to him at one point and watched him for a while.'

'What was he doing?' she asks excitedly. She's a big fan of his.

'He was…mmmm… he was picking at his polystyrene cup.'

'Oh.' She doesn't seem too impressed. Then she adds, 'Come on, come on, tell me all about the scenes you were in, Alice. They sound really romantic'.

'Yes, they were,' I agree happily, thinking of how Mel had stared deep into Julia Robbins's eyes. I'd just got a quick glance at them because I was supposed to be chatting to the woman in a bonnet. But one glance was enough.

After Annie has quizzed me about Mel and Julia for at least half an hour, I tell her about my swim in the river. 'Ah, yes, that sounds like the old Alice,' she smiles.

'What do you mean?' I give her a quick, almost fearful glance.

'Oh – oh nothing. It sounds fun, that's all,' she replies, suddenly bashful. It's as if she's said something she hadn't meant to say. Something she's been thinking for some time. Friends do that sometimes. They let something slip and you realize they've formed some opinion about you that they haven't shared. They may allude to it indirectly, but they don't want to be too blunt. Maybe they sense you're not ready to hear it, but it tends to leak out anyway.

I don't press her for an explanation about the 'old Alice' she's referred to. I know what she means. She has known me for so long she can remember happier, carefree times. Younger days when swimming in my undies wasn't that uncommon. Days when she and I laughed wildly as Aaron chased us with a frog he'd caught. We weren't even frightened of frogs, we just liked the squealing. Afterwards we'd let the frog go. We'd watch it hopping away and Annie would say, 'Maybe we should have kissed it.' But, like her, I don't want to talk about all that now.

'Yes, swimming in that river was fun,' I agree. 'Afterwards, when we had a drink outside a pub, I didn't even have any knickers on.'

'Good for you!' she chuckles approvingly. 'When you meet your Mr Wonderful you must do that again. Whisper to him that you're not wearing any knickers when you're in a restaurant. He won't want dessert, I can tell you. It will drive him wild.'

'Really,' I say. Annie has many useful tips regarding seduction. 'Maybe I should try it with Eamon.'

She doesn't reply.

After Annie has gone I decide to pay Mrs Peabody a quick visit. I must say I'm curious to see how Cyril and his new partner Dora are getting on. I rather hope they've found true love like Mel and Julia. But, as soon as I go into Mrs Peabody's sitting-room and look into their cage, it is rather clear they haven't.

Cyril is staying very stubbornly in a corner. He seems to be taking no interest whatsoever in his new partner.

'He's just shy,' Mrs Peabody explains. 'He's not used to company you see, dear. Just give him time.'

What Mrs Peabody can't discern because of her poor eyesight is that Cyril is not only 'shy', he is also darting frequent hostile looks in Dora's direction. He looks like he'd like to eat her. Literally.

'Maybe his years alone have made him too fussy,' I comment, aware that this is something that has often been said of myself. 'Maybe he's holding out for Pamela Anderson.' As I say this a soft 'feck' emanates from Dora and Mrs Peabody goes over to her.

'Yes, p e c k – peck – dear,' she says carefully. 'You just need to get that first letter right.' Then she turns to me. 'Let's have a little sherry, shall we?' She's grown rather partial to sherry recently, and I must say I'm quite fond of it myself.

'OK,' I agree swiftly. She fetches the bottle and I get the glasses. As we sit, sipping our Harvey's Bristol Cream, I reflect that I, and Mrs Peabody, and even Mira and Eamon seem to be drinking rather more than we used to. Eamon really dug into the alcohol on our recent

161

dinner date, and Mira has become very keen on red wine. She's taken to reading up about it in the Sunday newspapers and says if you're prepared to spend 'just that little bit extra' you can get surprisingly good vintages. We have it with dinner almost every evening now. We sort of waddle into the sitting-room afterwards and slump contentedly on to armchairs. I think we're going to have to buy a bit more Aqua Libra. I really don't want us to turn into the kind of people who look at their watches and say, 'Ah, it's 11 a.m. Time for a little tipple before lunch.' That kind of thing can happen quite easily and I'm beginning to understand why. Drink takes the edge off one's worries. It makes things seem more simple. Mellow. It hides things from you. Am I hiding something from myself? No, of course not. It's just a habit. That's all it is.

'Liam is such a nice young man, isn't he?' Mrs Peabody suddenly announces as I struggle to open a packet of peanuts she has offered me.

'Mmmm – well – he's certainly...' I pause. What is he 'certainly'? Irritating? Yes, that is one word I would use to describe him.

'He was over here just now helping me move the garden seat,' Mrs Peabody continues. 'He just pops by like that sometimes. He's very obliging.'

'That's nice,' I say, wishing she'd shut up about him.

'He was telling me that he was born in Ireland but his parents emigrated to America when he was four. He was brought up in New York and returned here in his late teens.'

'Oh, how interesting,' I comment politely, though I don't find it interesting at all. I am staring at Cyril and Dora. I think Dora is more interested in Cyril than he is in her. She looks at him quickly, hopefully sometimes, but he doesn't respond. For some reason this reminds me of James Mitchel. Oh, bugger it anyway, why did I phone him?

'Liam's a primary school teacher,' Mrs Peabody is now telling me. 'He works in the inner city. I think he finds it a bit sad sometimes.'

'Why?'

'Well, most of the kids he teaches come from poor backgrounds. He wishes things were easier for them. He says they're lovely now, but he doesn't know how they'll turn out later. There's just so much he can do for them.'

'Oh, I see.' I must say I'm a bit surprised to hear that Liam is a teacher. That puts him in a slightly different light. He seems to have a social conscience too, but he and Elsie don't seem to have much of a conscience about each other. I wonder if I should tell Mrs Peabody this, but I decide not to. Her friendship with him is obviously important to her. She probably sits there and tells him about me. I hope to goodness she doesn't go into too much detail.

'Well, Mrs Peabody, I suppose I'd better go,' I say, after I've emptied my glass for the fourth time. She tends to fill it up when you're not looking. Bits of it have spilt – her aim isn't as accurate as it used to be. I give the table a quick rub with my paper hankie and help her bring the bottle and glasses back into the kitchen. Then I waddle back to the cottage. Why on earth did I drink all that sherry? I should have held on to my glass – that way she couldn't have got at it.

As soon as I reach the kitchen I make myself a strong cup of Gold Blend coffee. I think I only buy that brand because of the romantic ads for it, which of course is quite ridiculous. Men don't seek you out in that manner. They don't track you down just because you have their preferred blend of dry roasted coffee beans. Life would be so much easier if they did, but they don't. My goodness, we humans are so impressionable. Dear old Mrs Peabody gave everyone 'Ferrero Rocher' chocolates last Christmas because the ads convinced her they were the 'Sign of Good Taste'.

As I drink my coffee I re-read a letter from Eamon. It arrived on Friday and contained an architectural sketch. Eamon has decided that if we do marry he will build me an artist's studio. It will be at the back of his house and the designs for it look wonderful. He's obviously given it a lot of thought. I look at the sketch again, trying to get excited about it – I've always wanted a studio of my own – but I find myself yawning instead. It must be all that alcohol. Perhaps I should eat a biscuit.

As I reach into the cupboard for the chocolate digestives I look at Tarquin. He's dozing on his cushion. Every so often he stretches his paws luxuriously and gives a little yawn. He knows a lot about contentment. I'd better learn something about it too. For the cheery, carefree, playful Alice who swam in that river seems very far away suddenly. Was it reading Eamon's letter that suddenly changed my mood? No, of course it wasn't. I'm thrilled about that studio. Delighted. It shows what a really nice man Eamon is. I bet James Mitchel wouldn't build a special studio for me. No – no – I mustn't think about James Mitchel now. If I'm not careful I'll slip into my Cyril mode.

I turn on the radio, desperate for distraction. I'm hoping for something chatty and cultural but Cyndi Lauper singing 'Girls Just Wanna Have Fun' blasts around the room instead. I'm about to turn the dial to another station when I decide not to. At least it's cheery. I turn down the volume and tap my fingers to the beat.

'Girls Just Wanna Have Fun tum tum tee tum' I find myself humming as I rise and reach for a J-cloth. The counter tops are in need of a good wipe. Tarquin likes sitting on them, even though I scold him about it. His paw marks are clearly visible. I squirt some Mr Proper at them and start to scrub, and as I do so I find myself tapping my feet and jiggling around a bit. It's like there's a dance inside me that's itching to get out. Yes, this is more like the 'old Alice' Annie spoke of. She was obviously there all the time. She was just waiting for her cue. I feel honky and funky suddenly. I feel like a woman in an open-topped convertible cruising along a palm-fringed highway on MTV. As I begin to gyrate to the music, Tarquin stares at me warily. He has studied me long enough to know these movements are not connected with Whiskas.

This is great. How long is it since I danced alone like this? I see the moustache I wore on the film lying on a shelf and grab it. Should I put it on? Yes, why not! Just for a bit of fun. 'Men always make passes at girls with moustaches,' I sing as I look out at the garden happily. Even the nasturtiums seem to be dancing in the light summer breeze. I twirl the J-cloth dramatically in the air above and shout 'Ye ha!' and then I realize something… I realize Liam is watching me. I halt in mid-twirl. I stand very still and watch him back.

Just for a moment it seems as though the world has stopped turning. As though there is only us, staring at each other, over the boundary wall.

'The little bollocks,' I mutter to myself. 'The cheek of him, watching me like that.' I duck and cower beside my distressed-pine table. How long has he been standing there? Oh, no, and I'm wearing the moustache too! The humiliation of it! Tarquin looks at me sympathetically.

165

Then he heads towards his food bowl and gives me a hopeful look.

'Can't you ever get off the subject of food!' I reprimand him irritatedly. 'You're just like James Mitchel and ceramics.'

After some minutes it occurs to me that I cannot spend the rest of the afternoon sitting on the floor by the cooker. It's quite ridiculous. I rise and peer gingerly up at Liam's window. Oh, thank goodness, he's gone. I must put up those net curtains soon. I simply cannot have Liam snooping on me like this.

As I get on with my cleaning I feel a bit self-conscious. It is just possible that Liam is now peering out at me secretively – though this is highly unlikely of course. Even so I seem to feel the need to compensate for my prior wantonness. I try to summon the serene poise of, say, Nigella Lawson, as I scrub and polish and dust. If there was a cake in the room I'd definitely decorate it.

Oh, no, the phone is ringing! Mira must get it. Is she in her bedroom? I really hope she is. 'Mira – phone!' I screech. I couldn't talk to James now, even though I know he'll never phone me. I know this with great certainty, and yet every time I reach for the receiver I'm sure it's him. I even practise my lines before I pick it up. I can now say 'Hello, James' in four different ways, and I'm still not sure which is the right one.

'Mira!' I shout. 'Mira – the phone!' Oh good, she's heard me. She's answering it. She's saying, 'Yes, Alice is here.' On hearing this I dart into the sitting-room. I grab a piece of paper and scribble on it fast. The note says, 'If it's James Mitchel say I'll phone him back.' I thrust it under her nose. Mira just glances at it and then hands the phone to me.

'Who is it?' I hiss. We have been through this little drama many times recently and I think Mira's getting a bit tired of it.

'It's someone you'll want to speak to,' she replies enigmatically, then she goes out the front door in her huge furry slippers. She must be going to the corner shop. I stare after her fearfully. Surely she would have told me if James himself was on the line. Yes, I'm sure she would, and yet a small doubt lingers. I pick up the phone and say 'Hello' in the singsong tones of a hotel receptionist.

'Hello, Alice!' a male voice greets me cheerily. Oh, thank goodness! It's Matt. 'Alice, I have a small proposal for you.'

'What kind of proposal?' I enquire, somewhat edgily.

'Oh, not the kind of one you've had already,' he laughs. 'This one's entirely different. In fact you might even find it fun.'

Chapter 20

I'M NOT FINDING IT fun actually – this 'Personal Exploration' day that Matt has enrolled us in. I know he meant it kindly. I know he thinks it might help me clarify my feelings about Eamon's proposal, but I'm simply not in the mood for it. I've done quite a number of these workshops in the past and Matt has too. Though they can be enlightening they also seem to involve eating rather a lot of lentils and sitting around trying to be authentic.

'Have you ever felt you are living someone else's life?' That's what the leaflet about this day said. 'Have you ever felt submerged in other people's expectations? That someone else is handing you a script that is not your own? Do you fear being true to your own passion? Then this workshop is for you. Please bring a light blanket for the meditation sessions.'

This 'Personal Exploration' day is being held in a rather nice country house. It's quite small but full of interesting pictures and wall hangings. I wish I'd had more time to explore it before we all had to come into this big room. We're sitting on big cushions now. We've already done breathing exercises and a bit of yoga. We've also moved around for a while to music to loosen us up and held hands in a circle. Now we're back on our cushions again and the workshop leader, Samantha, a woman with henna-dyed hair and numerous silver bracelets, is addressing us.

'A lot of people feel that they took some wrong turnings in their lives,' she says soothingly. 'But we need to accept where we are right now. Appreciate it and see what it can teach us. In the end all roads merge into one.

Don't worry too much about your destination, because your journey is part of it.'

'So wise,' Matt murmurs in my ear.

'Yes,' I agree as I shift uncomfortably. My cushion is against the edge of a radiator. I decide to move it and hope the woman in the blue kaftan doesn't think I'm encroaching on her territory. She has her eyes closed and doesn't even notice.

'I'd like to ask you why you've come here,' Samantha continues with studied serenity. 'People can have very different expectations of days like this so I'd like to know what it means for you.' She looks at a woman called Julie. The answers are obviously going to be in a clockwise direction.

'I've come here because my children have grown up and left home and my husband's out a lot,' Julie says sadly. She's wearing a pink tracksuit. 'Most of my friends have jobs and I feel at a loose end. I need a purpose again.'

'Ah yes – the empty-nest syndrome.' Samantha looks at her sympathetically.

'I'm mainly here because I'm thinking of becoming a graphic designer,' a man called Pete then reveals. 'I work in a department store at the moment but it's not my thing.'

Samantha smiles unconditionally at him and then looks at Matt. He's mainly here because of me. I wonder what excuse he'll give for his attendance. I start to pull at the tassel of a cushion.

'I'm here because I'm gay,' Matt announces bravely. 'I find it hard to deal with some people's prejudices and I thought that a day like this might be – mmmm – empowering.'

Samantha positively beams at him. 'Empowering,' she repeats happily. 'Yes, Matt, that is an important word. We'll be using it quite a lot today.'

Silence. Dear God, they're waiting for me to speak. Why am I on this 'Personal Exploration' day? Should I tell the truth and admit that Matt pushed me into it. No. It would sound so wimpish. What about telling them about James Mitchel and Eamon? No. Too personal. My painting – that's it.

'I – I'd like to do more painting,' I say. 'I don't have as much time for it as I'd like and I miss it.' There. That sounded nice and succinct.

'And what are you working at now, Alice?' Samantha asks.

'I'm a journalist.' As I say this I am aware that a slight frisson has gone around the room. 'But I'm not here to write an article about this workshop,' I add quickly. 'Honestly I'm not. It's a personal thing.'

'Of course it is,' Samantha agrees calmly, but her gaze does linger on me cautiously for a moment before she smiles at the woman in the blue kaftan.

After everyone has spoken Samantha announces that she's been looking for some common threads amongst our answers, and one of them appears to be 'passion'. I'm not quite sure how she arrived at this conclusion. Maybe it has something to do with the fact that she's written a book called *Passion: Honouring the Flame Within*. A heap of copies were on a table in the hallway. The back of the jacket claims that it can 'Change Your Life'. So many things are supposed to change your life these days. There seems to be a deep seam of unrest running through the first part of the twenty-first century.

'I want to share something from Kahlil Gibran with you before we break for tea,' Samantha says. Everyone looks more chirpy as she mentions 'tea'. There is a definite shift in mood. Samantha picks up a small book, which I see is entitled *The Prophet* and which I have in my own bookcase. I haven't read it since I was in my twenties. She explains that she wants to read out an extract from the section on reason and passion.

'Your soul is sometimes a battlefield, upon which your reason and your judgement wage war against your passion and your appetite.

'Would that I could be the peacemaker in your soul, that I might turn the discord and the rivalry of your elements into oneness and melody.

'But how shall I, unless you yourselves be also the peacemakers, nay, the lovers of all your elements?

'...Therefore let your soul exalt your reason to the height of passion, that it may sing;

'And let it direct your passion with reason, that your passion may live through its own daily resurrection, and like the phoenix rise above its own ashes.'

'Lovely,' murmurs Matt.

'Absolutely,' I agree, wishing I wasn't quite so aware of the clinking of cups in the dining area. That last quote was really nice. Suddenly everyone's jumping up from their cushions and heading eagerly out of the room. I must follow them, I don't want to be caught straggling. 'Just fifteen minutes,' Samantha calls loudly after us. 'I'd like us to all be back here at 11.30.' No one looks round. A nice cuppa is our passion at this precise moment. That and an oatmeal cookie and a visit to the loo.

In the dining area I opt for the real tea – not the herbal variety – and grab a wad of biscuits. I munch them quietly. One of the nice things about this kind of gathering is that one is not impelled to talk. People respect your 'space' and that kind of thing. I look over at

Matt. Good, he's chatting with a nice young man in a yellow pullover. I decide to drift out of the room with my big indigo mug and do a bit of exploring. I open a stripped-pine wooden door and find myself in what must be the library. There are shelves and shelves of books and a dog, who is snoozing on a sofa. He's an English sheepdog. Just like the one Paul McCartney used to have. I love big dogs like that. Maybe if I marry Eamon I could keep one. I think it would be nice to have some animals around the place, and his house is certainly large enough to accommodate them. His rooms can seem very silent sometimes, as though they've absorbed some of his own tendencies. Yes, I'd definitely need a dog. I hope Tarquin might be persuaded to move in too.

'Hello, doggy,' I say to the English sheepdog. 'What's your name?' He looks up at me patiently, clearly used to this kind of pointless questioning. I look round the room.

The colours they've used are similar to the sitting-room in my cottage. How fond I am of my little cottage. As I think this I sit down on the sofa sorrowfully.

I'm beginning to realize that I'll really miss my cottage and garden if I marry Eamon. They're like old friends. I've known them for so long now. There's a cosy feel to my small, slightly shabby little home which Eamon's just doesn't have. I've even wondered if I should suggest that we stay there – but it wouldn't be practical. If we have children we'd need the extra space. His house is in an extremely desirable area. It has a Jacuzzi and the garden is large and a horticulturalist's dream. There's even a view of Dublin Bay from the front bedroom. It's a wonderful house really. I simply must try to get more enthusiastic about it. I could add my own little touches. Yes, of course I could. Even though Eamon said he's had a lot of it freshly decorated there must be some additions I could make. And, of course, there's the artist's studio he plans to build for me. That would be all my own.

I start to pat the sheepdog absentmindedly. Maybe Samantha is right. Maybe 'passion' is an issue for a lot of us at this workshop. After all 'reason' is the reason why I'm drawn to marrying Eamon. And if I do this I'll simply have to find an outlet for the passionate side of me. The side that James Mitchel has made me so uncomfortably aware of.

I look up at a large painting of a lavender-covered field which is hanging above the fireplace. Painting – yes, maybe that could be the answer. I could paint wild, passionate, wanton pictures in my wonderful studio. I'd enjoy that. It would be fun. After having painted them frenziedly it might even be quite soothing to wander into the sitting-room and find Eamon watching golf on the television.

Golf...no, I mustn't think about the golfing honeymoon Eamon has suggested just now. It's so far from the passionate honeymoon I've often dreamed of that I can't bear to think of it. I rise and start to mooch around, looking at the book titles. Then I notice a crumpled paperback copy of *The Naked Ape* wedged against the wall. I haven't seen that book since I was eleven. Annie and I read it together. It fascinated us. It was the first book that offered us any explanation for sexual passion. Passion, there I've used that word again. There seems to be a lot of it around today.

I take the book down from the shelf and look at it. It had seemed so bold and brazen with its naked cover when I was eleven. It's awakening all kinds of memories. Happier days when sex was something deeply mysterious. 'See this book, dog,' I say. 'It's pretty saucy stuff. It's deeply giggly.'

The sheepdog just sighs contentedly and stretches.

'My friend, Annie, and I used to read this book,' I explain. 'We thought it was incredibly naughty.'

The dog scratches his ear.

I and *The Naked Ape* and my cup of tea head for an overstuffed armchair. 'Maybe I'll just have a little browse through it,' I think, but I don't. I'm remembering the first time I looked at its pages. I'm remembering how daring I'd felt. How furtive...I'm in Annie's attic. We've got torches. We feel like bandits. We're crouching over the book that is currently on my lap and giggling...

No. No, I mustn't start daydreaming now. I must go back to the workshop. It's probably already started.

I'm late again like the White Rabbit. I scurry out of the room.

'Ah, there you are, Alice, I was wondering what had happened to you,' Samantha says serenely as I rejoin the workshop and head for my big cushion. 'We were just discussing the importance of the "inner child".'

'Oh, OK,' I smile at her warily. Then I add, 'That sounds interesting,' because I don't want to appear uncooperative.

'In fact we've just started a little exercise, Alice,' Samantha continues. 'I want you to remember a time in your childhood when you felt really carefree. Really happy. I want you to write about it as though you're telling a trusted friend what happened. You'll find a notepad and pencil beside you. Take as long as you need.'

I look around. Everyone else is scribbling. Oh no – it's just like being late with an article. I pick up the pencil grimly and start to chew it. What on earth am I going to write about? Then, as Samantha smiles at me kindly I get my answer. Of course! I'll write about Annie and me and *The Naked Ape*.

'I'm remembering a spring afternoon when my friend Annie and I read a book called *The Naked Ape* in her attic,' I scribble, my pencil scurrying eagerly across the page. 'One of the advantages of knowing Annie when I was eleven was that she'd sneaked a copy of *The Naked Ape* off her parents' bookshelf and they hadn't yet missed it. We devoured the sex bits with horror and glee. They excited us, somehow, though the whole thing sounded awful. The details of enlargement and engorgement, lubrication, flushes, pelvic thrusts and vaginal contractions, not to mention sperm and other squishy stuff, all seemed deeply embarrassing. The only way to do sex, it seemed to me, was to choose someone who would kindly overlook the whole thing later. Which in my case was a boy called Aaron, even though we weren't as close as we'd been when we were younger.'

I pause and wonder if I should have stayed with the sheepdog in the library. Suddenly these recollections don't seem so 'carefree' and 'fun' after all. Maybe I should just doodle a bit and wait for the others to finish. I look at Matt. He's really getting into this exercise. Oh well, I might as well give it a go too.

'Aaron had been my best friend for years,' I scribble. 'But now that he was older there was something less soft, something wilder, about him. He was suddenly taller than me. He seemed to have spurted up overnight, like those mustard and cress seeds he used to grow. He didn't care about birds or ants like he used to. And he was nearly always too busy to go to the river. Football had become his big thing. Whenever I watched him and his friend Eric McGrath pretending they were George Best he

175

didn't even look at me. I somehow knew that having sex with Aaron just wouldn't feel right, so I suspected I'd never ever have it with anyone at all.'

I look at my notepad fearfully. Why have I described Aaron in such detail? These reminiscences are supposed to be just about Annie and me and *The Naked Ape*, only now I'm remembering them I see that they aren't. The important bit happened later, after we'd left that attic. It had very little to do with *The Naked Ape* at all.

I turn the page on my notepad, and as I do so I feel as though I am pushing a door open into my own past. To a day when my childhood was dappling into something different. A day when I could feel the severance and yet could glory in what remained.

'After we'd read the sex bits in *The Naked Ape* at least five times that spring afternoon, Annie put it back on her parents' bookshelf with amazing lack of detection,' I scribble. 'This seemed to reassure her in some way because she suddenly announced that she'd been thinking about sex and she'd decided something. She'd decided that the only thing that could possibly make people want to bump and bounce off each other so slurpily and scarily was love. And if love made you want to do something that ridiculous it must be a big and wonderful thing and she wanted it. I looked at her for a while after she'd announced this, not knowing what to say. In fact I didn't say anything. We left the subject quickly, almost carefully, as if guided by one of those beams of insight that can come at any age. Suddenly we wanted to leave all that 'stuff' until later, because we knew that's where it belonged. And so we ran off to the river to see if there was any frog spawn yet, and found Aaron and Eric McGrath there too. We paddled and giggled and when I was climbing up a muddy bank Aaron held out his hand to help me. And it felt firm and warm and right. And I looked into his face and I knew

I loved him. And I knew he loved me too. And it had nothing to do with The Naked Ape and those strange words that had so perplexed me. It was just that there, that afternoon, there was no one else I would have preferred to be with. No one else who knew me so well. And I somehow knew too that time was dappling our certainties. I knew that sometimes none of this would seem true. And then we walked for a while until we came to the narrow bridge. The one with no sides – just a plank across the water. I had crossed it so many times before. Completely unafraid.

'That was the last time I crossed that bridge without looking down. In later years I would walk further to the footbridge, not even considering it. But that day I followed Aaron's firm, steady footsteps. Revelling in our daring. And then we went to the Delaneys' shop and bought four of the marshmallow mice we liked so much. The marshmallow mice with proper tails. We were – so happy – so happy to find that we were young again. Young in the old way that we knew.

'And then Aaron and Eric drifted back to their football, and Annie and I went to her house to watch The Monkees and wish we could meet Davy Jones. And though we knew time was making things different, a small sweet strand from the past had somehow reached us like a narrow bridge over our different dreams. Reminding us that what had now nearly gone had been so very precious, and that we knew it. And it was in some deep part of us all and would always be there.

'That spring a woman in the village read my tea leaves and told me I would marry "the man next door". I was sure that she meant Aaron. By the time summer came

Annie had decided she wanted to be a jazz singer in a smoky New York night club. I didn't know what I wanted to be, but it didn't matter. The tadpoles changed into frogs and I hopped around our lawn saving them from the mower. And then, shortly after my twelfth birthday, Aaron's parents announced they were emigrating to Australia. They sold their house and shipped their furniture to the other side of the world in huge wooden crates, and I never saw Aaron again. So much was changing. They even built bungalows on the meadow by the river where we used to play. And then, that autumn, I went to boarding school and in a way my childhood ended. And on my first day home during the autumn break I discovered the Delaney sisters no longer sold pink marshmallow mice with proper tails.

I stare numbly at what I have written. Where did all these words come from? Why did I write them so urgently, so passionately? There is no comfort in them. None at all. They seem so mute and abandoned as they lie there. Lost. Bewildered. Like me.

I hear sniffling sounds and look round. The woman in the pink tracksuit is crying. Samantha does not seem too surprised.

'Some of you are probably feeling a sense of loss,' she announces, as she shifts her long slim legs so that they are curled beneath her on the cushion. 'That is quite natural. You've been remembering something precious. Something, perhaps, that you'd almost forgotten.'

'When's lunch?' the man who wants to be a graphic designer interrupts. He doesn't seem to be sharing the general mood.

'Soon, Peter,' Samantha answers firmly. 'I just want to address some issues that seem to have arisen first.'

'Could I open a window?' asks the woman in the blue kaftan. 'It's getting a bit stuffy in here.'

'Of course, Laura,' Samantha replies. 'You may need to use a chair.'

'I'll do it,' says Peter gallantly.

'To get back to what I was saying,' Samantha says. 'We all have lost parts of ourselves, and we can reclaim them. Find a way to incorporate them in the person we are now. That carefree, playful child that you were remembering is still inside you and can teach you so much.'

Though I know what Samantha is saying is important I, and a number of other people in this room, are now looking at Peter as he struggles to open the window. It seems to be jammed in some fashion. He's pushing and pushing and it's not shifting. 'Try the other one,' Samantha suggests, and he does. This time the window opens and Julie isn't crying anymore. She's been distracted. We all have. We want lunch. We can smell it. The dining-room is just down the corridor.

'Is there anyone who would like to discuss what they have written?' Samantha is now asking, rather pleadingly.

Silence. I look at her sympathetically, sharing her disappointment, even though of course I could relieve it. I could speak about Aaron, but I just don't want to.

'Can I tell you after lunch?' Julie asks tentatively.

'Yes, after lunch' – a number of people echo her suggestion. I watch them shifting restively on their cushions. Reason and passion. Poetry and prose. We are all such a mixture of things. Even the ones who were looking nostalgic are now glancing eagerly towards the door. Samantha glances at her watch.

'Yes, you're right. It is lunchtime,' she smiles tolerantly. 'Bon appetit, but do try to be back here by two o'clock. We've got a lot more personal exploration to do this afternoon.'

'Save me a place, will you? I want to go to the loo,' Matt whispers as we all rise from our cushions and our conundrums.

'Yes, of course I will,' I reply, as I follow the others out of the room. We're almost running with glee. The simple solace of vegetarian risotto suddenly seems enormously enticing. In fact, our 'inner children' are so excited that there's a minor spat about who is to have second helpings of the bread and butter pudding.

'Wait. Wait,' Samantha addresses us firmly. 'There's another bread and butter pudding over there on the sideboard.'

'Why didn't you tell us?' Peter demands petulantly.

'If you'd looked you would have seen it, but you only saw the one in front of you.' She smiles at him and then for some reason glances at me as she adds gently, 'Perhaps that's a small insight in itself'.

Chapter 21

THAT 'PERSONAL EXPLORATION' DAY was more interesting than I'd thought it would be. I think the last 'exercise' we did was the most helpful. Samantha asked us to make a list of all the things we'd like to do but are frightened of for some reason. She said it might help us reconnect with some of our own 'passion'.

'You may even find yourselves putting love on that list,' she told us. 'A lot of people are frightened of loving. Of the intimacy a close relationship brings. They are scared of being truly known in case they are rejected.'

'Well, that's not me anyway,' I thought, remembering James Mitchel.

The list of things I'd like to do but am too scared to try could have filled an entire shorthand notepad. Thankfully we were only given one A4 lined page each, so I just made a random selection. Among them was my desire to do an art course in Paris. There's a college there I'd wanted to attend when I left school. In fact, I almost went there until piles of people pointed out to me that living in a garret isn't quite as romantic as it sounds.

'Why not try journalism?' Uncle Sean suggested. 'You loved writing essays at school. You'd enjoy the variety. And you could keep your painting as a hobby.'

'Yes. Yes,' everyone chorused. 'What an excellent suggestion.'

'Mmmm – maybe,' I said. It certainly seemed a sensible solution, even though on at least three occasions I almost buggered off to Paris with a haversack. Annie and Laren thought I should go, but in the end I didn't. I was scared of being alone in a big strange foreign city.

Painting seemed a whimsical thing suddenly, journalism was far more sensible and solid. My French wasn't fluent enough anyway. The reasons why I shouldn't go to Paris grew and grew. But they have never entirely convinced me. I'm not sure they ever will.

Another thing I put on that list was that I'd like to visit my parents' graves again. I used to visit the graveyard occasionally, but then there came a point when I found it too upsetting. I'd like to give them flowers. Show them they are remembered. But it seems so lonely standing by their headstones. Maybe if I marry Eamon he could come with me.

By the time I'd finished writing my list it covered every inch of the paper I'd been given. As I re-read it the bit that most surprised me was the sentence that said, 'I'd like to ring Laren MacDermott.' I realized I'd been feeling deeply curious about her. We'd been such good friends. It seemed a pity just to 'lose' her telephone number like that…even though I hadn't. It turned up the other day in a pocket of one of my jeans. It was stuck together and hard from the washing machine. The numbers were faded, but I could still just make them out.

Now I'm in the sitting room with Laren's telephone number in my hand and wondering if I can summon up the courage to dial it. I've spent all morning puzzling over a particularly problematic assignment Sarah has given me so this diversion is, in a sense, quite welcome. Phoning Laren could be fun, as long as I don't care if we find we have nothing in common anymore. Yes. Why not. We could always talk about her apparent detestation of terrapins.

I dial the number quickly. She probably has an answering machine. I listen to the ringing tone and look at Tarquin playing with his catnip mouse. No reply. She's obviously not there. In a way I'm rather relieved. I'm just about to hang up when she answers. 'Hello!' she says brightly. 'Hello, Laren here.'

'Hello, Laren,' I say softly, suddenly unsure about the wisdom of this reconnection.

'Is that you, Alice?' she asks. I must admit I'm rather surprised she recognized my voice.

'Yes, it is,' I reply.

'How funny, I was just thinking about you. I was wondering if you'd lost my number.'

I'm about to say that I did, but decide not to. Why not be honest? There's enough acting in the world as it is. 'Well, to be truthful, Laren, I was a bit nervous about phoning you,' I say hesitantly. 'I was worried that – you know – we might find we don't have much in common any more.'

'Oh, I'm sure we do,' Laren laughs reassuringly. 'Don't be too fooled by my public image, Alice. I'm not quite as intimidating as you might think.'

'Would you like to meet up for a drink sometime?' I ask. 'Then we could have that "proper chat" that you suggested.'

'I'd love that,' Laren replies. 'But I'm afraid it will have to wait until next month. We're flying to Japan today. We're doing a tour in East Asia.'

'Wow, how exciting!' I exclaim. 'I've never been to anywhere as exotic as that.'

'Come with us,' Laren suddenly announces.

'What?' I frown.

'Come with us to East Asia.' She makes it sound as though she's inviting me for a cup of coffee in Bewley's. She has obviously grown used to this type of last-minute suggestion, but I haven't. We have been leading very different lives.

'But – but, aren't you leaving today?' I enquire cautiously.

'Yes. This evening. We have a fantastic tour manager, I'm sure he could get your airplane tickets in time. All you need to bring is your passport. It wouldn't cost you anything.'

'Laren that's incredibly generous of you,' I reply, dumbfounded.

'Not really,' she replies. 'You'd be quite busy. I need an assistant and anyway it can get quite boring just being cooped up with the band.'

'I – mmmm – I –' Laren's suggestion is deeply tempting, but I realize it's not feasible. I can't just sod off like that. However much I'd like to. 'Laren, I'm afraid I don't think I can come with you,' I say. 'I have a number of commitments here. But it's wonderful of you to ask me.'

I hear a man calling to Laren in the background. 'Hang on a minute, Malcolm,' she's shouting back. 'I'm talking to Alice.'

'Well, don't be long,' I hear him saying. 'We've got an interview with that fellow from *The Irish Times* in ten minutes.'

'Laren, I'd better not keep you,' I say. 'I'll phone you when you get back.'

'Yes, please do,' Laren replies enthusiastically. Then I hear Malcolm calling out to her again.

After I've hung up I feel strangely exhilarated. 'Come with us.' That's what Laren had said. I could have gone off to East Asia for an entire month. The fecklessness of it. The spontaneity. No one has ever said something like that to me before. I feel like I've been put into another category. I am a woman who could arrive at an airport with just her passport. Perhaps this calls for a change of hairdo.

After about five minutes I begin to wonder if I should phone Laren back. Immediately. Say 'Yes. Yes, I will come with you.' Sarah, of course, would be deeply pissed off. She's quite strict about holiday arrangements on the magazine. Heaven knows what she'd do if I just disappeared like that. She might take a very firm stand. And then there are the articles I've promised to do for the local paper. And Eamon...

Eamon will be returning shortly. He's not quite sure when, but it may be by next month. He told me this in a postcard which arrived today. The job in Peru took less time than they'd expected. He will be expecting me to have an answer to his proposal and I haven't yet. Though I am frequently convinced I am going to say 'yes', there are occasions when I am equally convinced that I'll say 'no'. 'Maybe' is the answer that seems most truthful, but it wouldn't sound too good in the wedding ceremony.

As I accept the fact that I cannot run off with Laren I sigh deeply and head towards my computer. I'm glad I phoned her anyway. She sounded so pleased to hear from me. Maybe she can become a friend again. A weird friend, but then I'm rather odd myself. Odd – yes, that's a word that could also apply to the assignments Sarah has been giving me lately. They're enough to make anyone want to go to the other side of the world.

Having already asked me to trudge through the gloomy territory of supermarket singles evenings, Sarah now wants me to do the same thing with singles dances and personal ads. She seems determined to send me deep into the love jungle. She even wants me to place a personal ad of my own in a newspaper 'for research' – or at least answer one.

I'm getting decidedly suspicious about the match-making themes of these assignments. I'm beginning to suspect Annie has told Sarah about Eamon – they were friends in college. I even saw them having lunch together some time ago. I can almost hear Annie saying, 'She simply mustn't marry him, Sarah. We've got to do something about it.' Annie won't admit to this of course. She's keeping a coy silence on the subject.

I don't want to do it. I really don't want to answer a personal ad. Even though the men go on about sharing champagne in exotic locations – they want you to be 'slim' and 'attractive' and heaven knows what else in return. Occasionally they even specify 'freckles', or an actress they want you to look like. It's absurd.

The ones in the publication I am currently reading seem mostly from very rich middle-aged men. They want someone with a GSOH, which we all know means 'Good Sense of Humour', only I somehow didn't until the other day. I suspected that it might be an abbreviation for some kind of household accessory that I plainly didn't own. Because some of these men sound very picky. I wouldn't put it beyond them to require a certain type of Scandinavian wood-burning stove.

How on earth would I answer one of them?

'Dear Box Number 52,' I scribble.

'I have a GSOH, GFCH (gas-fired central heating), a cat and a Mitsubishi colour portable. My jumpers tend to bobble shortly after purchase, but people have told me I can look pretty if I try. I watch too much telly, but am willing to have my habits changed, and like the sound of that champagne you mentioned. My romantic experiences have made me deeply appreciative of more predictable pleasures, such as gardening, so please don't answer if you're horrible. I really couldn't take it.

Yours sincerely, Alice

I stare at what I've written. Though it's true, it's far too facetious. It doesn't seem fair anyway. Meeting some man under false pretences. Just using him for research. I must try to hang on to some scruples.

Scruples. I first heard that word when I was five. 'What I like about Mrs Smyth is that she has scruples,' my mother said about an elderly friend of hers whom we often visited. Mrs Smyth had spent a long time in India. She referred to that vast continent as frequently and casually as if it were the corner shop. For some reason I was sure the 'scruples' my mother was referring to were the unusual biscuits Mrs Smyth favoured. Firm of texture and tasting slightly of cinnamon, they were strangely pleasing.

'I like Mrs Smyth's scruples too,' I announced, glad to have found a point of such obvious agreement. 'They're so nice and crunchy.' Whereupon my mother and father laughed and I sulked off and sat in the middle of a large hedge and pretended I was adopted.

I toss my scribbled personal ad into my overstuffed handbag. I'm not going to think about scruples now. I'm going to make another phone call. That 'personal exploration' workshop seems to have made me a bit more daring. Yes – I'll phone James Mitchel.

Good, he has his answering machine on. I take a deep breath and say brightly, 'Hello, James. This is Alice Evans. I left a message for you some time ago. There's no need to phone me now because I got the information I needed. Thanks anyway.' Then I bash the phone back on to its receiver.

I have a good reason for doing this. James Mitchel is a very good fantasy and I don't see why James himself should deprive me of it. This way James's not returning my call no longer irritates me because I have instructed him not to do so. Out there on the furthest realms of plausibility I may even begin to believe, like Annie, that there were extenuating circumstances for his silence. That he lost the number. That the recording was unclear. That he was shy. Or tried to phone when I was out and then didn't try again because he was very, very busy. These excuses are fine as long as he does not say them. For they belong to another man. The Good James Mitchel. The one I made up and still have a small affection for because I like – and in some ways even need – his little glimmer.

Having taken this decisive action about James, I address the vexed matter of the singles dance and personal ads article. The deadline for it is looming and I must work out a course of action. 'If I go to a singles dance I may meet women who have answered personal ads,' I think. 'I could get quotes from them about it. That would do.'

I see from an ad in the *Evening Herald* that a dating agency is organizing just the kind of dance I need tomorrow. You have to book in advance. It costs fifty euros, which seems quite a lot, but this includes a free drink and disco. I phone up and make my booking.

I've persuaded Mira to come to the singles dance with me. It is not, of course, something she wanted to do. She's weaving a particularly complicated wall hanging on her portable loom at the moment. And there's one of those deeply obscure foreign movies on the telly that she loves.

We don't spend long getting ready for the dance. We grab the first slightly dressy things we see in our wardrobes, grumbling as we do so. Of course, Annie would say that I should doll myself up but I know, I just know, I won't meet Mr Right at an event like this. He wouldn't have time for it. He'd be planning his next expedition to the tropical rainforests or something.

'I hope I don't spend the evening discussing Finland,' Mira says as we enter the hotel. 'I've only been there once but I always seem to end up talking about it.'

The hotel is quite plush. As I walk across the foyer I feel the words 'Desperate Single Woman' are emblazoned on my back – maybe followed by 'thirty-eight' in brackets.

'We shouldn't have come here,' I whisper. 'See the way that clerk is looking at us.'

'Nonsense,' says Mira, who wouldn't care if he was. 'He hardly looked at us at all.'

We leave our coats in the cloakroom and go to the Ladies. We haven't even bothered to put on some make-up yet. That's how much we care. 'We don't have to stay long, do we?' Mira looks at me pleadingly.

'I don't know. I need to talk to some women about their – you know – experiences of this kind of thing.'

'Oh, all right,' she sighs. 'You'll find me in the downstairs bar if I get really fed up.'

We walk towards the 'function room' with some trepidation. It's big and modern with wine-red velvet seating and a parquet floor. There's a space in the middle for dancing, and a small bar at one side. The proper bar is downstairs. The bar where single people – there must be some of them – haven't yet been drummed up into this undignified desperation. This antsy, itchy, scratch-me state about being alone. Not that the people here look desperate. 'Purposeful' seems a more appropriate description. The lighting is not too low, so people can see each other I suppose.

The room is quite crowded. A glamorous young woman greets us at a little desk. She ticks us off the attendance list and then hands us our name-tags. We clip them on doubtfully and look around. Lots of people are looking around like we are. Staring at each other in a way that is not usually socially acceptable. There are more women than men so the men are looking slightly smug. Even that plump, balding, sweaty fellow with the lurid shirt in the corner has an air of ease about him. 'Yes, I am a man,' he seems to be saying. 'One of that rare, special species.'

'See anyone interesting?' I ask Mira, forgetting for a moment that this is entirely beside the point. That I am here purely for the purposes of research.

'Of course not,' Mira sighs, looking for a quiet corner. She finds one. Then she opens her bag and takes out a book.

'Not here, Mira.' I stare at her, astounded. 'You're not going to read here, are you?'

'Yes, I am,' she replies firmly.

I go off to get some drinks and when I return I find that the plump lurid-shirt man has found her. She's saying, 'I've only been there once. For a holiday.' Dear God, she's got on to Finland already. 'Here's your drink, Mira,' I say, giving her a sympathetic smile.

Some of the women here are dressed quite sedately. They're talking to each other in cheerful clusters, veterans of the considerable consolations of sisterhood. Others, however, are really dressed for action in short sexy skirts and clingy tops, in tiny dresses and tight pants. Many of the men, subtle creatures that they are, are crowding round them.

No one is crowding around me in my Indian mother-earth number. A dress so loose you could hide a few illegal immigrants in it without detection. This, of course, doesn't matter because I am a journalist on assignment.

Even so I can't help feeling that it's a sobering reminder to me that my dreams of meeting some 'Wonderful Man' are highly unrealistic. I am thirty-eight. I am not young and nubile anymore. I am easily overlooked and I find it hard to get used to it. Because when I was in my twenties these men would have looked at me with interest. Some of them would have been chatting to me at this very minute. Perhaps offering me a drink or a dance. My dress wouldn't have made any difference. Perhaps I should buy myself a clingy top.

I head towards the women and not the men. I ask them original questions, like whether they come here often. I tell them about my article and take out my little notebook while they tell me their tales. 'I've met some very nice men at these dances,' a woman in her forties, called Fiona, tells me cheerfully. 'They've really transformed my social life. I go out on lots of dates these days. I usen't to before.'

'Why?' I ask, hoping my shorthand can keep up with her. She's talking rather quickly.

'Because nearly all my friends are married, and so were most of the men of my age that I used to meet. I stopped going to discos and things like that because the people were so young. I felt like their mother. I almost put myself on the shelf, and then I decided not to.'

'What did you do?'

'I decided to face facts,' she says. 'I decided to seek out people who are in the same position as myself. It felt a bit awkward at first, admitting that I was lonely. But then I discovered that it's a very common thing.'

'Yes, indeed,' I agree, looking at her thankfully. It's great when you get someone who's this succinct with their views.

'I've been to all the latest films,' she continues. 'I eat out a lot and do some ballroom dancing. I have company now, and that's what I wanted.'

'But…' I hesitated. 'But don't you sometimes wish you could meet – you know – someone special?'

'Oh, I gave up on marrying George Clooney at least ten years ago,' she says, laughing heartily and rather too loudly. This, I realize, is one of her anecdotes. A nice way of getting off the subject, but I don't want to…not just yet.

'But surely you'd like to meet someone that – that you could…'

'Love?'

'Yes.'

'Of course I would,' she replies quickly, almost impatiently. She glances at my name tag. 'Doesn't everyone, Alice? The thing is, I don't know if I'll find that person. Maybe I missed him. A nice, kind bloke, that would do me fine these days. Someone who likes football.'

'Oh, so you like football?'

'Oh, yes.' Her face lights up. 'Manchester United, Alice. They mean more to me now than George Clooney ever did.'

'Good for you, Fiona,' I find myself saying. I am deeply impressed by her. How well she has adjusted to her situation. She has 'faced facts' just like I'm doing with Eamon, my 'nice, kind bloke'.

'But if I do meet someone special, Alice,' she is now adding, 'I hope that I'll recognize him. Not let him slip by without at least telling him how I feel. That kind of thing takes courage, but I think it's worth it.'

'Yes, absolutely,' I say, feeling a bit better about my phone call to James Mitchel, even though he did ignore it. Her words have made me wonder if there's someone else around who's 'special' that I haven't recognized. Sometimes I get a distant sense there is. It must be wishful thinking. I've done a lot of that over the years.

As I leave Fiona I notice a nice man in a navy suit is approaching her. She has such a very jolly smile. She'll always have people round her. Some men aren't just looking for women in clingy tops – I must remember that. Some men look deeper. They don't care so much about the wrinkles. They are attracted to the spirit of a person. The essence. The truth. That's what I want really, someone who sees the truth of me…but how can I share it with him if I don't really know it myself? Who am I? I'm just not sure any more. And anyway, the only person who studies me carefully these days is my irritating new neighbour Liam. I saw him looking at me again this evening, from his upstairs window. He obviously has voyeuristic tendencies. I'm beginning to feel rather sorry for his girlfriend, Elsie. I simply must put up those net curtains in the kitchen window. The thing is they need to be altered to fit the window properly and I'm not that good at sewing. I'll have to get them done professionally. I don't know why I keep putting it off.

I approach some other women and continue with my questioning. All through the conversations they look around hopefully. Some are more brazen than others, fixing a man who has caught their interest with a long look, a small but significant smile. As the dancing starts they drift away from me into mixed gender clusters.

Occasionally I see a man glancing at me, and then looking away uninterestedly.

Eamon didn't look away when we met at that beach barbecue. He looked at me for so long I began to wonder if I had a bit of charcoal on my face. I wasn't even wearing a clingy top. Just an old sweatshirt and jeans. I suddenly feel a wave of affection for him. Gratitude. I swirl it around me like a cape, hoping it will guard me from the night's strange chill.

A tall, swarthy man with greying hair and eyebrows that command uncomfortable attention suddenly says, 'Hello, Alice.' I stare at him, bewildered, and then I remember my name tag.

'Hello – er – Malcolm.' I peer at his own name, which is stuck to his jacket.

Malcolm informs me that he is a farmer from Mullingar. He is looking for a woman with good morals who likes heifers and loud music. He's just bought a new car and is very close to his mother. This is obviously his chat-up line, which explains the space around him. He wants to meet 'someone' because 'there's nothing to greet me when I get home. Only the light bulb I put on when I went out.'

'So, Malcolm,' I venture. 'Are you enjoying yourself?'

'Sort of, but I wish they'd put on Status Quo.'

'Gosh – or should I say GSOH,' I smile. 'Slade's more my style.'

'Really?'

'No. Sorry. I was just joking.'

Malcolm doesn't laugh, but he's a nice enough fellow, and quite snazzily dressed. He's sincere and not as linear as he first appears. He's doing his best, but I'd baffle him.

'We're not compatible, Malcolm. I'm too complicated for you,' I say, after we've danced to Tina Turner singing 'What's Love Got To Do With It?'

'Aye – you're probably right,' Malcolm agrees.

'But I do hope you meet your "someone",' I add.

'And I hope you do too, Alice.' He gives me a brave grin and then moves purposefully towards a cluster of women in clingy tops.

I've got loads of quotes in my notebook now. Where's Mira? She seems to have disappeared.

Mira has retreated to the downstairs bar. She's tucked away in a corner seat. She's still reading her book. It's by Anthony Powell and is part of a series called *A Dance to the Music of Time*. There are twelve books in the series and she's on number ten. That's the kind of person she is.

'Mira, what are you doing?' I ask. 'They were playing quite nice music. You could at least have danced.'

'That fellow in the lurid shirt kept pestering me,' she sighs wearily. 'When I told him that I was an eccentric spinster he just laughed. He seemed to see it as something of a challenge. He wanted me to spend the weekend in his caravan on Ballybrittas beach.'

'No one asked me to share a caravan,' I smile encouragingly. 'You're an attractive woman, Mira. All my friends have said it. Even Eamon.'

'Did he?' She looks up at me, surprised.

'Yes, when he first met you he said he couldn't understand why you didn't have a boyfriend. Of course, you were involved with Frank at the time, but I didn't mention that.'

She looks at me gratefully. 'So, what did you think of your first singles dance?' she asks, as we leave the hotel and walk towards her car.

'I suppose you could say I have mixed feelings about it,' I reply. 'I found it sensible, and yet somehow lonely – a bit sad.'

'Why?' she asks, as she unlocks the car door for me.

'There was the feel of the marketplace to it. You know, people sizing each other up in such a very obvious way.'

'Yes, I know what you mean,' Mira agrees. 'But there's a lot to be said for those kinds of gatherings. If you have the temperament for them.'

'What do you mean?'

'It's practical and simple. People are being upfront about their needs.'

'So why did you run down to the bar?'

'I don't need a man, Alice.' She smiles at me indulgently. 'Surely I've made that plain by now.'

No, she hasn't made it plain at all – but I don't say this. Frank, her married ex-lover, has snuck into this car suddenly. I can feel him. She loved him so much. When he came to the cottage she looked so happy. Like a little girl. There was such an understanding between them. Such a closeness. The cottage felt full of kisses when he visited. They'd disappear into her bedroom with a bottle of wine and I'd hear them laughing. I could hardly believe it when she told me she wasn't going to see him any more.

'I can't share him,' that's what she'd said. 'I can't be the person waiting in the background for leftovers. It's like grabbing hors d'oeuvres, hoping they'll make a meal, but they don't. I love him too much just to have a little bit of him. He'll never leave his wife, and do you want to know something really weird, Alice? His loyalty is one of the reasons why I love him.'

Yes, there was a time Mira used to talk to me about Frank. But she doesn't any more. For example, even though he's snuck into this car suddenly the only remark she's made is 'Fancy a takeaway pizza?'

'Yeah, let's get one,' I reply.

Sometimes, late at night when I go by Mira's bedroom door to the bathroom, I hear her sobbing. I want to rush in and comfort her, but I know she doesn't want me to. So it is in these abrupt gear changes from, say, men to pizza, that we acknowledge Frank. Because what she wanted to say about him has already been said. So now he sometimes fills our silences on nights like these. He is there amid the talk of pineapple and green pepper and sweetcorn pizza topping. I really wish she'd forget about him, but it seems that she just can't.

'Don't force the feeling away. Let it leave when it feels less.' Someone told me that about grief once. They were words I needed to hear. It's so hard, missing people. The little rituals of love and belonging – the sand to pearl accretions of understanding – had taken such time. But for what? I shed such bewildered tears. But sometimes, now, it seems that the tears Mira and I do not shed as we stay in our silences, our rememberings, are the deepest, the saddest ones of all.

'I think we should get some jasmine and train it up the wall at the back,' says Mira, as we drive home with a box of hot pizza in the back seat.

'Yes,' I agree, thinking how I should go to a jeweller's and at least have a peek at some engagement rings. 'Yes, that would be nice.'

197

Chapter 22

I'VE BEEN LOOKING AT engagement rings in jewellery shops. The assistants are very solicitous. Almost respectful. I've seen quite a nice solitaire. Just one diamond in a simple gold setting. I'm sure Eamon would like it. He's fond of understatement. It would be nice to show off my ring. Flash it around a bit. I wonder who I should invite to the wedding... if I have one.

I wouldn't want it to be too fussy. Just a gathering of family and close friends. I wonder if the California Cafe would do the reception. They have a nice function room which would be just the right size. I'd design the invitations myself. Do a line drawing of something suitable – though I'm not quite sure at the moment what that might be. I'd like my cream dress to have a slight pink tinge to it. I'd like it to be in raw silk and rustle a bit when I walked. I'd want it to have small embroidered blossoms that would match my sweet pea posy.

Dear God – how can I have decided all this? There is a vast conspiracy to make people marry. I see that even more clearly now I've shown some interest in the subject. It's like joining in on some huge conversation that's 'members only'. Once the subject is broached it seems to acquire a momentum all of its own. And, of course, that 'singles dance' was most sobering. I rather wish I hadn't gone to it now.

I also wish I didn't have to go to the laundromat tonight, but I do because our machine's being serviced. So I empty the contents of the dirty clothes basket into an old plastic laundry bag and lug it gloomily down the road. I have a book with me called *The Road Less*

Travelled by M. Scott Peck. I've been trying to read it on and off for years. I put the washing on and settle back into a chair. As I do so a tall man who has had his back to me peers over my shoulder. I can see a bit of his jacket, but not his face. 'Life is difficult. This is a great truth, one of the greatest,' he reads.

'Do you mind?' I look up at him irritatedly.

'Not at all,' he replies. Dear God, it's Liam. 'That's a cheery book you're reading, Alice,' he continues. 'Are you "on assignment" here too?' He's stuffing some very grubby items of clothing into the machine as he says this. My usual politeness seems to have left me this evening. I decide to ignore him.

'Once we truly know that life is difficult – once we truly understand and accept it – then life is no longer difficult,' I read. 'Because once it is accepted, the fact that life is difficult no longer matters.'

'Would you like a liquorice toffee?' Liam is now asking. I pretend not to hear him. I don't know why he's being so forward suddenly. He hardly knows me. If I encourage him he'll be turning up at the cottage next – wandering around – poking his nose into things. Maybe Sarah is right and men are a bit like dogs. What I want to say to Liam now, and very sternly, is 'Sit'.

'Self-discipline is a wonderful thing. I love to see it in others,' Liam observes as I look down at my book again and read: 'Most do not fully see this truth that life is difficult. Instead they moan more or less incessantly, noisily or subtly, about the enormity of their problems, their burdens, and their difficulties as if life were generally easy, as if life should be easy.'

I can feel Liam studying me. 'Oh, it really isn't fair,' I think. 'I just wanted to find a quiet corner and read my book and he has to show up.' I read on, skipping quickly over the more challenging sentences: 'Discipline is the basic set of tools we require to solve life's problems…It is in the whole process of meeting and solving problems that life has its meaning.' Yes. Yes. OK. OK. I turn back glumly to the contents page and see a section called 'Love Defined'. I turn to it eagerly – some sort of explanation at long last! On mid page I see the following words: 'One result of the mysterious nature of love is that no one has ever, to my knowledge, arrived at a truly satisfactory definition of love.'

Oh, just great.

I'd close the book now if it wasn't such a useful way of not getting into conversation. So I just gaze at it until 'Love Defined' becomes the blur it is anyway and think how I should really have put my whites into a separate wash. Out of the corner of my eye I see that Liam is stuffing more items into a machine and, as he does so, I can't help noticing he has a rather lurid pair of Mickey Mouse boxer shorts.

'Ah-ha! Caught you!' he exclaims suddenly.

'Caught me doing what?'

'Admiring my underpants.'

There are two other people besides us in this laundromat and they are now sneaking looks at us. 'Your underwear is a matter of complete indifference to me,' I reply in as withering a manner as I can manage. The cheek of him! Though I knew he was irritating, I never guessed he'd be this brazen. It's probably his background. He probably thinks I find his New York humour entertaining, but I don't. I don't at all.

'Do you have some change for the detergent? I've only got euros and I need two fifty cent coins.' He gives me a pleading look.

I sigh and reluctantly look into my overstuffed handbag. I hand him the fifty cent coins carefully, determined that our hands shouldn't touch.

'You are so, so kind, Alice,' he grins, offering me a euro coin with quite unnecessary ostentation. 'We all need kindness in this difficult life.' I give him my 'fuck off' Laren Brassière look and open my book again. I stare at it studiously.

'Laundromats are great places for meeting people,' Liam is now saying. 'I've had some great conversations in laundromats in my time.'

'Really? It's not a phenomenon I myself have encountered,' I reply. Then I add rather pointedly, 'How's Elsie?'

'Oh, you've met her, have you?' He seems somewhat surprised.

'I've seen her around,' I reply enigmatically.

'She's away at the moment, actually.'

'Ah, that explains why he's being so friendly,' I think. 'While the cat's away and all that. Well, he's not going to foist his Lothario tendencies on to me.' I stand up.

'Excuse me, Liam,' I announce. 'I don't feel very plural at the moment. I'm going to a café where I can read my book in peace.' I stress the 'peace' bit and stare at him stonily. Funnily enough he doesn't say anything as I leave, even though I can feel him watching.

The California Café's a bit of a walk away, but it's a mild evening. I order myself an Earl Grey tea and a chocolate brownie, which I decide to eat guiltlessly. It's for my 'inner child' – that's what it is. It's part of the important process of recognizing the 'many selves' inside of me. I go to a quiet corner and chomp it greedily. As I do so, I open my book again. I glance at some more chapter headings in the 'Love' section. 'Falling in

"Love"', 'The Myth of Romantic Love', 'More about Ego Boundaries', 'Love is Not a Feeling'. Whatever love is, it's beginning to sound like an awful lot of hard work. Maybe Eamon is right when he says we don't really need it. As I drink my tea I take out an old envelope from my bag and decide to list the reasons why I should or should not get married. I begin with the 'Yes':

'Yes, because I am a contrary and complicated person, though I seldom admit to it, and need a sensible man to teach me sense,' I scribble.

'Yes, because if I had a baby I'd be up to my neck in nappies and immediately become a more mature and worthwhile person who could say things like "I never realized how wonderful children are until I had one. My baby has given me a completely new perspective on life."

'Yes, because acquiring a husband would prevent my married women friends suspecting that I might grab theirs.

'Yes, because when you're single people often assume you're available at the drop of a hat to sort out their problems while somehow naively believing you don't have any of your own.

'Yes, because I could leave the magazine and paint at home instead.

'Holidays in Provence.

'Someone to spend Christmas with.

'No shortage of pine shelving.

'Excellent and expanded horticultural possibilities.'

I turn the envelope over and under 'No' I simply write: 'But I do not love him.'

What a peevish, pernickety sentence it seems suddenly. What a small, foolish, sullen reason not to become part of that huge conspiracy of compromise and comfort which marriage surely is. Icing may be sweet, but marzipan has far more texture. Even my mother discovered that eventually. One day all James Mitchel will be is a slight sugary aftertaste. No more real than Laren's infatuation with Leonard Whiting. Someone I simply made up because I couldn't bear to face the truth: that I'm simply not temperamentally suited to all that high-flown romantic stuff. It simply takes up too much time, and it only lasts four years anyway. I stare at my list again and then find myself scribbling:

'Buy new sofa.

'Bleach knickers.

'Continue spiritual quest, but more gently.

'Re-pot geraniums.

'Find backs of earrings or buy new ones at that jewellery craft shop.

'Lose weight from bum and other flabby areas.

'Become tidier.

'Go out more often (where to?)'

I am deeply engrossed in this new list and about to write more when I glance at my watch. Dear God, I've been in this café for nearly an hour.

Back in the laundromat the first things that come out of the machine are my grubbiest bra, some very unflattering knickers, some laddered navy wool tights and the clay-stained T-shirt I used to wear to pottery class before I bought the posh new ones to impress James Mitchel. I have no wish to impress Liam. I really don't care what impression I make on him. He's hardly looked at me since I came back anyway. He's reading a book as he waits for his clothes to dry. It's called *By Grand Central Station I Sat Down and Wept*. So he's reading a 'cheery little book' too. I refrain from mentioning this, though I can't help sneaking some glances at him. He really is very handsome in a slightly dishevelled way. He doesn't seem to have shaved this morning, but the stubble suits him. He looks so solemn now, so unselfconsciously absorbed in the story he's reading. I sense there's a serious side to him. One that I have scarcely glimpsed. I think I've hurt his feelings a little. I was so offhand with him earlier. I'm not usually like that with people. What is it about Liam that makes me so defensive? He was probably only trying to be friendly.

Clothes seem to expand when they're clean. As I struggle to stuff mine back into my blue plastic bag Liam looks up at me for a moment, and then goes to check if his own clothes are dry. He is behaving with such coolness now that I feel impelled to speak. To soften the tone of our meeting.

'So, how's your garden, Liam?' I ask.

'Oh, all right I suppose,' he answers unenthusiastically, as he removes a woman's pink blouse from the drier. That's all he's going to say. He's almost ignoring me. I begin to feel rather uncomfortable. It's best to try to keep on good terms with one's neighbours.

'I'm sorry I was a bit off-hand with you earlier,' I say. 'But I was a bit preoccupied about something.'

'Yes, you certainly were,' he replies, making no attempt at tact. Americans can be so blunt sometimes.

'Well, anyway, I'm sorry if I appeared rude,' I continue, 'I'm not usually like that.'

'You said what you felt, Alice.' He turns to me and gives me a placatory smile. 'There's no need to apologize for being honest. I "vant to be alone" sometimes myself.'

'Well, I just thought I'd explain,' I say, picking up my blue plastic bag and lugging it towards the door.

'And I'm glad you did,' he replies, as he begins to stuff his clean clothes into a large Nike sports bag.

Once I get outside I begin to wish I'd brought another bag with me. The one I have is rather old and the plastic around the handles has stretched. How silly I was not to check it before I came out. Eamon would have. He's such a very methodical person. I lift it gingerly and, just as I'm about to head home, I hear a thud and look down to see that my plastic bag, sans handle, has landed on the pavement. I grab my bra, which has escaped, and stuff it back. Then I pick up the bag and attempt to hug it to my chest. I wish my arms were longer. My hands are sweaty now and are slipping on the plastic. As I start to walk away in a splayed-footed duck-like fashion I sense someone is watching me and turn around. Oh no, I should have guessed it, Liam is watching me. He's laughing. 'Would you like a lift, Alice?' he is now asking.

I stare at him, flustered. In normal circumstances there is no way I'd want to share a car with Liam, but I'd better say 'Yes' if I'm ever going to get this laundry home. I approach his Citroën slowly. Then, as he opens the passenger door, I have a sudden desire to flee. To drop my laundry and race away down the almost empty street. It's ridiculous. What is it about Liam that makes me so uncomfortable? So defensive? It's as if I'm frightened of him for some reason, but surely there's no need to be. After a conspicuous hesitation I enter the car gingerly. This makes Liam smile. When he looks at me from his upstairs window he sometimes smiles like that. I stare ahead stoically, determined not to share his amusement. It's just a short drive home. Surely I can put up with his company for ten minutes. As Liam stuffs my laundry bag into the back seat I say 'thank you' in a prim, polite manner.

'You're welcome,' he replies in the bland tones of an airline steward, though he is grinning at me mischievously. As he climbs into the driving seat he adds, 'Sorry that the car's so untidy. I've been meaning to give it a good clean for ages.'

'Oh, don't worry,' I reply. 'You should see my cottage.'

'I'd very much like to see your cottage, Alice,' he answers, deliberately misinterpreting my remark it seems to me. I stare out of the window grimly. Then, as Liam switches on the ignition, I almost jump out of my seat. He must have been playing the radio at full blast when he drove here, because it's now blaring so loudly I put my hands to my ears.

'Sorry,' he grimaces, turning the dial to a civilized volume. As he does so I recognize the song that is now filling the car. It's k d lang singing 'Constant Craving' and it's reminding me of James Mitchel. I look down at my lap sadly. I really don't want to hear that song right now. Not here. Out of the corner of my eye I see Liam giving me a swift, studious glance. Goodness, he's turning the radio off. I didn't even have to say it. He must be very perceptive. Maybe that's what drew Elsie to him. There must be some reason they stay together, despite their infidelities.

'Mrs Peabody is a great old character, isn't she?' Liam is now commenting as we take the coast road homewards. I look out at the sea. The sea changes colour at least ten times a day. I love looking at it – charting its changes.

'Yes, she is,' I agree.

'She talks a lot about you.'

'Mmmm – I suspected as much,' I sigh. I wonder what on earth she's been saying. I decide not to ask.

'She really gets into the old Harvey's sometimes, doesn't she?' Liam continues.

'Ah – so you've noticed that too,' I smile. He's obviously shared a number of sherries with her, like me. 'It's best to hold on to your glass,' I add. 'That way she can't keep refilling it.'

'Yes, I kind of sussed that one, Alice.'

I look at him with muted warmth. Sharing this car with him isn't quite as uncomfortable as I'd thought it would be. He's not being so forward now, so brazen. Even the leather patches on his faded tweed jacket don't seem so irritating anymore. He's obviously not going to try to turn me into one of his infidelities. I'm too old for him anyway. He wouldn't fancy me at all. Amazingly I'm feeling quite comfortable with him. Almost cosy. 'What do you make of Cyril and Dora?' I enquire, mainly to be conversational.

'A definite case for no-fault divorce,' Liam says firmly. 'Though, of course, I haven't been able to tell Mrs Peabody this. She's convinced that they are "love birds".'

'Yes. She keeps telling me they are "company for each other", but frankly I think Cyril was happier on his own.'

'You know something, Alice?' Liam says, turning to me earnestly. 'Sometimes I feel like sneaking into her sitting-room and letting them both out. I hate to see any creature in a cage, but they're used to it now – and they like their birdseed. Anyway, they'd need a warmer climate.'

'Indeed,' I agree, almost forgetting my previous awkwardness. It's rather a relief to have someone to discuss all this with. Mira has never been that close to Mrs Peabody. She doesn't have that many other visitors.

'I was the one who encouraged her to get the larger cage for them,' I add, speaking quickly.

'It's a very nice cage,' Liam comments. 'Almost a little aviary.'

'Yes, it is nice,' I agree. 'But I'm afraid it doesn't quite make up for the Australian outback.'

We're almost at my street now. As Liam changes gear his hand briefly brushes against my leg and, suddenly, my old awkwardness returns. Did he do that on purpose? Surely not. And yet a small suspicion lingers. He is definitely a most perplexing person. I lean towards the door and notice that we are pulling up outside my cottage. I reach for the door handle the moment the car stops. My sharp, urgent exit is beginning to feel like a getaway. In fact, I'm about to leave my laundry behind when Liam says, 'Here, don't forget this,' and hands me my big blue bag. There's something almost tender about the way he does it. Concerned.

'Thanks for the lift,' I say, winching up an appropriately grateful expression.

'It was a pleasure. Really.'

I give him a guarded smile and close the car door before he has time to say anything else. Then, hugging my bag, I walk quickly away.

Back in the cottage I dump the laundry in my room and turn on the television. It is only later, when I'm hunting for one of the long T-shirts I use as nighties, that I discover something very puzzling.

Somehow – and I can't work out how – I've brought Liam's lurid Mickey Mouse boxer shorts home with me.

Chapter 23

I'VE JUST GIVEN LIAM'S Mickey Mouse boxer shorts to Oxfam. I'd no wish to keep them and I couldn't march up to him and say, 'Here's your underpants.' It might have created the wrong impression – especially if Elsie was around. I still can't work out how they got into my bag. Maybe boxer shorts have a life of their own, like socks and the TV remote control.

After I left the Oxfam shop I dashed into a newsagent's to buy a card for Eamon. It's his birthday soon. I'm still in the newsagent's now – it has an excellent selection of various 'greetings'. Too good a selection perhaps because after a quarter of an hour I still haven't found a card that seems quite right. I need a marzipan card – one that's not too sweet and not too neutral. Something pleasant and in no way perplexing. The thing is, the romantic ones are far too schmaltzy and the golf ones are rather garish. The ones with teddy bears aren't his style either. There seem to be numerous photographs of gorillas in various poses – but heaven knows what he'd make of them. It occurs to me that I really don't know what kind of card Eamon would like to receive. I could stay in this shop for hours, hacking my way through the various nuances, panic mounting. Eventually I grab one featuring a tranquil lake.

As soon as I get to my desk Gerry asks me if it's August yet. 'Yes, it is,' I answer, adding the date, year, century and country just in case he might be unsure about them too. As Gerry studies me warily, Humphrey darts towards my desk and borrows my stapler. Then Cindi appears and asks me about my weekend.

'It was quite quiet really,' I answer wearily. She's obviously itching to tell me the latest saga in her complicated life. The thing is, I don't really know if I can listen to her. My own life is making its demands felt very firmly this morning. More firmly than usual.

I turn on my word processor. My singles dances and personal ads article has to be ready by tomorrow. I've got to phone various dating agencies and some women I've tracked down who answer personal ads on a routine basis. A number of people I phoned on Friday weren't in. I left messages for them to ring me, but I'll probably ring them again anyway. Research of this nature requires a great deal of persistence.

'Having a cuppa?' Cindi is looking at me curiously now, obviously not understanding why I have not, so far, offered to make her one.

'I'll probably have one later. I'm in a bit of a tizz about this article.'

'Which one is that?' asks Cindi, who now sounds slightly put out. Article deadlines have never prevented me from listening to the details of her complicated life before. She went on for a full half-hour that time her hair got caught in a metal hinge on the filing cabinet.

'The article about singles dances and personal ads,' I reply.

'Ah, yes.' Cindi is still staring at me.

'Sorry that I can't talk now.' I give her an apologetic smile. 'It's just that I've got piles of people to phone. I've got to give this article loads of oomph. Sarah's still angry with me.'

'Why?'

'Because I didn't answer a personal ad myself.'

'Why didn't you?'

'I just couldn't face it.'

'Oh well, I'm sure the article will be interesting anyway.' Though Cindi is smiling, her jaw juts out as she says this, as if I've broken some tacit agreement. I only listened to her because I wanted her approval, but it's becoming rather clear that she hasn't been too concerned about gaining mine. I wonder if she's ever even wondered what I want or need these mornings myself. I haven't even asked her for that assertiveness book back because I thought it might offend her.

'See you then,' Cindi calls out a trifle sharply as she exits, taking her approval with her. Part of me feels like jumping up and running after her, and it. I need approval. I need piles and piles of it. Or maybe I don't. For, as I sit here staring at my computer it suddenly occurs to me that though Cindi may now like me a little less, I seem to like myself just a little more. Suddenly the image of Laren Brassière floats before me and I allow a little scowl to settle serenely on my mouth. I'm rather looking forward to having that 'proper chat' with Laren now. The fact that she has altered so much is almost comforting. I've grown used to the idea of her metamorphosis, it no longer unsettles me. It fact, in some ways I almost find it hopeful. Proof that people can change their ways, if they really want to.

The morning passes in a phalange of phone calls and paragraphs. I want to make this article even-handed. I want to give practical information and a description of the dance, as well as offering a fair representation of the various viewpoints. The thing is, as the day continues the article seems to take on a strange life of its own – especially after a rather liquid lunch with Matt. I don't refer to my research notes nearly as frequently as I should. By the time I've reached the middle of the article I have even ceased to care whether it makes sense. The who, what, when, where, how and why of things is rarely the whole story. Articles tend to need a slant, a cohesive 'angle', and I am growing tired of geometry. My rebellion mounts and I attempt a small mutiny. I type the words in a sort of frenzy. The final paragraph reads as follows:

'In short, it doesn't really matter what you've done or who you are. Just make sure you're wearing a short dress or clingy top. Get his phone number somehow and ring it. Ring it even if he doesn't want you to. Reach the point where you're not even sure you want him anyway. Find things you love and then start doing them. Talk to God occasionally. Empty churches are most restful. Sing in the bath. Watch Colin Derling on Gardeners' Questions. Take up weaving if necessary. And buy yourself a really nice pair of slippers. Wear them on dates if you feel like it. If he really is 'Mr Wonderful' he won't mind.'

'Ah, well,' I think as I email the article to Sarah. 'At least it's a refreshing change from *The Rules*' – that American book about dating that takes demureness to extraordinary extremes. I walk out of the office blithely, but as soon as I'm on the bus home I start to fret. That article is definitely over the top. Maybe I should email a revised version of the piece to Sarah tomorrow. Yes – that would be sensible.

I decide to pop in on Mrs Peabody before I go home. She's on her own so much. She really does need company. But when I go into her sitting-room I see that Liam is already with her. He's wearing a denim shirt and looks even more young and fetching than usual. His hair has grown longer lately and is a bit tousled. His faded jeans hug his long, slim and rather athletic legs, which are stretched out languorously. He seems very much at home. His deep brown eyes look at me so intently that I have to look away. 'Oh, sorry for interrupting, I'll come back later,' I say quickly. But Mrs Peabody insists that I join them.

'Alice, I'm so glad you helped me find a partner for Cyril,' she announces happily. 'Look at them – they're inseparable. It's so sweet.'

Liam regards me with raised eyebrows. Just a moment ago Cyril lunged at Dora and she had to hop quickly out of his way. They're bickering over a sprig of millet. Their pecks are in no way affectionate. Liam obviously feels a change of topic is called for. 'You've lots of photographs on your dresser, Mrs Peabody,' he remarks. 'Is that dashing fellow in the tweed jacket your late husband?'

'Yes. Yes he is,' Mrs Peabody replies animatedly. 'See the big one in the centre – that's of Eric with his great chums Ian and Michael – they were off bird-watching in the Wicklow mountains.' Liam gets up to have a look. 'It's a great photograph. Did you take it?'

'Yes. Yes, I did. It's so strange to think they are all no longer with us. Sometimes I can't quite believe it.'

Liam pats her shoulder kindly. 'It's dreadful missing people isn't it, Mrs Peabody? I can never get used to it myself.'

I look around the room and its reminders of Eric. Mrs Peabody has kept many of her husband's personal belongings, including his carpet slippers, which are by the fireplace, his silver snuffbox and his old *Reader's Digests*. In fact, there is so much of Eric around I sometimes almost feel I've met him.

'Let's have some sherry,' Mrs Peabody suggests eagerly.

I get an urge to giggle, and I can see Liam is struggling to remain solemn himself. 'Would you mind if

I had a cup of tea instead, Mrs Peabody?' he asks gently. 'That Darjeeling of yours is so delicious.'

'Yes, I'd like that too,' I add quickly.

'Tea it is then,' Mrs Peabody agrees, though there is a definite trace of disappointment in her voice. She starts to rise from her chair with considerable difficulty. I'm about to assist her, but Liam rushes over before me. He offers her his arm in a most gallant manner and she leans on it, smiling up at him almost flirtatiously. I follow them into the kitchen. We both watch as she reaches into cupboards, her hands feeling for the shapes of the crockery before she extracts it.

'How's your eyesight these days?' I ask.

'Those glasses I got were a great help at first, dear,' she sighs. 'But after a while they just seemed to make everything more blurry.'

'Maybe you should give them another try,' Liam suggests.

'I have, dear,' she replies. 'They're no use at all. And anyway, I've lost them.'

'I'll help you look for them,' I volunteer.

'No, no, dear. I'm better off without them. Really.'

Liam and I look at each other concernedly. Mrs Peabody is handling the crockery in a rather precarious manner. As she loads it on to a tray I half expect to hear a clatter at any moment. 'I know where things are you see, dear,' she's explaining happily.

'Yes, of course you do,' I agree, stealthily shoving the tin of tea bags towards her. She's been hunting for it for the past minute. I stand stock still as she pours boiling water into the teapot, ready to lunge.

'I'll take the tray out for you,' I announce firmly. As I reach for it Liam reaches for Mrs Peabody's arm. 'Here, let me escort you,' he says grandly.

She looks up. 'You are such a nice boy, Liam,' she smiles.

'Thank you, Mrs Peabody. You're a rather ravishing young lass yourself,' he replies, giving me a quick wink as he does so. He waits patiently as Mrs Peabody touches the corner of her favourite armchair, watching protectively as she works her way round cautiously to the seat. Then we all sit down and sip our tea and try to ignore Dora's frequent 'fecks'. She's saying them quite loudly and Mrs Peabody seems determined not to be offended.

'She's a great little talker, isn't she?' she observes. 'Listen to her saying "peck" − such a clever little thing. She hasn't got the pronunciation quite right yet but there's a definite improvement.'

I'm going to laugh in a minute if I'm not careful. I'm going to splutter into my tea and spray its droplets all over the furniture. I try to distract myself by looking out the window. As I do so I spot a pair of glasses half hidden by the curtains. They are on the ledge and are slim and stylish. As I go to fetch them I notice another slightly thicker, tortoiseshell-rimmed pair peeking out from under a pile of ancient newspapers. I pick them up too.

'I think I've found your glasses, Mrs Peabody,' I say, bringing them over to her. 'There seem to be two pairs. Which is the right one? They look very similar.'

Mrs Peabody peers at them. 'This pair, dear,' she says, putting the slimmer ones on. 'They're still no help, I'm afraid,' she squints. 'I can't even see Cyril's cage.'

'Well, try these on then.' I proffer the other pair.

'No, no, those used to be Eric's. I can tell by the tortoiseshell frame.'

'But they've both got tortoiseshell frames, Mrs Peabody.'

'Have they? Goodness.'

'Try them on – please do,' I urge.

'Oh, all right, if you insist,' Mrs Peabody sighs. She puts on the glasses and surveys the room again. She says nothing for quite some time.

'Oh well, it was worth a try,' I think, a trifle dejectedly.

Then I hear Mrs Peabody exclaim, 'Well, goodness me, Alice, you're right. They do make a difference!' She's beaming delightedly. 'I must have got my glasses mixed up with Eric's. Oh, thank you, dear. You don't know how much this means to me.'

Mrs Peabody's hands are fluttering on her lap. She's almost jumping out of her chair with excitement, and Liam and I are pretty ebullient too. How wonderful – Mrs Peabody will now be able to see her crockery and find her tea bags. She may even not have to sit so close to the television that she's almost in the cast of *Coronation Street*. 'Well, this certainly calls for a sherry,' she declares joyfully.

'Yes, indeed it does,' I agree.

As I return with the glasses I notice that Mrs Peabody is staring most intently at Cyril and Dora's cage. 'My goodness,' she is saying, 'these two are not at all the lovebirds that I'd thought.'

'Oh dear,' I mumble apologetically. 'We should have told you.'

'Yes, we didn't want to disappoint you, Mrs Peabody,' Liam adds. 'You seemed to find the idea of their romance so cheering.'

'Maybe even budgies lose interest in romance, Mrs Peabody,' I say earnestly, desperately trying to comfort her. 'I mean even I'm not as interested in romance as I used to be. It's begun to seem so – so laden with illusion.'

Just as I've announced this, Cyril decides to break his months of silence. He squawks 'bollocks' very loudly and as he does so Mrs Peabody and Liam exchange gleefully delighted glances. They've even begun to laugh. They're not just laughing at Cyril, they're laughing at me, I know they are. It's just not fair. I meant what I said about romance. I really did. Still, I must say I find the timing of Cyril's expletive rather disturbing.

'Oh, come on, Alice, don't look so serious,' Liam is chuckling. He's staring straight into my eyes with a strange softness. I look away quickly. I don't like him looking at me like that. It's as if he thinks he knows me, but he doesn't. Very few people do. I don't trust people easily. I don't expect them to understand me. I am so scared of their misinterpretation that I prefer to dissemble. Smile my dolphin's smile.

I'm smiling gamely now as I finish my glass of sherry. I am pretending to share Liam and Mrs Peabody's delight in Cyril's pronouncement. That's how you keep people away – you don't show them what you feel. Only I don't think I'm fooling Liam. He's the one who's solemn now. Concerned. I smile more brightly. Why aren't I fooling him? I can do it with most people. I drink my sherry quickly then I make my excuses and leave.

As soon as I get home Mira says that there's a letter for me on the hall table. 'Fancy some spag bol?' she adds.

'Yes, please.'

I go into my room, where I put on an ancient jumper that's covered in paint splashes. Then I set up my easel and get out a landscape I'm working on. Having done

217

this I go to the hall table and pick up my letter. It's rather stiff and probably contains some invitation. I seem to have got on to a number of obscure mailing lists recently.

Yes, I was right, it is an invitation. It's to an art exhibition which is being held this Friday. The exhibition features ceramic sculptures by – I have to read the sentence again – by James Mitchel! Mira must hear something strange in my silence because she pads out into the hallway in her huge furry slippers. She looks at me and then at the card I'm holding.

'So you've opened your letter.'

'Yes' – I lean against the wall and take a deep breath – 'yes, I have.'

'Who's it from?'

I hand it to her.

'Ah, the "last good man" himself,' she smiles wryly. 'What's the PTO at the back about?'

'What?' I grab the card from her, then I turn it over and read:

'Hi there, Alice.

Hope you can make it to my exhibition. I'm inviting former pupils from my pottery class, so you'll meet some old friends there. I got your address from the college. I've been staying in a cottage in the wilds getting ready for this exhibition, so I only heard your phone messages when I got home the other day. Glad that you got the information you needed. Best wishes and hope to see you soon, James.'

The words are almost dancing in front of me, like they're in the Rio Carnival. James Mitchel has written to me. He's going to be right here, in the same city as me, at the end of this week! I read through his note again, hoping I may have missed some sense of pining, some sense of urgency. I haven't. If only it was in French.

'So, are you going to go?' Mira is studying me curiously.

'I dunno. No. I mean – maybe – yes. Probably.'

After dinner I try to get on with my painting, but thoughts of James Mitchel keep intruding. Cyril was right, I haven't really lost interest in romance – that is, James Mitchel – at all. Poor Eamon, how disloyal I'm being to him. I so wish I could love him the way I love James. He's a good man. He deserves that. But I can't say 'yes' to his proposal if I could have James instead. Yes, I must go to that exhibition. If nothing else it may clarify my feelings a little.

As I paint a field filled with lavender – a field I often see when I look out the window of my imaginary villa in Provence – I decide that what I admire most about James is his conviction about himself. The answers he has reached. I suppose I hope a little bit of them are going to rub off on to me, though I do realize that men like him sometimes just leave smudges. Long before James Mitchel there was that yoga teacher, and that bus conductor, and that bassoonist. All very different, but similar in one vital way. They had an altitude to their attitude. Even their confidence seemed to have the weather-beaten, but durable, quality of granite. Contented in their solitude, they were a sort of emotional equivalent to Mount Everest. Unassailable to all but the determined, and perhaps foolhardy. Compared to them, most of my past boyfriends weren't even hills.

I didn't know James Mitchel did 'ceramic sculptures'. He's got so many interests he's a veritable Renaissance Man. Where does he get time for all this stuff? I wrote an article about time management once and left it so late I almost didn't make the deadline. He has so much to teach me. I must have him. I must.

219

No, no. That isn't right. I mustn't get too needy with James – I know he'd find that off-putting. I must remain nonchalant with him. Have some altitude to my attitude myself. That's what men like him really admire. Having trekked for miles through their internal Himalayas, they don't really want to have to peer down into the foothills for their Significant Other. They don't want to retrace their steps to find her. They want her right up there with them – in some sweet, calm place where they don't really need each other anyway.

I really must buy myself a clingy top.

Chapter 24

I'M AT THE OPENING of James Mitchel's art exhibition.

It's a swelteringly hot night. I almost feel I'm in the tropics. The large whirring fan overhead looks like it belongs in Casablanca. I put lots of ice in my wine and then cup the glass in my hands, letting it cool me.

My 'look' this evening is not what you might call subtle. In fact, I could be taken for a participant in one of my own articles. Annie helped me with my make-up. 'You didn't get those lips sucking oranges,' was Mira's parting comment. Who knows, by the end of this evening I might be licking mayonnaise from James Mitchel's inner thigh area. I want to look sexy and attractive. I want James Mitchel to see my curves but not too much of my bottom, which is a bit too big. Thankfully my new clingy top covers it and my navy cotton trousers have a flattering line to them.

I'm used to receptions – or 'deceptions' as Cindi calls them. I find large helpings of wine and hors d'oeuvres alleviate the small talk. 'Yes, I have the press release and the photos, thanks,' I say. 'Was that caviar vol-au-vents that went by just then?'

But tonight is different. I am not 'on assignment' – though in a way, of course, I am. I must somehow make an impression on James, but I'm not sure how to go about it. I'm standing in a corner of the gallery feigning enormous interest in the exhibition catalogue. My nose is stuck right into it, but every so often I look up, rather furtively, and search for him among the crowd. I feel so self-conscious, as though what I'm up to is obvious to everyone. I must see him first, preferably from afar, so that I can ease, with a shore appraisal and then a gentle paddle, into the great sea of longing he brings up for me.

I grab another glass of wine from a tray as though it is a life jacket. Alcohol. I need alcohol. I've seen him. He's over there chatting with a bunch of calm, cheerful people, a wineglass in his hand. His hair is shorter and he's got a brown corduroy suit on and a cream cotton shirt, which shows off his tan. He feels me staring at him and looks over. I look down, gulp, into my catalogue which is now damp from my sweaty palms.

This is ridiculous. I sidle over to a sculpture of a naked man. There's a lot of nudity in James's sculptures. They are mostly of men and are very well done. Almost embarrassingly detailed in fact. The sculptures of women, many of them in abandoned poses, are also hard to stare at in my present state. James Mitchel knows a lot about the human body, that is becoming very clear. He's studied its crevices and corners, its curves and conduits. How I wish he'd study mine.

Out of the corner of my eye I see that James is moving towards this side of the room. I head for the table with wine bottles on it. I fill up my glass, a little unsteadily. I'm beginning to experience a distinct sensation of floating.

How many glasses have I had – four – five? I take a fistful of peanuts from a bowl.

'Is that you, Alice?'

Oh, my God, that's his voice. I stand very still for a moment, steadying my face. Then I try to turn around, nonchalantly, only I seem to tip a bit to one side.

'Hello, James! Great exhibition.' I gesture rather too wildly and spill some of my wine.

'So, how are you?' James is smiling his calm, sweet smile. I find myself staring at him, drinking in his features. If he was wine he'd be vintage Bordeaux. 'Done any pottery recently?' he continues. He seems slightly perplexed by my silence.

'No. No, I haven't actually. Your sculptures are wonderful, James. I didn't know you did this kind of thing.'

'Ah well, Alice. I'm sure there are a lot of things we don't know about each other.' James gives me one of his wry, knowing looks. 'I'm so glad that you came.'

'So am I.'

'Have you bumped into Mildred yet? She's over there.'

'Oh, is she?' There's a pause. A pause in which James might decide to wander off. A rotund lady in a chiffon dress is studying him purposefully. She looks as if she's about to grab him away from me at any moment. Other people are touching his arm and saying, 'Well done.'

'So, how is the pottery studio in West Cork going?' I ask. He mustn't get away from me, not just yet.

'I haven't done much with it, but I hope to soon. I've been getting ready for this exhibition.' James is looking around a bit, probably aware that there are a number of other people he should be talking to. I wish he'd show more signs of lust. Lust would do to start with. We could get round to the other stuff later. I'm not usually this superficial but even meaningless sex with James would be wonderful. He'll be gone in a moment. If I want to see him again I'll have to act now. I take a deep breath and try to summon up the lines I've been rehearsing.

'James – regarding your pottery studio – I may be able to help you with a bit of publicity for it.'

'Really. How?' James is looking most interested.

'You'll be making some household ceramics, won't you? You know, like tableware?'

223

'Yes, along with other things.'

'Well, there's a "Style" section in the magazine I work for, and I might be able to get them to include a write-up about your range.'

'Really! That would be great.'

I can't believe what I'm about to say. But I must. I must. It should sound spontaneous. I've been practising it all day. 'Tell you what, James,' I smile gaily, 'why don't you come to dinner the next time you're in Dublin. Bring some samples and photographs of your pottery with you. We could have a proper chat about it all then.' I take a deep swig from my glass of wine and brace myself for his answer. Dear God, my bra strap is showing! I tuck it back into place.

'Thanks, Alice. What a kind offer.' James seems genuinely grateful. 'Give me your number again, will you?'

I hand him my card and then the rotund lady in the chiffon dress grabs him and pulls him away from me. I don't mind. A quiet, grateful smile has settled on my features. One does have to take the romantic initiative sometimes, one really does. And I just have! Me, Alice Evans.

And then I realize something. I should have said I would phone him to make the dinner arrangements. This way James Mitchel has to phone me. But what if he doesn't? He didn't last time. I lean dejectedly against a wall and am about to leave when I see Mildred. I go over to her. She's gazing longingly at a particularly nubile male nude.

'Quite an exhibition, isn't it Alice?' She eyes me meaningfully.

'Yes, it is,' I agree.

'In fact, if these sculptures were paintings,' Mildred begins to chortle delightedly, 'I'd say they were extremely well hung.'

Chapter Twenty-Five

JAMES MITCHEL PHONED YESTERDAY. He's coming to dinner tonight! The thought had me bolting out of bed at a ridiculously early hour this Saturday morning.

I can't believe how unkempt this cottage seems. Even though Mira and I clean it quite regularly, we seem to have overlooked innumerable domestic details. At first glance anyone could see that it's the home of a woman with a tidemark around her bath, and life. A woman with tea-stained mugs and ancient grey bras. This gross generalization acquires the purity of higher calculus when I feel it, and I'm feeling it right now. At least it's the weekend, so I have time to clean the place up. But I'm still in a terrible tizz.

'Oh, Tarquin,' I say, 'how am I going to get this place ready in time?' He just looks up at me longingly, with deeply resigned eyes. He hopes we're discussing food. He begins to rub himself against the leg of a chair. He now shows his affection for me by caressing inanimate objects but still hasn't summoned up the courage to let me pat him.

I rush out to the corner shop and buy Cif, bleach, lavender Ajax, lemon floor cleaner and a box of J-cloths. When I get home I arrange them in a row on the kitchen sideboard and vow to keep them there because they look so impressive. Then I squat beside the cooker, trying to reach the globs of muck that have gathered slyly between it and the washing machine.

'Hello.' Mira pads into the kitchen with a yawn and reaches for the tin of Earl Grey tea. She's about to spoon some into the teapot with the cracked spout when I shriek with alarm.

'You can't use that!'

'What?'

'The teapot. It's got bleach in it. It was all brown and stained inside.'

'Oh, for God's sake, Alice,' Mira sighs wearily. 'James Mitchel is hardly going to go around inspecting the insides of our teapots.'

'It just makes me feel better to know it's clean,' I announce defensively. 'We've become sluttish, Mira. We've let things slide. Even our underwear isn't white any more.'

'How were we to know that the blue bedspread would run like that?' Mira counters. 'You're getting into a state, Alice. I wish Eamon was back from Peru. He wouldn't stand any of this nonsense.'

'How can I attract a Wonderful Man if I don't even have a decent sofa?' I wail. The state of this cottage has suddenly become synonymous with my entire life. Things spilling out of cupboards, unsorted. Murky corners I am somehow going to have to steel myself to face.

'Oh, for goodness sake,' Mira says sharply. 'The kind of man you need wouldn't care about that stuff – he'd be far less high-maintenance. He'd want you for yourself.'

I stare at her glumly. She is, of course, right. A pristine sideboard would, in a way, be so much easier. And how desperately politically incorrect it is of me to want to lure a man in this manner. I really must start rereading Gloria Steinem. My feminism definitely seems to need a bit of dusting.

'You'll be here tonight, won't you?' I look at Mira anxiously.

'Yes. I said I would.'

'I've invited Matt too.'

Mira studies me quizzically. 'I'm surprised you want company. I thought you'd want James all to yourself.'

'I – I do really. It just seemed better to do it this way.' As Mira puts her orange juice, tea and toast on a tray and heads back towards her bedroom, I recommence my scrubbing. She's right. I'd love to have James here, alone. I'd love to stare at him tenderly over a candlelit meal. The thing is, attraction and anxiety can make me blab a bit, especially if there's wine involved. I'd probably tell him all sorts of things he'd be better off not knowing yet. I'd frighten him off. After all, he does think he's coming here simply to discuss a write-up in the magazine.

With Mira and Matt here I'll be prevented from love lunging. This way I'll get to know James gradually, which is something I haven't managed to do with many men in the past. If I really like a man I tend to want him right in my life, immediately. Having probably gone without romantic intimacy for ages, once I think I've found it I go on a bit of a binge. I guzzle it. I luxuriate in the feeling that I somehow know all the things that we haven't, as yet, said. I paint my passion canvas carefully. It sets me alight inside just to look at it. What a wonderful person this man must be to evoke all these blissful feelings. I feel I know him so well. And then one day he says something like 'Wildlife TV programmes are so boring' – and I realize I don't. I realize I should have waited for him to paint his own picture, but I've been so needy I haven't even given him time to reach for a brush.

Nat King Cole singing 'When I Fall In Love' is drifting out of Mira's bedroom as I give the final rub to the lino directly opposite the toilet seat. Sitting on that seat I have, for some time now, noticed that some dust has been gathering where the lino meets the wall. I have watched it accumulating with a vague lack of interest. Now I have to use a cloth to extricate the more persistent bits. As soon as I have done this I realize that, when James Mitchel uses the loo, he will probably be facing the opposite direction. So more cleaning is required, including under the loo seat itself. Dust there would be a dead giveaway. Evidence of the current marked absence of men in my life.

I'm about to go into the kitchen to make myself a cuppa, when I notice the sofa. The cheap sofa that doesn't know how to behave itself. Mira and I have been meaning to get a new one for ages. I go over to it purposefully and start to tussle with its cushions, bashing them into some kind of shape while reprimanding them sternly.

'You are not to slide and sag gradually until you reach the floor this evening,' I tell them. 'I know it's a little game you like, but you've done it once too often.'

'Is someone there? Who are you talking to?' Mira calls out.

'No – no – I was just – just...' I decide to come clean. 'I was just telling the sofa to behave itself.'

Mira lets out a low groan, but says nothing.

Having dealt with the sofa I sit on it and take stock.

Oh dear – I should have asked if there is anything James doesn't eat. I've seen him eating a chicken sandwich in the college canteen, so he can't be vegetarian. I know, I'll buy some 'Chicken Louisiana' from the deli in the supermarket. It's all prepared and you just have to cook it. It should be OK with boil-in-the-bag basmati rice and salad. And garlic bread. I mustn't forget the garlic bread.

And ice-cream. And my vase. I mustn't forget some freesias for my vase. And I must remember to take my personal growth books into my bedroom – especially *Chronically Single*. The litany of 'must dos' starts to drone on in my head like the BBC Radio 4 shipping forecast.

James Mitchel is late. As I wait for him I wander edgily around the sitting-room. I'm trying to pretend that I am a visitor and seeing it for the first time. Lots of people say this cottage has a kind of country charm, but I'm never quite sure if they mean it. There's lots of pine and plants and colourful cushions, and Mira is very good at finding pretty hand-crafted accessories and nice lampshades. I tend to be drawn towards objects that are bright and playful – like that antique tin toy motorbike and luridly coloured collection of Disney pencil sharpeners. Mira calls them my 'Kitsch Collection'. Sarah says they're presents for my 'inner child'. I have 'a lot of the inner child about me' she says, which is perhaps just as well, because I'm not at all sure if I'll ever have an outer one.

I bet any child of James Mitchel's would have his beautiful deep brown eyes.

The doorbell rings. I rush over to the mirror to make sure I'm not showing too much cleavage in my new coral pink silk blouse. Good, my lipstick is still there. I practise a quick, casual smile and then sniff the air fearfully. Geranium aromatherapy oil is combining with Fidgi perfume, lavender Ajax and freesias in an overpowering manner. When I'm nervous I tend to over-indulge olfactorily. 'I must open a window fast,' I think, as I approach the door.

It's Matt. 'Hello, darling,' he says, bending to kiss my cheek. He looks all Merchant Ivory, as usual.

'Hello.' I grab the bottle of wine Matt has proffered and race into the kitchen with it, suddenly aware that the garlic bread needs to be taken out of the oven. I put it on too early. It will be all dry and hard soon if I don't rescue it. I take it out and put it on the sideboard, then I peer anxiously at the Chicken Louisiana, which is bubbling away in a saucepan.

'Like some help?' Matt calls out from the sitting-room.

'No, you just relax. It's a very simple meal.'

'What is it?' Matt comes into the kitchen and starts to snoop around.

'It's Chicken Louisiana. You can buy it pre-prepared at the supermarket. What are you looking for?'

'I'm looking for a bottle opener. That Valpolicella I got you needs to breathe for a while to be at its best.'

'There's one in that drawer. Oh shit.'

'What is it?'

'I forgot to open a window.' I race back into the sitting-room. Matt follows me in a more leisurely manner.

'What's the smell?' he asks.

'Is it – is it very strong?' I look at him anxiously.

'It is rather. What is it?'

'I'm not quite sure at this stage. A bit of everything really.'

Matt sniffs the air again. 'Don't worry, Alice, it's not unpleasant, just intriguing.'

Mira appears from her bedroom, where she's been meditating. She hoovered the sitting-room earlier and did offer to help with the cooking. The disparaging remarks about James Mitchel's visit now seem to have eased somewhat. In fact, I suspect she's rather intrigued and can't wait to meet him herself. 'Poor Eamon,' she mumbles every so often. Apart from that she's behaving herself quite well, even if she is currently wearing her leather motorcycle jacket, huge furry slippers and ancient jeans. Her hair colour is now not unlike Laren Brassière's. I look at her.

'Mira, aren't you going to change?'

'Maybe.'

Matt nudges my elbow. 'Alice, what about putting some candles on the table?'

'Do you think we should?' I frown.

'Yes,' he says decisively. 'They give the place a softer feel.'

'But they might look too romantic.'

'No, they won't. We'll keep the corner lamp on.'

As Matt scurries off to find some candles Mira starts fussing about the boil-in-the-bag basmati rice. She doesn't approve of short-cut cooking.

'Stop scolding,' I tell her. 'There's some parsley over there that you can chop up if you like.'

Suddenly we're all rushing around like actors putting the finishing touches to a set. I go into the sitting-room and stare at the table. Yes, Matt is right. The candles do look good. Lots of people burn candles at dinner parties. They are not inextricably linked with seduction. I'm glad I remembered the paper napkins. They don't quite go with the tablecloth, but at least they're there. I didn't buy a sailing magazine, but *Country Living* looks fairly bracing on the coffee table. I pour myself a glass of wine and am wondering – for the umpteenth time – if I should change into something a little less eager, when the doorbell goes. I jump, somehow tremendously surprised. The evening has begun to seem more about anticipating James's arrival rather than him actually being here. I try to move calmly towards the front door. 'Why on earth am

I doing this?' I think. But as soon as I see James I get my answer.

He is, as usual, looking adorable. He seems a bit windswept, but then he always does. He's got a big bag with him, which I assume contains the pottery samples. He's also holding a small brown parcel, which he thrusts into my hands.

'Hello, Alice. Sorry I'm a bit late.' He gives me his wonderful wide smile. I try to remember my manners.

'Come in. Come in,' I beam, trying not to sound flustered. I don't know if it's my imagination, but it seems to me James gives the sitting-room a small but significant sniff as he enters.

Mira, bless her, is sitting on the sofa, ready to deflect any attempt James might make to sit on it himself. She's wearing a rather plain but very pleasant designer dress she found in an Oxfam shop. She finds lots of wonderful second-hand designer clothes. She's that kind of person.

'This is my housemate, Mira,' I announce.

'Hello.' Mira gives James a welcoming smile. 'Alice told me your exhibition was most impressive. We can't wait to see your pottery.'

James looks as though he's about to sit beside Mira on the sofa, but I steer him firmly to the leather armchair.

'Like some wine?' I ask.

'Yes, please,' he says.

I realize I haven't opened the package he gave me. I tear off the wrapping to reveal a box of After Eights. 'I wanted to get some Chianti but I didn't have time to get to the off-licence,' James explains, watching me.

'Oh, we love After Eights – don't we, Mira?' I enthuse.

'Yes. We absolutely adore them.' She gives me a meaningful look.

I'm glad I've got my back to them as I pour the wine because I might get flustered if they watched me. I scrubbed these glasses really well, but they still don't have the dazzling sheen I'd hoped for. Oh, my God, the garlic bread.

'Here you are then,' I plonk the wineglasses down on the coffee table and scurry into the kitchen. As soon as I've got there I realize this sudden exit might have seemed rude so I peer back into the sitting-room and say, 'Excuse me for a moment.'

In the kitchen Matt is tasting something fastidiously on a spoon. He can be quite shy about meeting new people and is clearly stalling for time by preparing vinaigrette sauce. I put the garlic bread back into the oven and then check the plates are warm enough. They are. I stack them on a tray and bring them into the sitting-room, where I almost bump into James. He's looking for the bathroom.

'It's just down there. On the left.' I point to the corridor off the kitchen and suddenly remember I haven't checked the Chicken Louisiana recently. It's been on for so long now that it may have to be attributed to someplace deeper south. I put the plates on the dining table and race back into the kitchen. I peer into the saucepan and am relieved to see the chicken does not appear overcooked.

'I turned it down to simmer,' Matt says smugly. 'Do you have any balsamic vinegar?'

'No.'

'I've told you that you should buy it,' Matt scolds, but I don't reply. I've realized something. I've realized that I have told James that the bathroom is on the left side of the corridor when in fact it's on the right. I streak off after him. How could I have made such an obvious

Freudian slip? I've directed him to my bedroom! And he's gone into it. I know this because I see him coming out.

'The bathroom must be in there,' he says with suspicious solemnity as he points to the door opposite him.

As soon as he's gone into the bathroom I go into the bedroom myself. A bedroom which cannot be mistaken for Mira's because it has a big picture, painted by Josh on prominent display. 'To Alice with Lurve' Annie has written at the top in huge blue letters. Wouldn't you know it – even though I removed all my most embarrassing objects from the sitting-room, James has discovered them anyway. *Smart Women, Foolish Choices* is actually on my bed, along with a pile of off-white underwear. Even the penis pencil sharpener Sarah bought for my Kitsch Collection is on display. I rush over to my handbag and peer in at the numerous calming herbal remedies I keep in a side pouch. I take some out and gobble them down.

It takes me a few minutes to summon up the courage to return to the sitting-room. When I do, I find that Matt and Mira have already brought the food in from the kitchen.

'Ah, there you are,' Mira says gaily.

Suddenly I feel like the director of some strange art house movie. A film with no script. We all sit down and I regard my cast cautiously.

'This Chicken Louisiana of yours looks very tasty,' says Matt as he piles a little heap of it on to his plate. As he does so, James Mitchel looks at him curiously. Dear God, I haven't even introduced them.

'James this is Matt,' I say. 'He's a friend of – of ours.'

'Yes, so Mira said,' James smiles as he unfolds his napkin. His glass of wine is empty. I fill it.

'Do help yourself to anything you need,' I say. 'Please don't wait to be asked if you want wine. Or – or anything else.' I don't add 'me', but I'd like to.

'I've had a look at the magazine you write for, Alice,' James says. 'It's very interesting. I looked out for your name but I didn't see it. What kind of articles do you do?'

Oh God – he would ask that. Should I? Should I tell James why I don't use my real name for my articles any more? After all, if I tell him I write about sex he might think I'm an expert on the subject. It might impress him. But then again it might not.

'Mmmm – I write about lifestyles mainly,' I mumble. 'Matt made some delicious dressing for the salad. Have you tried it?'

'Yes, I have. It's excellent.' James gives Matt another odd glance and Matt looks back at him in what I suppose could be described as a strange way. Even despite my numerous preoccupations I am aware of some sort of vibe between them. Could it be – surely not – that they are slightly jealous of each other? That in some small way they are vying for my attention? Matt can be a bit possessive about our friendship at times. And perhaps James Mitchel expected – wanted – to have this dinner alone with me. I must make it clear to him that Matt and I are just friends, because Matt is not obviously gay. And he is, as I've said, extremely attractive.

'It's so good to see you again, James. I needed an excuse for a dinner party. Matt and I met at college. We've been friends' – I linger on that word for a moment – 'for ages.'

Having said this I realize it does not contain the sort of internal logic that statements – however throwaway – usually require. There is really no link between wanting to have a dinner party and the fact that Matt and I met at college. I could, of course, try to find one. Happily, James speaks before I am driven to further inanities.

'And it's good to see you too, Alice. This chicken is delicious.'

'Thank you.' Then there's a rather uncomfortable silence in which I hope he's not going to ask me for the recipe.

'So, what do you do Mira?' James asks.

'Oh, I've done piles of things over the years, James. I'm currently in training to become an eccentric spinster.'

'Really?' James regards her quizzically. 'And what does that involve?'

'Mira teaches English as a foreign language,' I interrupt quickly. 'She can make English sound incredibly foreign – she'll teach you to speak as though you come from Guatemala if you want.'

James is supposed to laugh at this, but he doesn't. I look down at my plate. I take a deep swig from my wine glass. Silence. A silence which I feel impelled to fill. Suddenly, unaccountably, I find myself announcing that I'd like to live in Provence. Dear God, I've started to blabber. I wish Matt would speak. What on earth is wrong with him? His shyness with strangers doesn't usually last this long.

'So, what do you do?' James says suddenly in a direct, almost challenging manner. He's staring straight into Matt's eyes. Matt looks down at his salad as if reluctant to answer.

'He's an architect,' I answer protectively. 'And he's very, very good at it.'

'I'm sure he is,' says James with an enigmatic smile.

'Yes he took it up after Trinity. He's worked on some lovely places. Even Prince Charles wouldn't disapprove.' I look at Matt hopefully. When dinner guests don't speak up for themselves I feel impelled to do it for them. Surely my eulogy will have warmed him up a bit. Surely he's going to say something. He doesn't.

'I need a bit of architectural advice about the pottery studio, actually,' says James. 'I want to extend it. Maybe Matt might help me with it.'

Matt shifts uncomfortably in his chair. 'I'm rather busy at the moment,' he mumbles after what seems a very long and cumbersome pause. 'I wouldn't be able to get round to it for quite some time.'

'There's no hurry,' James says slowly. 'I just thought I'd mention it.'

'And how kind of you to mention it, James,' I think. 'After all, you hardly know this man. It's typical of you. Typical of your generous, trusting nature.' I give Matt a reproachful look, but he won't meet my gaze.

The conversation meanders on in a not very riveting fashion. I begin to wish I'd come clean about my articles. They might have spiced things up a bit. Intimacy is not as easy to rustle up as Chicken Louisiana. Maybe I should have had this dinner with James alone. The candlelight is making him look even more delicious. I wonder if I could get Mira and Matt to go off somewhere so I could feed him the Häagen-Dazs dessert we are currently eating. Slowly. And on a silver spoon.

As Mira goes into the kitchen to make the coffee, Matt moves in a rather dejected manner to the sofa, and James does too.

'Oh dear,' I think. 'Please sofa, behave yourself just this once.' I sit on the leather armchair.

'Mira says these paintings are yours.' James is pointing to some of my landscapes. 'I was admiring them earlier. They're very good.'

'Do you really think so!' My toes are curling with happiness.

'Yes, indeed. You should have an exhibition.'

'Perhaps she could have one at your studio,' Mira comments, as she returns with the coffee. She's been trying to encourage me to paint more for some time now, but she shouldn't have said that to James. It's far too pushy. I give her a reproachful glance.

'Thank you, James,' I say quickly. 'I'm so glad you like me – I mean my – paintings. They're just a hobby really.' I smile, loath to tell him about the short, blunt 'Thank you, but...' letters I have received from numerous galleries. 'Morale is ninety per cent of every victory' – Tony Benn said once. When it comes to having my paintings 'taken on' by a gallery I frequently have to remind myself of this fact. James Mitchel has morale in EU proportions. He's got piles of it. Almost a surplus. I lean towards him, hoping some of it will drift towards me. 'I can't wait to see the pottery samples you've brought,' I add. 'Shall we look at them now?'

They're lovely. Each carefully wrapped item that James removes from his Nike sports bag is more beautiful than the last. The colours are gorgeous, and somehow unexpected. They're light and wonderfully crafted. He's been showing them to various shops. He already has orders.

'Do you have any photographs of these?' I ask. 'They'd look great in the magazine.'

James reaches into his bag again and takes out a hard-backed envelope, which he hands to me. It contains colour transparencies of his pottery range, and a comprehensive press release.

'Gosh, you are organized, James!' I exclaim. I'm pleased, but also slightly disappointed. If I'd had to get photographs done I would have had an excuse to phone him. Arrange for the return of the samples. Ask him questions I see he has already answered in the press release. Still, he has been friendly this evening. We do know each other a little better now. It takes time to know people. I often forget that. It's like painting a picture of something – you have to look at it. Really look. Be as aware of the shape of the spaces where it isn't, as of the shape itself.

I look over at James warmly and then I notice something. The space between him and Matt on the sofa seems to have diminished. The sofa cushions don't normally sag in the middle, but they obviously have thought up a new ruse. And the funny thing is, neither James nor Matt seem uncomfortable with this proximity. They are helping themselves very liberally to more wine. Matt's been drinking a great deal of wine this evening and it seems to have loosened him up considerably. In fact, he is almost coquettish. Maybe I should go over to him with some Aqua Libra. James is leaning towards him, talking animatedly about something. James has never talked to me like that. His face radiant. Excited. At one point he places a hand on Matt's arm in an extremely familiar, almost intimate, manner. Their knees are touching. Mira, who has also been following the proceedings, looks over at me. Eyebrows raised.

'Oh fuck,' I moan, very softly. The cheery scatter on the dining table now seems like the detritus of some dream. For I now suspect something. In fact I know it. I know that it is Matt who is going to lick mayonnaise off James Mitchel's inner thigh area.

Even coleslaw – if that's what he'd prefer.

Chapter 26

MAYBE I SHOULD JUST become a hermit. Move into a shack halfway up a mountain. I could have BBC Radio 4 humming in the background. That would be company, of sorts. There'd be no people to invite to dinner parties. No mayonnaise and no James Mitchel.

I could probably just about support this exile by writing articles for the magazine. Oscillating between features that benefit from a certain distance from the subject matter, such as 'Why Men are Marvellous', to more autobiographical offerings: 'I've Tried Celibacy and it Works!' Or 'Feeling Sheepish? Then Keep One'.

Becoming an eccentric spinster like Mira also seems quite attractive at the moment. If I am to be an eccentric spinster I'd prefer to do it somewhere warm. A gradual development of, say, strong unfashionable views might be quite bracing. Of course, one doesn't have to be eccentric to be single. Some of the most sensible women I know are living on their own. It's just that Mira and I like to do things with a certain dash. We have the cat already, but we'll need at least another ten to do spinsterhood in style. I'd like to paint wonderful landscapes. I'd have a straw hat too. I'd potter around my garden a lot. My garden full of bougainvillea and frangipani and oleander and lavender – and other words you can almost smell. I'd listen to the World Service and fire off letters to its management correcting the announcers' pronunciations. I'd have a bee in my bonnet about certain words. I might have real bees too. A virile lad from the local village would help me with them, and Mira and I would admire his firm and beautiful young body as he stooped before the hives. Afterwards we'd share tea under the loggia and his dear young face would frown as he talked about his complicated love life. We'd just smile and listen, as if hearing a half-forgotten melody. Sweet but not insistent. Something from long ago.

Another possibility, of course, is following the religious inclinations of Gilbert – my mother's first love. He became a monk...maybe I should become a nun. I could forget about Eamon's proposal and become a spiritual bride of Jesus. That would simplify things enormously.

I'm thinking about all this as I sit at my desk. Then I see Gerry. 'What date is it, Gerry?' I ask. He stares at me as though I'm talking Swahili. 'What date is it?' I repeat. He starts to rummage around his desk for his diary.

'It's – it's the fourth,' he announces eventually.

'Thank you.' I give him a small tight smile.

I hear the steady pad of Humphrey's Hush Puppies approaching. 'Can I borrow your stapler for a minute?' he asks.

'No.'

'What?'

'No, you can't borrow my stapler, Humphrey. Here, I've got you one of your own. It's the same model. I've tried it and it works.' I hand it to him. He seems somewhat startled.

'Thank you. Thank you, Alice,' he says. 'There really was no need.'

'Yes, there was,' I think, as he sprints away. Humphrey has been borrowing my stapler for four years. He doesn't even bring it back. I have to retrieve it.

When Cindi appears she takes one look at me and decides not to comment. 'Oh shit, I didn't buy any milk,' I hear myself say to her.

'I've got some,' she says. 'Would you like me to make you a cuppa?'

'Yes, I would actually,' I reply, handing her the new mug I've bought. It's got small pink rosebuds on it. Then I yell 'no sugar' after her as she scurries away.

Sarah senses something is up almost immediately. I have the kind of face that doesn't hide things too well. However much I smile my dolphin's smile, it doesn't fool people. Not that I am smiling, actually. As I sit down in Sarah's office I clear my throat, and she asks me if I'm growling.

'You've got your "difficult man" face on today, Alice,' she says. 'Would you like to talk about Ea... I mean, it?'

I look at her sharply. She was about to say Eamon, wasn't she? How does she know about Eamon? I've never told her about him. Annie must have told her about my proposal. I guessed as much.

'What did you want to see me about, Sarah?' I ask briskly. I just can't confide in her right now about Eamon or anyone else. I just can't tell her that any day now Matt will be in West Cork helping James to erect his extension... in more ways than one I'm sure. Matt has found his Wonderful Man. The one I thought was mine. Well, they can both bugger off now as far as I'm concerned.

It happened almost the moment they met, apparently. That vibe I felt between them wasn't jealousy, it was attraction. An attraction Matt was desperate to hide because he didn't want to upset me. Well, he has upset me. He rang to apologize, profusely. He said he was determined to be very cool with James, but not talking made him drink far too much and his resolve slipped. He wants to take me out for a meal at a marvellous restaurant. He says he'll scour the country for a wonderful man for me if I let him. Well, I'm not going to let him. If either James or Matt ever has the cheek to visit me again I'm going to have my new 'All Men Are Bastards' diary on prominent display. James Mitchel isn't even entirely gay – he's bisexual. He chose Matt over me – despite my new silk blouse.

Anytime I go into Sarah's office the phone rings almost immediately. As I wait for her to finish her call the headline 'When the Man You Love is Gay' flashes in front of me and I realize that if Sarah ever manages to wheedle the whole James Mitchel saga out of me she'll think it is a great angle for an article. 'My Man Made Me a Lesbian.' Yes, that would certainly have loads of oomph too. 'Can Mr Mediocre be Mr Right?' Dear God, where are all these headlines coming from? Maybe Sarah is right to use articles that are wildly contradictory. Whatever you write about romance, it will be true for someone.

As soon as Sarah finishes her phone call she looks at me with a slight glint. Her earlier softness seems to have left her.

'Look, I can't talk for long,' she says briskly, as though I'd suggested this meeting in the first place. 'But I have to have a word with you about your singles dances and personal ads article.'

'Oh, yes.' I stare at her nervously. 'I meant to get that back from you to revise it a bit.'

'I'm glad to hear that, Alice,' she says sternly. 'Because, frankly, the last part of it doesn't make any sense.'

I don't reply.

'I mean the bit about saving frogs was interesting. And the neon tetras sound nice, if you like tropical fish. But really Alice, suggesting that women pester men who have no interest in them. And why bring Colin Derling into it?' She's flicking through the pages of my article impatiently. Every so often she looks up at me with narrowed eyes.

'Annie told you about Eamon, didn't she?' I sigh. 'I know you had lunch together recently.'

'What?'

'I saw you together in that café down the road. Annie told you that Eamon has asked me to marry him. I know she has. I can almost hear her telling you, "She can't marry him, Sarah. We've got to do something about it."'

Sarah stares out the window.

'You two have always tried to manage me romantically – you even did it when we were in college,' I continue indignantly. 'That's why you've been sending me off on these stupid assignments. You've been trying to matchmake me with some – some stranger.'

Sarah stops shuffling the papers. She looks embarrassed for about half a second before announcing, 'Really, Alice! What a suggestion.'

'It's true. I know it is,' I protest. 'Well, I'll tell you something, Sarah. It hasn't worked.'

'Look, Alice,' Sarah gives me a flinty glare. 'You of all people should know that I usually have very little patience with this kind of insubordination. In fact, if you were anyone else I'd...' She leaves the sentence unfinished and fiddles with her lavender pot-pourri. 'But since I know all this is very unlike you,' she continues slowly, 'I'll overlook it just this once. I'll see it as the small cry for help – which I think it may well be. But if

246

you argue with me about your next assignment, Alice, I'm going to have to take a very firm stand.'

'Yes, yes, of course,' I agree gratefully.

'So I won't even tolerate one word of remonstration when I ask you to have one thousand words about...'

'Oh, dear God,' I think. 'She's going to ask me to date a transvestite.'

'One thousand words about herbs and their culinary uses by tomorrow morning.'

I am dumb with bliss.

'Oh yes, and I need an interview for the next issue,' she continues briskly. 'Any suggestions?'

Somehow the first person who comes to mind, almost instantly, is Laren Brassière.

Back at my desk, I try to be busy, though initially I don't seem to get much done. Of course, looking back I'll probably see this is not the case. 'Life is a Process' – I wrote an article called that once. It was about how you should give yourself credit along the way and not only when things were all wrapped up – if they ever are. It was wise, but now I can hardly believe I'm the woman who wrote it. It's not enough to know things, you seem to have to remind yourself of them over and over again.

'A thought is only a thought and can be changed,' I think, glad to have remembered something from Louise L. Hay's *You Can Heal Your Life*. Dear God, I even dusted behind the lavatory bowl for him.

Thank God for tarragon, parsley, sage, rosemary and thyme. By the end of the day I've finished the article. I even nipped home to fetch my herbal reference book at lunchtime. I worked really hard on it. I hope Sarah will be pleased.

On the bus home from work I decide to try for a little James Mitchel sob. I want to forget about him fast, and this may help. Buses are good places for weeping. Especially on the top deck, if it isn't too full. You can sort of stick your face right by the window and shade your crumpled features with a strategically placed hand. There's a satisfying poignancy about it. But I don't cry. I can't. I haven't cried for ages now. I don't know why.

Mira, however, is crying when I get home. Big blubbering sobs on the sofa. 'What is it?' I ask, alarmed. She just looks down at the carpet dejectedly. 'What is it?' I repeat, putting my arm around her. She leans against me, her face blotched and bewildered.

'I, I saw Frank,' she mumbles.

'Where?'

'In the California Café.'

'Did you have lunch together?'

'No. He was with someone else.'

'His wife?'

'No. Alfreda.'

'Who's Alfreda?'

'The woman he's living with,' she announces wearily, reaching for a Kleenex. 'Now I know why these are called man-sized.'

Little by little it emerges that Frank has left the wife and daughter he would 'never ever leave'. Not for Mira at any rate. She's known this for some months. That's why she tore up Frank's last letter. The letter telling her about Alfreda and his new-found love.

'Why didn't you tell me all this before?' I ask, aghast.

'I just didn't want to…it was so, so humiliating. He said he'd never leave his wife, Alice. Never. I almost didn't believe he had until – until I saw…them.' She says 'them' in a very sinister fashion. As though Frank and Alfreda have merged to form some sort of despicable slithery beast.

248

'Oh, poor Mira.' I rub her back comfortingly.

'The little shit.' She spits the words out like a snake.

'Yes, absolutely, the little shit,' I agree. 'Punch that cushion, Mira. Get it out.'

'I don't feel like it.' She seems tired suddenly.

'Well, what do you feel like doing then?'

'I dunno.' She pulls the tassel of a cushion absent-mindedly. 'James Mitchel turned out to be a bit of a bollocks too, didn't he? Poor Alice. You must be so disappointed.'

I look at Tarquin, who is as usual anxious to be fed. 'I don't know if I'd call James Mitchel a "bollocks" actually, though I'm sure Cyril would.'

Mira manages a hollow laugh.

'He never really led me on,' I continue resignedly. 'Though I desperately wanted him to. It was a bit Jane Austen really. But without the marriages. Anyway, I don't think I ever really believed I'd get him. Not deep down.'

'I found him much too solemn,' Mira remarks with the sisterly bias we often use in such situations.

'Yes, he didn't seem to have much of a GSOH,' I concur. 'And Tarquin didn't like him. Did you notice the way he sloped off as soon as he arrived?'

'And his socks were an extraordinary shade.' Mira wrinkles her nose with distaste.

'Absolutely,' I agree. 'And what's more, that box of After Eights he gave me was past its sell-by date.'

'Well, there you have it,' Mira announces authoritatively. 'He's obviously not a Wonderful Man.'

I smile at her gratefully, wishing I could share her conviction, but my smile fades as I see her tense, disappointed face. She's looking so sad. I wish I could say something wise. Something uplifting. I wish I could offer some insights, but I'm just as mixed up about love as she is. 'Mira, I really admire you,' I decide to say.

'Why?' she looks at me disbelievingly.

'The way you've been getting on with your life. Taking up new interests. Though you may miss Frank, he didn't deserve you.'

'Mmmm – wish I could believe that,' she sighs.

'You must Mira,' I say earnestly. 'If you don't appreciate yourself how can you expect anyone else to? We both need to do more of that, Mira. Give ourselves more credit. I myself am far too self-critical. I know that because I frequently criticize myself for it. After all, Jesus did say "love thy neighbour as thy self".'

Mira smiles wanly. Good, I'm cheering her up. It will take time for her to get over Frank, but I think she will. She's already looking a little less miserable. In fact, she's just looked at her watch and announced, 'Gosh, we're missing Colin.'

And indeed, dear Colin Derling is on the television again talking excitedly about brassicas. We are soothed by his calm eagerness. The steady purposefulness of his words. We rest deeper in the sofa, like travellers after a long and weary journey. And for half an hour Frank and James Mitchel seem very far away. Almost inconsequential. Almost a half-forgotten melody. Sweet but not insistent. Something from very long ago.

Chapter 27

MIRA AND I ARE laughing in the sturdy manner favoured by romantic veterans. We watched the film *Truly Madly Deeply* on the television last night and sobbed so dramatically it seems to have cheered us up. In fact, we have spent a most entertaining Saturday morning wondering if we should play some prank on Frank and his new love, Alfreda. We've even considered telling the members of the South Seas Club that Frank is kindly providing his new apartment as the venue for the next bi monthly beach party. We have also been scouring an erotic catalogue that arrived at the magazine. We thought it might be fun to order their most outlandish items and hand deliver them to his office. They'd be in an unsealed box marked 'Sexual Accessories – Every Fetish Catered For. Strictly Private and Confidential.' How the women at reception would titter. They'd peer into it, of course. It would become part of the company's folklore. I was even prepared to get some friends to keep ringing his personal number. 'Hello, is Mira there?' they'd ask. After some days I myself would phone and say, 'I'm ringing on behalf of Mira. She wants to know if there are any messages for her.' That would have been a good one.

In the end, Mira decides not to go through with these pesterings. Instead, she's going to send him a succinct note in his own handwriting. She's cut out some words from the many passionate missives he's sent her. 'Frank, you are a SHIT,' they read. The last word has to be cobbled together from individual letters and really stands out. We look at it with considerable gratification, then I

251

accompany her as she posts it. Afterwards, we go to the California Café and have cappuccinos and two large slices of carrot cake. I have to check before we go in to make sure Frank and his new love Alfreda aren't sitting cosily in a corner. In some way our little escapade has soothed me too. Provided an outlet for some of the anger I've been feeling towards Matt. I still can't quite believe that he whipped James Mitchel from right under my nose. He sent me a huge bunch of flowers the other day and I brought them round to Mrs Peabody. I couldn't look at them.

'Please don't hate me' – he'd written on the note that came with the flowers. I tore it up. I do hate him. At the moment anyway. I'm so used to being able to turn to him. To confide in him. But I can't very well ring him up and say, 'Matt, a horrible man has stolen James Mitchel from me at my own dinner party. In fact, now I come to think about it, that horrible man is you.'

Added to all this emotional baggage is my growing concern about Mira. Matt's disloyalty and James Mitchel's defection have made me even more aware that she might feel abandoned if I marry Eamon. We are a couple in a way. A team. I know she'd want to stay on in the cottage if I left. She once said she'd buy it from me if I ever wanted to sell it. I wonder if she'd advertise for a housemate. I wouldn't like her to be all on her own.

'Mira, would you mind if I married Eamon?' I ask as we sit in the California Café together. The bluntness of her note to Frank seems to have put us both into a straight-talking mood.

'Of course I wouldn't. I'd be pleased for you,' she replies reassuringly. 'He's a very nice man.'

'Yes, you've always liked him, haven't you?' I say, remembering how comfortably they've chatted together anytime he's visited. He's never silent with her for some reason. 'What is it you like about him?' I look at her hopefully.

'He's sincere, Alice,' she answers. 'He's kind, and attractive. And he can be very interesting.'

'Very interesting in what way exactly?' I probe, beginning to wish I saw his attributes as clearly.

'Well, he knows an awful lot about cars for a start.'

'Yes, he does,' I concur disappointedly. I've never found discussing the merits of the latest automobiles at all riveting, but Mira does. She's quite mechanically inclined.

'And he's very generous. Remember that lovely dinner he treated us to on my birthday? Frank never bought me a dinner like that. The wine was wonderful.'

'Yes, it was,' I agree. 'Eamon knows a lot about wine, too. And restaurants.' As I say this I almost add 'I wish he knew more about me' but I don't. It's not fair. It's not his fault that there's no shorthand between us. You either have that kind of thing with someone or you don't. 'He even has a list of the best restaurants in his diary,' I add. 'He updates it every year.'

'Does he?' Mira smiles fondly at this revelation. 'That's another thing I like about Eamon. He's very methodical.'

'I must say I find that side of him a bit irritating at times,' I sigh. 'He's ruled by his Blackberry. Everything is done according to schedule and he insists we arrive everywhere at least ten minutes early.'

'There's a lot to be said for it,' Mira comments. 'Frank was so higgledy-piggledy.'

'What a strange expression that is,' I remark, but Mira does not reply. She is staring softly, dreamily into her cappuccino. Talking about Eamon seems to have comforted her for some reason. 'Of course, if I did leave the cottage I'd come back and visit regularly,' I find myself saying. 'I'd really miss you, Mira, and dear Mrs Peabody and…' Who else was I going to add to that list? Cyril? 'I wouldn't want to sell it immediately,' I add, 'though you'd be the first person I'd offer it to.'

'Thank you, Alice,' Mira smiles.

'I'd pay for someone to help with the garden.'

'Oh no – I'd like to look after it myself.'

'Really?' I glance at her gratefully. 'That would mean a lot to me.'

'What about Tarquin?' she says suddenly. 'Would you want to take Tarquin with you?'

'I don't know if he'd want to move,' I reply. 'Cats can be very fussy about that kind of thing.'

'Yes, I suppose we'll have to leave it up to him,' Mira says. 'I'd be getting more cats anyway. Eccentric spinsters need plenty of them. One isn't enough.'

'Are you always going to be an eccentric spinster, Mira?' I look at her concernedly. In fact I am looking at her the way my parents used to look at me when I told them, yet again, that I hadn't found my Mr Right.

'Probably,' she replies. 'Unless I find a deeply eccentric bachelor who likes motorbikes. Did I tell you I want to get a motorbike, Alice?'

'No, you didn't,' I smile. I'm getting used to her varied enthusiasms now; in many ways I find them cheering.

'I myself am taking up a new interest, Mira,' I say as we leave the café.

'Oh, what kind?'

'Golf,' I say softly.

'Really!' Mira exclaims. She looks most surprised.

'It was Eamon's suggestion really,' I explain.

'Mmmm,' Mira says thoughtfully. 'I used to be rather disparaging about golf, but I think you see its charms as you get older. In fact, lately I've sometimes wondered if I should take it up myself.'

I look at her. Though she's often advised me to 'simplify' my days, she certainly isn't following her own suggestion. Still, these new hobbies do seem to stop her brooding. Boyfriends take up a lot of time and now she's ditched them she's leading a very multi-faceted life. Almost an enviable one in some ways. 'I'm sure Eamon would be happy to give you some lessons, Mira,' I say. 'In fact we could all go golfing together. I'd like that.' I look at her eagerly.

'Oh, you know what they say about three being a crowd,' she sighs.

'Oh, no – three wouldn't be a crowd with us. We wouldn't be that kind of couple.'

'Really?'

'Yes. Absolutely,' I reassure her. 'In fact, to be honest, I wouldn't even mind if you came on our honeymoon.'

Mira splutters with mirth. 'What a funny suggestion!' she giggles.

'I'm not joking, Mira. I mean it.'

She grows solemn. She kicks a stray pebble on the road and looks away from me. A bleakness has strayed into our silence suddenly. I must say something. Maybe it's time I revealed that Laren Brassière has turned out to be an old schoolfriend of mine. Yes, that would certainly distract her.

Mira is so ecstatic about my knowing Laren that we talk about it the whole way home. 'Can I meet her? Will you invite her round?' she asks.

'Well, I'd like to meet her on my own first,' I reply. 'I'll be interviewing her for the magazine soon. I'll see how that goes before inviting her to dinner.'

'It could be lunch,' Mira suggests quickly, obviously remembering my last dinner party.

'Yes, I suppose it could be lunch,' I smile.

Back in the cottage Mira gets on with her weaving. It's not her windsurfing night and she's completed her motorcycle maintenance classes. 'Fancy a glass of wine?' she calls out.

'Oh, OK,' I reply as I stand at the kitchen window. I'm looking out into the garden, and then my gaze drifts upwards, almost hopefully. What am I looking for? Am I looking to see if Tarquin is slumbering on the boundary wall? No, I'm not. I am looking at Liam's upstairs room. It's as if I want to see him there, watching me. Dear God, where did this wish come from?

I turn away and sit dejectedly at my distressed-pine table. 'How lonely I must be,' I think. 'Wanting near strangers to take an interest in me. James Mitchel didn't take an interest in me. He was only concerned with ceramics really. He never fancied me at all. How silly I was about him. How very immature.'

Mira comes in and pours out a large glass of wine for me. 'Thanks,' I murmur dully.

'What is it, Alice?' she frowns. 'You look doleful.'

'I was thinking, yet again, how silly I've been about James Mitchel,' I reply.

She pats my shoulder comfortingly. 'No, you weren't, not really,' she says. 'I can see why you liked him. He's very attractive and…and I think he likes you too.'

'Thanks, Mira, but there's no need to say that,' I reply. 'It's not true. You know it isn't.'

'Yes, I think it is, Alice,' she says earnestly. 'He has an affection for you. I could see it in his eyes. It wasn't a passionate thing. It was more paternal. And he meant what he said about your paintings. He wanted to encourage you.'

'Yes, he is an encouraging person,' I say a bit more brightly. 'He said wonderful things about my coil bowl.'

'Well, that's something isn't it?' She looks at me tenderly.

'Yes, I suppose it is,' I agree.

'And you still have Eamon,' she adds consolingly as she turns to leave the room. 'He's much nicer than James Mitchel, Alice. Really he is.'

'Thanks,' I mumble then I glance at Tarquin, who is looking at me most sympathetically. He's very intuitive is Tarquin. When I marry Eamon I hope he decides to move with me. When I marry Eamon... Goodness, have I actually made the decision to accept Eamon's proposal without realizing it? I must have known it all day. I have my answer. It's just as well since Eamon will be returning home in ten days – he emailed all the details of his arrival to the office. He obviously wants me to meet him at the airport. I must say I do rather wish my decision to marry him hadn't happened in such a muted, practical manner. Maybe I should get a bottle of champagne – have a small party. I could send Eamon an email too. Mel Nichols and Julia Robbins do that in the film I worked on – I saw it in the script. He proposes in a letter and she telegrams him one word, 'Yes'. They'll probably use great music in the background when he reads it. It will swirl around the cinema and everyone will feel incredibly moved. That's what I need right now – good background music. Something to lend this moment the significance it deserves. I know, I'll go out and buy a

Snickers bar at the corner shop. That's by far the easiest option.

By the time I return to the cottage I have eaten my Snickers bar. I tore the wrapper off as soon as I'd paid for it and munched it greedily. I took big mouthfuls – its naughty, sticky sweetness melting on my tongue.

Now I'm padding into my bedroom in my new furry slippers. I bought them the other day. They're pink and soft with a little bow at the front. I love them but I won't wear them to the corner shop. I'll leave that kind of thing to Mira.

In my room I frown at the huge teddy bear Matt sent me. He's got a sly look to him. Matt's been sending me lots of presents lately. Chocolates, Badedas bath oil, books about contemporary art. I haven't acknowledged their receipt. They're dumped in a corner of my room. Maybe I should give them to Oxfam.

I decide to get on with a bit of sorting. I found a big box of oddments from my parents' house at the back of the cupboard the other day. I can't keep them all. I'm just about to lug the box out of its hiding place when I notice *The Road Less Travelled* lying under a chair. I still haven't finished reading it. I should. I'm beginning to suspect that it is rather wise.

I pick it up and curl up on to my duvet. I'll read a bit of it now. Yes, that's what I'll do. But for some reason I don't open it. I find myself staring at the cover instead. *The Road Less Travelled* – yes – maybe life is a journey. And if it is how have I ended up where I am? Didn't I see the significant signposts, notice the right turnings? How did I miss love along the way – wasn't I watching closely enough?

Oh well, Eamon is a very nice man, as Mira says. And if we have children I could love them. That's why I'm marrying him really. To have a family. I wonder if I'd make a good mother. I'd try my best at it. I really would. Louise L. Hay says we're doing our best in her self-help books. We're all doing our best with the information we have garnered. That's why it's so important to keep an open mind, I suppose. To keep learning, exploring. To understand everything is to forgive everything, that's what the French say. Just as I'm thinking this I hear the doorbell.

'I'll get it,' I call out, leaving the snugness of my duvet. I walk towards the door as quickly as my soft furry slippers will allow. It's probably Annie. She said she might call round this evening. But it isn't. It's Liam.

'Hello, Liam,' I say, rather warily.

'Hi there, Alice,' he replies. His normally calm face seems slightly tense. He's just standing there. Is he waiting for me to invite him in?

'So, how are you then?' I ask, stalling for time.

He ignores my question. He's staring at the ground. What's wrong with him? He's not usually like this. 'Alice, I – I think you'd better call in on Mrs Peabody,' he says at last.

'Why?' I ask, feeling a slight tremor of panic.

'Because – because – oh dear, I'm sorry to have to tell you this.'

'What?' I demand, by now almost jumping with agitation.

'Oh, Alice,' he reaches out and touches my shoulder gently. 'I think your cat has just eaten Cyril.'

Chapter 28

POOR OLD CYRIL HAS shuffled off this mortal coil and ended up in Tarquin's stomach. I wish he'd had a more dignified departure. It's so sad. He was a very nice budgie in his way. Now that he's gone we seem to discern his positive attributes more clearly. He always had a lovely plumage. And he did enjoy his birdseed. Though he could only say one word, his diction was perfect. Maybe his spirit is soaring over the Australian outback. That's what I told Mrs Peabody anyway. I hoped it might cheer her up.

Mrs Peabody is very distressed. She blames herself. She left the sitting-room window open when she was out in the back garden. Tarquin must have climbed through it because when she returned she found the cage on the floor and Cyril had gone. Tarquin had some feathers in his mouth and Dora was squawking plaintively on the top of the dresser.

I feel so angry with Tarquin. I know cats do this kind of thing, but it's awful. 'You horrible cat,' I tell him. 'We should have called you Fred. You won't be getting those tuna chunks you like for dinner. Cats who eat poor little budgies don't deserve haute cuisine.'

I must say, Liam has been very kind to me about Cyril. I suppose you could say we are united in our grief. Mira hardly knew him. Apart from Mrs Peabody we were probably his closest 'friends'. Dora and he never really hit it off. She is certainly not in mourning. In fact she's looking far more contented these days. Being single obviously suits her.

'You mustn't feel guilty,' Liam said the other day when we met each other at the corner shop. 'There are lots of cats in the neighbourhood. Mrs Peabody shouldn't have left that window open when she was out.' As he spoke Elsie came in to buy a newspaper. He introduced us. She smiled at him most tenderly. They do seem very fond of each other. As they left I heard her saying, 'So that's Alice, is it?' in a rather pointed manner. I don't know why she said it like that. Maybe I misheard her.

When I got back to the cottage that evening I discovered that James Mitchel had sent me a letter. In it he thanked me for the 'lovely' dinner and said he wondered if I'd like to exhibit some of my paintings in his new studio. In normal circumstances I would have been over the moon, but the suggestion was so obviously prompted by his defection with Matt that I almost dismissed it. However, Annie and Mira have been adamant that I should grab this offer. 'Remorse can be very useful sometimes,' Annie commented rather ruthlessly. 'Go for it, honey. And get him to print the invitations.'

'I know Matt would want you to do it,' Mira added. 'He's so fond of you, Alice. It's a little fig leaf.'

'Fig leaves are frequently used to cover genitals,' I told her. 'And I doubt if Matt needs that kind of foliage when he's with James Mitchel.'

'I think she means olive branch,' Annie interrupted. 'Look, I don't know what I'll tell James, OK?' I glared at them. 'Now, please, excuse me. Eamon will be returning tomorrow and I need to wash my hair.'

Eamon is home. I met him at the airport earlier this week. I stood at the arrivals area and rather envied the cosmopolitan folk who had just disembarked from various jumbo jets. Even though most of them looked solemn, there was still a tinge of adventure to them. A touch of the exotic. There was a nonchalance about their recent peregrinations that was deeply impressive – especially to someone whose most recent trip abroad was a short shopping trip to Chester via ferry. I watched the way their faces suddenly transformed when they saw their loved ones. The broad smiles, the relief, the laughter. I began to wonder what face I should prepare for Eamon, but in the end I didn't actually see him arriving. I'd gone to check whether the flight was on time and when I returned it was he who tapped my shoulder.

'Alice!' he said.

'Eamon!' I replied. He put down his bags and put his big strong arms around me. It felt nice. Comforting. I was glad that he was home. We went to have a drink and I told him I'd decided to accept his proposal.

'Oh, Alice, I'm so glad,' he beamed and then he ordered a bottle of champagne. It went 'pop' just like it's supposed to. It fizzed into our glasses – its bubbles dancing.

'Yes, yes, this is right,' I thought. 'This is what you do when you become engaged. I've become engaged. Me. Alice Evans!' I snuggled against Eamon's shoulder contentedly. I've watched so many of my friends getting engaged, and married. I've been to their babies' christenings. I've been the onlooker at these occasions so often that I began to suspect that was my role. And now Eamon wanted me. A kind, decent man had chosen me to share his life. I gazed at him gratefully. He looked particularly handsome that evening. He had a tan and sunstreaks in his hair. His expensive linen suit was perfectly tailored. When people glanced at us they gave a little smile. Any reservations I might have had evaporated as he refilled my glass. The champagne came from a particularly good vineyard apparently. He'd specifically asked for it.

'We should have this champagne at our wedding,' he said and I agreed with him. 'Shall we have the reception in Cassidy's Hotel?' he then enquired.

'Yes, that sounds nice,' I replied. I didn't mention that I had considered holding the reception in the California Café. Eamon likes to do things with a certain style and it would have been too informal for him.

'I know the chef at Cassidy's,' he said. 'He does the most marvellous seafood.'

'Good,' I said. 'I'll leave the menu to you. You know more about four-star cuisine than I do.'

Eamon took my hand and pressed it warmly. 'When would you like to get married, Alice?' he asked. 'We'll need to book the church and hotel and musicians in good time.'

'The musicians?' I frowned.

'Yes – I thought it might be nice to have a string quartet playing while we are eating. Though if you don't want them that's fine.'

'Oh, why not,' I said. 'I like Vivaldi. Maybe they could play something from The Four Seasons.'

'I'll request that they do so.' Eamon got out his Blackberry and keyed in a note. 'So, Alice,' he continued. 'What date should we set for our wedding?'

'Sometime soon,' I answered. 'Let's just get it over with.' As soon as I said that sentence I realized it hadn't sounded right. I'd obviously drunk too much champagne. Eamon frowned. 'I mean, we've known each other quite a long time,' I added hastily. 'There's no call for a long engagement, is there?'

'Indeed,' Eamon said. 'Have you a particular florist you'd like me to contact?'

The more we talked, the more obvious it became that Eamon had given this wedding a good deal of thought. His methodical nature required that we discuss every aspect of the occasion at some length. I must say I didn't feel like talking about it all just then, but it was also rather reassuring to know he was prepared to look after most of the details.

'Oh, I haven't shown you your present,' Eamon suddenly announced, as we were about to leave. He opened his perfectly packed suitcase and removed a paper bag.

'It's lovely!' I exclaimed as he revealed a brown hand-knitted sweater. The minute I saw it I knew it was a size too small, but of course I didn't mention this.

'Llama wool,' Eamon said happily. 'Feel the texture.'

'Mmmm – super,' I smiled. 'Most unusual.'

I am now sitting at Eamon's kitchen table wearing my new llama wool sweater. It hasn't stretched yet and is, frankly, rather uncomfortable. There seems to be some dried foliage woven into it – it was probably knitted outdoors. It also smells of something, llama probably. I haven't said any of this to Eamon. We're having breakfast. I'd forgotten how quiet Eamon is at breakfast. When we marry I think I may start wearing a Walkman. I'm currently reading the special offer on the back of a cereal pack. I could get a transistor radio if I get into muesli in a really huge way before the end of the month.

Eamon is reading the sports page of his newspaper as he munches his toast. Any small exclamations he makes tend to be prompted by a golfer called Nick Faldo. He's probably reading a report of the game we watched last night on television.

'We don't have to watch this you know,' he'd said. 'I could record it. We could rent a DVD. You like the romantic stuff, don't you?'

'No, let's watch the golf,' I replied quickly. 'This is more restful.'

It was quite relaxing actually, watching the crisp, purposeful men, striding over vast tracts of tailored grass. The announcer's voice sounded almost sleepy, like a bee humming softly in a faraway blossom. We all have to find our sweetness somewhere, and sprawling quietly on Eamon's firm, upholstered sofa, did have a muted contentment to it. A kind of calm.

We made love later in his big bright bedroom. The sheets smelt new. Magnolia I think the colour is. I just lay there and let him caress me. Eamon's a gentle lover. Though it was very nice I felt detached somehow. Like I was a small island and he was one too. I found myself wondering if I should double-glaze the studio he's promised to build me. In fact I got so preoccupied with this that the 'hardness of Eamon's manhood', as they say in some women's books, was almost inside me when I realized I hadn't put my diaphragm in. I leapt out of bed.

'What is it?' Eamon asked, understandably peeved.

'My diaphragm. It's in my bag.' He watched as I fetched the pert round plastic container. The sort of container that at another stage in a woman's life might contain accessories for, say, 'My Little Pony'. I put spermicide on to it and squeezed the springy rubber together, attempting insertion. It sprang from my hand and leapt across the room. 'I'm sorry, I'm a bit out of practice with this,' I said as I retrieved it and tried again. Eamon watched with mounting frustration. After the fourth attempt he said, 'Do you really need it anyway? If we want a baby why not start now?'

I looked at him guardedly.

'Come on, Alice.' He reached forwards and touched between my legs in just the right spot. 'Yes! Yes!' my hormones screeched. 'Go for it – come on!' they shouted like American cheerleaders. I listened to them. I relented. Wantonly, excitedly, I tossed my diaphragm on to a chair and lay down beside him. There is something about attempted procreation that is extraordinarily seductive, if you're in the mood for it. And I was.

Afterwards, when I was in the bathroom and some of his sperm was sliding slipperily down the inside of my thighs, I wondered if I'd done the right thing. I thought of the photographs in magazines I often stare at the pictures of serene women holding their newborns besottedly. I'd probably do that too – just not with the panache of, say, Angelina Jolie. 'After all, Eamon and I are nearly man and wife,' I told myself. 'And he'd make such a good father.'

Then I picked up my diaphragm and blithely tossed it into the rubbish basket.

Chapter 29

I'VE DECIDED TO ACCEPT James Mitchel's offer to have an exhibition in his studio. Matt phoned the other day and persuaded me. I was very cool with him at first, scarcely speaking, but he seemed so desperate to make amends that I found I didn't want to hate him anymore. Forgiveness is a gift you give yourself in a way. Holding on to grievances takes away the lustre from one's days. It can become a habit and, after all, falling in love with James Mitchel wasn't Matt's fault really. It just happened, the way these things do. And I'm no longer sure if James was my Mr Wonderful anyway. I think I must have had a fully formed infatuation that I 'made earlier' as they say on cookery programmes. One that was just waiting for somewhere to land. I know it sounds strange, but I think I may even have mixed James Mitchel up with Jesus. When I went into that church I so wanted to talk to him. Hold his hand. Gossip. Maybe even have a cup of coffee. But Jesus was moving in ways that were too mysterious for me, so I worshipped James Mitchel instead.

Matt's the one I miss now, not James. And at least that dinner party fiasco has led to this offer. I'm getting an exhibition out of it – some form of compensation. Since Eamon and I may well be starting a family soon the timing is just right. I wouldn't have much time for my art with a baby in tow. I might as well take this opportunity while it's there.

Preparing the paintings is an excellent distraction from my wedding – I am not a traditionally thrilled bride. I hate all the fuss and lists and discussions about who we should invite. Thank goodness Eamon is taking care of most of these details. He seems to enjoy that kind of thing. I already have quite a number of paintings that could be exhibited. During the past week I've been frenziedly getting on with some new ones. Liam says a friend of his will frame them for me at a discount.

I must say, Liam is turning out to be quite a nice neighbour. He's encouraging. I no longer get encouragement mixed up with attraction and anyway he's as much as told me that he's mended his ways – that he's no longer going to be unfaithful to Elsie. I discovered this the other day when he asked me why Mira was looking so sad. I told him, in strict confidence of course, that the man she loves had gone off with someone else, though I didn't give him the background details.

'Oh, poor Mira,' he said. 'Loyalty is so important. You can't have a good relationship without trust.'

'Absolutely,' I said, beaming at him. I feel much more comfortable about being with him since he said that. We're almost friends now, though I wish he'd watch *Neighbours* on television and not me. I still see him watching me from his upstairs window sometimes. These days I usually smile back at him and wave. People can get into funny habits and that's obviously one of his. I don't think we'll ever be that close. Strangely enough I haven't even told him about Eamon. I've meant to, many times, but just as I'm about to say it we end up talking about something else. Anyway, he himself rarely mentions Elsie. We tend to talk about Mrs Peabody and gardening and my paintings. But I no longer feel the need to put up those net curtains. Especially now that I've learned he and Elsie are going to be husband and wife.

I discovered this when I was looking at wedding dresses in a shop the other day. As I browsed around I noticed Elsie looking at them too. 'Hello!' she said when she saw me. 'Liam has been telling me about your exhibition. He's very excited about it.'

'Yes, he's been very helpful,' I smiled, then I added slyly, 'They have quite a good range in here, don't they? Are you choosing a wedding dress for yourself?'

'Yes, I am, Alice,' she said. 'I find this stuff's a bit formal. I don't want to look like a meringue.'

'I know exactly what you mean,' I sighed. 'I wish we could just wear jeans and a jumper.'

'I saw you looking at the bridesmaids' dresses just now,' she said. 'Is a friend of yours getting married?'

'No, I am,' I said, slightly smugly. I wished I was wearing my engagement ring – it's the solitaire I chose some time ago but I keep forgetting to put it on. 'My housemate Mira is going to be my bridesmaid,' I added. 'I'd like to find her something nice.'

As I spoke I realized that Elsie was looking at me extremely oddly. She definitely seemed somewhat surprised. 'The turquoise dresses over there are quite pretty,' she commented, rather curtly it seemed to me. Then she made some desultory remarks about raw silk and slunk off towards the veils. I think she must be a rather moody person. I hope Liam has made the right choice.

I did choose a raw silk wedding dress actually. It's cream with a slight tinge of blush pink. It has rosebuds round the bodice and is rather charming. Mira is very pleased with her dress too. It's much the same as mine, only less flouncy. I'm rather relieved that the dress business is sorted out. I'm getting married in twelve days' time…

Twelve days' time… I must say I do sometimes feel a pang of panic about my forthcoming nuptials. Nearly every bride does, I think. It's not uncommon. I think that's why I threw away my diaphragm really – it was one way of making sure I didn't chicken out. I've been avoiding Annie. She's still trying to persuade me to wait for Mr Wonderful. 'The dress is beautiful,' she told me. 'Keep it and find another man.'

'Oh, shut up, Annie,' I said to her. 'You can just feck off if you're going to keep saying that kind of thing.' I was amazed at my own rudeness, and so was she. She left shortly afterwards.

I have been a bit irritable lately. There's so much going on and I suppose I feel under a bit of pressure. I haven't even been very nice to Eamon. When he rang to ask whether I wanted the ceremony videotaped I said, 'Well, I doubt if I'll want to watch it again – but you can if you want.' I hurt him. I know I did. He went all silent and I didn't even apologize.

'What's wrong, Alice?' he asked.

'Nothing,' I said petulantly. Afterwards I flung paint at a canvas, not caring where it landed.

Actually, Eamon's in the cottage now, and I've scarcely spoken to him. I've told him I'm busy preparing the list of invitations for the exhibition and he's just remarked, rather pointedly, that he wishes I'd shown the same interest in our wedding guests.

'Look, I wanted a simple ceremony. It's you that's turning it into a Cecil B. De Mille job,' I bark at him. 'And why have you invited your business associates to the reception? I thought it was just supposed to be for family and close friends.'

'We discussed all this, Alice,' he says wearily. 'You didn't seem to mind before.'

'Well, I do now,' I reply, unreasonably. Then I go into the bathroom, hoping that my periods have arrived. They're due around now. In fact they're a bit late. I'm beginning to wish I hadn't thrown away my diaphragm. I bought a box of condoms the other day and insisted that Eamon use them.

After I come out of the bathroom I go into the kitchen and pour myself a glass of wine. As I sit there alone I hear Eamon and Mira talking very easily and comfortably together. Amazingly, she's telling him about Frank. She rarely confides in people and he's being very understanding. Very kind. When I return they look up at me almost reluctantly. I feel like an intruder. 'Fancy a bit of Wensleydale?' I ask, trying hard to be civil. 'I bought some today at Superquinn.'

'Yes, that would be lovely, Alice,' Mira says. When I come back with the cheese I find them earnestly discussing motorbikes. Eamon wants to get a motorbike apparently. He never told me this. As we polish off a bottle of wine he also reveals that he'd wanted to be a musician when he left school. He was particularly 'drawn to the cello' apparently.

'Ah yes, I've always loved the cello myself,' Mira comments. I watch them talking. It's amazing. Eamon is being so open. Why isn't he like that with me? 'Well, I'd better leave you two lovebirds to talk,' Mira says eventually, getting up to go to her room. I wish she hadn't used that description. It suddenly feels so entirely, so almost ridiculously untrue. In fact, at this precise moment the only birds I would liken Eamon and myself to are Cyril and Dora. My forthcoming marriage is beginning to seem like a cage suddenly. I am not prepared for the wave of dread that overcomes me. It's as if I'm seeing the whole situation for the first time. I look at Eamon and I realize he is almost a stranger. A nice man, yes, but not someone who will ever understand me. And why should he? Because I don't understand him. I've been so horrible to him lately. Is that the kind of wife I'll be? Irritable, complaining, hard? It was starting already. How could I have fooled myself quite so completely? Persuaded myself that I was being 'sensible'?

As Mira leaves the room I find myself thinking about a question I've been wanting to ask Eamon for some time. Since he's in an open mood this evening, maybe he will answer it.

'Eamon,' I say, 'a friend of yours told me you "disappeared" earlier this year. That you were gone for some days without telling anyone. Where were you?'

He looks at me stony-faced.

'Were you with someone?' I continue. 'I need to know. Tell me.'

'I was on my own, Alice,' he replies slowly. 'I just wanted to get away for a while.'

'Are you telling me the truth?' I persist. 'It sounds so unlike you.'

'That's what happened,' he sighs. 'I'd been having some disagreements in the office. I thought "Fuck them — I'm going off to clear my head." Haven't you ever felt like that?' He studies me sadly.

'Frequently,' I say. 'But I never thought you would.'

'Well, I did.'

'Why was there mud on your clothes?' I pester. 'Why did you come back unwashed and unshaven? You even had a tent in your car.' I almost add 'you made love to her under the stars, admit it. You were with a woman you love truly, wildly, helplessly'— only I don't. I want him to tell me this himself. For some perverse reason I dearly wish that it's the truth.

'What exactly are you implying, Alice?' Eamon regards me icily. 'Why don't you believe me?'

'Because I think you were with someone,' I say, angry now. 'You were – go on – admit it.'

'The fact is, Alice, that I went for a long hike up the mountains. It was wet out. I got muddy. I'm sorry if it's not an exciting enough answer for you, but it's the truth.' Eamon is staring at me, crestfallen. I've never seen him look like that before.

I feel abjectly apologetic suddenly. 'I'm sorry, Eamon,' I whisper miserably. 'I do believe you. Of course I do. It's just…'

'Just what?'

'Oh, I dunno. Pre-wedding nerves or something. Please forgive me.'

He leans over and gives me a quick kiss on the cheek. Then he gets up. 'Of course I do,' he says. 'Look, I'd better go now. I promised the lads I'd meet them for a pint in O'Driscolls.'

As I watch Eamon leave I know he's keen to get away. When we marry I think he will often want to meet 'the lads for a pint in O'Driscolls'. But then again, many men do.

'You'll be glad to know I've given Eamon a thorough vetting on your behalf,' Mira calls out from her room as I watch Eamon's car leave. 'I know you're still a little doubtful about this wedding, Alice, so I gave him a little ESK quiz.'

'What do you mean?' I frown.

'I tried him out on Empathy, Sensitivity and Kindness. He came through it with flying colours.'

'Oh,' I say. 'Thanks.'

273

'I'm so pleased you're marrying him, Alice,' Mira says as she returns to the sitting-room. 'He's special. Quite a find.'

'I'm glad you think so,' I say, trying to smile gratefully. It's becoming rather clear that Mira is far more delighted about my wedding than I am. I can't quite account for it. Maybe she's enjoying 'romance' by association. And if she is, she can't be quite as confirmed an eccentric spinster as she claims.

I go to my room and pick up a letter from Matt that I have not yet opened. I rip open the envelope and gaze gratefully at his large, even handwriting. 'So pleased you've decided to exhibit your paintings at James's studio,' it says. 'I'm getting the invitations printed. They'll be ready by the time you come back from your honeymoon. Did you get the set of dinnerware we sent you? James designed it especially. It's got small tropical fishes on it – I told him you like them. He sends you his love, and I do too.'

I look at the note numbly. I'm remembering how the small fishes in Laren's bedroom used to remind me of hope. How it can glint and sparkle at you suddenly, at the most unexpected moments. I stare dully out the window.

Oh, how I wish it would glint and sparkle at me now.

Chapter 30

I AM GETTING MARRIED in seven days' time. We've already had the rehearsal. Two hundred people are coming to the wedding. Some of my cousins are even flying in from Boston. Eamon's house is jam packed with expensive presents. The cake's been made and iced. Mrs Peabody has bought herself a most elaborate hat and even Annie has been persuaded to attend. Matt and James are coming too. I haven't invited Liam. I don't really know him well enough and anyway he's been a bit cool with me over the last few days. I don't know why. Perhaps he's getting pre-wedding nerves too. I should tell him about the 'Rescue Remedy' I've bought. It's in the 'Bach Flower' range. I take four drops of it in water at regular intervals. It does seem to help a bit, and I need it. Especially after what Eamon told me yesterday. He said he'd just heard that he, that is 'we', might be posted to Colombia before Christmas. It's a year-long assignment.

I must say being in some far-flung location with Eamon, and perhaps a newborn baby, does not seem at all enticing. Though I may have admired the cosmopolitan folk I saw in the arrivals area of the airport, being forced to join their number has an entirely different feel to it. Mira, however, exclaimed 'how exciting!' when I told her. Apparently she's always wanted to go to South America. In fact one of the reasons she took a TEFL course was because she planned to spend some time abroad, only she somehow ended up teaching English to foreign students here.

I asked Eamon if he could tell his employers that he didn't want to go to Colombia, but he said he'd already discussed this with them and they'd insisted. Then, when I suggested that I myself could stay in Ireland he got rather angry. 'My work takes me all over the world, Alice,' he said. 'You've said you want to leave the magazine. You said you like travelling. I thought you'd enjoy coming with me. What's the point of getting married if we're going to be separated half the time?'

'Yes, indeed, what is the point of our getting married?' I almost replied. It certainly didn't make much sense to me anymore, apart from the fact that I may be pregnant. My periods still haven't arrived. I'm trying not to think about it, though I did wander into Mothercare the other day. I've always wanted to buy a pair of those tiny woollen bootees. I get quite dewy-eyed when I see them. The tiny pants and cardigans looked so endearing too. 'What are you doing in here? It's silly,' I told myself. 'My periods are probably late because of all the excitement. And anyway, Eamon's using contraception now so it's highly unlikely that I need these particular items just yet. But if I do I should buy them before I go to Colombia.'

Colombia … I didn't even know where it was. I had to look it up on the map. I can't believe Eamon and I never discussed the possibility of him being sent abroad. We don't seem to have thought the whole thing through at all. But since I am now pretty much stuck with the situation, I am desperately seeking distraction. And that is one of the reasons I'm going to interview Laren MacDermott today.

I'm having a quick cuppa before I head off to see her. I'm using one of the deeply flawed mugs I made at pottery class. Their shape is nice and they're a very pleasing colour. If you're only looking for what's wrong with things you won't notice what's right. I know this because I see now that there's a lot of good things about the life I've been leading. I wish I'd seen this before. It would have helped me wait – wait for the man, the marriage that's right for me … if it ever came my way. And even if it didn't, I probably could have come to terms with being single. Found its many and ample compensations. I think being single would be far better than being trapped in a loveless marriage, which is a situation I will probably find myself in. After all, the main thing Eamon and I have in common is that we are lonely, but 'Great marriages cannot be constructed by individuals who are terrified by their basic aloneness', I read in *The Road Less Travelled*. I finished reading it the other day. 'The only way to be assured of being loved is to be a person worthy of love, and you cannot be a person worthy of love if your primary goal in life is to be passively loved,' it said on another page. I wish I'd read it earlier.

I think these last few months have really changed me. I've been searching so hard for answers and am only now beginning to wonder if I've been asking the right questions. What Matt said to me some time ago is right. If you watch your life closely enough it will guide you. Show you what you need. You have to do it with an open mind – not one full of prerequisites and prejudices. In some ways the little girl I used to be was wiser than the woman I am now. She lived in the moment. She wasn't peering at the past or glancing fearfully at the future. She's still there in a way. I think she's watching the preparations for this wedding with great anguish. I've tried to comfort her, but she won't listen. I don't think she trusts me any more.

I prayed last night. I knelt by my bed and asked for guidance. 'Please, please help me, whoever you are,' I said. 'Send me some sign. Some signal. What am I to do? Surely I can't call off the wedding now – everything's been arranged. I may be pregnant.' There was no reply. It was like phoning James Mitchel.

I'm walking to Laren's apartment – she lives nearby. As I do so I look to see if I can glimpse the kingfisher Annie saw the other day. She just got a glimpse of blue as it flashed by her towards the river. We haven't had a kingfisher in these parts for quite a while. Quite a few people have mentioned it. It's also been spotted on the top of a tall tree by the University Botanical Gardens – the place I wrote about some time ago. I look and look, but I don't see it. Oh well, maybe another time.

Laren lives in an apartment in a tall Georgian house overlooking the sea. I press the button marked 'LB', state my identity, and she buzzes me in. I'm rather nervous. I hope we find we have something to talk about. Oh well, at least I'm interviewing her so I can ask her questions.

Laren is waiting for me in the doorway. She's wearing a red tracksuit and is looking surprisingly normal. 'Hello, Alice!' she says warmly and throws her arms around me. 'It's great to see you.'

'It's great to see you, too,' I say, my voice slightly muffled by her hug.

'It's just like old times,' she exclaims happily.

'Yes, indeed,' I say, wishing it was the truth.

'Come in. Tell me all the gossip,' she says, taking my jacket.

'No. No – I want to hear about you,' I say quickly, anxious to deflect her curiosity. 'How did the tour go?'

'Fine,' she says. 'I'm glad to be back though. It's nothing like as glamorous as you'd think.'

'What do you mean?'

'There's too much travelling and sitting in hotel rooms eating junk food. It can get a bit claustrophobic, being cooped up with the same people. The most exciting bits are the concerts.'

'Oh,' I say, rather disappointed. Somehow the idea that Laren was leading an incredibly exciting, glamorous life had cheered me recently. Now I find she was probably pining for her Dublin apartment all along. I'd even begun to find her weirdness rather intriguing. In fact, I was rather hoping she'd greet me in a bodystocking and be wearing piles of make-up, but instead she's looking quite like her old self. She hasn't uttered one expletive since I arrived. Even her hair is tied back sedately. It's nothing like the expensive crow's nest that aided her camouflage at that concert.

She ushers me into a large, sparse sitting-room. The colours are stark – mostly black and white with rips of red and yellow. There are many cupboards and no clutter. The framed posters on the wall seem to be of mangled machinery. As Laren goes to make us some coffee I peer at them and see they are, in fact, sculptures. There is a skylight in the middle of the room with a dusky glass table and two striped deckchairs beneath it. As Laren disappears into the kitchen I place my small expensive tape recorder on the table and then pick it up again to make sure I've got the blank tape in on the correct side. I check my bag for extra batteries and hunt for my biro. I turn to the list of questions in my notebook and am about to read them when I see a large aquarium partially obscured by a rampant cheese plant. I go over and peer into it. Terrapins. At least twenty of them resting on rocks and small logs and small stones. Some are partially submerged by water. They are staring at nothing stonily.

'Milk?' Laren asks.

279

'Yes, please. No sugar.' I pace the room, making notes. Though I hope Laren and I will get a chance to have that 'proper chat' we spoke about, I also need to try and do a decent profile of her and people like these kinds of details. 'No curtains or books,' I scribble in shorthand. 'Deckchairs. A cello by the window...' I pause and look at the large solemn instrument. Somehow I find it hard to associate it with Laren. 'Huge batik cushions clustered tidily in a corner,' I note. 'Large palm tree lamp. Silver-framed photos of Ava Gardner, Ginger Rogers, Betty Grable and Greta Garbo on a white shelf. A large teddy wearing sunglasses.'

'Is that the same teddy you had when we were in school?' I call out, hoping for some slight trace of continuity.

'No. A fan gave him to me in Japan. The other had no attitude.' She laughs as she says this and sashays in from the kitchen with two large navy blue mugs. I sit on a striped deckchair as she places them on the glass table. Laren then reaches for a large cushion and lies down on it.

'God, I'm tired,' she groans, lighting a Gauloise. 'Hand me that mug of coffee, will you?'

I pick it up carefully – it's full to the brim. Suddenly this afternoon seems too full in its own strange way, as though something might spill.

We sip our coffee in silence for some moments. 'Oh dear, I shouldn't have come here,' I think. 'We've nothing to talk about. Maybe I should turn on the tape recorder and get on with the interview.' Just as I'm reaching for my notebook Laren turns to me and gives me a mischievous smile. 'So, have you found your Wonderful Man yet, Alice? Remember how we used to talk about him in my room?'

'Indeed,' I smile. 'I rather wish we'd talked about something else.'

'Why?'

'Well,' I say, remembering some of our classmates, 'it might have been more character forming to join the Girl Guides, like Fidelma Higgins, or become infatuated with ponies like Sophie Brennan. And the clarinet seemed to do great things for Paula Clark.'

'Paula's living in Bulgaria now.'

'Really?'

'Yes, she's running a restaurant with a woman called Gertrude. They're lovers. She came to one of my concerts and told me all about it.'

'Oh.' Some months ago this news would have astounded me, but now I find it doesn't. 'Does she still play the clarinet?' I find myself asking.

'I dunno, Alice, she didn't say.'

The radio is on in the background as we speak. I listen and hear that a woman has rung in to discuss the photograph on the cover of the telephone directory. The photo includes a close-up of a hand and the woman says the nail-varnished index finger looks like a woman's, but the thumb seems different. 'It doesn't seem to have nail varnish on it and is bigger. Could it be a man's?' she enquires.

'The things people ring up about!' Laren gives a hollow laugh as she turns off the radio. Then she grabs the telephone directory from a shelf. We look at it. The hand's proportions are indeed rather strange. 'It's probably just the angle,' Laren says. 'That can happen sometimes with photographs.'

'Yes, that's probably it,' I agree. 'But then again, they could have used a toe nail from the Loch Ness Monster.' We both chortle a bit at this, our awkwardness fading.

Silliness is a great breaker of barriers. Suddenly it does feel a bit like old times, being here with Laren.

'You never told me if you'd found your Wonderful Man,' Laren says, as she sits back on her cushion.

'No, I'm afraid I haven't found my Wonderful Man, Laren,' I reply. 'But it doesn't really matter because that romantic stuff only lasts four years anyway. My father told me that years ago, and I'm beginning to suspect he's right. It's just nature's way of making people procreate.'

'Mmmm —' Laren sighs. 'But it's fun, isn't it. That passion. That — that wonder.' She stares at the ceiling for a moment and then turns to me cosily. 'There must be someone who stands out, Alice. Some man in your life who was special.'

'Yes, a number of them did stand out, Laren,' I smile wryly. 'But not quite in the way I'd hoped for. Do you want to hear about the transvestite, the bigamist or the bisexual?'

'Well, I have a certain fondness for transvestites,' Laren says. 'For example, Eddie Izzard is deeply fanciable, though I'm not sure what category you'd put him into. That's probably why I like him.'

'So you want to hear about Ernie then?'

'No, I want to hear about your favourite man, Alice,' Laren says, correcting me firmly. As she says this she looks like a young girl again. Curious. Eager. She was always asking me questions like that when we were teenagers. Wanting to know my favourite pop song or brand of jeans or film star. It was one of our hobbies, naming our favourite things. They changed quite regularly, so the answers were rarely predictable.

'Apart from my family, you mean?' I ask. Clarification is important with these questions. Almost imperceptibly we seem to have drifted into the past, into our old ways. I half-expect Laren's mother to appear at any moment to offer us some biscuits.

'Yes,' Laren confirms.

I stare into my mug of coffee. I can hardly believe the answer that has come to me, but it seems entirely true. 'This may seem very stupid, Laren,' I glance at her cautiously. 'But I think "my favourite" wasn't even a man yet. He was a boy. A boy called Aaron.'

'Oh yes, Aaron,' Laren says, slightly disappointed I think. Maybe I should have answered her with an anecdote. Given her some outlandish reminiscence of a wild affair with Brad Pitt. 'You used to speak about him at school,' she adds, speaking softly now. 'He and his family emigrated to Australia, didn't they?'

'Yes, they did, when I was twelve,' I say, amazed that my eyes have started to mist. I reach into my bag for a hankie. 'This is ridiculous, Laren,' I say, bashfully. 'I'm being far too sentimental.'

'No, you're not,' Laren pats my shoulder comfortingly. 'He was special. A soulmate.'

'He's married with a family now,' I sigh. 'Funnily enough, he's living in Alice Springs. I got his address some years ago and we wrote some letters to each other. It was nice, but it wasn't the same.'

'We can have more than one soulmate you know, Alice,' Laren says consolingly. She seems so gentle now. So different from the woman who strode about so outrageously on that stage. 'One day you'll find another Aaron,' she says. 'Someone who shares his qualities.'

As she says this I realize the only person I've met who reminds me even slightly of Aaron is Liam. This realization is so unexpected that I clench my hankie tightly in my hand until it becomes a damp, tight ball. He has the same playfulness, the same humour, the same

283

way of noticing things. But he's too young for me and he's marrying Elsie and…and he wears leather patches on his jacket. Yes, he's obviously not for me.

'Remember that woman in your village who said you'd marry the man next door?' Laren suddenly asks disconcertingly. As she says this I take a deep breath and look at her. It's obviously time to tell her about Eamon.

'I'm not marrying the man next door, Laren,' I say. 'Actually, I'm marrying a man called Eamon in seven days' time.'

'Gosh!' Laren exclaims, looking at me with startled eyes. 'Why didn't you tell me this before?'

'I dunno, we sort of got sidetracked,' I mumble. 'We're having a posh reception at Cassidy's Hotel. Here, I've brought an invitation with me.' I hand it to her. She stares at it for some time.

'Lovely design,' she says eventually.

'Yes, Eamon knew the printer.'

'I'd love to come, Alice,' she smiles, placing the invitation slowly on the table.

'Oh, I'm so glad,' I say. 'Bring Malcolm with you.'

Laren looks at the floor. 'Actually, Alice, Malcolm's moved out. We're getting divorced.'

'Oh no, I'm so sorry!' I exclaim.

'There's no need to be, Alice,' Laren says softly. 'We were driving each other up the wall. We should never have got married really. In fact, looking back I'm not quite sure why we did.'

'I see you still have the terrapins,' I say, feeling a sudden desperate urge to change the topic of conversation.

'Yes, he's going to collect them one of these days. Funnily enough, I've grown fonder of them since he's left.' She lights a Gauloise and inhales it thoughtfully.

'Do you regret marrying him?'

She frowns. 'I think it's pretty pointless regretting things,' she says slowly. 'Maybe there are some things we need to do, even if it's only to learn they're not for us. And anyway, he helped me to see that there's such a thing as a wise folly.'

'What do you mean?'

She leans on an elbow and looks at me earnestly. 'There are some things that can seem foolish and wise at the same time. The sensible, moderate part of you shrinks from them, and yet another part of you knows they are exactly what you need. It's a risk. You don't know how it will work out. But you know you'll always regret it if you don't try.'

I lift my mug of coffee and sip it cautiously.

'I spent so much of my life trying to make things safe, Alice,' she continues. 'That's why I married Malcolm really. We met in Edinburgh. He was in a band. He was very protective and I was grateful. I was terrified of the uncertainty of life. I wanted to find a little corner where I could hide.'

'Been there, done that, bought the T-shirt,' I smile.

'In fact, I wrote songs about how I was feeling and Malcolm liked them. He persuaded me to join his band. So I had to come out in the big wide world and sing at concerts. It was rather perverse really. Doing the very thing I dreaded. You know how insecure I was at school.'

'Oh, poor Laren,' I say.

'But it got easier,' Laren continues. 'Sometimes you have to practise being brave. After a while I began to create another persona, Laren Brassière. I called her that because I'd always wanted a bigger bust. She was everything I wasn't. Her songs became more feisty. She really didn't give a shit. Hiding behind her I didn't care if

285

people liked me or not. In fact I encouraged them to find me outrageous. It was strangely liberating, but now I've had to let that go too.'

'What do you mean?'

'Well, it was beginning to become a trap. I was still hiding really. Not being myself. It's so easy to slip into roles and then people, and eventually you yourself, believe they're you.'

She plays with her lighter. 'I used to think life was like a jigsaw, Alice. I thought you spent your time looking for the pieces to put together and when you had them all, things made sense. But the thing is, when you get to the sky bit – the real mysteries – the colours tend to look the same. You just have to keep exploring, I suppose. Experimenting. Because in the end it's not about shapes or patterns but what fits in your heart.' She looks at me earnestly. 'Do you know what I mean?'

'Yes,' I nod sadly. 'I think I'm just beginning to.'

'And so now I'm going to have to become Laren MacDermott all over again,' she sighs cheerfully. 'Not the old Laren, of course, but the one that seems right for now. Do you think I can do it?'

'Absolutely,' I smile.

'I'm going to give up singing for a while. People think that's crazy. They seem to think if you're good at something you're kind of stuck with it forever – that you have to keep doing it. Being the person it demands. But I've other dreams I want to follow. A friend of mine has set up a hostel in Paris for battered women. I'm going to help her run it. That is my wise folly.'

'What?' This news certainly surprises me.

'It's not a new thing, Alice,' she explains. 'I've done a lot of benefit concerts for women's hostels, both here and abroad. I have this wish to protect women somehow.

Maybe it's because I so often feel lost and bewildered myself.'

'Do you?' I look at her, surprised. 'You seem so confident now, Laren. So assertive.'

'Do I?' she smiles. 'It's good to know I'm a good actress.' She picks up my invitation from the table and starts to flick it in her hands. Part of the gold edging is coming off on her fingers. 'I suppose I do feel those things sometimes, Alice,' she says dreamily. 'More often than when I was a schoolgirl anyway. But I still get that feeling sometimes.'

'What feeling?'

'You know, that everybody, simply everybody, has their lives worked out apart from me. It's ridiculous, of course. I know they haven't. But part of me still believes it.'

'I know the feeling exactly,' I sigh. 'In fact, I was even rather scared of meeting you today because of it.'

'Oh, Alice, we're a pair, aren't we?' Laren giggles. 'I don't think we've changed as much as we might think. I wrote a song about us you know. About how we used to stare at neon tetras in my aquarium.'

'I know you did. I heard it,' I smile. 'It was nice.'

'Let's have some wine,' Laren announces suddenly.

'Would you mind if I didn't, Laren?' I say slowly, putting a hand protectively on my stomach before I've realized I'm doing it. 'I – I don't feel like it just now.' As I say this I decide not to mention that I might be pregnant. I can tell her in good time if it's true.

'OK, but I think I'll have a glass myself,' she says, padding barefooted into the kitchen. When she returns she sits on her cushion again. 'I've something to tell you, Alice,' she says, leaning forwards on her cushion conspiratorially. 'One of the reasons I'm going to Paris is because of a man called Gustave.'

'Mmmm – sounds intriguing,' I reply.

'Yes, and before you get envious I should mention he's seventy and a retired professor. He's got wrinkles and a beer belly and hardly any hair. He makes the most awful puns and doesn't even speak English properly. But he's my Wonderful Man, Alice. Isn't that amazing!'

'How did you meet?' I ask, flabbergasted. Gustave sounds as unlike Leonard Whiting as a man could get.

'It was in a bookshop in the Latin Quarter. I looked at him and he looked at me and that was it. Just like in the films. We had a coffee together and that's how it started. Isn't it funny, Alice – the things that are most important are often the hardest to articulate. In fact, sitting here I cannot tell you why I love him. But I do.'

'Oh, Laren, how – how spendid!' I say. Though I never dreamt Laren would fall in love with a man like Gustave, she has and I feel pleased for her. Genuinely delighted and relieved that one of us at least has stayed true to our earlier yearnings.

'Oh, Alice, I hope you and Eamon will be very happy,' she's saying now, suddenly hugging me fiercely, protectively, as if somehow fearful.

'We're going to the Algarve on our honeymoon,' I find myself mumbling. 'The Algarve's supposed to be nice, isn't it? Have you ever been there?'

She doesn't reply and after that we get on with the interview. I refer to the questions in my notebook and Laren answers them as best she can. Her answers are not the whole story, of course. Language is only what can be named. That's one of the reasons life can seem so mysterious sometimes I suppose…all the things we haven't words for.

'Thanks so much, Laren,' I say, as we finish the interview. 'That was great. We'll have to get a nice photo of you now. Would you mind if a photographer came round here?'

'No, not at all,' Laren replies.

I start to collect my belongings. Then, as I get up to leave Laren looks at me strangely. 'Alice, if you ever need a place to stay in Paris you could stay with me and Gustave,' she says. 'He has a beautiful house near the Champs-Élysées.'

'I doubt if I'll be needing a pied à terre in Paris for a while,' I smile resignedly. 'But if I do, I'd love to stay with you both.'

'Isn't there an art college in Paris you wanted to go to?' Laren continues.

'Yes, there is,' I say. Remembering it now is like recalling a lost dream. One of quite a number I seem to have accumulated. As Laren and I say goodbye and promise to ring each other soon I suddenly feel desperately sad, but I mustn't cry. If I started crying I'm not sure that I could stop, and I have no wish to flood her apartment.

On the way home I look for the kingfisher again and think of Cyril. Poor old Cyril, how he would have loved to fly beside the river, to test his wings. Perching on a branch of some tall tree would have seemed so wonderful after the confines of his cage. But that one time he did escape his cage he just flew back to it. He just didn't have the courage to face his own freedom.

We seem to have even more in common than I'd thought.

Chapter 31

I HAVE MADE A startling discovery. My mother did not throw out the romantic novel that so fascinated me when I was eight. The book she brought with her to the B&B with the bouncing bedsprings. The one called *Moonlight* with Tarquin Galbraith and Posy looking like they wanted to eat each other on the cover. I found it just now when I was packing. It was in a box of oddments from my parents' house.

I pick it up with disbelief. When I open it I see my mother has written something on the inside page. 'For Alice if she ever finds this, and I hope she does,' it says. 'For even at eight she knew that people need their dreams.' In the middle of its pages is a picture of my mother and father that had been taken at some dance. They are grey-haired and old. My mother's cheek is pressed against my father's face. Her eyes are closed and there is a small smile of happiness on her lips. It seems to me, as I look at that photo, that there is much more love in it than in the picture of Posy and Tarquin. This is the love of long attainment. So different to the romantic notions I'd had when I was a girl that I hadn't even seen it was there. But my parents had their first four passionate years too, and I won't even have those with Eamon. How – how could I have thought I could be contented without them?

I sit in my bedroom, numb with yearning, the tears I couldn't cry with Laren welling up in my eyes. I go into the kitchen. As soon as I get there I can't remember why. So I sit down and throw myself despairingly at the table. Every so often I reach for the man-sized Kleenex. I may well have to swim out of here, but I don't care. And then someone taps me on the shoulder. I look up. It's Liam.

'What is it, Alice?' he asks, his face clouded with concern.

'Nothing,' I sniff abjectly. 'How did you get in?'

'You left the front door open.'

'I couldn't have.'

'You did.'

'Why are you here?' I look at him cautiously.

'I saw you crying from my window.'

'I knew I should have put up those net curtains,' I mumble.

'What?'

'Oh, nothing,' I sigh.

Liam sits down beside me. He puts his hand on mine. I do not pull away. His kindness is making me sob again. 'Do tell me what it is, Alice,' he says. 'I can't bear to see you this sad.'

'I'm getting married.' I try to say it calmly, but it comes out as something of a wail.

'Yes, Elsie mentioned that,' Liam says solemnly.

'I've had a lot to adjust to lately. I suppose I've just got some pre-wedding nerves,' I explain, rather unconvincingly.

Liam doesn't reply.

'How silly of me to leave the door open like that,' I find myself adding. 'Anyone could have walked in.' He just smiles. He's looking at me tenderly. There's a kindness to Liam. An understanding. I knew that the first moment I saw him, though I pretended that I didn't. There's a shorthand between us. It's always been there and it frightens me. He's the kind of person you can't hide from. The kind of person you could love…

No. No. What am I thinking? He's just the man next door. He's too young for me, and anyway he's about to marry Elsie. But he is a good neighbour. I turn towards him gratefully.

'Liam, thank you for trying to cheer me up,' I say, dabbing my eyes in a businesslike manner. 'Would you like a cup of tea?'

'Well, actually, I was going to suggest we go for a walk,' he replies.

'A walk?' I frown. 'A walk where?'

'To the University Botanical Gardens – the place you wrote about in the local paper. I visited them yesterday to get a bit of advice about my philodendrons. I saw something I think would please you.'

'Oh, have they got their rare plants on display?' I ask, feeling slightly less desolate. 'I was rather intrigued by some of the orchids the head gardener mentioned.'

'You'll just have to wait and see, Alice,' Liam replies. 'Do come with me. It would do you good to get out and about.'

'Just for an hour then,' I say, glancing at my watch. 'I've piles of packing to do and I've got to practise my putting.'

'Practise what?' Liam asks, eyebrows raised.

'My putting. Eamon and I are going to play golf on our honeymoon.'

Silence. 'I didn't know you played golf, Alice,' Liam says eventually.

'Well, I don't really. I mean, I haven't up until now. A lot of people seem to enjoy it.'

'Yes, it's a very nice hobby,' Liam agrees. 'I play a bit of it myself.'

'Do you? Maybe you could join us sometime.'

Liam doesn't reply.

At the Botanical Gardens we walk around the glass-houses admiring the orchids and the many other exotic plants. The succulent section has really grown since I saw it last. And there's a new 'passiflora' – that is, passion flower, which is a most unusual colour. It's nice strolling under palm trees and vines.

'This walk was a good suggestion, Liam,' I say. 'Plants are so very uplifting.'

'Bollocks,' he replies with uncharacteristic vehemence.

I look at him sharply. 'So you've found you don't like gardening then. I suppose it's not to everybody's taste.'

'Bollocks.' This expletive fills the glasshouse, only Liam isn't saying it. He's holding my arm. He's pointing to the top of a palm tree.

'Look up there, Alice,' he whispers excitedly. 'See anything familiar?'

I look. All I see is the tree itself. The trunk, the branches, the huge green leaves. What seems like the beginnings of small fruit. And then – is it? Is that a small blue bird perching on the very top looking coyly down at us? 'Bollocks!' he's screeching, louder than ever.

'This can't be true,' I say. 'This kind of thing doesn't happen. Pinch me, Liam. I'm dreaming.'

'No, you're not, Alice. It's true.'

'Cyril!' I exclaim, overjoyed. 'It's Cyril!' I'm tugging at Liam's jumper. 'Look Liam, look – it's Cyril.'

'I know, that's why I brought you here,' he smiles.

Cyril is flying around the glasshouse now, showing off a bit. Dipping and diving, soaring and gliding. He recognizes us. I'm sure he does.

'How did he get here? It seems so – so strange.'

'Not really when you think about it,' Liam says. 'The gardens are only five minutes away from his previous residence, and there are bird feeders all over the place. What's more, there's a small aviary beside one of the glasshouses. Cyril probably hoped he'd make new friends.'

'But – but I thought Tarquin had eaten him,' I say, dumbfounded.

'So did I,' Liam says, grinning. 'But if you remember, Mrs Peabody only saw the feathers in Tarquin's mouth. That's the only evidence she had. Cyril must have escaped somehow. The gardener here said that when he arrived he looked as though he'd lost some feathers. They've obviously grown back.'

'Oh, clever Cyril,' I call out. 'Good for you! You're a hero.'

'Yes, he's certainly a clever budgie,' Liam agrees. 'He flies into the glasshouse through an air vent. They even leave out seed for him. He's found one of the few places in Dublin where he can live in freedom. He's found his version of the Australian outback after all.'

'Goodness, who would have thought it,' I say, gazing at Cyril in wonderment.

'He does fly around outside as well. Some people think he's a kingfisher when they see that flash of blue in the distance.'

'Yes, that's what Annie thought when she saw him,' I say, leaning against Liam happily. 'Thank you so much for bringing me here, Liam.' I give him a grateful kiss on the cheek.

My joy is making me forget for a moment that he and I are just neighbours. Special moments like this demand intimacy – a sense of wonder shared. Liam must be feeling this too because he's gently wrapping his arms around me. They feel so warm. So comforting. This is nice. I could do with a good hug. We're pressed so close together. I can feel his breath in my hair. Goodness, I haven't felt like this in ages. So at ease, so right with someone. I could stay here all day like this. It's wonderful.

'Oh, Alice,' I hear him say, sadly, longingly, as I pull away from him. We're looking into each other's eyes. No one has ever looked at me the way Liam is looking at me now. For a moment I am not aware of anything else, just his deep dark, beautiful eyes staring into mine. And what he sees there must say 'yes' because he is now leaning towards me. His mouth is hungrily, yearningly, seeking out my own. We are kissing each other. Long, deep, passionate kisses that send tingles through every little bit of me. We're melting together like pieces of each other's jigsaw. We fit – we make sense. It's like…

No. No…what can I be thinking of! I tear myself away from him. I wipe my mouth, desperate to remove his kiss.

'We can't do this!' I say, horrified. 'We are both nearly married. What about Eamon? What about Elsie?'

'What about Elsie?' Liam says, his voice slightly gruff, his eyes glinting with frustration.

'Oh, for God's sake don't be so callous!' I wail.

'I'm sorry, Alice. I truthfully don't know what you're talking about.' Liam is now looking at me curiously.

'Elsie – the woman you're going to marry!' I toss the words at him dramatically. 'And now you've been unfaithful to her again!' Contempt has come into my voice now. How could I have let him seduce me?

'Alice, I think I'd better explain something,' Liam says solemnly.

'Yes, I think you'd better,' I reply.

'I'm not going to marry Elsie, we're just sharing a house. She's my cousin. I thought you knew that.'

I stare at him. 'But – but I heard her shouting at you. She was saying you'd been unfaithful…'

'She's an actress, Alice. Didn't I tell you that? She was rehearsing some lines from a play.'

Silence. I can't believe what I am hearing. So that's why Elsie was in that film. That's why she was kissing that man. But somehow I was so sure. So sure that Liam was someone else's. It seemed inevitable. A man like him just couldn't be free. And now I find he is. Free as a bird. Free as Cyril. 'I really wish I'd known that,' I mumble miserably.

'Yes, I really wish you'd known it too, Alice,' he sighs as, calling out 'goodbye' to Cyril, we both turn dejectedly homewards.

As we reach my gate Liam says sadly, 'Well, Alice, we probably won't be seeing much of each other after this.'

'S'pose not,' I mumble miserably.

'I'll be moving out of the area soon anyway. I'm only renting the house on Half Moon Lane. When Elsie gets married I think I'll find somewhere closer to town.'

'But I thought you liked Monkstown.'

'I do, very much, but it will remind me of you, Alice.' He reaches out and touches my cheek tenderly. 'I'll still visit Mrs Peabody, of course. I've told her about Cyril. She's delighted.'

As he says this I notice Mrs Peabody herself peeping out at us from her sitting-room window. She's smiling at me rather knowingly. I frown back at her and she disappears.

'Oh well, I suppose this is goodbye then,' I sigh.

'Yes – yes, Alice. I suppose it is.'

I move towards him and he hugs me again. A big strong loving hug that I wish could go on forever. We stay, pressed closely, yearningly, for at least a minute and then, when I look up, I see something. I see Eamon and Mira staring, gobsmacked at us from my own window. Liam sees them too.

'Oh shit!' I exclaim. I scurry away from Liam up the pathway.

'Who is he?' Eamon demands as soon as I get in the door. 'Who is that man you were with?'

'My neighbour,' I answer curtly, deciding not to be too apologetic. It might make Eamon even more suspicious.

'A very close neighbour by the looks of it,' Eamon says sarcastically, anger glinting in his eyes.

'He's a good neighbour, Eamon,' I reply, in firm, even tones. 'And you know what that song says – we all need them.'

'Some more than others it seems,' Eamon says, sitting with sudden dejection on the sofa. Mira pats his arm comfortingly.

'We were just saying goodbye,' I say. If I'm not careful I'll start to blabber. 'It was an affectionate hug. That's all it was. He's American and they tend to do that kind of thing more than we do.' Silence. 'Though, of course, the French and Italians are very demonstrative too,' I add, quite unnecessarily. I don't think Eamon and Mira are in the mood for a discussion about the social characteristics of different races. 'Anyone fancy a glass of wine?' I add. 'It's a good one. The woman in the supermarket specifically recommended it.'

'No,' says Mira, most disapprovingly. 'Where were you, Alice? Don't you remember? We were all supposed to go to lunch together. Eamon had booked seats at a lovely restaurant.' She looks at him sympathetically.

'Oh no! I completely forgot,' I exclaim. 'I really am very sorry.'

'So am I,' says Eamon, only I don't think he's just referring to our lunch.

'Could we still go?' I add hopefully.

'No, it's too late now,' Eamon replies.

'Yes, I suppose it is,' I say, slumping into an armchair. Silence. I must say something. 'I'll tell you where I was,' I say. 'I – that is Liam and I, went to the Botanical Gardens.'

'Oh, how nice,' Eamon says dully.

'You won't believe this, Mira, but we saw Cyril.'

'Who's Cyril?' Eamon says sharply.

'He's a budgie,' Mira explains reassuringly. Eamon glances at her gratefully.

'Tarquin didn't eat Cyril at all,' I continue. 'He escaped.'

'Good for him,' Eamon says with a deep sigh. He's getting up. He's leaving.

'I could make us lunch here,' I say quickly, guiltily. 'Do stay, Eamon. I could make us some spaghetti with pesto sauce. You know you like that.'

'Thank you, Alice, but I think I'll go and play a round of golf. I can have a sandwich at the clubhouse.'

As Eamon departs swiftly in his new Audi, Mira turns on me furiously. 'How could you?' she's saying. 'How could you treat the poor man like that?'

'I'm sorry I forgot about lunch,' I mutter, head lowered.

'I'm not just talking about lunch.' Mira is almost shouting at me. 'You've been treating Eamon dreadfully lately. And then – and then – hugging Liam right in front of him like that. Since when did you and he get so close anyway?'

'Just lately,' I whisper.

'Well, I tell you something, Alice – Eamon is distraught. Don't you care for him at all?'

I look at her, a cold truth suddenly dawning. 'Not as much as you do, Mira,' I say softly. Then I walk slowly, sorrowfully, towards my bedroom.

'What a ridiculous thing to say!' Mira shouts after me, obviously furious. 'I'm just being nice to him because of you. I won't speak to him at all if that's what you want. I was only trying to be helpful.'

'She doesn't even know it yet,' I think, as I sit on my cane chair. 'She's such a loyal friend she wouldn't be able to admit it to herself. And even if she did realize how much she likes him, she wouldn't do anything about it. That's the kind of person she is.' I pick up the teddy Matt sent me. He doesn't look sly anymore. I hug him to me, burying my face in his fur. It's been such a long day already, and it's only four o'clock. What's more, as I look down at my feet I realize something. All afternoon I have been wearing my pink furry slippers, and I don't care.

Suddenly I know I can't stay in this room all evening. I can't. I have to get out. Get away. Mira doesn't see me as I leave. She must be in her bedroom. I'm walking in a daze along the road. When I reach the river I look down at the swirling water almost longingly. It's deep at this place near the bridge. It wouldn't be that far to fall To fall? Oh no – what can I be thinking of! Fall where? Surely that's not the answer. It can't be.

I have been so foolish. So foolish. All along I've been blaming other people for my unhappiness. Sarah, James Mitchel, Eamon. But I've caused most of it myself. I'm shivering now, trembling with fear. How can I have reached this point of utter desolation? Something inside me is curling into a tight ball of pain. Surely this misery can't last? I can't bear it. What I want now is just not to feel anything. I look at the river again. It seems the colour of endurance. My heart is breaking and yet I can still say 'Nice evening' to the woman who runs the newsagent's as she passes by.

How I'll have to smile and smile at my wedding. How I'll have to hide my deepest, dearest longings in some place – some place where even I can't find them. It would be so much easier if they went away, but I don't think they ever will. They'll make me hard. Brittle. Angry. One day Eamon will wish he'd never met me. Why couldn't I have just said 'no' to him? That would have been the loving thing to do. Why didn't I go to that art college in Paris after school instead of being persuaded out of it? Why was I so slow to admit that Liam cared for me, even buying net curtains to try to keep him out? Why? Why? Why? Those questions will go on for ever if I don't do something about them. But do I have the courage? The conviction? I feel like I'm on the edge of my own life and I dare not, I simply dare not look down.

All my life I've been afraid of falling. Falling into some place where no one could reach me. Falling in love even – real love. The kind you can't escape from. That leap of faith has eluded me. Terror has been locked inside me for so long that it has made me Almost Alice – only part of the person that I could have been. And it is this realization that has brought me to this river. Made me clutch the parapet with shaking fingers. I look at the river again. The comforting blankness of its depths. And then suddenly, almost from nowhere, the words of a poem come to me. A poem by Christopher Logue I thought I'd forgotten. I only read it once, very long ago. The words are drifting with the breeze now, dancing with the light dappling through the trees...It's about people being called to the edge and replying that they can't. They're too frightened. 'We might fall,' they say. But amazingly, remarkably, they do come to the edge.

'And they come,
and he pushed,
and they flew.'

Chapter 32

THE CHURCH IS ALMOST full. I peeped in a moment ago –
Mira and I are hiding round the back of the building.
Somehow we got here a bit too early. The service will be
starting any moment now. We're just waiting for our cue.
Inside the church I saw heads in big hats bobbing around,
whispering, fidgeting, looking behind them quickly,
furtively. I'm really nervous, but I suppose that's natural.
It's a big occasion.

I made love with Liam again last night. We've been
seeing a lot of each other lately. It was wonderful. I'd
forgotten how good sex can be with the right person. No
wonder Sarah keeps asking me to write articles about it.
The first time I made love with him was the day after
we'd kissed each other in the Botanical Gardens. The
'long day' when I'd argued with Eamon and stared for so
long at that river. When I left the river and turned
homewards I felt quite different somehow. I saw all the
things that didn't matter and let them fall away.

Liam and I really thought we were saying 'goodbye'
when we hugged each other outside the cottage and Mira
and Eamon saw us through the window. By the next day,
however, I wasn't at all sure of the wisdom of our
parting. So when he 'just happened' to be passing the
cottage as I was watering the dahlias, I called out 'Hello'
in a very friendly fashion. Though there were many
things I yearned to say to him, I found myself asking him
about his philodendron. He suggested that I might pop
around and have a quick look at it. He also wanted advice
as to whether his buddleia required pruning. I was rather
surprised that he was being so conscientious about his

garden since he planned to move soon, but I happily complied with his wishes. As we wandered through the greenery he asked me if his clematis had clematis droop, but it just needed a thorough watering. Liam didn't have any kind of droop either, as it turned out.

His house is very colourful. Even though it's rented, he's done his best to make it 'home'. He has all sorts of little objects dotted around the place, including a collection of old tin toys. He also collects old jazz records and played Bessie Smith for me on an ancient gramophone. In the kitchen there are a number of framed photographs of the Mississippi delta. He's very fond of the Mississippi delta for some reason. In fact, he's very fond of many things. He is what one might call a natural enthusiast. Maybe that's what makes him seem so young. He's not that much younger than me actually. Only five years. He kept rushing off to get things to show me. At one point it looked like he was going to play the guitar, only I managed to sidetrack him on to the subject of lobelias. Then he darted into the kitchen announcing he was going to make pancakes, but they stuck to the pan. So we had thick slices of toast and jam and three-quarters of a packet of chocolate chip cookies. I think it was around that time that we opened the first bottle of wine. Liam is interested in wine. A lot of my friends are these days. He said that one day he'd even like to have a vineyard somewhere warm.

'Really,' I said. 'In Provence?'

'I dunno yet,' he replied, refilling my glass. The candles were making everything glow warmly. He'd lit about four of them and it was only three o'clock.

He's a good listener. He loved hearing about the Delaneys' shop and how Annie and I and Aaron used to play by the river. Then he told me about his childhood in

New York. All the sights and smells and sounds he yearns for sometimes, and the people he loved who are no longer around. He told me about his work at the school too. How great the kids are. How honest. I loved listening to him. It wasn't hard at all. The wine was delicious. I suddenly wanted to be closer to him. As close as we'd been when we kissed so deliciously, so naughtily, under the palm trees. I must have fancied him for ages, but just didn't want to admit it. I was too scared. Jumping to the conclusion that Elsie was his girlfriend was very convenient. It gave me an excuse to hide from my feelings, but I didn't want to anymore. I knew this when Liam asked if I'd like to see the rest of his house that afternoon and I said 'yes'.

He took my hand and led me upstairs. I found myself lingering in his big and rather overcluttered bedroom. I was admiring the pictures, the kentia palm, the eclectic selection of books, the Victorian brass bed that he'd found at some auction. 'It's a very comfortable bed,' he said, as he sat down on it and patted the cotton Indian bedspread.

Of course, I had to sit on it myself to find out if he was telling the truth and that's how, five minutes later, we found ourselves semi-naked and entwined in a passionate embrace. It seemed inevitable somehow. Like something long postponed. He looked into my eyes and said, 'Oh, Alice,' in such a sweet, relieved, tender way that I almost cried.

It was so lovely, our lovemaking. He removed my clothes carefully, nuzzling my shoulder, breasts, cheek, arms, as he did so. 'You're obviously a layered person like me,' he commented as he got to my rather ancient vest. I didn't care that it was ancient. I would have with James Mitchel but with Liam I don't feel there are all sorts of things I need to feel shameful or embarrassed about. Things that I should hide. I didn't feel shy when his hand moved downwards, and reached in between my thighs. I didn't feel bashful when he felt my excitement, my wetness. He moved his fingers expertly. Aided by my slipperiness. Then they reached inside me, probing, gentle, searching.

'I hope you're not looking for my G spot because I'm not entirely sure where it is,' I mumbled into his ear. 'Sometimes I think I've found it and then I'm not sure.' He giggled and I did too. We both knew it didn't matter if he found it. We had found each other. That in itself was still a source of some amazement. He kissed me from my forehead to my toes and then up along my legs. 'Would you lick mayonnaise off my inner thigh area?' I found myself asking. 'Yes, yes of course, if you insist,' he chuckled, nuzzling my pubic hair enthusiastically. 'Oh, you smell so good – can I?' Before I knew it he was kissing my soft pink folds, his tongue dancing deep inside me.

I writhed and moaned and clenched the bedspread.

'Am I doing this right?' He paused and looked up at me playfully.

'Need you ask?' I groaned. 'This is better than any article I've written on the subject. I should be taking notes.'

'I want you. I want you so much.'

I looked at him gratefully. I was sure that was the kind of thing Tarquin Galbraith said to Posy in my mother's slim bright novel. 'Yes, Liam, I kind of guessed that,' I smiled, looking at what I'm sure Posy would have called the 'hardness of his manhood'. It was a very nice 'manhood' – I reached out and massaged it, while Liam closed his eyes blissfully. Then he turned towards me longingly. 'Can I?'

'Yes, absolutely,' I confirmed. He reached for the packet of condoms urgently. I waited. It was worth the pause. How wonderful, how full it felt. He searched my face as he entered me. He looked almost protective, but determined too. Fierce with feelings. I heard myself cry out, moan. I gripped my fingers into his back as I climaxed. Waves of bliss were rippling inside me, for a sweet moment melting us together. He quickened his thrusts, arching, bucking, urgent. He called out my name at his own sweet release. When I opened my eyes and looked into his they were heavy with surrender, with love, with closeness. But I can't think about all that now.

We've moved to the church porch. The church looks lovely. They've done a wonderful job with the flowers and Mrs Peabody's bonnet looks very cheery with its big pink bow. Josh is getting terribly excited. Annie has just beamed at me and is now furtively offering him sweeties.

Sarah is already sniffling. I saw her dabbing her eyes a moment ago with a lace hankie. She always cries at weddings. She's a big softie really. And a very good features editor. I really have begun to admire her far more than I used to. I think she's right to use wildly varied articles. I mean, if we ourselves can be wild, wise, kind, stupid and uncaring all in one hour, surely we need publications that entertain us with our own inconsistencies. That give us some insight into them.

Ah, there's Matt, looking so smart in his turquoise bow tie. He's been ushering stragglers to their pews. James Mitchel is watching him fondly from his pew and is looking as gorgeous as ever. 'What's for you won't go by you' – that's what my Mum used to say in her later years. James Mitchel certainly went by me pretty dramatically. I'm no longer angry with him for not being Mr Wonderful. Because we're not put here to be what someone else wants – someone else's idea of perfection. We are here to be ourselves, and that's not easy because we change. Sometimes bits of us go ahead, and the rest of us has to catch up. Sometimes the sweetness of life leaves us for a while and yet, with our dolphin smiles, we find ourselves pretending it's still there.

I look at my sweet pea posy. It was grown in my garden. I rather wish I was in my garden now. Where on earth is Eamon? Ah – here he is – rushing in, fiddling with his shirt collar. Looking the immaculately groomed groom that he is. He gives me a warm smile, and then Matt steers him in the right direction.

I glance at Mira. She's looking lovely. Really quite radiant. Her dress looks beautiful on her. It shows off her figure well. Oh goodness, the organ music has started.

We try to move forwards slowly, serenely, like we were told to at the rehearsal. People are looking at us, smiling. Oh, dear God, I hope I don't stumble, or drop my flowers or get tangled in my dress. And what if I suddenly need to pee? I've been four times already in the past hour.

The priest has got on his benign 'here come my flock' smile. I hope he isn't planning a long sermon. Some of them really get the bit between their teeth when they see a full church. Warbling on about 'these two young people' and all that. I think there should be a little buzzer one could press if they go past fifteen minutes. Jesus, I hope you're taking close interest in these proceedings because I think we all need a bit of help here. Mira seems surprisingly calm. She's wearing baseball boots, only you can't see them under her long, flowing raw silk dress. 'Marriage involves a lot of standing around. Comfortable shoes are essential,' she told me. Oh well, at least she's not wearing her huge furry slippers. She's always going to be rather eccentric. It suits her.

Of course, this is all a very spiritual, uplifting ceremony. It's full of sanctity and solemnity and not at all the time when one might find oneself wondering whether, for example, one has let the cat out. Tarquin has a way of darting into another room and hiding. He's become very crafty lately. The vicar is getting to the 'I do' bit. The bit where one has to speak. I tense, hoping the words come out right. They do. Mira and Eamon say them perfectly. Many months have passed since I myself was supposed to get married. This is their wedding, not mine.

I had to do quite a bit of matchmaking to get them to this altar. Mira had become quite attached to being an eccentric spinster and Eamon seemed set on becoming a bachelor after our own wedding was called off.

'I can't really be bothered with all that stuff now,' he told me reproachfully.

By that stage I'd told him about Liam and he was understandably hurt. Not as hurt as he would have been if he'd been in love with me, but hurt all the same. Mira was furious with me. I had a very unsettled few months trying to cope with their varying emotions. I became determined that Eamon and I would remain friends and that he would become someone's Mr Wonderful. He deserved it. Stealthily, slyly, I drew him and Mira together. On numerous occasions I invited him round for 'lunch' and disappeared off on a pretend errand as soon as he arrived.

'You talk with Mira,' I'd say. 'I just have to get some lettuce.'

After a while it became obvious, even to them, that they were a match, though they weren't at all sure about the wisdom of giving romance another try. The fact that they have is a 'wise folly' I suppose. I think there are a lot of them around.

I'm so glad I managed to bring them together, especially now as I watch them kissing. A long delicious kiss. Yes, definitely, that's how it should be done. My eyes start misting. I am profoundly moved. So is Mira's dad. He's standing near her. He walked her up the aisle. Half the church are now reaching for their Kleenexes. Most people are pretty romantic really. Deep down. There's not much that can be done about it.

I couldn't do it in the end, marry Eamon. I'd asked for guidance about my dilemma and I got it. Loads of it. Almost an EU surplus in fact. I looked at Eamon and myself long and hard and I just knew our marriage wouldn't work. It might have looked all right on the outside, it might even have seemed sensible, practical, wise. He was a definite 'catch', but there was another catch too. We would have driven each other up the wall. And anyway it was becoming painfully obvious that he felt more comfortable with Mira. He's her Mr Wonderful. He's even bought her a motorbike. Attraction is such a strange thing. Their wedding reception at Cassidy's Hotel is going to have a 'South Seas' theme to it. Eamon even managed to fly in some Hawaiian-type flower garlands. We're all to wear them apparently. It sounds fun and very unlike the rather sedate reception we ourselves had planned.

'We can't cancel the wedding now, it will look so foolish,' Eamon said at first when I told him I no longer planned to marry him. 'The reception menu's been chosen, we've hired musicians. And what about all the invitations? The wedding presents?'

'We'll just have to send the presents back. And we'll just have to contact the hotel and everyone else – we'll have to explain.'

'But what will we tell them?' Eamon was in a state.

'Just the basic details. They don't have to understand, Eamon. As long as we do.'

'It's Liam, isn't it?' he frowned at me. 'Why didn't you tell me you felt that way about him? I would have understood.'

'I didn't know until the other day,' I explained. 'And it's not just Liam really. It's lots of other things as well.'

After that conversation Eamon said he thought a round of golf might cheer him up and I asked if I could join him. He was, of course, rather startled, but I could also see that he was pleased. I enjoyed playing golf with him actually. I didn't think I would, but I did. I can see why people like it now. When I got into a bunker he helped me to get out. He showed me the right swing and the ball landed on the green. As we wandered over the manicured grass Eamon admitted that he was relieved we had called off the wedding. 'You didn't seem happy about it,' he said. 'Frankly, even before I saw you with Liam, I had started to wonder if it was wise.'

'So I suppose cancelling it is a wise folly,' I said. He just looked at me and laughed.

My exhibition at James's studio went really well. I sold quite a few paintings. It's encouraged me to take my painting more seriously. I'm taking a year off from the magazine and have enrolled in an art course in Paris. I plan to teach English part-time while I'm there and also do some freelance articles for various publications, including the magazine. Sarah says I can make my own suggestions.

I know Paris. I like it. Not everything about it, of course, but enough. I'll take sneering lessons if necessary. I plan to stay with Laren and Gustave when I first arrive. I want to visit Provence, of course, but I won't make a big deal of it. I think I may have turned it into someplace a bit too perfect. It's easy to do that with places and people. I did it with my Wonderful Man. Now I'd just like to explore it a bit. Accept it as it is.

What I'm trying hard to do these days is to be a bit kinder to myself. I see that I put myself under a lot of pressure about a lot of things and it wasn't really necessary. I am what I am and I am learning to accept myself. Appreciate myself. Show myself the kind of love I want to offer others. And I do want to offer love as well as receive it. I really do.

I don't know if I'll ever get around to having a child myself now. My periods arrived shortly after I broke off my engagement with Eamon, and in a way I was a bit disappointed. But even if I don't have a child there are plenty I can borrow. Annie's son, Josh, sometimes comes to the cottage with his friends and I give them painting classes. It's great fun. I put newspapers on the floor so we can splash around rather wildly. Everything Josh paints, even a duck, ends up wearing a Manchester United T-shirt. He keeps saying that I should marry his mother. He still doesn't understand the penis thing. Not really – but then maybe I don't either.

I visited my parents' graves the other day. I placed flowers by my grandparents' and Aunt Phoebe's headstones too. I told them I was going to Paris and, strangely enough, I got the sense that they were rather pleased. They hadn't wanted me to go there when I was younger. Maybe they see things differently now, wherever they are. And they are somewhere, I'm pretty sure of that.

Liam wants to visit me in Paris. I want him to, I really do. He's going to rent the cottage while I'm away. Mrs Peabody was most reassured when I told her this. They've become great buddies and Liam and Tarquin have become very pally too. In fact Tarquin lets us pat him now. One day he just didn't run away when I reached out to touch him. He sat there, terrified, but he stayed.

I wonder if Liam and I will stay together. I wonder if what we feel for each other will last. Who can really tell? Of course it would be wonderful to have those first four romantic, passionate years – to stretch them out a bit if one could. The 'less giggly and obvious' bit sounds pretty good too. And the companionship. The friendship. The marzipan. We'll do our best. We'll give it a try and see what happens.

Lately I've begun to suspect something. I've begun to suspect that contentment doesn't have as much to do with circumstance as I'd thought. And that 'perfectionism and happiness don't sit too comfortably together' as James Mitchel said. I also think that life may be a bit more like felt pictures than I'd realized. You have to be prepared to move things around if necessary. Even your beliefs.

For example, as I look at Mira and Eamon here, in this church, signing the register, I find myself believing that their love may be 'giggly and obvious' for a good deal longer than four years. Believing has a lot to do with it I think. Trust. Hope. That leap of faith. I know this because just the other day Liam patted my bottom rather naughtily when I was replanting my lobelias. As we

312

looked at each other and laughed I realized something very wonderful and very unexpected.

I realized that we looked just like Mr and Mrs Allen did in the B&B with the bouncing bedsprings, all those years ago.

Grace Wynne-Jones was born and brought up in Ireland and has also lived in Africa, the US and England. She has a deep interest in psychology, spirituality and healing and she also loves to celebrate the strangeness and wonders of ordinary life and love. She has frequently been praised for the warm belly-laugh humour and tender poignancy in her writing and has been described as 'a novelist who tells the truth about the human heart'.

Her feature articles have appeared in many magazines and national papers in Ireland and in England and her radio play *Ebb Tide* was broadcast on RTE 1. Her short stories have been published in magazines in Ireland, England and Australia, and have also been broadcast on RTE and BBC Radio 4. She is the author of four critically acclaimed novels: *Ordinary Miracles*, *Wise Follies*, *Ready Or Not?* and *The Truth Club*. She has written and broadcast a number of talks for RTE's 'Living Word' and 'Sunday Miscellany' and has been included in the book 'Sunday Miscellany A Selection From 2004 - 2006' (New Island). She also contributed to the travel book 'Travelling Light' (Tivoli).

Please visit her website for more information:

www.gracewynnejones.com